Praise for

Then Things Went Dark

'Shocking, addictive and utterly exquisite! Fitzgerald
delves into the ugly side of our obsession with reality TV
and fame, and does so in a gripping page-turner. With
characters you'll love to hate, it feels like a TV series
in itself' L.C. North, author of *Clickbait*

'A clever, queer whodunit that will grip readers until the final
page' Rebecca McKanna, author of *Don't Forget the Girl*

'The perfect holiday thriller!' Natali Simmonds, author
of *Good Girls Die Last*

'Sharp, gripping, fun and utterly brilliant' Beth Reekles,
author of *The Kissing Booth*

'A delicious, murderous thriller that feels like you're
watching a live episode of reality TV unfold in your living
room' Lucinda Berry, bestselling author of *If You Tell a Lie*

'A complex game of scandals and scheming, alliances and
betrayals that pops off the page' Kimberly Belle, internationally
bestselling author of *The Paris Widow*

'Fitzgerald plays a scathing, thrilling game of worst-case
scenario, poking fun and critiquing dystopian reality
TV tropes while also forcing the reader to take a
look at themselves and ask, "Why am I still watching?"'
Iman Hariri-Kia, author of *A Hundred Other Girls*
and *The Most Famous Girl in the World*

'Deliciously dark and moreish; Fitzgerald has created
a cast you love to hate, and I could not put it down.
Reality TV fans will be all over this!' Lizzie
Huxley-Jones, author of *Hits Different*

Bea Fitzgerald is an international bestselling author and content creator, writing romantic YA fantasy and dark, messy adult fiction. She has worked in publishing for a number of years and shares her love of Greek mythology – and ancient tragedy – online at @chaosonolympus. Bea is passionate about stories and fascinated by the way they endure. She spends her days working with incredible authors and her nights trying to become one.

Then Things Went Dark

BEA FITZGERALD

MICHAEL JOSEPH

PENGUIN MICHAEL JOSEPH

UK | USA | Canada | Ireland | Australia
India | New Zealand | South Africa

Penguin Michael Joseph is part of the Penguin Random House group of companies
whose addresses can be found at global.penguinrandomhouse.com

First published in Canada by Sourcebooks 2024
First published in Great Britain by Penguin Michael Joseph 2024

001

Copyright © Bea Fitzgerald, 2024

The moral right of the author has been asserted

Set in 13.5/16pt Garamond MT Std
Typeset by Jouve (UK), Milton Keynes
Printed and bound in Great Britain by Clays Ltd, Elcograf S.p.A.

The authorized representative in the EEA is Penguin Random House Ireland,
Morrison Chambers, 32 Nassau Street, Dublin D02 YH68

A CIP catalogue record for this book is available from the British Library

HARDBACK ISBN: 978–0–241–69543–2
TRADE PAPERBACK ISBN: 978–0–241–69545–6

www.greenpenguin.co.uk

To Margaret and Raymond Biggs:
Thanks for all of those games of Scrabble

Author's Note

Then Things Went Dark is a work of fiction that engages with topics that might be personally impacting. I would like readers to feel comfortable engaging with my books, so I've listed the following content guidance.

Then Things Went Dark contains depictions of:

- Abuse within a relationship
- Death, murder and suicide
- Alcohol and drug abuse
- Violence
- Stalking
- Blood, injury and descriptions of a corpse
- Mental illnesses and mental ableism
- Accusations of child abuse and paedophilia

Twelve million people watched Rhys Sutton die. AHX pulled the episode from its streaming platforms in seconds, but it was too late. If they'd kept it up, they could have broken the record for most watched video in history. As it was, the video was ripped and posted, ripped and posted, again and again until everyone could say they'd seen it, but no one could find a working link.

The news reported it without footage. Social media posts showed his promo shots, sweat glistening on his dehydrated muscles, hair coiffed into a perfect point, teeth shining white against his tanned skin.

Within days, Rhys had finally achieved the level of fame he'd always desired. His ex-girlfriend spoke to the tabloids. His former bandmates reunited and planned a tribute tour. His parents blinked into cameras as they spoke of loss.

And millions of people forgot that just a day before his death, Rhys had been the most hated man on television.

12.4 million views. No murder had ever had more witnesses.

All most people want is to be remembered. Oh, no one admits it, of course. But remembrance is everything people strive for. Every dream and desire. Who hasn't scratched their initials into a desk just to make a mark upon some small piece of the world? What is a longing for love if not the desire to know your life had impact? That you were a single red strand in someone else's grey life.

Well, I don't want to be remembered. Remembrance implies reflection. I want to be immediate, to be fleeting and now. I want to control a room, to command a single second of time and to be gone the moment it's over.

The mark of any good show is that you cannot remember it, no matter how much you yearn to. That from the very second the curtains close, the whole thing slips through your fingers like grains of sand until all you're left with, if you're lucky, is the feeling. You should be struck by the sense that something incredible is gone. No matter how much happiness it brings you, any good performance should be tinged with loss.

What differentiates icons – true icons – from celebrities is that they are not simply a person of renown; they're a moment, an impression, a fixed point of creation.

When I'm gone, I don't want to be a memory. I want to be a feeling that lingers long after my bones are gone from this world. I want to have impact. I want to *be* impact.

– Rhys Sutton, Audition Tape, *Iconic*

'Can I smoke in here?' Kalpana asks, already pulling a cigarette from a hemp case and fumbling a lighter in her shaking hands.

'This is a police station, ma'am,' the taller officer says, standing behind a chair he now leans against.

'Yeah, in Portugal,' Kalpana says. 'You have a bunch of weird laws about these things.'

The officer takes a breath. 'No – you cannot smoke in here.'

Kalpana narrows her eyes before slipping the self-rolled cigarette back into its case. 'All right, can we make this quick then? We haven't even started yet, and I already need a break.'

'A man is dead,' the shorter officer says, voice quiet, but with the sort of edge that cuts most witnesses. For Kalpana, it barely registers.

'Yeah – because he was an idiot. It was an accident, wasn't it?' she asks, fingers twitching on the table without a cigarette to keep them steady.

'Well, that's what we are here to find out.'

Isko's head rests in his hands, or rather his hands cover his face – it's difficult to tell which.

'I'm sorry,' the taller officer says. Isko isn't sure whether they failed to say their names or if he'd just been sobbing through their introductions, but he catches a French accent, then clocks that this is no local investigation. Though, of course, why would it be?

'No, no, I'm sorry – I just . . . I will be together soon . . . I just . . . to see a thing like that, I –' his voice catches and he dissolves into tears again. 'I can't believe it. Which is ridiculous, I suppose. It almost feels like nothing else *could* have happened.'

The detectives share a look, the shorter man's laced with a contempt that he doesn't bother to mask as he turns back to Isko. 'What do you mean by that?'

Isko looks up through watery eyes, dazed and disoriented, like he is shocked to find himself there, with these men. It is as though he does not remember leaving the island, like a part of him is still clawing at the beach, begging it to give back all that it took. 'Do you know what happens when you put people like us together – people with so much passion it bleeds? So much desperate need to be something, to do something, to become something? Do you know what happens when you put us all in a house in the middle of a deserted island?'

There is a pause as both detectives weigh their options.

'No, I'm not sure that I do,' the tall detective says carefully, rounding his words around the edges of his disdain as if he can mask it altogether.

'Something like this happens,' Isko says so intently it sounds almost profound. 'We are people who live for our passion. Is it any surprise that we might die for it too?'

Jerome regards the detectives calmly, his gaze level, his back straight. But his hands clench and unclench on the cup in front of him, so tightly that the plastic strains.

'You have to catch whoever did this. And quickly, if you don't mind.'

The smaller detective – still tall, six foot at least but a full head shorter than the other – levels Jerome with a glare every bit as harsh as the cameras ever were. 'I had no idea you were in such a rush, Mr Frances. With a few days left on that island, my understanding was that your schedule had just opened up.'

'You haven't given us our phones back, but it doesn't take a genius to imagine the way we're all being dragged through the mud right now. I have investors to think of, share prices to –'

'And you think someone did this?' the detective interrupts. 'That's what you said, yes, *catch whoever did this*? You think this was intentional.'

'I'm not sure Interpol usually gets involved with accidents. You clearly have reason to suspect foul play.'

The detectives do not, in fact, suspect foul play. But the internet does, so here they are, making a show of investigating. An easy case to close, to file away, to forget about.

'The circumstances were unusual,' the tall detective says. 'And the profile considerable. But it might not be a case at all. It could very well be an accident.'

Jerome is not quite quick enough to mask his disbelief – or perhaps it's intentional. Perhaps it's altogether fake.

'But you don't think it was an accident, Mr Frances?'

He does not even hesitate before it bursts from him in a rehearsed stream. 'I think everyone in that house was a psychopath. You have no idea what it was like being stuck with them – always harping on about the most absurd things, so self-indulgent and pseudo-intellectual. So I'll answer your

3

questions and I'll help with whatever you need because they are horrible, pretentious people who couldn't admit to themselves that they were base, fame-hungry assholes.'

'I –'

'And they would absolutely kill to win.'

'Now, Miss Yaxley-Carter –' the shorter detective starts, and Araminta chafes at his accent: British, home counties even – someone who should definitely know who the hell she is and treat her far, far better than this.

'I'm not saying anything until my lawyer comes,' she hisses, resisting the urge to kick at the table. She cannot believe she is here in this dark room with its cold metal chairs and bolts where handcuffs can be latched.

'We have been in touch with your family,' the British detective says. It is a simultaneous thing: her despair and her relief. For all that she has done, all that she has fought for, here she is once again, cushioned and comforted by the protection the Yaxley-Carter name – and its money – affords. 'Your lawyer is on her way.'

'Then I'll see you both when she arrives.'

'That's perfectly fine,' he says. 'We're more than happy to wait.'

She nods tersely.

'So you studied sculpture?' the taller detective asks with genuine interest.

'My lawyer,' Araminta growls through gritted teeth.

Theo looks up as the detectives enter. They look exhausted – far more tired than when they'd first introduced themselves.

4

'Mr Newman,' the taller detective says. He's French, straight from Interpol – Detective Inspector Cloutier, he thinks, though he can't be sure. The introductions were so rushed, and any voice that hadn't been on an island with them for the last few weeks was like a new language. 'Can you please confirm for the tape whether you want your lawyer present? Your management have been quite insistent; they've even sent –'

'No,' Theo says. 'It's fine. Is there an update? Are you still planning on keeping us here?'

'We're not keeping you here, Mr Newman; we just have a few questions,' says Detective Inspector Kennard, the British one – though he's from Interpol too. Which means he's here to pin a murder on someone. The detective steps forward, not waiting for his reply.

'How would you describe your relationship with the deceased?'

'With Rhys?'

'Is there another deceased contestant we should be aware of?' Kennard grumbles.

'Yes,' Cloutier speaks over him. 'How would you describe your relationship with Rhys Sutton?'

Theo shakes his head, utterly lost. 'God, that's the question, isn't it?'

Iconic

Season 1, Episode 1

Araminta: *My name is Araminta Yaxley-Carter and honestly I'm not sure why I'm here.*

Araminta's laugh is lighter than the dainty step she takes from the boat. Her heel sticks into the sand and she stumbles forward, her muted laugh eerily out of sync with the voiceover version that plays.

She kicks the shoes off, tossing them onto the beach, before she reaches for her suitcases.

Araminta: *I'm just kidding. I guess what I want most from this is a platform to do some good. I've benefitted from a great deal of privilege in my time, but the last few years have been tough — I've lost loved ones, suffered some rather public heartbreak and, through it all, built a life for myself. I suppose if anyone can take any inspiration from that, I'd feel incredibly honoured.*

As she drags her suitcases across the beach, the speedboat pulls away, leaving her alone on the island. The camera spins the view, and Araminta approaches a huge house dropped among the palm trees. It is an architectural monstrosity: layers of chrome and glass stacked atop one another, everything right angles and slashing edges. It is surrounded by a bleach-white deck with cameras drilled into every pillar. The island itself is tiny, a sharp cliff at one edge, a desperate crawl toward the ocean at the other.

Across the screen, her name unfurls in glowing letters: *Araminta Yaxley-Carter, Influencer, London, UK.*

Araminta: *But I've also lost myself. In my fight to lay foundations for my life, I've forgotten what I once wanted. I used to be an artist, a sculptor, and that's been pushed to the side. Don't get me wrong, I'm incredibly proud of the work I've done on my social media channels — especially working as a mental health support ambassador — and I've taken great joy in the creative projects of my newly launched home rejuvenation series. But I'm also an award-winning artist. I'm here to prove that I really can do it all — and what is that but incredibly iconic?*

Araminta reaches the villa, entering a living room that is as artificial as everything else — painted gold accents, pink and green paired without thought, and everywhere indications that they are in paradise: pineapple lamp, palm-tree-print wallpaper, ocean sunsets hung in frames. It isn't a house; it's a set and a messy backdrop to the woman in the bright white dress whose bare, sandy feet leave trails on the polished floor.

'Hello?' Araminta calls. 'Oh, I'm first? Gosh, I thought they'd have someone far more impressive than me first.'

She wanders the room, taking in its every inch without a single expression flitting across her face. Internally, she's doubting her decision to come onto the show at all. She has to spend four weeks here? In this violent clash of a house?

She spins with a smile. When she speaks her voice is warm honey, practised for speeches in front of ring lights – and now for television. 'I guess I'll go snag the best bedroom then.'

*

Isko: *I'm Francisco Andrada, but everyone calls me Isko. I'm from Cebu City, but I spent most of my childhood in Vancouver before training in Paris and Porto, then travelling the world, working as a chef on super yachts and also privately for individual clients. For so long, I've been driven by sheer passion for my craft — to learn as much as I can, to explore new opportunities, to cater to new people with new taste buds. Food is an incredible thing, sensual and tactile — more than an art form, it is a thing that, across cultures and throughout history has, I think, made us human. Good food is good life.*

Isko lounges in the boat, sun glinting off his sunglasses, and salt spray of the sea tousling his hair as the boat speeds along. He waits a moment as it finally stops before lowering his glasses in a practised move he knows will make the final cut.

His suitcases appear heavy as he drags them from the boat, artfully battered cases that say he is rich and well travelled. He bought them last month, brand new, and took a hammer to them himself.

Isko Andrada, the screen says, *Chef, Vancouver, Canada.*

Isko: *For a while, food was an intimate thing for me. I loved being a private chef, catering for a handful of people in such a specific, acute way. But recently I've craved something larger. I keep coming back to what a unifier food is — and maybe I'd like to be more in touch with that collective experience. My food is excellent. I know that's not an acceptable thing to say, but I've won awards, trained in the best academies, served the rich and famous. Let's face it — modesty is for the untalented. And I'm here because I am very, very talented. And also because my fiancé bet me that I couldn't survive on an island for a month without having a tantrum about under-ripe produce or a poorly shaken martini. I think he might be right, but I'm just stubborn enough to try.*

9

Isko meets Araminta in the kitchen, where she searches for alcohol, thinking to put out a spread to greet the others.

'Anyone whose first thought on a deserted island is to hunt for booze is my kind of person,' he jokes, and the screen cuts back to the boat.

Rhys: *I'm Rhys Sutton. I'm an artist of various guises, but right now I'm an actor. I've been a musician – you might remember my band, Hurricane Bay. I've been a director. I've been a writer. But acting is something else, something beyond all of those. You're not searching to create art; you're trying to become it.*

Rhys relaxes in the boat like it's a deck chair, so calm and uncaring, unlike the others, who had leaned forward eagerly, searching out a glimpse of the island. He is all sharp lines and jutting angles – not handsome, exactly, but striking. Everything about him seems deliberate. He is precision personified, and it's clear that if he is an actor, then he was designed to play the villain. No hero looks so interesting.

The camera pans out, shows the speck of a boat approaching the island. Framed by so much ocean, it looks spiteful, like this rock has avoided being submerged by all that water through sheer force of will and some violent refusal to drown.

Rhys Sutton, Actor, New York, USA.

When Rhys reaches the house, he finds the others in the living room checking cabinets, after finding nothing in the kitchen.

They introduce themselves and share their quest for liquor.

Rhys takes one look around the room before leaving.

He finds the cellar door so easily it's difficult to believe he hasn't been in the house before.

Rhys: *Why am I here? [Laughter] Well, why not?*

Kalpana: *Most of my work is done under the name Kalpana. I'm an eco-activist, feminist, protest poet and, according to one* Crier *article, 'an upstart menace and young refusenik.' And I'm here because I want to challenge what we believe our icons to be. I don't think they need to be singers and footballers – I think they can be people who are trying to change the world for the better.*

Kalpana sits bolt upright in the boat as though she has forgotten she is on screen. She stares at the island approaching, and there's something in the shock of her pink hair and the steeliness of her gaze that issues a challenge.

Kalpana Mahajan, Activist, Perth, Australia.

Kalpana: *I want a larger platform for the work I'm doing. I want my voice heard. Being on this show is a start – winning the prize money and putting it toward the causes I care about? That's even better.*

The wheel of her suitcase catches on a wooden plank, and she pulls it with such force that the plastic casing cracks. Whatever, she thinks; it's not like this is the footage they'll show. A drone hovers near her anyway, her constant companion. She's signed up for a term in the panopticon.

She resigns herself to the fact she won't be able to do much here – lectures will be cut from the edit for time, and she doesn't want to preach. She has to play the longer game – buy an audience while ignoring the show's carbon footprint – and when she's done, when she's outside, she'll have ammunition for months.

The others cheer as she enters, several bottles of wine already uncorked.

Araminta is first to introduce herself, and Kalpana shakes her hand and nods, even as her worst fears are confirmed – that no one else is here for the noble reasons she is.

So she reaches for the wine and forces a smile for the cameras.

Jerome: *My name is Jerome Frances, and I'm a tech entrepreneur. I'm here for the challenge. That's always been what's driven me. I launched Soltek when I was twenty, and within two months, DateRate was the most downloaded dating app in history. I did all that with just a small loan and a major in political science! It's now a multimillion-dollar company with a dozen apps under its belt. My motto is 'Work hard, play hard,' and that's what I'm here to do.*

Jerome leans back in the boat in a parody of relaxation. The pose should read as chilled, as self-assured and confident. But he is not used to manipulating his body, not used to physical pretence. His arms are too rigid, two straight lines along the edge of the boat, leg crossed at the knee, not the ankle. His fedora is pulled forward, and he waits until the boat docks before pushing it back to reveal his face.

The camera operator clearly decides it's a forgettable one, quickly cutting away to a sweeping view of the beach, Jerome a dot moving across it.

Jerome Frances, Entrepreneur, San Francisco, USA.

Jerome: *So yes, I am going to be that arsehole who says: look at all my accomplishments. And you know what? I'm pretty iconic.*

'Hello!' Jerome greets everyone as he walks into the house.

The others barely pause in their conversation. But Kalpana is pouring wine and jolts as she sees him, the Cabernet spilling across the glass table in bright red splatters.

Kalpana: *Oh, you did not just put me on an island with Jerome fucking Frances.*

Theo: *I'm Theo Newman, lead singer and guitarist for RiotParade. You could say we're pretty successful [laughter]. Yeah, it's all happened so quickly, but here I am, I guess. Last week we won a Treble so I'm riding that wave. 'Destroy My Name' was actually the first song we wrote together as a band rather than just me and a notebook, so maybe we should all be here, not just me.*

They barely show Theo on the boat. A quick glance, an abrupt cutaway.

Viewers don't know it's because he spent the whole journey curled over the side, emptying his stomach. He has a fantastic agent. She got in quick. And you don't want to piss off the agents on the first episode. You save that for the third.

When he steps from the boat, the sun is setting. The sweat sticking to his skin lends him a glow so gentle, forums query whether he oiled up for the moment or whether the post-production team was just really thirsty for his muscles to gleam.

Theo Newman, Frontman of RiotParade, Manchester, UK.

Theo: *I'm here because we've just made it to the point where we're getting widespread attention, and well, I keep being plastered across the media like I'm another coked-up celeb. And I guess, here, at the start of all I'm hoping to become, I'd like the opportunity for the public to know who I really am.*

13

Theo reaches the house and pushes his sunglasses up through the short, tight curls of his windswept hair.

Theo: *I get it – we're all raised on images of rock stars, but for me it is all about the music. I don't care about your drugs and your alcohol and the scantily clad women clawing at my door. I care about the riffs, about the lyrics that break your heart, about the drum beats you feel in your bones. I care about the art of it all. I'm not just another rock star spitting out some cliché lines for the charts. I want to make something that matters.*

He opens the door, the camera zooming in on the black flicks of a tattoo twisting along the deep brown skin of his wrist.

The others freeze when he walks in, clocking his unbuttoned shirt, the patches on his suitcases, his deep-set collar bones and the arches of his cheekbones.

A glass shatters.

Theo: *So I guess I'm here to set the record straight.*

Araminta: *Theo freaking Newman. Here I was thinking the most famous among us would have a few thousand followers on Instagram, not platinum records. And he just walks through the door like it's nothing . . . I mean, I've met a fair few celebrities but . . . Christ, I mean those abs really aren't airbrushed, are they?*

Kalpana: *You'd have thought they'd just watched Jesus walk on water, the way they all reacted to Theo Newman.*

'Hey, man.' Rhys is the first to react, jumping to his feet and thrusting his arm out. 'Rhys. Rhys Sutton. Actor.'

Theo drops his bag and shakes the hand, his other clasping Rhys's elbow.

'Theo,' he nods.

Jerome rushes forward with an eagerness that leaves the

14

others cringing. 'Yeah, no shit,' he says. 'Can I get you a drink?'

'Nah, I've got it,' Theo says, grabbing a beer from shelves on the side that the others had somehow entirely missed on their search for drinks.

'That's Jerome, by the way,' Kalpana adds, forcing her hand into his as he leans for her cheek. 'He's a . . . what would you call it? CEO?'

'Entrepreneur,' he answers curtly. 'I'd prefer not to get bound up with too specific a job title. I'd rather show flexibility, get my hands dirty – I don't want to ever stop grinding, you know and –'

'I'm Kalpana,' she continues. 'I'm an activist.'

'I love how everyone's dropping their careers with their names,' Theo says with a smile that seems too easy for the number of cameras in the room.

'Would you call them careers?' Isko asks, eyebrow quirking. 'It seems like such a debasing term for what we do – to give yourself so fully to something then limit it to one mere aspect of your life? I'm Isko, by the way.'

Kalpana laughs. 'I'd agree that my passion isn't a career but a life I live, but I'm not sure I'd say the same of – what was it you do? Ice cupcakes?'

Isko: *Please tell me you got Kalpana breaking the glass on camera? Like, this dude had just walked through the door.*

Kalpana: *Yeah, I dropped the glass because Jerome started jumping up and down – not because I was beside myself over this dude. Firstly, I'm a lesbian. Secondly, I need more than someone walking through a door to get me going.*

'Araminta,' she greets, air kissing both cheeks. 'Lovely of you to join us. Do you think that's all of us?'

'I can't see anyone following Newman,' Rhys says with such assuredness there seems to be no question as to whether anyone else is expected. He glances around at the room they have settled themselves in and determines it too plush, too kitsch and utterly underwhelming. 'Should we take all this outside?' He nods to the drinks they're all clutching. 'It's a nice night.'

It's not. Now that the sun has set it's cold. Bitterly cold. The kind of chill that creeps from the wide expanse of the Atlantic Ocean and descends onto the island with malignant intent.

Reality TV like you've never seen it before, AHX boasted on their posters, their ads, their posts and their previews. But it looks like any other: pretty, young people in a villa, in paradise. Only this is not the Caribbean or the tip of some Mediterranean island; this is a rock off the coast of Portugal, encircled by the biting Atlantic Ocean. There are no carefully positioned cameramen to give the illusion of their isolation – only complete and utter abandonment. It might not look all that different to the other shows, but the jarring disparities in even the tiniest of details suggest it is ill-conceived, perhaps even destined for tragedy.

Outside the house is a shaded patio scattered with lounge furniture for any situation the producers have thought, or rather hoped, might occur: canopied beds big enough for four people, circular benches around a fire pit, large dining sets and smaller tables for one-on-one conversation – or even dates.

Beyond the patio and the long, straight-edged pool, the beaches stretch until they hit the ink-black ocean, distinguishable from the sky only because the waves are too rough to reflect the stars. There is just tumultuous darkness. Trees gather on one side of the house, the jut of cliff on the other.

Close to the house, through the garden, is the smoking area, the only place they are assured there are no cameras, the TV execs not wanting to glamourize smoking. And apparently everyone here smokes. If there's a vice, they all want in. Or maybe they all took it up quite suddenly, and it's the idea of a space without cameras that they're truly addicted to. At any rate, microphones will be necessary – every conversation captured and broadcast. Beyond that is a short, grassy verge before the sand begins again, running into the shore – waves crashing onto the beach like an attempt to swim out will be met by the ocean forcing you back, the island an inevitability.

The contestants gather around the fire pit and urge their shivers still, dreaming of the sun rising and baking the island.

But the camera doesn't catch the chill, just the contestants leaning in closer to the fire, to each other, and already the chemistry is palpable, like they might throw themselves into the flames just to be nearer.

'So we need to address this, right?' Araminta asks, swirling her straw in her drink before glancing up at Theo with a self-mocking smile. There is at once something indulgent to it – that she is embracing the embarrassment of being starstruck – and something almost coquettish in the practised look from beneath thick lashes. 'Theo, why are you on this show? Haven't you already proven you're an icon?'

Jerome turns to her sharply. 'Well, I think quite a few of us are proven icons, actually.'

'Come on; you know what I mean.'

She angles her body back to Theo, like she is ready to give him all of her attention if he would like to take it.

'*We're* doing wonderfully; it's true,' Theo admits. 'But *I'm* not. The show sounded like a fun opportunity to get out of the music bubble and prove that I can be more than a label's puppet.'

Rhys laughs in a short blunt bark. 'Seriously, dude? Back when I was in a band, I would have killed to be a label's puppet. Aren't you living the dream?'

Theo shrugs, but his fingers tighten on the neck of his beer. 'Integrity means a lot to me, and I don't want to be defined by the corporate music world. I'm looking to cement myself so solidly that each reinvention – on my own terms – retains the whole. You think Bowie or Freddie Mercury would have been the icons they were with music labels like they are now? You think they would have done the required three social media posts per day, or would they have done something wild and freeing like this?'

Isko: *I don't see him turning down those record contracts . . .*

Rhys: *Are we all coming across so deluded? Do all our attempts to prove ourselves iconic sound as ludicrous as a guy with one hit single comparing himself to the greats?*

'Are we not all here for such things?' Isko asks. 'Except for you, I suppose, Jerome.'

'What's that supposed to mean?'

Isko's gaze is as shrewd as it is graceful, like every pointed remark is a step in a well-rehearsed dance. 'Well, we are all passionate about something in a way that feels greater than ourselves. Things that take skill and talent.

18

You would like to make money in technology – is that not a rather distinct difference?'

Jerome scoffs, spluttering on his drink like he has no idea where to even start. 'First of all, I would not *like* to make money – I already am. Secondly, it does take talent, but you know what I value more? Hard work, and that's where I'm beating you all. Skill and talent? Passion? All right, sure, let's pretend I don't have that, but I'd love to hear how the heiress in the corner is fitting your metric.'

Jerome: *I've built an empire and there's a girl sitting right there who inherited one, but you want to come for me for lacking something? Who let this guy out of the kitchen?*

Isko shrugs. 'I wasn't going to provide a ranking, but sure, I'd say she's down there. No offense, honey, but the rest of us have made *careers* out of our passions. Yours is a hobby.'

Araminta doesn't deign to look at them, her composure so undisturbed it's possible she hasn't even heard.

Araminta: *It's hardly the first time, is it? And they're not exactly wrong – I have inherited a lot. I'm sure I probably haven't fought as hard as everyone else. But to imply I haven't fought at all? That I'm untalented? That speaks far more to their insecurities than my deficiencies.*

When she speaks it's a little too calmly, like someone who has learned that ice can burn more harmfully than fire. 'Well, *honey,* I have many strings to my bow, so I don't see not wholly dedicating myself to one of them as a problem. I don't really know how to like things casually; everything I do is all-consuming.'

Jerome laugh. 'Yeah, people can be so passionate about posting photos to Instagram, can't they?'

'You mean of the houses I've lovingly restored as part of a flourishing home rejuvenation series that I'm hoping to launch into a full-fledged business?'

'Rejuvenation? Do you mean renovation?' Kalpana asks.

'No, that's not what I do. It's about finding and replenishing energy in a home,' Araminta starts, but the others are already smirking and she cuts herself off. 'If you don't understand it, fine, but don't mock those to whom it means a lot.'

Kalpana: *Dear god, she's gentrified gentrification.*

'And I'm not defending my social media, Jerome,' Araminta continues. 'Out of everyone here, I've helped people the most. I've been working with charities on there for years and –'

He interrupts her with another choking scoff as he inhales his whiskey. '*You've* helped people the most? Look, Araminta, I really don't want to play a card like this, but DateRate has revolutionized dating.'

'Oh my god.' Kalpana can't contain herself – or maybe she makes no effort to. She glances away from the camera just for another angle to catch her eye roll.

Theo: *I haven't really been on the dating scene much lately – is he saying what I think he's saying? Oh, 'rate'? Jesus, does the bloke know that's only one letter away from –*

'What?' Jerome challenges. 'What's so worthy of your disdain, Kalpana, about making dating safer for women by enabling them to rate the men they match with? It's –'

'Are you serious –'

Kalpana and Jerome are both cut off by bright pink and green lights flickering to life around them, accompanied by what they can only assume is the show's jingle.

On the pale stone wall of the villa, a TV screen flicks to life.

Araminta reaches to refill her glass, twisting around the others for the bottle. It's terrible wine. But it's better than trying to do this sober.

When she turns back, the *Iconic* logo fades as their host appears in a wash of bright studio light, so many miles from them. She is blinding veneers, a heavy contour and a smile distorted by uneven creasing along her Botoxed skin. She is a recognizable face: Eloise Taverner, veteran of reality TV, there from the very first days of Big Brother. She is not merely *a* host, she is *the* host. Eloise is AHX saying they believe this show is the next hit – and they're willing to put a lot of money into making it so.

'Contestants, welcome! We're so thrilled to have you here! I hope you're enjoying getting to know each other, because this gorgeous island is your home for the next month. But don't relax into your sun loungers just yet, because we're about to put you through the ringer. To succeed, you have to be one in a million – but can you even be one of just six?'

They try not to look, knowing it is what the cameras crave: an assessing of the competition. But they can't help it, and the camera catches furtive glances, reflections in windows and flickering side-eyes.

'You've all made a name for yourselves in your respective fields. But this isn't *The Apprentice* – we're not here to ask if you can be the very best in your area of expertise; we're asking if you can transcend it. Can you take your skillset, your talent and your ingenuity, and become someone whose name will live on forever? Over the next three weeks, we're going to see what you're made of. And with a quarter of a million dollars on the line, this is no time to be anything short of exceptional. Between weekly competitions and daily mini-challenges, our viewing audience is going to decide which among you is truly *Iconic*!'

Araminta prepares an excited smile, but it falls when she realizes that no one else is even pretending to want that money. Oh, certainly no one would pass on it, but no one *needs* it. Theo's band might have only just burst onto the scene, but it's making waves – platinum-coloured waves – and Kalpana's intent to give it to a worthy cause makes her own living situation perfectly clear. Araminta herself has stock in Soltek, practically all she has left after estranging herself from her family, and $250,000 is barely a drop in Jerome's proverbial ocean. She's been #gifted enough designer clothes to recognize the five-figure sums Isko is wearing, and Rhys doesn't even blink as Eloise lists those numbers.

She knows why she's here – rebirth, reinvention, a declaration that she is *perfectly fine, thank you very much*. So why are the others here if not for the prize money?

If, like her, they're here for the limelight, then how might they try to snatch it away from her?

'And to our viewing audience, not only is every camera on this island available to livestream on the AHX website, you'll also have plenty of opportunity to vote for challenges and rewards to really get involved with the competition. In fact, right now you can go online or download the *Iconic* app to vote for which traits you expect your idols to have. Then watch over the next month as we test our contestants on each and every one. But before we get to those mini-challenges, it's time for the bigger tests. That's right – as well as daily tasks, we'll also be asking our contestants to give it their all in a weekly challenge. So let's start with the first, shall we?'

Smoke billows from one of the nearby tables as it slides apart, a box rising from within.

The contestants offer the obligatory shocked gasps and excited squeals, though really they're anxiously contemplating whatever the first task might be.

'This competition is a chance for all of you to step up and become something new, something more. We're really going to push you to the limit to see if you can be all that we expect of our heroes. But before you can rise up, you must embrace where you are now.'

The box falls open, revealing a stack of cards and six ballpoint pens, which the producers pair together with a record scratch, the anti-climax played for a comedic effect that no one finds funny.

'You can't allow anything to hold you back. So now, around this fire, we want you to write down the things in your past that you wish you could toss into the flames. You are going to free yourself.'

The screen shuts off and no one speaks, the silence abrasive against the crackling heat of the flames.

Finally, Rhys rises and gathers the pens and cards.

'Looks like five each,' he says as he hands them out. 'I suppose you're going to have to choose your dirty little secrets carefully.'

'I'm not really sure that I have any anymore,' Araminta says with an awkward laugh as she takes them from him. 'I think the press has exposed every awful thing I've ever done.'

Isko: *Oh, I'm sure that's not true at all.*

'Is that what we're doing then, secrets?' Kalpana asks. 'Can we include regrets? Fears?'

'I suppose it's anything that might be holding you back,' Theo says. 'Anything you worry about other people knowing.'

Jerome uncaps his pen and starts scribbling with such ease the others simply stare. 'We're taking this seriously then – no one writing anything meaningless.'

Araminta chews on her lip as she stares into the flames, trying to think of things to dredge up and toss in. 'I think if we established anything earlier, it's that we all care about this an awful lot. We're taking it seriously.'

They fall back into silence – no giggling laughter, no awkward attempts at humour, no grandiose efforts to make the things they are writing seem larger than they are. They let the intensity of their consideration speak for itself.

Kalpana: *I did wonder, while I was giving it everything I had, are the others really doing the same?*

Isko: *It felt ludicrous, knowing that while I was sharing such deep parts of my past on the page, for all I know, Kalpana might have been composing a poem and Theo writing song lyrics.*

Araminta: *It was rather freeing to be honest, all that pressure of the others and the cameras and knowing it's all going to go up in smoke.*

Theo: *I don't think anyone else really did it, actually. But I did. I felt like I owed it to myself.*

Jerome: *I don't have skeletons in my closet, but I did my best.*

Rhys: *Oh, I absolutely left those cards blank [laughter]. No, I'm just joking, but it was difficult to focus when everyone else was taking it so very seriously. I can only imagine the sort of things they* *worry might destroy them. My money is on Kalpana and a closet full of fast fashion.*

When they're done, they stand over the flames, cards in hand.

Isko shuffles his nervously. 'Okay, are we ready –'

The lights flash again, an alarm blaring.

'Oops, sorry contestants!' Eloise flashes back to existence. 'You didn't think it would be that easy, did you? There's one more thing we didn't mention: if you want to be the best of the best, you have to accept the scrutiny of the public. You cannot simply erase your past – not when everyone's watching.'

There is more smoke and the bottom of the box falls away, revealing six hammers and a handful of nails.

'You're going to nail your confessions right into the villa wall, secrets facing in.'

'What?' Kalpana breathes.

'You are going to have to rely on your fellow contestants to resist their curiosity. Because the only way to get that secret out is to rip it down. If you look, everyone will know someone's been snooping. Here's lesson number one: when you reach this high, it's a cutthroat world. And you need to be careful who you trust.'

Theo grips his cards close. He looks as though he might throw them into the fire anyway and accept whatever punishment they give him.

'The rules of your first weekly challenge are simple – take a card down, lose a point. Take your own down, lose everything. And with $250,000 on the line, every decision counts. Any cards remaining at the end of the week will be the writer's to take down and do with as they please.'

25

Jerome: *Knowing that I just wrote what I did and having to not only trust that the others won't read it but also that they took it just as seriously, wrote things just as damning? Yeah, someone isn't making it out of this alive.*

Isko swallows his own outrage and turns to Araminta. 'Well, you first, princess. You said you had no secrets left, right. You can't care all that much.'

She doesn't stop to glare at him, just reaches for the hammer with a shaking hand. Ironically, there's something about holding the tool that calms her. It could be a chisel. The villa wall could just be another block of stone.

She begins bashing her cards in, and soon the others join her, dancing around for space, trying to put their cards somewhere inconspicuous, where they're less likely to be the one chosen if someone was to be tempted. They are so focused on memorizing which are their own that they struggle to keep track of where the others are pinning their secrets, four nails to each card, so no one can even peel the corners back.

Araminta: *I put things I've never told anyone on those cards. Now my secrets are held in the very walls of this place. I . . . I was never expecting to put so much of myself on the line.*

When they're done, they deposit the tools back into the box, which promptly locks shut before anyone can think to take those hammers and pry the nails back out again.

'We could just tell each other now,' Rhys suggests. 'It would take the tension out of it all, wouldn't it? We could just suck it up and then move on.'

'No,' Theo snaps. 'We aren't doing that.'

Kalpana stares dead ahead. 'Until someone betrays us, I'm sticking with my cards being blank.'

'Can't we just all tear them down? If we all lose, then no one does – we just stay where we began,' Isko proposes.

But no one answers – because as much as they dread it, they can't ignore the fact that leverage over their opponents is a siren song calling to them.

And their secrets – their lives – on the line or not, they are here for a reason, and it's not the money. They need the attention, need the viewers and the gossip and intrigue. And none of them can deny that this is good TV.

They stare at the wall, thoughts spiralling: How will the viewers ever trust them when those cards are proof they're keeping secrets from the screen? Is the audience already churning through social media feeds, desperate for an inkling of what they might have to hide? And if they faced disqualification and gave those cards up to the flames, how might the audience turn on them?

In the quiet, Rhys laughs.

'Well,' he says. 'Don't say I didn't warn you.'

They retreat inside and pour more drinks, hurrying to get to know each other, distracted from their secrets by more important matters: their competition.

Theo and Kalpana spend hours in the corner discussing the optics of passion, of sacrifice, of all the things they've given up to get to where they are.

Jerome attempts to flirt with Araminta in a way that is relentless and, somehow, always about himself. Eventually even Rhys has had enough and steps in to rescue her, but before he can, she turns to Jerome with big round eyes and asks why they simply cannot print more money. He launches into a monologue, a distraction that frees her.

She winks at Rhys as she notices him watching, impressed. Meanwhile, Isko takes the opportunity to observe the others like the audience incarnate, his grip tightening on his merlot with every self-indulgent comment or performative giggle.

Isko: *Maybe my fiancé was right – maybe I really can't survive on this island for a month.*

And when they finally retire to bed, the screen fades to black.

But it's not the credits – the black is alive, and gradually shades of grey flicker to life. A night camera, whirring to life, capturing a figure outside.

A figure who tears something from the wall, slips it into their pocket, and creeps back into the house.

The credits roll.

@addiebrookes72

Is anyone watching this #Iconic show? These people met each other for like ten minutes and started digging into each other lmaoooo this is going to be messy and I am READY

@SusiB123

Why is everyone on #Iconic acting as though Theo Newman is Beyoncé and not some guy in a band who only went viral last week? Going on a reality TV show to avoid being a one hit wonder is trashy as hell

> **@TheosLittleRioter**
> @SusiB123 OH ABSOLUTELY NOT!!! Just because YOU didn't know who they were until Destroy My Name just means you have AWFUL taste in music.

Urgh, are people like this what we have to deal with for our faves going mainstream?

Cloutier leans over his partner's chair to better see the screen and watches as Rhys Sutton dies.

'Jesus.'

Kennard shuffles away from him and drags the footage back. It's grainy, black and white – desperate drones hauled to the action, nighttime footage, and a boy staggering, yelling, almost incoherent.

'He's drunk,' Cloutier says, though he doesn't need to. Even if they didn't have footage, he knows enough about the show to know they were drunk most of the time.

There's a sharp rap at the door of the dingy room they're using as their office in this tiny precinct. At their beckoning, Detective Maes appears, eyes tired, coffee clutched tight in her bony fingers, and, tucked under one arm, a slender folder that she tosses onto the table in front of them.

'Here's your report on episode one.' She nods at the screen showing the paused still of Rhys in his final moments. 'That's viral, by the way.'

'So I've heard,' Kennard says bitterly. 'It's what all the fuss is about, right?'

'Is there any update from AHX?'

Cloutier shakes his head. 'No, they're still saying the only way they won't release the final episode is if we can prove a crime took place.'

'Damn, how long do you have?'

'Three days, and then they air it,' Cloutier says. 'And if, on the slim chance there really was foul play, we'll never get a conviction with that episode out there. There won't be a jury in the world that won't be prejudiced.'

'So three days to arrest someone and force AHX to pull the final episode, or they destroy any potential to get justice?'

'They're arguing that it's already out there. And they're not wrong; we can't get the injunction through because it's already on every news channel and all over the internet. People even streamed it live.'

Maes sighs. 'Yeah, I was one of them.'

'Really?' Kennard scoffs. 'I wouldn't take you for a fan.'

'I have teenagers, George. All three of us saw it – along with a few million other people, apparently.'

'How were that many people even watching?'

'Instagram,' she says. 'Facebook, TikTok, Twitter, Snapchat, Tumblr – you name it, the message was shared. We only watched the edited episodes each night, but Lila had, like, a hundred texts from her friends telling her to join the live stream on the AHX website. It was running 24/7 and you could tune in to different cameras. They all said shit was going down. Even her friends who didn't watch the show were streaming it.'

'So millions of people watched him die,' Cloutier says, beginning to list things on his fingers. 'We're in a race against millions of armchair detectives, everyone at Interpol is losing their goddamn minds and asking for updates every twenty seconds, and if we don't solve it in three days, AHX is going to blow it.'

'Can they blow something that's not even worth investigating?' Maes asks. 'I watched it live. And I've watched that clip a dozen times,' she says, nodding at the screen. The footage doesn't show his last breath – it would be much easier for all of them if it did – just the moment before where, if you look closely enough, you can tell he knows this is how it all ends. 'He's just a kid who got too drunk. Do you really think a crime took place?'

'I think it's unlikely,' Cloutier says with a shrug. 'But a case is a case, and I'm not going to waste my own time by not taking it seriously. If Interpol wants to investigate it, that's what I'll do.'

'I disagree,' Kennard says, and Cloutier stiffens at the rebuttal. 'I didn't think there was anything there until I spoke to the witnesses. They're definitely hiding something – and maybe it's murder.'

Iconic

Season 1, Episode 2

Araminta stretches on the golden sand with the sun low in the sky, and the *Iconic* logo slowly unfurls across her elongated body.

Post-yoga, she walks straight past the pinned secrets with barely a glance. The camera zooms in, lingering on the nails of that snatched note and the scraps of paper still clinging to them.

She enters the kitchen, hair frizzing in her ponytail, her skin dewy from exercise, and piles fruit and vegetables into a blender.

Jerome joins moments after she sits down, his shirt crooked and eyes bleary with sleep.

'Morning,' he mutters, fetching a cup of coffee. 'Look, I wanted to apologize about yesterday. I'll be honest; I got defensive when Isko came at me like that and I threw you under the bus. It wasn't right – especially for someone who considers themselves a feminist. So if I hurt your feelings, I want to say sorry.'

'Oh, that's okay . . .'

'Did you know I took a class on women's studies in college?'

'Umm . . . no, I didn't.'

'Yeah, really great stuff. Really eye-opening. It influenced much of what we do at Soltek.' He comes to join her at the table, stifling a yawn as he collapses into the chair. 'You know, it's not often someone's up before me. I really believe in rising with the sun – chasing the day and all that. No such thing as success at a late hour, am I right?'

She takes her time chewing on the seeds sprinkled atop her acai bowl. 'Sure.'

'I don't drink very often, that's probably why you beat me. But you look so together and you drank twice as much as I did, and I'm struggling to stay vertical.'

'Keep drinking then,' she suggests. 'I was always told the problems with alcohol only come when you stop. It's a vindictive lover, throwing your belongings out the window when you leave her.'

'I was always told to eat my vegetables.' Rhys appears in the doorway. 'Evidently our parents had very different styles.'

'There is something to "hair of the dog,"' Jerome admits.

'There's another secret to my hangover cure,' Araminta confesses. 'It's called aspirin.'

Rhys laughs. 'Well, I'm allergic, but I still don't believe it's powerful enough that you seriously woke up early, exercised, and made a healthy breakfast after last night.'

Araminta shrugs, a slight smile on her lips, eyebrow quirked. 'I thought I made it quite clear last night when I listed my many successes, but in case it passed you by: I'm amazing.'

Rhys is still laughing after she leaves to shower.

'Gwyneth Paltrow might want to look out,' Rhys says.

Jerome had watched her leave and now turns as though only just remembering Rhys is still in the room. 'I had no idea *goop* was a personality.'

'I think I can work with it.' Rhys stretches as though winning her heart, or at least her body, requires a level of dexterity.

'You like her?' Jerome asks.

'Rather her than Kalpana. I feel like she'd want to peg me against the wall to prove a point. Which I'm not averse to but I prefer to be on the other end of sex with a vendetta.'

'I'm not convinced she swings that way, dude.'

'I'm everyone's sexuality, Jerome. I'm the intersection where all lines cross.'

Jerome chuckles like it's the funniest line he's ever heard.

Rhys gives no indication he was joking.

Later, when the sun has had an hour or two to burn away the night's chill, Kalpana steps into its umber glow. She wears a long shawl in bold splashes of purple and red over a beaded orange bikini, large octagonal sunglasses perched on her nose, pink hair twisted into a clumsy knot, and the cameras skirt over her like they don't know what to do with her. She is model beautiful but haughty and aloof and quirky to the point of disinterest. The audience is immediately on guard, grating against the implication she is trying too hard, and against her sneering superiority.

Kalpana clutches an iced coffee, condensation clinging to its sides; it nearly slips from her hands as she staggers at the sight of the wall.

She sees the missing card immediately.

Kalpana rushes toward it, pressing her eyes close like she might be able to see through the cards. She can't, but she recognizes her own after a moment – always too much pressure on the pen, the cards too thick to press out individual letters, but she can see the hard bulges of her writing. Not hers missing then, but whose? And who took it?

She would like to shout, to make a fuss, to hold them all accountable. But while she poured her heart onto those cards, one of them was less of a destructing secret and more of a hidden admission meant only for herself: *I am terrified to be here.*

A camera winks at her from a nearby pillar, and she can feel its glare like the hot air clinging to her skin. She is hyperaware of herself – of her posture, of her clothes, of her every breath.

Kalpana: *I didn't know whether to pretend I hadn't even noticed. What if people suspect me just because I bring it to everyone's attention?*

In the end, she runs for Theo.

Theo: *I think it's mine. I mean . . . it could be. I was standing there . . . I feel genuinely, actually sick. Not just that it's out there but that someone here took it – it might even be Kalpana. I . . .*

'I can't believe someone would do this,' he says. They are seated around one of the patio tables. The scent of the cypress trees washes off the beach, and even though it's early still, the sun glares so intently that they can feel the heat even beneath the shade of the roofing. 'I thought . . . I don't know what I thought.'

'You thought we were all better than this,' Kalpana says, seething. 'So did I. I thought we were all actually looking for a platform to prove ourselves on.'

Theo takes a breath and stares out at the horizon of the

36

ocean. 'It doesn't matter. It's a challenge, right? To prove that you're above this? Well, I am. I'm here because I care about music. The others can do what they like, and they can even drag me into it if they want to. It doesn't change the fact that I just want to talk about what I love most.'

Kalpana narrows her eyes and takes a long sip on her drink to avoid saying anything.

Kalpana: *It would be the perfect cover wouldn't it, if you'd taken someone's card to pretend it was your own card taken?*

'All right, let's talk music then,' she relents. It's hard not to – she is drawn to passion. And secure in the knowledge that her cause is the most noble, certainly the one most likely to change the world. She can indulge those who dedicate themselves to something lesser because she can see nobility in art too. It's the very thing she fights for, after all – for capitalism to stop draining and spitting artistic talent back out like oil in pipes. 'Why choose that as your medium?'

'It's never a choice, is it? One day something simply moves you, touches you deeply, and changes you forever. You're a poet too, right?'

Kalpana nods. 'Yes, but the real thing – the kind with meanings and intention. Not some scrawled content on Instagram.'

'Why do you get to decide what counts as real poetry?'

Kalpana tosses her hair from her face. 'I don't, obviously, and I have a lot of respect for it as a gateway to get people into poetry. When I was growing up, my dad worked in a shop – it's not like my house was full of poetry books and I discovered it through blogs and social media. But all art exists on a scale, and I think it's ignorant to disregard the history of the art form like Insta-poets do. Movements happen for a reason. For me, it's not that I'm an activist and a poet – my poetry is activism and my activism is poetry.'

Theo nods, satisfied and smiles.

Theo: *This is exactly what I wanted from all this: conversations about art and passion that are filled with so much devotion, to outside ears they sound ridiculous.*

'We're all just trying to find different ways to talk about life, at the end of the day,' he says. 'We're all trying to spin our experiences into something collective.'

Kalpana considers him, wondering if perhaps he might truly have meant his earlier statement – that he cares so much about all this, his own secrets really are inconsequential. She admires that as much as she fears it because it's an ideal she would spout but not one she could ever commit to.

And if he keeps shining such a bright, incomparable light, who knows what it might expose.

She needs to speak – needs to say something profound – because she cannot be left behind here. 'I think all of us – whether it's making art or food or an app or a post – when you boil it all down, isn't it just screaming into the void: *Tell me I am not alone?* Maybe that's what we're all doing here – we're all seeking that human connection.'

'Oh my god, we get it!' Rhys laughs as he jogs over, sea water clinging to the lines of his torso and the strands of his hair. 'We're all some ideal of passionate perfection! We all like whatever it is we're claiming we like! We don't need to talk about it *all the time.*'

He snatches a glass of water from the table and downs it.

'Some of us like talking about it,' Theo says grimly, eyes cutting to Rhys like he is something distasteful that the sea has discarded on the beach. 'Some of us are only here to talk about it.'

Rhys smiles in a way that is gentle and unsettling.

'Not to get away from the paparazzi? The bandmates?'

Theo's jaw clenches. He runs his eyes over the man, knowing all he wants is a reaction and trying to work out why, even as he resolves not to give it to him.

When he speaks it's with a dismissive finality: 'I don't know what you're talking about, Sutton, so why don't you run off to whatever it is you were doing and leave us to discuss whatever the hell we want.'

One by one, they notice the missing card.

Isko: *It's not one of mine so who cares.*

Araminta: *Of course. My only surprise is that it happened so quickly.*

Rhys: *We should have just shared them all, like I said.*

Jerome: *I don't see anything wrong with it, to be honest. If you're in a competition, there's no fault to be found in getting to know your adversary. Losing one point now could gain you ten in the future if you leverage it right.*

Isko returns from the smoking area to find Rhys on the deck chair he had departed. He's clearly just been swimming, and while most of the water has evaporated, it pools in the lines between his abs.

Isko is by no means out of shape, but Rhys's muscles are so finely chiseled that he allows himself to admire them. For a moment, he imagines what it would be like to lap that salty water up with his tongue. A drone hovers nearby, and he's sure the footage will make the final cut.

'I don't bite, you know,' Rhys says. 'Unless you're into that.'

'Of course I'm into that.'

Rhys pushes his sunglasses down his nose to examine him. 'A lucky man, your fiancé.'

'Indeed,' Isko says, pulling his shirt off and taking the next sun bed over.

Rhys: *I'm an equal opportunity lover. I suppose pansexual if you want to get technical. But I honestly don't much care for the person beyond the body. Sex and personal relationships are two very different things to me.*

'How long have you been together?' Rhys asks.

Isko shoots him a look. 'Do you actually care?'

'No,' Rhys says bluntly, not tearing his eyes from Isko's.

Isko: *Rhys is a flirt. But I'm not complaining.*

'Then what are you really asking, Sutton?'

'I'm going to be very bored with a month on this island. And if there's one thing I hate, it's being bored.'

'All right, guys?' Araminta greets. A loosely woven white smock is thrown over her bikini that shows every curve of her skin underneath it. Someone as pale as she is shouldn't wear white, but she makes it work. It washes her out, yes, but there's something striking about it all that suits her.

Isko really wishes he weren't noticing this now, but of course he is – this was the sort of thing he was paid to notice, not just as chef but friend and fashion-adviser and everything in between. But Araminta is not his former employer. Juliet Moncrieff is fun and flippant and careless, and she knew what she was doing in all ways except the

40

one that damned her. Araminta is contained and poised and purposeful in a way that hints at covering up a mess. And yet, Isko already feels that growing itch to be liked by her, to glow in her acceptance. And he can't have that.

Isko: *And then Araminta arrives because of course no moment on this island would be complete without the princess. And I'm in an open relationship, by the way. Just so that's clear.*

'Mind if I join?' She doesn't wait for a response before she puts her cocktail glass on the table and pulls her slip off, perching on the edge of the seat next to Rhys as she slathers sunscreen on, her fingers dipping beneath the thin black cord of the microphone twisted around her body in a way that is almost explicit.

'Need a hand with that?' he asks.

She scrutinizes him before nodding. 'Yeah, actually, if that's okay.'

'I'm going for a smoke,' Isko snaps.

Rhys: *That time, I wasn't actually flirting. I have way better moves than the cliché sunscreen approach. But if it works? Well . . .*

Araminta jolts as he touches her and Rhys runs his hands across her shoulder blades more than is necessary. After a moment she leans into his touch.

'SPF fifty huh?' he asks, flipping the bottle over.

'Have you seen me?' Araminta asks, lying her arm next to his. A network of veins is visible beneath her skin, whereas Rhys was tanned before arriving on the island.

'Vividly.' His smile is a slash of teeth.

As he finishes, she rises to open the umbrella near her deck chair. She's taking no risks with this hot sun and she looks shocking there, on the screen, when every other reality show has bronzed gods glistening in the heat. She returns to her seat with her cocktail and takes an agonizingly long sip, pulling away with a whine.

'Long day?' Rhys jokes.

'I'm so bored! Why didn't they give us anything to do?'

'I think that's the point – they want to force us all to talk to each other.'

'Sticking us all on an island with nothing but other high-achievers and a well-stocked wine cellar?' Araminta asks, looking at him over her sunglasses. 'They're birthing chaos.'

Rhys tilts his head to the side and grins at the camera. 'Good thing I thrive on chaos, then.'

'I can't do this anymore,' Araminta declares after just half an hour of sunbathing. She leaps to her feet and pulls her crocheted dress back on. It's hideously uncomfortable – who thinks knitwear is perfect for a beach? It catches the sand, it's too itchy against her bare skin, and it's far too warm despite the loose weave. But she's paid her stylist enough.

And her publicist.

And her manager.

All those people who she can hear screaming in her head that no one wants to watch this. This show is her chance to rebrand herself, to force the world to reckon with the talent she knows she has. She wants to make herself synonymous with Rodin and Michelangelo rather than FaceTune and Pretty Up. But to do that, she needs as many viewers as she can get and she needs to be the fan favourite and she needs to make sure she's getting screen time and votes for the challenges and she can't rely on an edit, she needs to give them content they can't ignore.

All this talk about returning to her artistic roots, but she's an influencer to her core, and her heart beats to the sound of *content, content, content.*

'Come on,' she tells Rhys.

He snorts a half laugh. 'Give me those come-hither eyes and I'd follow you anywhere, but I would appreciate some sort of explanation.'

She smiles, intimately, indicative of some sort of collusion. She uses this trick often – forcing a closeness into being that doesn't exist. 'I refuse to play into this absolutely shameless attempt of Eloise's to cause friction. She wants us to be careful of who we trust? Screw that; I'm going to force us to trust each other – at least a little bit. And in the process, I'm going to find out who we're trapped on this island with. Aren't you curious?'

Rhys's answering smile is one of delight. 'Whatever you have planned, I am thoroughly here for it.'

The others are scattered around the island, uneasy and reluctantly summoned. Though they force smiles for the cameras, there's an edge of irritation as they gather on those long, reclining sunbeds, the canopied ones that feel like soft padded islands of their own. They can barely look at one another without their suspicions soaring and anxiety taking hold . . . but they sit in a circle anyway.

Araminta fetches bottles of liquor – the sort that a cable network would try to hide but not this show, streaming carelessly with no regulator to complain to.

She pours tequila into the shaker without measuring.

Kalpana's jaw twitches as she declines the cocktail passed to her and reaches for the whiskey instead. She swigs it straight from the bottle.

Kalpana: *Everything Araminta does is so performative – can't even gather us all without doing a little cocktail dance for the camera.*

'Let's get to know each other,' Araminta suggests.

'I think I know enough,' Isko sneers, but he takes a cocktail from her anyway.

'What did you have in mind?' Theo asks.

Araminta laughs and glances away. 'You'll think it's ridiculous, but well, we have little else to do. What do we think of "Never Have I Ever"?'

Kalpana's nose wrinkles. 'Must we?'

Jerome gives her a look over the top of his glass. 'Why, something to hide?'

'I'm down,' Theo says.

'Of course you are, Rockstar.' Rhys rolls his eyes. 'For you this is a bragging game, right?'

'Like it's any different for you,' Theo retorts and for a moment they stare, trying to work out if this is a challenge.

'I'm game,' Jerome interjects. 'Though fair warning that there isn't much I haven't done. My college days at Stanford were particularly wild.'

'I'm sure,' Araminta says dryly, taking up her own drink. 'All right, you know the rules – take a sip if you've done the thing. Never have I ever kissed someone.'

'That's too easy,' Rhys says once they all lower their glasses.

'Oh, we'll get there, but I'm starting small.'

'Never have I ever slept with a friend's partner,' Kalpana says.

Araminta, Rhys, and Theo drink.

'But they were polyamorous; they both knew and were fine with it,' Araminta says.

44

Rhys raises his glass to Theo. 'Looks like it's just us two that are trash then.'

But Theo shakes his head. 'It's really not something I'm proud of.'

Rhys snorts. 'Shame is an indulgence of one's own self-importance.'

Theo: *I hate him. I might actually hate him.*

'Never have I ever had a threesome,' Jerome says, an eagerness to his tone that implies he was not happy to be left out of a moment.

When everyone drinks, he hesitates just a moment before joining, his eyes startled and watchful.

'Let me correct myself,' he rushes and his eyes land on Araminta. 'Never have I ever had a threesome with a married couple who are friends with and the age of my parents.'

Araminta's glass doesn't move but the tension braids between them like a thick rope, fraying only with the strain of who might break it first.

'Come on, Araminta,' Jerome says delicately. 'We've all read the articles.'

'Speak for yourself,' Theo says, glowering at him but catching the eye of the camera over his shoulder instead. It makes a better shot.

The others are almost wary, fingers curled into the fabric of the chair, distracting themselves from their unease with a sip of a drink or adjusting their hair. They had not considered this unequal footing: that some contestants might be in the public eye and that some amongst them might already know something about their competition.

'It was a foursome, actually,' Araminta says matter-of-factly. Unlike them, she had considered this at length,

45

and when she is faced with it, the petty accusations run off her skin like every headline ever did. 'Their chauffeur also joined but he wasn't famous so the paps cut him from their shot. I guess they thought he was just giving us a ride and not giving us a ride.'

Rhys laughs and that delighted grin is back.

Rhys: *I might have to marry this woman.*

Kalpana takes a quick sip before she speaks – unlike the others, she uses words that are not pointed but quick and sharp like a surgical incision. 'Never have I ever been sued for endangering women and then tried to slut shame one on live television.'

Jerome turns so abruptly his drink spills over its lid with the jerky movement. He seems on the cusp of saying something but cannot manage to pull the words together past his shock and rage.

Araminta swivels to face her with wide, startled eyes, and for a moment Kalpana worries she has overstepped, pointedly attacking back without checking with her first.

But Kalpana doubles down. 'Go on, aren't you going to drink?'

Jerome's eyes flicker with fury: not merely that she has said this, but that there is only one way she could know. He glares her down as he says: 'Never have I ever taken one of the cards from the wall.'

The pivot takes everyone a moment – a moment in which they almost miss Rhys taking a long sip from his cup.

'Oh my god, what?' Kalpana cries.

'Of course it would be you,' Isko says with a half laugh.

Isko: *There's something attractive about such recklessness,* *about the idea you might make terribly bad decisions for one moment of fun.*

'Whose card was it?' Jerome asks.

Rhys tries not to make it clear, but his eye catches on Theo. He'd been expecting anger – not resigned expectation – and it takes him by enough surprise that he hesitates. They all clock it.

'Mine,' Theo confirms, voice quiet and breathy, like a long exhale of relief. 'Go on then, you might as well get it out.'

'Are you sure about that, Rockstar?' Rhys asks, brow furrowing in a way that might be concern if he weren't the one who created the wound Theo now bleeds from. 'This might as well be dynamite.'

'If you've read the card, it's a bomb that's already ticking. No sense lingering in anticipation.' Theo's voice is tight.

'I could promise not to tell anyone.'

'I'd never trust you.'

Rhys takes the folded card from his pocket, its edges jagged. It is astonishing to see it like that – all this suspense and here it is, an ordinary scrap in someone's pocket.

He holds it out to Theo. 'If you want it known, you read it.'

Throughout, Theo has been nowhere near as angry as anyone else might be. But now he is positively outraged, tendons in his neck tight, nostrils flaring.

He snatches the page from Rhys and turns to Kalpana, presenting the card to her like he cannot bear to look at it.

'Please,' he says. 'Don't make me humiliate myself further. Isn't this bad enough already?'

47

She hesitates, but he seems resigned, so she nods and takes it. With a wavering voice, she reads: 'I think I hate my bandmates.'

No one was expecting it – not the simplicity of it, no inner turmoil, but a simple fact, nor that it might inexplicably have nothing to do with any of them.

But they do recognize it for what it is: career suicide.

The edit lingers on their silence, the waiting mics and tense cameras clinging to the heavy stillness.

And finally, under his breath, Rhys breaks it: 'Boom.'

Slowly, Theo stands and strides away.

Theo's destruction ignites something in them, secrets spilling like a dam has burst. They pour so quickly it is difficult to push past their onward flood to the realization they are hardly secrets at all and certainly not as catastrophic as Theo's. But they pretend they are – they gasp and frown and needle information like if they throw enough of themselves into it, they might snatch attention back from Theo, whose unravelling they cannot allow to draw the cameras away from themselves.

Araminta spins tragedy, as though it is not well documented and readily available. Her absent millionaire father brought back to panic attacks and heartbreak – the things that might make her absurdity relatable.

Jerome's are all sex, like he can see Theo's fall in popularity and snatch the vacancy for expected island playboy.

Rhys's are horrendous – affairs and lies, thefts and drama – cementing the pain inflicted on Theo as another in a long line, the sort of things that will have the camera glued to him.

Kalpana's horse has never been higher, moralizing so intently they struggle to even pretend to believe it – that she has never used palm oil, not had sex in a year, that the Australian on a Portuguese island has never even travelled in a plane. Isko abstains completely, running across the island in a fruitless search for Theo, desperate to be the shoulder he cries on, begging to steal some of the lime-light of his scandal for himself.

By the time the TV alarm rings again, they have all drunk past the fear of the cameras and the proven consequences of those secrets glowing on the walls. Araminta's head is in Kalpana's lap, her feet in Rhys's. Isko is curled in the corner, practically horizontal, and Jerome stumbles to the kitchen for a drink he doesn't need.

Araminta blinks sleepily, Kalpana's fingers still in her hair, not even aware she had been toying with the blonde curls until she jolts as though caught.

Theo returns to the summoning call of the alarm, stony eyed and exhausted.

Theo: *I don't know what to say. I . . . I feel like I should deny it. To apologize and pretend it's not true. More than anything I'm just sorry to the fans. I'm sure we'll get through it – the band isn't breaking up – but, yeah, fame has not been good for us. I don't think I like who they've become, and I'm sure they don't like who I've become either.*

Eloise appears on screen, too shiny and polished for their drunk eyes.

'Good evening, contestants!' Even her voice is refined, the cheeriness too honed, the delivery too perfect. 'I hope you all enjoyed your first day on the island. Today we have a mini-challenge for you. Mini-challenges won't win you

49

points, but they might give you an advantage in the next group challenge. Only one of you will get to do a mini-challenge each day, and our audience have spent the day voting on who they want it to be.'

The contestants tense. If they are not here for the money but fame, then these challenges matter more than the grander ones – they are the popularity test, the metric of how much screen time they're getting, of how they're being received.

'And our first contestant is . . .'

Later they'll hate it, the way they lean forward in their seats, the anticipation. They'd like to believe it's for show, not a desperate need to be chosen. Not necessarily to be liked, but to be the gravitational centre the cameras and the public turn to. They do not merely wish to be famous; they wish to be *more* famous, to shine brighter and bolder and finally – *finally* – have the world agree on what they have always known: that they are essential.

'Araminta.'

It's not only disappointment, it's rage. Sudden and violent, Kalpana's fist twisting the fabric of her shawl, Rhys's jaw clenching, the sharp tendons in Jerome's arms.

They would rather cling to their anger as something righteous than admit their jealousy.

Araminta gives a modest, almost shy nod of her head.

Isko: *Of course it would be her – the last person who needs an advantage, or even the cash prize.*

'What do we actually expect of the greatest amongst us? Well, for one thing, we expect them to be talented in their field. So Araminta, today we've devised a test just for you. And what's a bigger challenge for influencers than handling a social media crisis? Head on down to the confession booth because we have quite the simulation for you!'

Araminta's smile has fallen long before the final word leaves Eloise's lips.

Araminta: *You know, there was a moment there when I thought I might actually get to sculpt something.*

Anger morphs into vicious, acidic glee – their competition torn down if not in blood, then humiliation.

Kalpana: *Oh, that's embarrassing.*

Araminta stands and smooths out her dress with shaking hands. Swallowing her indignity, she follows Eloise to the challenge.

The others break into laughter the moment she's gone.

Isko gives a wry shake of his head. 'Imagine being here, surrounded by such talent in so many important areas and thinking you can stand amongst them with something like *influencing.'*

Kalpana refrains from commenting.

Kalpana: *It's difficult because I don't think she's on par with us, but I'm also very aware that influencing in the way that she does is a woman-dominated activity that takes time and effort. Male influencers are seen as charismatic. Women are seen as hot – it's sexist.*

But the contestants don't see what the audience does: Araminta in the booth, handling the challenge with a steely determination. A fake company being truly cancelled online, and there is Araminta with a cold smile and quick eyes, tapping buttons, spinning their unethical supply chain crisis into not only a resolved solution but an opportunity for growth, generating messages of support and gaining thousands of new followers.

It's what she does, when she's at the end of the firing line, a crisis, an accusation threatening to drag her down. She doesn't just come out of it unscathed, she glows.

One day, a true tragedy might just make her radiant.

When she returns to the others, Eloise appears on screen to praise her performance. 'Having successfully completed your challenge, you may take down any two notes without point reductions or disqualifications.'

Araminta rushes to that wall.

Kalpana: *Oh fuck. Do you know the damage she could do?*

Jerome leaps to his feet almost instinctively, like he might run and tackle her. But all they can do is watch with tense, anguished anticipation.

Araminta rips two of her own cards down and throws them straight into the fire.

The contestants glance at each other, clearly thinking the same thing: what's she hiding that is worth more than exposing the competition?

Isko: *Odds are, most of those cards are going to stay on the wall. So, of course, taking someone else's card is worth more than burning your own.*

Rhys: *Just when I thought she couldn't be hotter, now she has secrets.*

Afterward, Araminta is quiet and subdued – the sort of collapsing thing that might be anger and might be upset, but the men do not even notice. Kalpana does though. With a silent nod and a few glances, an effortless exchange takes them away from all that chatter.

Together, they head to the smoking area.

Theo sits on the beach watching the dark, encroaching waves.

Theo: *I can't believe it only took twenty-four hours of being here for my life to implode.*

The others continue talking around the firepit.

'I appreciate it, you know,' Isko says to Rhys. 'The boldness in taking the card, in revealing it like that with a quiet sip.'

Rhys shrugs. 'Like I said, I hate to be bored.'

'You know, I'm the same,' he says, standing without taking his eyes off the other man. 'I'm going to bed. Are you coming?'

'Excuse me?' Rhys says, sitting up a little straighter, his shirt unbuttoned in a way that makes him look already dishevelled.

'I'm bored,' Isko says. 'And I do so hate to be bored.'

Rhys's eyes light up. 'All right then.'

The two vanish up the stairs, door echoing shut as the episode fades to an end.

@DestroyTheNameAlice

Oh my God WHAT??? Theo if you let this break up RiotParade we will NEVER forgive you! I followed this band for years, it means too much for too many of us and I can't believe you would do something like this! #Iconic

---

@FionaReeves_

Not me coming into Iconic thrilled at the existence of a reality show that doesn't revolve around romance just to scream as Isko and Rhys head upstairs #Iconic

---

@RiotParadeOfficial

Hi all, we're as surprised by the revelations on #Iconic as everyone else. It's difficult to come to a consensus when

Theo is still on the show and we can't talk to him but rest
assured, all bands have their difficulties and Theo still has
our FULL support. We'll work it out when you're back
home, pal – until then #TeamTheo – love Al, Dante
and Tyson

Kennard flicks through reports of the episodes, tracing
drama like motives. It's a tangled web, too many intersect-
ing lines, too many things he'd dismiss as inconsequential
if he hadn't seen for himself how they exploded on screen.
The suspects burned bright and bold, and he wouldn't put
it past a hot flash of temper to be all the explanation they'll
need. But that would be difficult to cover up. *If* Rhys was
murdered, to make it a mystery like this, with all these
cameras, he suspects he's looking for a plan, a rage that
seethed from the very first episodes.

He returns to Theo.

'I wouldn't have expected you to be the one to go after
the body like that. That was a very decent and brave thing
you did.'

Theo shakes his head, eyes wincing shut like he cannot
reconcile himself with such words.

'Especially with someone like Rhys.'

Nothing.

'So much happened on that show, but it was all rather

54

contained, wasn't it? Except for you, because for you there were repercussions. Your life was crumbling, episode by episode, and you were just stuck on an island, waiting for the dust to clear.'

Nothing.

'And I think many people would argue Rhys was the one who set it all in motion and made it all come crashing down at the end.'

Now a breath, and Theo looks up with reluctant despair.

'No, Rhys just got tangled up in messes that already existed. Sure, he may have helped bring them to everyone's attention, even made some false accusations. But it all would have come out eventually. Blaming Rhys would make him a scapegoat for other people's problems.'

But, Kennard notes, scapegoats can be led to slaughter all the same.

Maes takes her seat in the interview room, repressing a shiver. Metal table, one-way mirror, everything shiny and gleaming and so very cold. She doesn't miss this, but here she is, pulled from the digital team because Kennard and Cloutier thought Kalpana would respond better to a woman. They're probably right, however much she resents them for it.

Kalpana clutches her arms across her chest and regards Maes with a challenging gleam in her eye. It's like she can't believe she's here, that Rhys even had the audacity to die.

'You were the last one to speak to Mr Sutton.'

'Allegedly,' Kalpana snorts, leaning her chair onto its back legs.

It's quite a claim given it's the video racking up the highest views – the last conversation, possibly the last clue.

'Could you explain what you mean by that?'

'Theo tried to save him. Maybe he was conscious, maybe he said something.'

'The microphone didn't pick anything up.'

Kalpana gives her a withering look.

'Do you know of many microphones that work in that condition? Things that fall off cliffs tend to break.'

'Are you talking about the microphone or Mr Sutton?' Maes asks quickly. Maybe too quickly, because Kalpana looks like she's reappraising her.

Then she shrugs.

'You don't seem particularly upset about his death. The others are quite broken up about it.'

Kalpana's teeth grind.

'I tried to save him too, you know. Theo wasn't the only one.'

Apparently irritating her is the only way to get answers. 'None of you seem to understand that a man has died. In fact, the whole world is treating his death like the latest entertainment. We are not the whole world – we're the police. We are investigating a murder. If you weren't too busy posturing and thinking of your next witty retort, you might realize one of you is likely going to be put away for this. And you, Kalpana, given that little encounter *right* before he tipped over the edge, are our prime suspect.'

Kalpana's chair slams down as she throws herself forward, leaning across the table, lip twitching even before she speaks.

'Rhys Sutton was a horrible man who was too busy yelling at me to realize how close he was to the edge. And I'd expect the police to be smart enough to notice he was covered in blood when he found me. If you're looking to, what was it? "Put someone away" for this?' she sneers. 'I'd look at whoever broke his fucking nose and I'd start thinking the word *manslaughter*.'

Iconic

Season 1, Episode 3

Araminta: *So, um, things are kind of awkward this morning.*

The show title fades in under Araminta's stumbling words. Somewhere, her publicist smiles. Araminta has opened three of these episodes now, evidently the golden child of these producers. She had told her to go in there and cause some conflict, but she should have known Araminta would do it with the delicacy of a sculpture – one tiny chip at a time and always with her eyes on the finished piece.

Araminta: *I mean, not really awkward? Just confusing? Oh, I don't know.*

Araminta is in the confessional booth, footage they rarely flick to, preferring voiceover alone. The lights are bright on her face, the plush chair swallowing her. Dark shadows ring her eyes.

Araminta: *So Kalpana and I kissed last night. That's something I'm certain happened. I just . . . my memory's hazy – I was pretty drunk. I'm worried I said something or did something that might have made her think that I wanted . . . well, anything beyond a drunken kiss.*

The screen goes black, a hazy sort, like a camera is pointed at the night sky. No cameras operate in the smoking area, but the contestants still wear their microphones. Subtitles spill onto the screen over crackling audio.

*[***Araminta:*** *Oh god, sorry.]*

[**Kalpana:** *Ahh, you're a messy drunk. What is it? Damaged rich girl?*]

[**Araminta:** *Oh, piss off.*]

[**Kalpana:** *I'm just joking. Sort of. You're kind of fascinating; I can't resist.*]

[**Araminta:** *I'm more than just 'kind of' fascinating.*]

[**Kalpana:** *As the flames can attest, what secrets are you hiding, Araminta?*]

[**Araminta:** *. . . Well, for one, I can't stop thinking about the fact you haven't had sex in a year.*]

[**Kalpana:** *Why?*]

[**Araminta:** *Because . . . you know full well why. Look at you.*]

[**Kalpana:** *You think I haven't copped a root because no one has shown interest? [laughter] Please. I just haven't met anyone remotely interesting.*]

[**Araminta:** *Bullshit. You just called me fascinating.*]

[**Kalpana:** *Yes, yes I did.*]

[**Araminta:** *Oh.*]

And then the only sound is static.

Araminta: *If what we had could be considered a friendship, I'm worried I just ruined it.*

Two figures lie in a bed, the camera in stark black and white, the footage grainy.

White sheets are tangled around their naked forms, both asleep. Slowly, Isko stirs. He blinks wearily at the man next to him, and a lazy grin, the sort he'd never wear if fully awake, flits across his lips.

He falls back onto the bed, arm falling across Rhys, and closes his eyes.

*

60

Once again, Araminta rises first. And once again, Rhys finds her in the kitchen.

'So you really just look this good in the mornings?' he asks, dragging his eyes down her body purposefully, bright lines of her bikini, red this time, visible through her sheer wrap.

'Wouldn't you love to know,' she says, pouring her smoothie into a water bottle.

'Is that a trick question? Because you know I would.'

Araminta arches an eyebrow. 'How's Isko?'

'I imagine rather sated.' He stretches his arms above his head, T-shirt riding up and flashing those taut muscles of his, somehow more alluring for this snapshot than the generosity of a bare chest.

'I wouldn't want to wake without you,' she says before catching herself. 'If I were him, that is.'

'Noted.'

Araminta blushes and returns to her smoothie, attempting to distract herself by slipping the straw in her mouth. Rhys's eyes follow her hungrily, and it's unclear whether he is truly attracted to her – probable, as she is gorgeous, but who on the island isn't – or simply sees her as another prize to be won.

'Have you spoken to Theo?' she asks, changing the topic before he can make another comment – a comment Araminta would mark as creepy in another life but here, on this rock in the middle of nowhere, she suddenly finds enticing.

'It wasn't the first thing on my list for the day, no.'

'I don't imagine he's happy.'

'No, but how do you feel about it?' he asks, and the way

he looks at her makes her feel like he genuinely fears her disapproval.

She weighs her options. The truth is that she doesn't much care. She's glad it wasn't her, and if she could see some strategic purpose for it, she might have done the same. But she won the popular vote last night and doubts the voting public will be quite as forgiving. 'I think it was disgraceful. We have no reason to trust each other but we offered up such fragile parts of ourselves – parts we thought would be hidden when we wrote them. What you did was a violation. The competition might allow it, but I'm not sure my morality does.'

'Hmm,' he says, considering her. 'A very valid point. In which case you'll also think it awful that I don't particularly care what Newman thinks about what happened. But your opinion I do care for – and I'm far more interested in making it up to you.'

But before he can expand on how he plans to do that, Kalpana breezes into the room.

'Morning,' she says, grabbing a glass and filling it with, of all things, tap water. In a show like this, firsts are always noteworthy.

'Well, I'd best be off,' Rhys says, pouring a second cup of coffee and adding it to the tray.

'You're going back?' Araminta doesn't even realize she's spoken.

Rhys plasters the most innocent of grins across his face. 'Of course. Whatever did you imagine?'

'I –'

'Besides, round two,' he says with a shrug, disappearing before Araminta can mumble a response.

Kalpana shakes her head. 'I'm not sure who made the worse choice there, Rhys or Isko.'

Araminta hums her agreement, and she's not sure how a hum can sound disingenuous but it does.

'How are you feeling?' Kalpana asks.

'Tired,' Araminta replies quickly, like she'd prepared for this conversation, which she has — something indirect, something that says she's fine and doesn't want to talk about it but also doesn't mind talking about it if Kalpana asks, because she doesn't care.

'Well, luckily you're on an island with literally nothing to do for the entire day. Nap times abound,' Kalpana says, grabbing a banana. 'I'm going to eat this in the sun. See you later.'

Kalpana: *Look, I just wanted to feel something in this paradise. And Araminta would do. There's nothing more to it than I wanted her — but only in a very certain past tense.*

Araminta watches her leave, realizing that maybe she did want to talk about it. That maybe she had wanted it to mean something after all.

Isko leans against the doorway, white shirt unbuttoned, bronzed muscles glistening with sweat that can't be from the heat. His stance, the sunglasses pushed through his hair, the very way he glances at Rhys is nonchalant. Too much so.

'You want everyone on the island, yes?' Isko asks.

Rhys pauses doing up the buttons of his shirt as he contemplates the question. 'Jerome strikes me as the gay panic sort.'

'You know what I mean.'

63

'Are you asking me if we're exclusive, Isko? Pretty hypocritical given your current relationship status.'

Isko is already losing interest, staring at Rhys with the cold light of day. Rhys must catch his disappointment, because he straightens up and gives Isko his full attention.

'How do I fall into the game?' Isko asks.

'You're not a game.'

'Of course I am. We're all games here. So tell me how I fit into yours.'

'I didn't come here for that.'

'You took a card from the wall, Rhys; you're this game incarnate.'

'I took the card because I wanted to. Because I was curious and bored and thought it would be fun. I came here to be real, to be a part of something you can't find on any other channel or even in any other walk of life. I had sex with you because I wanted to, not because I think it will help me win this thing. In fact, I'm pretty certain the voting public will take as kindly to a casual sexual liaison between two men as they will to me hurting Theo Newman like I did. So if I were playing a game, you wouldn't be part of it.'

Isko shakes his head softly, as he realizes Rhys is telling the truth. 'I expected more from you.'

Theo skulks through the house, trying to work out his next move. How long should he be upset for? How should he try to rectify it? This whole thing is a precision pointed plan but he wasn't expecting those cards to be available for anyone to read. He'd known it was a chance, obviously.

You had to be a fool to suspect they wouldn't have a way of exposing it. He might have expected a camera hovering over his shoulder rather than a wall of secrets but he'd expected it all the same.

He just wasn't expecting it so quickly, and he wasn't expecting it like this.

It's out and he doubts the rest is yet – so what should he do?

He tries to avoid the others until he works it out, dodging Jerome around the pool to slip to the beach once more.

If he really had said that unintentionally, with no plans of breaking away from the band as he wants everyone to suspect – he'd try to rectify it, wouldn't he? But he doesn't want to appear too attached or it would defeat the purpose of distancing himself altogether.

He needs the world to know he hates them, that he is different from them, that no, he was never really associated with them, and one day this will all be part of a trivia game: *Theo Newman started in a band – ten points to anyone who can name it!*

He grabs a cushion from an armchair and screams into it, hurling it back with furious vigor that does not dispel his rage. He wants to kick and fight and never stop screaming. Has he not already raised his hands high and let himself land at the mercy of others? Is that not what got him on this show in the first place, a team of publicists saying, '*This might sound ludicrous, but we have an idea.*'

And here he is at the mercy of it all again. How many times must he lose control before the universe aligns itself once more to his whims?

He does not need everyone thinking *he* tore RiotParade

apart. He could tank his solo career before he's even launched it.

He has to stand by it. He can't be too angry at Rhys. He must be resigned and own up to the fact that Rhys exposing his feelings isn't the issue so much as what's driving the band apart.

He's going to have to publicly forgive Rhys.

The very thought leaves a foul taste in his mouth, but he washes it away with a particularly hoppy beer and returns to the pool. Isko and Rhys lie on separate lounge chairs. Araminta clings to the poolside, her head resting on her arms, her body the blur of her red bikini beneath the water. Jerome sits beside her, legs over the side, shirt unbuttoned over faint muscles.

'Maybe I should give up,' Araminta laughs, not stopping their conversation as Theo joins. 'Maybe the lesson I take from this isn't that I can be more, but that I have no reason to be disappointed with what I am. Better a content creator than a spoiled heiress, right?'

'At least you're a good one,' Isko says, eyes shut beneath his sunglasses like he's only half paying attention. 'Why be an awful sculptor when you can be an excellent influencer?'

'My sculptures are excellent, I'll have you know.'

'They should have challenged you with home rejuvenation,' Theo says with a sheepish smile. 'You could have fixed the energy in this place that, for some reason I'm struggling to recall, seems to have deteriorated.'

Rhys sits up, swinging his legs over the side of the chair to stand and clap him on the back. 'I think that one's on me to fix.'

Theo nods, and it seems the closest they might get to some sort of reconciliation.

Theo: *I don't want things to be strained between Rhys and I. It's a new day, and while I'm not happy he did what he did, the real issue is what I wrote. And I can't blame him for the way I feel about Riot-Parade. It's like I said: I am more than the drama.*

But he's not. And even as he smiles, he feels rage scalding his insides. His secrets, but not on his terms; his career, subject to the whims of this man's boredom. 'Anyone want a drink?' Rhys offers.

'Nah, I'm not drinking today; my body needs a break,' Araminta says. Theo takes Rhys's spot as he leaves, feet dangling in the cool pool.

'I'm surprised you're not doing a full detox,' Isko says. 'You seem the type.'

'Detox,' she scoffs. 'Is that still where we're at? You're from LA, right? Did you bring an IV drip to the island?'

'I'm *from* the Philippines – I *live* in LA. And not by choice, either. I trained in Paris and would have stayed there if I could. But my fiancé got a job he couldn't refuse and –'

'Wait, you have a fiancé?' Jerome interrupts. 'But I thought you and Rhys . . .'

Isko rolls his eyes. 'Rhys and I what? For Christ's sake, Jerome, I'm not fifty. Who does monogamy anymore?'

'Oh, yeah, of course,' Jerome says hastily.

'It's an open relationship.'

Araminta arches a barely visible eyebrow. 'Open in what manner?'

'Legs, mostly.'

'I meant, is your engagement one relationship of many or is it only open sexually?'

Isko wants a cigarette or a drink, something to do with his hands right now, something to split his attention. He's not a fan of this interrogation but can't think of a redirect.

'The latter – no emotional relationships outside of ours, just sexual,' he says, rolling his eyes again. He's so deeply tired of them already.

He always wondered how people watched reality shows where the conversation was the kind of boring drivel that made him think he could actually feel his brain rotting. Now he's stuck in one. He'd thought the people on those shows impossibly dull, that *Iconic* would be different, that they would be different. But it turns out, without any form of entertainment, they are all mundane.

'What does he do?' Jerome asks, an upturn to his voice that makes his politeness seem forced.

'He's an accountant.'

Araminta snorts. 'Oh, I'm so sorry. I just wasn't expecting that.'

Isko: *Oh really? This is how it's going to go? You have something to say about my fiancé? Spit it out then.*

'Wait, like an *accountant* as in . . . you know, OnlyFans, or as in someone with a calculator?' Jerome asks.

'He had to pass an awful lot of exams, you know.'

'An actual accountant. Christ.' Araminta shakes her head.

'Why is that such a surprise?' Isko's glaring over the ass of his sunglasses.

Theo laughs, not snidely but in a genuinely delighted way. 'Because we're a bunch of people so pretentious we were picked to be on a TV show about pretentious arseholes. And being an accountant is such a normal thing to be.'

'Please tell me he's called Tom or Harry or something,' Araminta says.

'His name is Alex.'

She cackles. 'Perfect.'

Isko points. 'You three are assholes.'

Theo frowns. 'Is that not what I just said?' He and Araminta shriek in their laughter, and even Jerome has a grin on his face.

Isko shakes his head and stands up.

'Oh, come on man, we're just joking,' Theo says.

Isko doesn't even reply, just storms off as they fight past their amusement to beg him to stay.

'I suppose it's nice, isn't it?' Araminta offers. 'I either pick someone I can't stand for long or never manage to choose someone who can stand me. I can't imagine a relationship lasting longer than a few months, let alone through a whole TV show.'

Jerome shakes a truly disappointed head. 'I should have known you're one of those girls that never picks a nice guy.'

Araminta: *Urgh. I give him two days max before he's begging Kalpana or I to let him into our pants and then calling us a bitch when we refuse.*

She leaps to her feet. 'You know what, maybe I do want a drink after all.'

As evening falls, Araminta finds Isko outside, catching the last of the day's warmth.

She taps her finger on the glass, the soft clinking audible on the microphones. She is nervous. Or rather, she would like to appear nervous. 'I wanted to apologize for earlier. I didn't mean to be cruel about Alex, I think it's great you

69

have someone in your life who means so much to you, and I am certainly not knocking accountants. Could you imagine how unbearable the world would be if everyone was like us? All awfully wrapped up in our own visions of ourselves?'

Isko hums in agreement, which is the closest to accepting her apology that he will come. He makes no further efforts to continue the conversation.

'So you don't remember me, do you?' she says, and it's clear this is her real reason for joining him.

He turns to her sharply. 'What? No. We've met?'

'I used to date Dean Rodríguez.'

'Ah,' he says slowly. 'So you . . .'

'Yeah, I spent a week on that yacht in St Kitts. You joined us sometimes, remember? I think I spent about a month afterward dreaming of your lobster benedict.'

Isko nods. He doesn't really remember Araminta, but there were plenty of rich blondes – especially on Dean's arm. And Dean had been friends with Juliet for so long it was easier to recall the moments he wasn't with them – on a yacht or at a party or at one of her homes. No wonder Araminta reminded him of Juliet – subconsciously, he must have recalled the two together.

'Well, I just wanted to say how sorry I am about what happened to Juliet,' she says. 'That must have been so horrible for you.'

'It was worse for her,' Isko answers grimly.

Isko: *[sigh] I don't particularly want to give this more attention, but yes, for the last few years I was a private chef to the pop star Juliet Moncrieff. I do, distinctly, believe she had no idea she was committing any sort of crime and was led astray by management that should have*

70

protected her better. But no, I never had any awareness or involvement in the financial fraud. Juliet was very kind, a friend as much as an employer, and when she's free, I'll be the first in line to cater the party.

'But still – you know, losing the life you had with her.'

He meets her eyes, a distinctly *fresh* shade of green that makes him think of kale smoothies and the accompanying nausea. But he sees the intensity in her gaze, the bold indication that yes, she means everything he thinks she is implying.

Because Juliet wasn't just a friend to Isko, she was a gateway, and if Araminta was there, then she knows that – knows the way Isko was part of it all: the glitz and the glamour, A-list celebrities and all their perks, enjoying a limelight that vanished the moment Juliet was arrested. And this is what Araminta is saying: *I know why you're here. You want it all back, and you think this is how you'll get it.*

She's not wrong. About any of it.

'What do you want?' Isko asks. Being so abrupt isn't particularly out of character, but he's thrown enough by being exposed that he forgets to at least time it appropriately.

Thankfully, Araminta laughs. 'Friendship? We got along fairly well two years ago.'

'Not well enough for me to remember it.'

For the slightest of moments Araminta seems startled, but then she's back to that particular blend of excitement and joy that is uniquely her. 'A valid point. I shall endeavour to be more memorable this time.'

'Why?' he asks again. 'Do you actually care for my friendship, or is obtaining it simply good for your image? I'm the only thing ruining your cherubic reputation, so you're attempting to get me on your side?'

Araminta's laugh is a cackle and a more genuine sound than any she has made so far, possibly more than anything else on the island yet. 'I'm sorry my *what* reputation? No. I want us to be friends because I'm a lot. It's pretty much my defining characteristic.'

'You're not exactly selling yourself.'

'See, this is what I need. I need someone to call me out on my bullshit. Otherwise, I'll take it way too far and no one wants that.'

'You need a mediator for the audience?'

'Yes,' she says. The way to win this is to be the voice of the ordinary viewer – which is quite hard to be when you're a Yaxley-Carter – even an estranged one.

Isko is the only one she can trust to be honest. He's been too critical to suggest he'd hide anything.

'And you want me because?'

'Because you don't like me. So you're not going to spare my feelings.'

'I don't not like you,' Isko says, scowling as though the thought has only just occurred to him. 'In fact, I'm liking you quite a lot in this moment.'

'Fascinating insight into your psyche.'

Isko: *Everyone on this island is playing a game. Everyone has a strategy. Araminta is the first person to admit that, and I appreciate that. Odds are if you tell me you're planning to stab me in the back, I'll close my eyes and turn around for you. It's not the wound that would hurt, but the pretence of it all.*

'All right, let's see how this goes.'

'Fantastic. So first things first, I kissed Kalpana yesterday and she's been so . . . casual every time I've seen her today that I can't work out her feelings about it.'

72

Isko doesn't express much, his smiles few and far between, but his eyebrows are in constant movement, normally – like now – a flight toward his hairline. 'I'll find out.'

'Is there anything I can do for you?'

'Why would I want anything from you?'

'Because you should want everything you can have and several things you can't.'

Isko sighs. 'Fine, but you can't tell anyone.'

'Your secret is safe with me and the thousands of viewers.'

Isko continues despite her. 'Rhys has barely spoken to me all day. Which after last night . . .'

'So you want me to . . .'

'Find out if I'm a good fuck, yes.'

Araminta nods and raises her glass. 'I'm on it.' She stands to leave, but he calls after her.

'And, *my dear friend*,' he says, 'I hope your friendship shows itself in these challenges. Taking cards down, for instance. Should you have the opportunity to remove any more, I'd appreciate mine meeting the flames.'

The alarm blares earlier than expected, though it's hard to tell, in a place without clocks where the only markers of time are the sun drifting across the sky and, far more importantly, the challenges.

'Good evening, contestants!' Eloise squeals. She is particularly glamorous today, decked in sequins like she is on a red carpet. They can never quite tell if she's pre-recorded or speaking to them live, but they suspect it's the former – her cheeriness at odds with their relaxed tipsiness.

'You're all doing a wonderful job of resisting the

temptation of the secret wall. Those points clearly mean a lot to you! But there's an easier way to win them – and maybe even make the penalty for reading a card worth it . . . Are you ready for another mini-challenge? Remember, these are voted on by the at-home audience and come with rewards that might make earning points at the next group challenge easier!'

Yesterday had been awful – the anticipation, the need for the audience to pay attention to *them* over everyone else. But knowing that more cards might be on the line . . .

'Tonight's contestant is . . . Theo.'

In other circumstances, they would be as furious as they were when Araminta was chosen. But after yesterday's revelations, how could anyone else but Theo even hope to be chosen?

But Theo doesn't look pleased; he looks terrified.

'Theo, for tonight's challenge the audience have voted to test your candour. If there's one thing we expect from our heroes, it's honesty. And being caught out in a lie can destroy the careers of even the most successful.'

Rhys: *Oh my god, these challenges are so funny. Like, can you name a single musician whose career has been ruined by lying? Just say you want to grill him more about the band!*

'So,' Eloise continues, 'as well as voting for you, viewers have been submitting questions. We have five – for every one you answer honestly, you'll get one minute in the confession booth . . . with access to the internet!'

Theo transforms, his fear dissipating to eagerness. That reward so tangible he could reach out and snatch it.

He needs this, needs to see where the land lies after his revelation.

Jealousy returns to the others like a vulture swooping on a carcass. They could find out what's working and what's not, learn who's the favourite they should pay more attention to, or put out a message on their own terms without relying on the edit . . .

Isko: *Alex. I could send him a message.*

Kalpana: *I'd do anything to speak to my family.*

Rhys: *If anyone says they'd do anything but search their own name, they're lying. We're all desperate to know how we're being received.*

'Your first question comes from Ian Badgley in South Africa. He asks: Theo, who's *Bitter Devotion* really about?'

Jerome: *Really? You can find that answer with a Google search.*

'Al's girlfriend,' Theo answers quickly. 'I liked her first and hated that she chose him instead. We got over it.'

Araminta: *It was clear from the start that they were trying to find the reason for the tension without asking too directly, but come on? A girl? Dig deeper – things are never quite so simple.*

'Morayo Ajayi from the United Kingdom asks: Why didn't you go to the Indy Chime awards last month?'

Theo's smile is a touch guilty but somewhat smoldering as he turns to the camera. 'I blew it off to go to the Victoria's Secret pre-launch party instead.'

'Mackenzie Pessoa from Canada wants to know: If you could re-record any song, what would it be, and why?'

'Anything off the *Troublemakers* album; I was outvoted on nearly everything.'

It's the first sign of any true discord, but Theo says it with only an edge of bitterness: he's angry, but not angry enough that he would hate his band for it.

'Marine Laurent from France has asked: What's the worst thing you've ever done?'

Theo laughs, taken aback. 'Honestly? Go on live TV and say that I hate everyone in the band.'

'And finally, from Dante, Al, and Tyson from RiotParade . . .' Eloise pauses to deliver a wicked smile. Theo's breath catches and they all freeze, gripped like any viewer as the bandmates are read out. 'Do you want to go solo?'

Theo swallows, his cockiness gone as he stares at the screen like he's watching his life fall apart on its glossy surface.

'I . . . I don't know,' he says, and then, realizing it's not enough, he forces himself to keep going. 'Right now, I want to make it work. But yes, I'd like to go solo one day.'

They're already smiling and nodding – even Eloise, who it turns out is live after all. They are ready to accept that as his answer.

So why does he feel the need to blurt out 'I don't see this band lasting forever' and ruin it all over again? He might as well have pried the nails from the wall himself and used them for his career's coffin.

Theo: *Shit.*

He thought it would be easy to spread the fall, but he's blowing up the band so quickly he might get caught in the shrapnel too.

'I . . . thank you, Theo. That was very honest of you! If you go to the confession booth, you may now enjoy five minutes of time on the internet.'

He rises, the others still lingering in their shock.

And when he reaches that confession booth, the mouse and keyboard in his hand, he does only the quickest of searches to confirm the news he's waiting for is yet to break. And then he pushes his own reception aside – because he does not need to see himself raked over the coals; he needs to give them something else to focus on.

So, one by one, he searches the others instead, looking for ammunition that might embed itself in someone else's skin.

@RiotParadeOfficial
Well . . . that didn't go as expected. Don't worry Rioters, this isn't the first time Newman's dropped the ball when the press has a tricky question, we're all still #TeamTheo # Iconic – love Al, Dante, and Tyson

---

@BexC23
Araminta and Isko: *team up*
Me, entirely ready for the two cattiest contestants to cause drama: !!!
Araminta and Isko: can I kiss? Am I good in bed?
Me: oh my god someone protect these sweet summer children #Iconic

---

@SorayaElla
Umm guys, anyone seeing this??? SHARE: #Iconic Star Jerome Francis on the cusp of bankruptcy, financial adviser claims in leaked emails

---

'Maes is doing well.' Cloutier nods from the other side of the glass, watching as she speaks to Kalpana. 'Do you think it will be enough?'

'She's better in there than behind a screen. I don't think the answers lie in the footage; it's in there, with them,'

Kennard says, gesturing to Kalpana like he'd been looking at anything other than Cloutier's faint reflection in the glass. 'And I think, without a confession, we'd struggle to get an arrest, especially on this timeline. All those other teams – forensics and digital – they're wasting their time.'

Cloutier laughs softly. 'Asshole,' he says with an edge of affection.

It's not just a word from him, and certainly not an insult – it's something more intimate, something about how Kennard's name sounds in French, something Cloutier would whisper before he . . .

'Don't,' Kennard snaps, turning to face him, though his voice slows with the weight of its reluctance. 'We can't do this again – not on a case this important.'

'I know,' Cloutier says, stepping back. He hesitates, like he's going to say something else before he simply repeats: 'I know.'

Kennard doesn't get the chance to say anything else before Cloutier's phone starts to ring.

He glances at the screen and recognizes the number.

'That's one of the show producers. I should probably take this.'

He doesn't waste time trying to convince them not to air the finale. Far better people have already tried.

'So the contestants were completely isolated?'

'No, not at all,' the producer says, a defensive edge to her voice that Cloutier's too familiar with. If Kennard were taking the call, he'd already have snapped that if anyone was going to sue them over this – and they should – it won't be the police. But he's not Kennard, and more importantly, he cannot afford to think about Kennard right now. 'Most of the cameras were wall-mounted, but some were operated by drones, which had a maximum distance. Even with the storm, we had several teams on boats surrounding the island, including medics who were en route when . . . well.'

'You must have known that was a risk,' he says, unable to stop himself. 'There would have been assessments that told you that you might not get there in time in the event of an incident. It's difficult to believe a show like this was green lit.'

'Well it was,' she snaps. 'And the contestants knew the risks. We have the paperwork. They all signed it.'

Oh, well if there was paperwork then it's fine . . .

'Besides,' the producer continues, 'they weren't alone the whole time. We delivered food every Saturday. We'd also set up the equipment for the challenges and take away waste, though the contestants were instructed to be inside during these visits.'

Sounds pretty isolated to me.

'And you had footage streams running twenty-four hours a day on your website, and then each episode that went out on TV would be a compilation of yesterday's events?'

'That's right.'

'Would that not lead to spoilers?'

'Some, but gossip like that just adds to the excitement, really. Besides, it's not really the sort of show you can spoil. Big moments, sure, but if I told you, say, that Kalpana and Theo spoke about the act of creating, it wouldn't really cover the *nuance,* and that's what people tuned in for.'

Cloutier is not so sure that's true. The allure is in watching the mighty fall, not in their posturing.

'All right, let's talk alcohol. You provided a lot.'

'So does *The Bachelor*; that's reality TV.'

'They have handlers, don't they?' *And fewer precarious cliff-tops.*

'Have you actually watched the footage? Rhys didn't even touch the drink he poured.'

Cloutier freezes. If that's true, then their only advantage is in talking to the suspects, not reviewing footage everyone has seen.

'And the challenges pitted them against each other, not only in who could do something better, but who could *be* better? Would that not cause undue tension?'

There's a moment of silence on the other end of the line – silence filled with the image of five people on a beach, a broken body on the sand between them.

'Apparently.'

Iconic

Season 1, Episode 4

This morning, Araminta's urge to run is so strong that that's what she does until she hits the ocean. As her heart-beat slows, she does her usual yoga poses, the cold water clinging to her skin.

After a while, her feet are numb, but her head is clear and she turns back to the house, only to find Rhys behind her.

'Sorry,' he says, his voice soft in a way it hasn't been before, as though, in the gentle early morning light and sea chill that raises bumps along his arms, he is rendered vulnerable. 'I didn't mean to startle you. I just woke early so I thought I'd go for a jog.'

Now that he mentions it, there is a glisten to his skin, like dew on a blade of grass.

'I was just heading inside,' Araminta says. 'I won't keep you.'

'Oh, I've already done several laps of the island. I just didn't want to interrupt you.'

'Until you did.'

Rhys laughs. 'You always seem like a different person in the mornings. I didn't want to stop that ... and then I couldn't resist seeing the transformation for myself.'

Araminta watches him, unable to tell if she's just been insulted. 'People don't change,' she says. 'They just hide parts of themselves away.'

'Well, I'm an optimist; I'd argue they reveal parts of themselves.'

But she can't say she agrees. She's not someone people warm to. The more she gets to know someone, the more she hides. The longer the relationship, the more skeletons in her closet.

'Well, let's go back then. I'm starving.'

He walks with her, their feet digging into the sand, each step a struggle, like the beach is trying to hold on to them.

'What can you have for breakfast that could possibly top Isko's meal last night?'

He'd cooked for them all – everything roasted in lime and salt, chili flakes and huge chunks of garlic, flavour she wanted to drown in. She'd envied him his ability to lean into a part of himself on this island. Short of making elaborate sandcastles, she can't find her passion here. Theo can sing, Kalpana can preach or write a poem, Jerome can come up with a new app or pitch, and she's not sure Rhys ever stopped acting.

The only thing that's left to her is the very thing she was trying to leave behind: entertainment, performance, scandal . . .

But who comes on a show like this to avoid all that?

Maybe she's been lying to herself, or at least not admitting the whole truth – that she wants to be seen as an artist, yes, but if not that, she'll take being seen as *someone* . . .

Maybe she never even wanted to leave it behind; she just wanted to control the narrative. And if they want content, she's the person to give it.

'Speaking of topping Isko,' she says. 'I'm surprised you didn't drag him upstairs last night.'

'This again? Anyone might think you're jealous.'

'I don't want to shag Isko. No, I mean . . . didn't everything with Theo make you feel reckless? Knowing you could lose it all so quickly? I certainly did – I wanted to run naked screaming into the ocean like nothing really mattered anyway.'

He levels her with the sort of steady gaze that indicates he understands her real question: Theo's down, and now the rest of us might actually stand a chance in this competition, so didn't you want to do something, anything, that might snatch attention and the public support he just obliterated?

'Any time you want to run naked into the ocean, you let me know.'

'*Rhys.*'

'I slept with Isko because I was bored,' Rhys says, dodging her real query but surprising her all the same with a genuine answer she never thought she'd get. 'I wasn't bored last night.'

'No, last night was anything but boring.'

Rhys laughs, the camera catching a glance at Araminta filled with genuine surprise. 'I thought you were going to berate me for sleeping with someone out of boredom.'

'Oh, Christ no, I'm not a hypocrite.' She gazes off at the sea before meeting his eyes again. The corners of her lips twitch. 'I wish I'd had reasons even half as good as boredom sometimes.'

'Go on then – what's your worst.'

She considers. 'Because saying "no" seemed like too much effort. Because faking interest seemed easier than being genuine.'

'That got dark quick.'

Araminta shrugs. 'And yours?'

'To see if I could.' He doesn't even hesitate.

'What would it take for you to sleep with me?' she asks, and it turns out Rhys was right because she's brazen in the mornings.

'An invitation.'

Araminta sighs.

'What?' Rhys asks.

'That's all any boy in the world needs with me. Where's the challenge? I need someone with standards.'

'I have standards,' Rhys says. 'You just happen to meet all of them.'

'Right,' Araminta rolls her eyes. They're at the door of the house when Araminta says, 'So was Isko any good?'

'Again with this? Really?'

Araminta doesn't speak, just stares until he answers.

Rhys glances around, checks they're alone before that relaxed grin appears on his face.

'Phenomenal,' he says, grabbing his towel from the side and heading off to shower. 'Then again, I do tend to bring the best performance out of people.'

Kalpana hesitates for so long, she convinces herself she's not going to do it.

And then she rips down one of the secrets.

Legal affairs.

That's it? She turns it over, wondering if she should take another. She was so certain this was where Jerome was standing, and this would confirm that, right? But the sharp, angular lilt is not what she imagined his handwriting would be, and the words themselves are so vague, she's suddenly unsure. Isn't Araminta estranged? And musicians are always embroiled in such scandal – copyright infringements or contract breaches or more mundane things. She knows nothing about Rhys but certainly wouldn't put it past him. And Isko –

'My, my!'

Kalpana takes the note down in plain sight, no plans to hide it, and still jumps when she hears Isko's voice.

'Kalpana! I thought you were better than this. Our noble little activist?'

She arches an eyebrow. 'Exposing dirty secrets is part of the job.'

'This is base and you know it. The rest of us are here for our own sense of self-importance. I thought you believed yourself better.'

She folds her arms across her chest to hide her sneering disbelief. Doesn't he realize she's here for both? They would never have put someone without a sense of self-importance on a show called *Iconic*. It wouldn't make for good television.

Though she's not sure she's given enough of that either. The most entertainment she can offer is the way she's scrambling for an excuse – her boldness predicated on her certainty the note would be Jerome's, revealing a smoking gun, or an absence so obvious it would be suspicious in and of itself.

But this is nothing. She has already hinted at what she knows about Jerome and cannot go after him without strengthening the case. Men like that have a way of refuting everything.

So she makes some vague effort to distract Isko from

the card in her hand: 'I'm not even sure I can say what I am and what I'm not at this point,' she admits. 'I feel so useless. I thought I could leverage this for some important cause, but no one cares to hear it.'

'Of course not. No one wants your preaching; we just want to know if you and Araminta are a thing.'

Kalpana spins to face him, eyes wide.

Isko: *It's not like I perform teenage tasks for spoiled rich girls often. All things considered, I think I was actually rather subtle.*

'Of course not. Why would you think that?'

'Something to do with that "running off to the smoking area to make out" thing.'

'If we kissed, I can hardly remember it,' she says. A brush of lips under the soft torch light in the midst of all this isolation? She's not lying: the memory is a blur. She's extrapolated it, stretched it, teased it for all it was worth until the moment, fully romanticized, was worthy of being pocketed away for future purposes. She'll stick it in a poem or spin it into a slogan.

'Are you craving a refresher?'

Kalpana: *Is that seriously what these people care about? Who's kissing who?*

'Do you really think one kiss is the greatest thing I can offer this island? That any of us can?' She can feel the card curling beneath her sweat-dampened fingers.

Isko doesn't answer because no, of course not, this is no standard reality show. They are not regular people seeking romance and relaxation. They're more – the entirety of the human experience condensed into six beings, bursting at the seams in their desire to portray it all, to offer the chaos of the world some semblance of meaning.

Admitting interest in a kiss feels like admitting they're all ordinary after all.

With Isko still watching, Kalpana turns back to the wall and pries a nail loose, pushing it back into the card – secret facing out for anyone to read.

If someone wants to write something so empty, then fine – they should have no problem with everyone reading it.

With only five minutes of internet access, there are only so many things you can search for. Theo can't wade past the outfit-of-the-day articles for Araminta to get to the real dirt and after three pages, he moves on. Rhys is a nobody – a few regional theatres, no social media – and while he hopes destroying the man might be on the cards, it appears it isn't on the internet.

And then he tries Jerome, and it's all there: a scandal blowing up the chat rooms and hashtags.

He runs out his final minute skimming the details, and now in the bright light of day, he's ready to expose it all.

He finds Jerome on the beach.

'Newman!' Jerome cries, sprawled across the sand, legs splayed, drink clutched lazily in his hand. 'Come, sit, talk. We should get to know each other better. I think I know some of your friends. Annaliese? The rapper? I met her at a dinner once and now we're very firm friends. Nearly something more than that, but we both decided against it. Oh, do you know –'

Theo lets him warble on, suddenly doubtful. He'd seen this too – pictures of Jerome with people who were famous or fame adjacent, collecting connections like trading cards. He imagines he'll be one of his name-drops one day. 'Are you excited for tonight's challenge?' Theo asks, suddenly wondering if that might be the better place for his big reveal. A camera hovers nearby, but perhaps he needs the others to be his audience, to let them run away with it and propel the drama further.

Jerome shrugs. 'The weekly challenges interest me but not the daily ones. All Araminta got was a marketing task.'

'She's an influencer.'

Jerome sits up. 'Interesting – you didn't take your internet time to research her then. If you only searched yourself, I imagine you'd be far more despondent right now. So which one of us was worth your time?'

Theo is careful not to look down or away. 'If I googled Araminta, I wouldn't think of her as an influencer?'

'Theo, she's one of the most prolific sculptors in the world. It just so happens no one cares about sculpture, so we all know her first and foremost from her bloodline and then her social channels.'

'I . . . how do you know?'

Jerome scoffs. 'It was very easy to find the line-up, Theo. People googling the show and the names attached, rumours spreading through back channels. It's the internet. You can find out anything.'

Theo: *I think we might have been overlooking Jerome. He's said nothing about anyone; but I think he might already know every filthy secret pinned to that wall.*

'So, Araminta,' he prompts.

'Award-winning artist, verified slut and a girl who only dropped daddy when she had enough success to know she didn't have too much to lose.'

'That's not fair. She probably didn't know –'

88

'About her father's funding of the Scottish Oil Pipeline? Maybe. But funny how she suddenly cared about displaced residents and obliterated nature reserves when she didn't care about the workers he paid three pence an hour, or when he destroyed unions, or the years of deforestation. She won a prestigious and very lucrative art prize, and the next morning, it was all over the internet that she had cut ties with the rest of her family and wanted nothing to do with their blood money. And of course, all the attention just made her richer, followers rocketing, brand deals flocking.'

Theo is torn. This was his plan, right? To deflect from his own imploding life by tearing apart someone else's. But this isn't what he intended . . .

Which Jerome knows.

Of course he does; he's doing this on purpose – has realized that if Theo is seeking him out when they've hardly exchanged a sentence or two, then he has to be the topic of last night's internet access. Jerome knows Theo has something on him and he's bombarding him with this instead, offering it up like a bribe.

And issuing a warning at the same time: *come for me and I'll throw you under too.* He probably has information on them all that's far more damning and buried far deeper than a five-minute google might allow.

'I don't know; family matters are messy,' Theo says, leaning into it, giving Jerome the opportunity to drag Araminta further, because if her reputation is on the line, then maybe his isn't. 'There might have been other factors – or it might have been the thing that pushed her over.'

Jerome shrugs. 'Maybe, but don't you have to look at

how calculating people might have been in the past to see them properly in this competition?'

'You have a point.'

'So that's her: sculptor, sure, but social media star who knows how to spin her image. No one knows quite how they're perceived and how to work it to their advantage like she does. You know the tabloids called her the Nymph of Knightsbridge? A plethora of famous hook-ups and sexual scandals and she comes out of it wearing white satin on a sun-kissed island. Her ex wrote a song about her – 'Peppermint' – and she made it go viral on TikTok, a whole 'why are you so obsessed with me' trend off the back of making people obsessed with her. She's a genius. And she's a liar.'

Theo should be pleased. Of everyone on the island, Araminta seems to be at the centre of everything. It's the very reason he googled her name first. That was supposed to be him. He can almost hear his publicist yelling at him to cause a scandal.

But he doesn't like to be threatened, even in the vague-edged way Jerome is parcelling out information.

And if Jerome *does* have something on them all, he's a threat that needs to be shot down.

Which, Theo realizes, he'll have to do far more carefully than the clumsy confrontation he'd planned. He'll inevitably retaliate and Theo needs to make sure he comes for someone else. He needs to be so far down the domino chain no one remembers the first one to fall was him.

Which means that when it comes to Jerome, he needs to give someone else the ammunition and let them fire the gun.

*

One by one they find the card.

Their fury turns to quiet unease when Isko reveals Kalpana took it. They'd all assumed she'd cling to the moral high ground, or the illusion of it at least. If even she isn't playing fair, then no one is.

But it does make Theo's decision of who to hand this information to awfully easy.

He finds Kalpana and invites her for a chat, positioning himself next to her in front of a camera, their microphones crisp and clear. But the stream mysteriously malfunctions and it does not make the episode edit. This is not how the producers want secrets to come out; better to wait for the shock reveal – which they're certain they can orchestrate.

When they return to the others, they act suspiciously normal, Kalpana launching into a spiel about living off a dollar a day to raise awareness of food poverty. Araminta blinks and, in a naïve way that feels laced with cruelty, asks, 'Oh, that's not much, is it?'

Isko isn't there to be her reality check.

But later, he finds her in the kitchen.

'I suppose we should report back,' he says, letting his hair fall into his face as he flushes with embarrassment at the words that just stumbled from his lips.

'I believe the word Rhys used was "phenomenal".'

'Just tell me –'

'I'm not exaggerating.' Araminta glances at him, her tone so nonchalant the conversation could have been about anything. 'That was the word he used.'

Isko considers this before turning to the alcohol. 'Whisky or tequila?'

'White rum.'

He tosses the bottle in her direction and her composure cracks.

'Well, what about Kalpana?'

Isko catches something in her voice that is not emotion, something beyond even intent. It's more like a vibration, a frequency he is attuned to, and he knows this is his opportunity to point a camera in his direction and spin something the audience will love.

'She doesn't like you,' he snaps – cold, cruel, and with a perfect edge of disinterest. 'She doesn't want you. Move on.'

He thinks that Araminta is a mirror, reflecting his own performance back – he forgets that she is the original.

He only remembers it when the mirror cracks. Tears glisten in Araminta's eyes and she rapidly blinks them away. Letting them fall might be a bit much. But she tilts her face toward the light and lets the cameras catch their existence all the same.

It's difficult to track time on the island, the days long and hot and plunging suddenly into the bitter, cold nights. But when the alarm trills, it seems to them all too early.

When they gather around the TV screen, it's not Eloise who greets them but a message:

We request that you stay in the villa while we set up equipment for tonight's challenge.

It doesn't make the edited cut. Nor do the two hours of the contestants anxiously huddled inside, gravitating toward windows while pretending they don't care all that much. Makeup is applied with shaking hands, drinks are hurriedly sipped, and by the time dinner rolls around, it's all they can do to pick at it – all except Rhys who does not give any indication of nerves, nor even that he might be expected to perform in a challenge anytime soon.

Meanwhile, those streaming the show are flooding social media with their speculation about the challenge and all the things that might be happening.

By the time the alarm rings again, the contestants are practically falling over themselves to hurry out the door and toward the patio screen: *Please continue to the beach.*

Lanterns light the path they are supposed to take, the sky rapidly darkening behind them.

'This can't be a mini-challenge,' Araminta mutters as her high heel sticks in a gap between the wooden slats.

When they emerge onto the sand, they've composed themselves like returning heroes. They're half expecting Eloise to be standing there in the flesh, but instead, a giant screen has been erected in the centre of a large plinth, six wooden tables set in a circle around it. The polished mahogany is so out of place on this bleached island that it's immediately obvious what the design team are aiming for: a courtroom. One where six defendants can stand.

'Contestants, please take a seat!' Eloise squeals excitedly from the screen. Unsettled, but attempting to appear confident – after all, icons do not doubt themselves – they fall into their seats.

Eloise's smile is empty; she seems to look right past them. She's too perfect, too immaculate. The contestants are beautiful but they are ruined too: the sun has burned patches around bikini edges, sunscreen has blocked their pores and foundation clumps on their warm, sweaty skin. Everyone is windswept, salt-teased and never quite clean enough.

93

'For today's challenge, the audience has voted to test your popularity. Ultimately, icons are decided first and foremost by how many people believe them to be one. Your task is simple: among yourselves you must vote for a leader . . . and then you must decide who is the least popular, least iconic and least worthy of their place on the show. That's right,' Eloise says, baring her teeth, though it might be a smile. 'Tonight, one of you is leaving the island. And you get to choose who that is. All you need is for five of you to come to a consensus.'

The screen switches off, and without Eloise to stare at, the contestants turn to face each other.

For a moment, sheer silence and utter shock.

Then: 'Araminta.'

Heads swivel to Rhys. Araminta gasps, her nails piercing her own leg beneath the table.

Rhys smiles gently, but his eyes reflect the torch light and it's clear unsettling her was intentional.

'For team leader,' he continues, flashing her a conspiratorial wink.

But any relief is short-lived when Jerome rushes. 'Absolutely not; she's first in line for the chopping block.'

'Is she?' Kalpana snaps.

'Of all of us, Araminta has had the most opportunity to become iconic of her own volition,' Jerome says. 'She's been in the public eye for years and has never made it off the D list. She's had everything handed to her, and she still needs to go on a TV show to even potentially make it. She's the least iconic of all of us.'

'She's the most talented person here,' Rhys snaps. 'She's the most successful, and she won the first popularity vote. If she's not the leader of this thing, it loses all credibility.'

Araminta leans on the edge of her chair, engrossed but hesitant, like she's waiting for the twist.

Araminta: *Oh god. I like him. I really do – and I know he's probably just playing a long con, or damn, I don't know – setting me up high so he can flirt with me and join me at the top. But it's working.*

'I second Araminta for team leader,' Isko says calmly, staring at a camera instead of his other contestants.

Isko: *A shaky alliance is better than none. I plan to protect it.*

'Third,' Theo says, seated to Jerome's right. The man startles, not expecting disagreement to come from that side. He turns and they lock eyes.

Jerome: *Theo voting for Araminta after everything I told him earlier? I wonder what secrets he's hiding. You know he was a rather last-minute addition to the line-up? That certainly might be worth digging into.*

Kalpana does quick math. 'Fourth.'

'Fifth,' Araminta says quietly, as though shocked at the sudden support. She is unwilling to believe she is truly so good at playing this game – there must be motives at play, cards being dealt. She's likely a strategic choice for now and someone to betray later.

A consensus of five is reached. And now they're on to the real test.

'Do we even need to discuss this?' Kalpana asks. 'All but one of us just came to an agreement – surely that outlier should be the one to go.'

Araminta rises from her table and goes to stand before the plinth at the centre – team leader, now the judge.

Whichever way she chooses, she imagines people will scramble to agree, lest they run the risk of everyone turning on them next. 'Everyone should have the opportunity to plead their case. But yes, I suppose we should start with Jerome.' She tries to stay calm, worried any hint of smugness in her words will damn her.

Kalpana: *Oh, this is going to be excellent.*

'Well . . .' Jerome looks so affronted, he's struggling for words. But when he finds them, he puffs his chest out with bravado. 'First of all, I disagree that Araminta is the most successful. I've made more money than anyone else here.'

'Money isn't our metric of success; it's yours,' Kalpana interrupts.

Kalpana: *I'm so sick and tired of these rich bitches thinking their wealth is proof of their success and not their privilege and luck.*

'Besides, isn't what matters most who still has trajectory, not who's peaked?' Theo muses almost innocently, with a curious expression and tilted head, but of course Kalpana seizes what he has teed up for her.

'And when you've stolen nearly everything from your business partner, can you even say you've peaked?'

Jerome blinks twice, almost comically.

'You motherfucker! Do you really think you can say a thing like that on live TV and not have me sue the ever-loving shit out of you?'

Rhys quirks an eyebrow. 'Well, that's certainly not a denial.'

'Of course it's a denial,' Jerome hisses. 'Thanks to Jobs and Gates, *everyone* thinks every charismatic tech CEO must have screwed over their coding partner. They all think that partner did all the work too – as if getting investors and pitching products isn't every bit as gruelling. I bought Alistair out, plain and simple. A tidy sum for him to launch his next venture.'

'Is that why he's suing you?' Kalpana asks.

'I . . . what?'

Kalpana: *The news broke yesterday, but I don't want to throw Theo under. Besides, better for Jerome to think I have some insider source.*

'A brilliant decision to come on a show like this,' she pushes. 'You've made what would be a footnote in a tech magazine into a trending topic.'

'Jerome,' Araminta says tightly, 'what is she talking about?'

'It's nothing, really,' he insists. 'There's absolutely no way it will go anywhere. And I really can't discuss it further without violating –'

'What about the girls?' Kalpana asks quietly.

Jerome turns to her, his panicked anger intensifying. 'What are you talking about?'

'Denial didn't work last time, did it?' Kalpana points out. 'I'm a feminist activist, Jerome. I've been involved in the class-action lawsuit on behalf of Soltek victims for the last year.'

Something she assumes the producers knew when they decided to put them both on this damn island.

Kalpana: *Ridiculous, isn't it, that this wasn't enough? That Theo had to come in with another lawsuit to make anyone pay attention to the women he's hurt.*

'Victims?' Araminta clutches her arms across her chest. 'How are there victims of a dating app?'

Kalpana rolls her eyes. 'Honestly, where the hell have you been?'

Araminta isn't prepared for Kalpana's vitriol directed at her, especially with her newfound power as leader. It bites. Besides, it does not matter that Araminta never wanted a simple kiss to become anything serious – that Kalpana didn't either has cut deep. And this is salt in the wound.

'DateRate,' Kalpana scoffs. 'Like a sexist app wasn't enough –'

'Sexist?' Jerome sputters. 'I created the app to protect women – so they could rate the men they date and ensure they're safe for the next girl.'

Isko's eyes dart back and forth, a slight smile on his face, though whether it's in enjoyment of the drama or relief that it's not being directed at him is anyone's guess.

'Sure, and didn't that just backfire to men rating women with *"Take her swimming on a first date. She's only a three, and she didn't even put out."* You enabled the most horrific, misogynistic reviews and turned dating into even more of a cesspool than it already was – women having to perform the perfect girl just so they don't get review bombed.'

'But he's not being sued for that, surely,' Araminta pushes.

Rhys: *Why does Araminta care so much?*

'No, he's being sued because there was an issue of people reviewing matches they hadn't actually met up with.'

'So?' Araminta asks, because Jerome has gone quiet. He's simply staring with narrowed, burning eyes, fingers curling around the table.

'So how did you fix that problem, Jerome?'

'Fuck you,' he growls.

'Still not sounding like a denial,' Rhys quips almost jovially.

'He made a Bluetooth link between the apps, so your phones had to be near each other to prove you'd met. Which meant people had to rate each other while actually on the dates. Men could literally see their rating and get violent, or intimidate their dates into a better ranking so they could get to the next girl. But even that wasn't enough, was it, Jerome? Because there was a technical error. Or were you just cutting corners? Or do you just have no clue what you're doing, and with an app so large, have no way to properly safeguard it? Either way users were given the technology to track each other's phones. And now several women who were stalked by their dates are suing him into the dirt. Soltek isn't going to survive this.'

'I'm going to sue you for so much slander –'

'With what money, Jerome? Because we're going to take all of yours.'

And mine, Araminta thinks with a quiet solemnity. That's what she took when she left everything behind – some social media accounts, a small six-bedroom flat in Kensington, a few suitcases of out-of-season designer clothes and the stock in Soltek that she'd been given five years ago on her eighteenth birthday, convincing herself that as a gift, the money was hers. And when it comes to income, it's seventy percent of hers.

Did the producers know that too, when they stuck her on this island with the rest of them?

Dear god, she needs that prize money. She needs to win. And so does Jerome. And now it all means something, to two of them at least.

'So we're happy to vote for Jerome, then?' Kalpana asks.

'No,' Araminta says too quickly.

Kalpana jumps to her feet as she turns to her. 'What?'

Everyone looks shocked – except for Rhys, whose eyes are creased with amusement.

'Theo's right,' she says. 'This is about who has potential, and Jerome could still crawl his way out of this. And frankly, if he doesn't, I want to see him crash and burn in person.'

She tries to inflect a degree of vitriol into her words, which isn't difficult. She's furious he's put both her income on the line and her reputation in having to come to his rescue. But whatever he's on this show for – to increase his profile, attract investors or gain public favour for a second chance – she needs him to do it. Her survival depends on his.

'So who are we voting out?' Isko asks.

Araminta realizes what she has to do and it's like a guillotine slamming down – cutting off a newly budding thing.

Isko is too valuable an ally to her, Jerome *needs* to stay, Theo and Kalpana will never turn on each other and are too riled up to push them further; she needs to turn their rage on someone else – and neither particularly likes the remaining option much anyway. No matter how much she's starting to.

'Rhys,' she says – and it's difficult to get those words out. Even harder to meet his eyes, and when she does he seems, if possible, even more entertained, like he's thrilled by this twist of events. 'The rest of us at least have a foundation – we've made steps toward where we want to be. But Rhys, I'm sorry but you've only had bit parts. I . . . I really don't want to, but if we have to choose, I think that's who we need to pick.'

'Seconded,' Jerome rushes, unable to believe his own luck.

Jerome: *It was tough; he's probably my favourite person on the island. But it's a dog-eat-dog world.*

Isko shrugs. 'I'm bored now. Whatever brings this absurdity to an end. I vote for Rhys too.'

Rhys: *Et tu, Brute?*

'This is ridiculous,' Kalpana says, seething. 'Jerome is –'

'Fourth,' Theo says with a nod. Keeping Jerome on after all this works in his favour; what better distraction from his own problems?

They turn to Kalpana, tense. If anyone was to raise their chin in defiance, ready to be the lone voice of dissent, it's her.

But if she did, she could be the one they all vote for instead.

'Fine, yes, fine,' she says quickly. 'But only because he was my second choice anyway and I believe in the power of the majority. I vote for Rhys.'

Rhys arches a cool eyebrow.

The screen flickers back to life. 'Wow, contestants, that was really something! And a result I'm sure none of us saw coming!'

They can barely look at Eloise. Araminta shuffles to the side of the plinth so they can see her better, but that just brings her closer to Rhys, and she can feel her whole body flushing.

'Congratulations on winning the popularity vote, Araminta. Your prize is . . . well, popularity is its own prize, isn't it? Adversity, however . . .'

The music that hums beneath her words suddenly jolts louder, a jarring, edgy thing.

'How do you feel, Rhys? About being voted off the show?'

Rhys turns to the others like he's buying some time to consider his answer. 'I'd be upset to leave the show under any circumstances. I really am here to rise to a challenge and prove myself. But to leave like this?' He glances at Araminta with the perfect expression of wistfulness, like she, and not the show, is the real chance he's missing out on. 'I'm devastated.'

Eloise nods sympathetically. 'Sometimes that's all it takes, isn't it?'

'All what takes?' Kalpana mutters, unable to bite her tongue at Rhys's performance of sadness for a moment longer.

Eloise beams. 'Why, to become an icon, of course. A motivation. Something to overcome. Your real lesson tonight, contestants, is that we all love an underdog. Icons don't let being down for the count stop them, and most of our heroes hit some real lows. Which is why Rhys, not only will you not be leaving the island, you'll be taking this evening's prize.'

'What?' Kalpana hisses.

A slow grin unfurls on Rhys's face until he reaches outright glee, eyes lit with sheer delight.

Rhys: *Incredible. Utterly incredible.*

'While we clear away this courtroom, we're going to be setting up something special in its place. A luxury spa for you and one other contestant. You'll have all of tomorrow morning to spend with whoever you pick!'

Jerome: *This is ridiculous. The prize should have been mine – I was clearly the one they wanted to vote for.*

'These traitors?' Rhys asks wryly. The cameras eat it up,

this gorgeous man smiling in the face of betrayal, that alluring joviality like all of life might be a little funnier with him by your side.

He turns to Araminta. 'It's like I said; I only really care about making it up to you. And evidently, I have some work to do. Care to join me?'

She gives him a flirtatious smile, like choosing him was just an effort to play hard to get. Then a shrug, like she doesn't care all that much anyway, like all this was little more than vapid, glib little @AramintaYaxleyC. 'Sure.'

The others are bemused, or irritated, or disinterested – perhaps some mix of the three.

But when they're inside again, locked away behind those villa doors as the crew get to work disassembling the set, they can hardly compose themselves.

The challenge has them riled, wound too tight, ready to burst – all that was unearthed on Jerome – for nothing? All the turning, the allegiances, the speed with which they would set aside their morals for the sake of survival.

And Rhys and Araminta – he for coming out of it victorious, and Araminta for the false veneer of popularity now ricocheting back at her.

Conversation is terse, smiles frosty.

Araminta and Rhys end up perched on the kitchen countertops, ostracized together.

'They're unbearable,' Araminta mutters as much to her drink as to Rhys.

'They're jealous.'

'Of course they are, but for what? They stuck a target on my back and now they're mad it's there.'

'At least they didn't fire at it,' he accuses.

Araminta blanches at the reminder of all she's done, and with it, she realizes she must seize this moment. She needs to reset this, needs to do the sort of dramatic thing that will have everyone rooting for them despite her betrayal. She needs the fact she turned on him not merely forgotten but turned into a part of the story.

And she needs a distraction, needs everyone so focused on what she's doing, no one will think to look too closely at her own financial records. She does not need Jerome dragging her down.

She touches Rhys's arm, just a brush, but intentional and weighty, and he blinks, thick, dark eyelashes fluttering.

'I'm sorry.' She's using that tone again, vulnerable but commanding, begging him to just go with it. 'You're the last person I'd want to hurt like that.'

Do they even realize they're closing the distance between them?

And then their lips are touching, small and sweet and barely a brush.

Araminta is going to win this damn competition, she decides. And she'll ignore the little jump in her stomach as she does so – the feeling of something flickering to life, a sparkling flame finally catching light.

Rhys draws away with aching slowness, lips pressed into a slight smile, like he's treasuring the moment. 'Apology very much accepted.'

@awkwardartist

OH MY GOD just seen that BET-RITE are listing odds on which characters are going to bang and when. Rhys and Araminta have the best odds, obviously, but I'm quite liking Rhys and Theo too – all that tension every time they argue is so damn homoerotic. Use my code for a free £10 bet betrite.com/Iconic #Iconic

---

@OrlaSaysStuff
YESSSS OMG!!! YESSSS! ARHYS IS GO!!! #Iconic

@MaisieRicardo
'I'm scared to go on my phone. I read the fine print of every app I download. I'm putting myself at more risk now because I can't bear to carry a cell phone with me' – Exclusive interview with the women suing #Iconic star Jerome Francis and Soltek www.attheforefront.com/soltek-lawsuit-victims-speak-out

Isko stares at the wall of the interrogation room, eyes wide, like he's still watching something else. If Kennard didn't know any better, he might think it was shock. But he's seen enough clips to know these people don't wear the truth across their faces.

'Mr Andrada, thank you for being here today,' he says. Like he had much of a choice. They're all under contract with AHX, after all, and if AHX wants to air that episode, it'd better look like it collaborated with the police. They'll be able to hold their hands up and say *Look, we paid for hotels for the witnesses and transport to the station – who cares that it was only for a few days?*

Isko nods. 'Of course, whatever helps. You think someone did this to Rhys? That it wasn't an accident?'

'We're still trying to form a picture of what happened on that island. What we do know is that you attacked Rhys the day he died.'

Isko glances down at his hands like he's surprised to see them in such a state: dark purple bruising, split knuckles, slender fingers warped by swelling.

'I've never hit anyone before,' he says softly.

'I believe you,' Kennard says. It's one of the few things he *can* believe; he's seen the footage, seen the clumsy form of Isko's fist. 'We're waiting on the autopsy, but if it confirms any sort of internal bleeding prior to his death – something that might have made him dizzy enough to topple right over the cliff, for instance, well, you can see how that would implicate you.'

'You think me hitting him killed him? Are you serious?' His demeanor slips, icy disdain shuttering across him.

'One punch can kill, Isko.'

'Yeah, so can alcohol and cliff edges,' Isko snaps. 'Rhys was wasted when I saw him.'

But he wasn't. So is Isko lying? Or was Rhys pretending to be drunk to manipulate them all?

'We'll probably be able to prove it,' Kennard tells him. 'But even if we can't – a tiny if – the footage is out there. Unless we find who really did this, plenty of people will think it was you. So it would be mutually beneficial if you were to help us out.'

Isko glares at him, vein pulsing in his forehead. He glances away, and when his eyes return there's a coldness there unlike anything Kennard's seen before.

'Is it true they're going to air the final episode?'

'Where did you hear that?'

'Everyone is talking about it. That's why you wouldn't let us have our phones back, right? So they wouldn't mislead us in the case? But the case is in your very halls. Funny, I thought this place would be better soundproofed.'

'You heard it from an officer?'

Isko laughs and says something Kennard will later translate as *'Every single person here is talking about it: the local cops, the cleaners, the hoteliers, the drivers – but of course none of you Interpol pigs speak Portuguese.'*

Kennard doesn't want to lose the thread of the conversation. 'Yes, Mr Andrada, they're going to air the episode in two days' time. An actual, real death televised as entertainment. If everyone weren't already speculating about whether you killed him – accidentally or not – they will be then. Unless we prove it was a crime, that someone on that island maliciously, and intentionally, killed him.'

'All right,' Isko says, finally relenting. 'I don't want that episode to air either. So what do you want to know?'

'There were cameras all over that island. I want you to talk to me about blind spots.'

Iconic

Season 1, Episode 5

On the beach, a white-canvased tent has been erected, and soft, artificial candles flicker inside. Two padded tables lie next to each other, a whole shelf lined with massage oils. Foot soaks bubble, creams and mud treatments lie in wait, crystal rollers form a rainbow on a bamboo tray and scented steamers fill the air with a soft haze.

Araminta and Rhys appear in white robes and take in the scene before them. Rhys's face lights up and he snatches an oil from the side like a child with a must-have toy. Araminta looks more hesitant.

'Rhys,' she starts warily.

But he turns to her with a practised smile, a hint of that ever-present mischievousness combined with an intensity that makes her knees weak. He has a way of looking at her sometimes that makes her feel captivated – like the ground has shifted, and he becomes her new centre of gravity.

'Where do you want to start?' he asks. 'Oil? Mud? I'll be very honest; I've spent most of the night lying awake thinking about every way I want to touch you.'

She arches a curt eyebrow. 'And does wearing my skin make the list?'

'Araminta, I'm being serious.'

'Unfortunately, I didn't doubt that you were.'

'Unfortunately?' He puts the oil down and turns to her,

the flirtatiousness falling away to a seriousness that is almost solemn. 'I'm sorry. I didn't mean to press; I thought we were both feeling something here.'

She draws her robe a little closer. 'We were – I mean, I am, but . . . last night was so much – all those emotions flying, and then you and I, isolated from the others like that –'

'Is that why you kissed me? Because that kiss . . . Araminta it's unravelled me.'

She wonders, briefly, how she always manages to attract statements like this. It's never 'I can't stop thinking about you' or 'I like you.' Her first boyfriend professed, 'This yearning, it's untenable' and her last, that 'My god, I could fill a lifetime writing songs about your smile.' He'd lied, of course. And knowing that 'a smile like an angel but she loves like the devil' was a line written about her was devastating. She couldn't even inspire a decent meter.

But now she's got 'Peppermint' in her head, and Rhys is waiting for a response.

'Why do you want to sleep with me so badly? If you want to get laid, I suspect Isko will be more than happy.'

'I think you're enchanting,' he answers so quickly it has to be rehearsed.

'I've dated poets, Rhys, you're not going to get me into bed with a false but lyrical platitude.'

'Believe me, if I wanted to seduce you with language, I could do better. But that's the honest truth – you're clever and creative; I love the way you're simultaneously flippant and direct, and there's something about the way you talk and the way you act, that is, for lack of a better word, enchanting.'

I flirt, she thinks. *That's all it is.*

'I have no interest in being another manic pixie dream girl on what I'm sure is a long list.'

'You don't want me in that way at all?'

She doesn't want to lie. But she doesn't know what the truth is because her feelings are buried beneath the competition, and when it comes to that, she's thought about screwing every single one of them, even Jerome. But Rhys . . .

Well, if her interest were solely calculated, all this would be easier. If it were just about getting votes and screen time, she wouldn't keep thinking about all the ways she wants him. And not just intimately: she wants his casual touches, his whispered words in her ears, his chaste kisses and his hand in hers.

Rhys smiles, the cocky smile that's so infuriating and so riveting all at once.

'Why, Araminta,' he says, teasing her silence.

She bites her tongue, still thinking this out.

'Rhys, the issue is' – she hesitates, because this is the calculated move – 'I do like you but I only had the nerve to kiss you because I felt vulnerable after that competition. I don't like the way the game gets inside my head, and I think if we date, the others will ruin it – or at least make it so I'm never sure what's real and what's their manipulation.'

'Come on, don't not date me for them,' he whines.

Rhys: *[Laughter] God, she's clever, isn't she? I didn't want a date, I wanted to hook up. And suddenly she had me begging for a relationship. If she carries on like this, she'll have me on one knee in weeks.*

'I want to date you, but I don't want them to know,' she says. 'I want to keep this secret.'

'Why?'

For the drama, Rhys. For the cameras and the audience and the challenges that leverage points and all that money at the end — a romance is ordinary, but haven't we proved secrets are destructive?

'Because I like you and I want to protect that feeling.'

'I'll think about it. Until then, let's consider this our first date.' He reaches for the cord of her robe and draws her close. 'May I? Because you seem like you could use a good massage.'

She nods and he slicks oil along her back, teasing the edge of her bikini, and then it is her turn and he is all hard muscle beneath her. They coat a thick mask from one of the jars onto their faces and mix cocktails from the mini bar; when they wipe it off, they move to the mud, layering it on each other, and they kiss clumsily, their hands sliding off their slicked skin. So they shower together, water cascading down them and kiss some more, and it is all slippery and wet and urgent.

And finally, it dawns on Rhys that he cannot have this date, with this girl, for those cameras, and reject her after. It will make him look awful.

'All right,' he says, holding her face in both hands, drawing away from her lips only long enough to get the words out. 'I'm in. And I won't tell a soul.'

'Hello, Rockstar.'

Theo's sigh is weary for the fourth day on the island. 'What do you want?'

'To sit.' Rhys collapses onto the lounger next to him. 'To talk.'

Rhys: *If I'm not going to spend the day gushing about*

Araminta, I need to distract myself with my second favourite hobby: annoying Theo with my mere presence.

'I can't imagine we'd have much to say to each other.'

'Oh, you're hostile today,' Rhys says with a grin.

Theo bristles. 'Look, Sutton, I forgive you the card you took from the wall, but that doesn't mean I want to spend time with you. In fact, I'd say we all made it perfectly clear how much we *don't* want you around when we voted you off the island last night.'

Rhys: *The thing about Theo is just how easy he makes it. It's like he doesn't know how to cope with people not fawning over him.*

'I'm flattered,' Rhys says, 'To get such a reaction from *the* Theo Newman? You were too cool to smile at the Turntable Awards but I elicit an emotional response?'

Theo ignores him.

'Come on,' Rhys says, trying again. 'I just want to get to know you better.'

Theo feels his jaw twitch.

'Oh,' Rhys's eyebrows shoot up. 'That terrifies you. Let's talk about that.'

'What is there to say, Rhys? Steal another card if that's what you want. Hasn't the whole world got to know me better at this point?'

'Deeper, then.'

'Don't you already have me figured out?'

'Well, I really don't think you're all that complicated.'

'And you are?'

'I'm not sure. I know that I want something real out of life, which is different from being tired of the fake. That's your reason for being here, right?'

Theo: *Rhys loves the sound of his own voice. He wants to* *pretend he's getting at some deep insight you've never confronted before but that's all he wants: to hear his own voice say something he thinks is clever.*

'I'm here because I'm tired of everyone thinking they know me because they've known the singers who came before me. I'm not just some doll created by my label to fit an algorithm and sell –'

'I'm pretty sure most musicians think there's no better way to get to know them than through their music. So let's not pretend you're here in noble defence of music itself. You're just a disappointed rock star hoping there's more from this life.'

Well, he's not exactly wrong, but hearing the words out loud sends a cold shiver down Theo's spine.

What if it's not just the desperate scramble to save a career? What if the only reason Theo cares is not that this means so much to him but that it has yet to be all that it promised? He's desperate and clinging to the hope that if he saves his dream, it might save him too.

'I'm fine.'

'You looked miserable at the Trebles. I bet you were already itching for the next award. Or maybe you're looking for happiness elsewhere. Albums going platinum or, just for a random example, TV show appearances?'

Theo swallows, does not want to let on that he's reeling, because the very thought that what he's fighting so hard for – what he's here for – isn't even something he adores, something he lives and breathes like he says he does . . .

He physically cannot face that potential truth, would rather embrace the lies, because at least he knows the person he's built himself to be.

Theo: *Of course, nothing he said was true. I think I'd be more worried if someone like Rhys did get me.*

'Come on – you know I'm right.' Rhys's smirk is replaced by an attempt at innocence that angers Theo even more.

'You know, Rhys, this is exactly why we all wanted you gone. You didn't steal anyone else's secret, but they voted for you all the same. You're not even nasty. You're just bloody annoying.'

'Oh, calm down, Newman.' Rhys stands and claps Theo on the shoulder. 'Try not to take all this so seriously, okay? It's only reality TV.'

'You're right,' Theo snaps, leaping to his feet. 'It's only reality TV. There's no harm to any of this.'

He rushes across the patio with purposeful, thundering steps. At the wall, he stares at the cards and rips another down.

'Let's see. You were standing here, weren't you?' Theo says, turning to Rhys, and shocked to find the man grinning as though enjoying the show. Maybe he really does think all is fair in love and entertainment.

Then he glances at the card. It's not Rhys's.

I'm sorry, Juliet. Your «chou»

It means nothing to Theo – except for the sign-off. *I trained in Paris* rings in his ears.

'I hope you don't mind, but I wanted to speak to you,' Jerome says, having drawn Araminta away from where she'd been discussing the ethics of art ownership with Kalpana. 'You saved me last night, at that public vote. Thank you.'

'Oh, no problem, Jerome.'

'I think we're similar, you and I. And I find myself rather impressed by you.'

Araminta draws her arms in tightly, like by shrinking away from him, she can put a little more distance between them.

Araminta: *Does he think I've forgotten the fact that I was his first choice to kick off the show? This is next-level negging.*

'You're someone who never had to be anything at all,' he continues. 'Your areas of expertise, though rather lacklustre, are admirable for their ambition,' he says, turning to her with his chin high like he has bestowed a gracious gift of a compliment upon her. 'I'd like to get to know you better.'

'Ah, um, sure, Jerome. I'd love for the two of us to be closer friends,' she says, wondering if she could use his apparent infatuation to her advantage. But she knows men like this. Being nice doesn't work; it just makes them think you're a bigger bitch when you don't reward the base dignity they offer with your vagina.

'Which is why I wanted to give you some advice. Be wary of Theo – he was spreading gossip about you yesterday. I think he looked you up when he had access to the internet.'

'Oh, really?'

She cannot think what he might find – she is not like the others with secrets hidden in the dark; hers are out among so much light that you might never find them for all the clickbait.

'Yes, which is pretty bold, isn't it? Given he bribed his way onto the show.'

'What?' she asks distractedly, too busy thinking through her own potential reasons for cancellation.

'Oh yes, they dropped someone else to make room for him. Probably didn't need to be persuaded for a name as big as his, but it certainly helped. They always think they're so subtle when they use shell companies. As if his record label could make a donation through a dozen different people and it wouldn't be traced back.'

Jerome: *I trusted Theo yesterday. Which was foolish, really. The man has a rather untrustworthy past.*

Araminta stares, but it is not Theo's secrets she is concerned by; it's Jerome, because clearly he's done something, hacked into somewhere he shouldn't have or encouraged Soltek to develop something they shouldn't. Either way, she's certain there's been some violation. Probably not the sort of thing that leaves a trail, nothing that can be traced back, but the sort that leaves whispers and accusations. Araminta, with all that stock tied up with this man's reputation, cannot bear the thought of being dragged down with him.

He needs to stop talking before he says something to the wrong person.

So she makes her excuses, and Jerome watches her all but run from him.

Jerome: *It's a classic pattern, but I refuse to be yet another nice guy who doesn't get the girl. It's all about sowing the seeds, doing the groundwork. After last night, she must be desperate to win back my favour. She must be realizing just how lucky she'd be to have me.*

Araminta nearly collides with Rhys as she rushes away. He laughs and draws her off the path into the sparse trees that, with enough shadow and luck, might hide them and might not, but that's part of the thrill. All that adrenaline pumping through her at the thought of the damage Jerome might cause has a better thing to latch on to, all her free-wheeling thoughts turning as one toward Rhys.

The rough bark presses against her back, Rhys pinning her against a tree and she fights the lust that's taking over her – that need to taste his salty skin and mark him with blooming bruises beneath her tongue.

'Rhys, they'll see us,' she whispers.

'How am I supposed to resist,' he groans, his fingers twisting at the ties on the sides of her bikini briefs.

In response she kisses him again because she can't resist either, not now that they've started.

'A second date,' he proposes. 'You wanted more than just secret hook-ups, yes?'

'But how?'

Rhys: *I'm not the sort of man to do things by half. With Araminta? I'm going to sweep her off her damn feet.*

The camera feels gratuitous. Its close-ups are intimate, and it cannot get enough of this: beautiful, scantily clad people, their yearning laid bare, and Rhys – gorgeous, beautiful Rhys – who has perfected the reverential look that makes viewers swoon, like he cannot believe his luck to even be permitted to look at this woman.

'Midnight,' he says, and with his lingering gaze, it is less a plan than a promise.

Before dusk falls, Jerome stares at the wall and all of its secrets. He admits he's tempted. Araminta, Theo, even Isko – he knew they would be here. They were in the limelight – or beside it – enough to find that information. But Rhys is a mystery. And Kalpana he should have paid more attention to given she's the one ruining his life.

But he doesn't think the secret to destroying her is on the back of that card.

No, he suspects she's the variety who simply needs enough rope to hang herself. Because isn't that what activists do? Put themselves on a pedestal? She could be brought down by one trip in a private plane, one misdemeanor, one confession.

'Truth or dare,' he proposes later, as they are all gathered around the firepit, waiting for Eloise to announce their task.

Kalpana doesn't even wait. 'I dare you to name a woman you actually respect.'

'Simone de Beauvoir,' he tosses back. 'I read so much of her at university, I even filled my walls with her quotes.'

Kalpana: *There's a thing that corporations do – and the male personifications of them, apparently – where they co-opt the language of those fighting against them. It's all talk. So no, I'm not surprised Jerome has come on this show ready to shout about what a feminist he is.*

'I choose dare,' Araminta says, grinning.

'I dare you to kiss us all,' Jerome rushes. 'In turn, blindfolded, and rate us. I think we'd all like to know what's so special about the Nymph of Knightsbridge.'

'Absolutely fucking not,' Kalpana fumes.

Rhys glances around with concern, viewers agreeing that it is less a jealous possessiveness than a recognition of Jerome's motives. 'Surely a dare ought to be one kiss. This is taking it a bit far.'

Araminta shrugs. 'I'm happy to do it.' Her eye catches on Rhys with a hint of amusement, like it is an inside joke, like she may be doing all this simply to kiss him again.

She wraps a scarf around her eyes and the boys line up, Kalpana seething and refusing.

Kalpana: *In case anyone was in any doubt about what a piece of shit Jerome is.*

They're all perfectly decent kisses, though it's clear Jerome, with the taste of rum on his lips, hopes his will set her ablaze. She rattles off numbers almost carelessly. She knows Rhys's kiss instantly. He bites her lip with the same pressure as earlier, like he might have left grooves he is trying to fill.

She never wants it to end but must admit that on a purely technical level, Theo's was better. Still, she calls out *ten* when she gave Theo *eight*. She needs the audience to root for them after all.

Jerome: *I'd like to say she was dreadful, but surprise, surprise — someone with that much practice is a good kisser.*

'Truth,' Rhys says.

'Are you angry with us all after last night?' Isko asks.

Rhys laughs. 'I'm flattered you see me as such a threat. To go to such lengths to get rid of me? I must truly be iconic. I was hurt at the time.' He catches Theo's eye before he continues. 'But there are no hard feelings. Some of us are very aware this is a game.'

Theo: *He's such a prick.*

'I'll take truth too,' Theo says.

'Why do you hate your bandmates?' Araminta asks with a gleeful smile that says this is not malicious; she simply cannot resist.

Theo sighs and pretends that he had not expected this question, had not seized the game as the perfect opportunity. The news must have broken by now. There's no way it would stay quiet for so long.

'When we started, it was all about the music, and for me it still is.' He shakes his head. 'For them it's about the fame, and frankly, I've seen some pretty disgraceful behaviour: women used as props and tossed aside just as easily, a toxic attitude toward drugs – a pussy if you don't and all that – they've screamed at staff they deem beneath them. I keep hoping they'll become the boys I once knew again, but I think I have to face up to the fact they're not very nice people anymore.'

He used to rehearse that answer daily, and the time on the island has given him just enough distance to stumble over the words in a way that seems natural.

Something that says I had no idea, I wasn't a part of it, but I never liked them anyway, and now that you don't like them either, you can root for me instead.

He looks around at the others nodding, offering sympathetic smiles, but Rhys just watches him with an amused smirk, like he knows learned lines when he hears them performed by an amateur.

'I take dare,' Isko says.

Theo: *I suspected he might do that, but I'm not asking him why he's apologizing to Juliet. I think he would have lied anyway.*

'I dare you to skinny-dip in the ocean,' Rhys says and the others cheer their enthusiasm for the challenge.

Isko's eye roll is even more exaggerated than usual. 'You are children.'

'Come on,' Jerome says. 'You have to do it – that's the rule.'

'There are easier ways to get me naked if that's what you want, Jerome,' Isko says, standing to unbutton his shirt.

'What? That's not . . . I . . . I'm straight, Isko – not that there's anything wrong . . .'

Isko: *I think he might still have been protesting by the time I got back.*

Isko drops his chinos along with his underwear, and more cheering follows, which he replies to with middle fingers raised – which get blurred along with all other unsavory aspects of himself for the camera.

He takes off toward the ocean, crashing into it and screaming, 'No one look on my way out – it's fucking freezing in here!'

Araminta grabs him a towel and when he gets back, he barely pauses to wrap it around himself before climbing onto Rhys's lap. 'Like what you saw?' he says, running a finger down Rhys's face.

'Oh, I've seen it before.'

'And the reminder?'

'I'll never say no,' Rhys laughs, pushing him off. It's clear only now that he crawled onto Rhys not to flirt but to make him suffer for daring him to do this, soaking him with the cold ocean water he'd brought back with him.

Rhys looks up to see Araminta glaring daggers at him. Not caring about the others – who are all carefully *not* watching Isko pull his clothes back on – he winks at her.

Rhys: *If she doesn't want anyone knowing about us then she's going to have to deal with the jealousy of watching Isko flirt with me – and green with envy is a very hot look on her.*

'Truth for me, I want my clothes on and lips to myself,' Kalpana says.

'What do you really think about each of us?' Rhys asks.

'I'm sure you don't want to know.'

'Hit me.'

She shrugs like she is not particularly reluctant to reel it off. 'I think you're arrogant and reckless in that 'I don't care if I hurt others; I'm just here to have a good time' sort of way. Theo, I think you're incredibly talented and care a great deal about music, but you're a little lost, both within the industry and where you want to be in it.'

'That's fair,' he concedes, though she's just repeating what he's said to her.

'Isko, I think you're even more detached than Rhys is. You want to win this thing but you want the victory to just land in your lap.'

Isko: *False, but I do not care what she thinks. Perhaps I am simply happy to wait for an opportunity to prove myself because I know, when it comes, I will not fail.*

'Araminta, I think you're all over the place. You've got passion and you've got talent but you're too rich to have ever been forced to apply yourself. Maybe the world would see you as an artist if you weren't trying to also be an influencer and a home renovator and whatever hobby has you distracted this week.'

Araminta: *She has no idea. Everything I have, I built. And yes, I had several steps up, but I still worked, and I'm here because I never stopped working.*

'And Jerome, I think you're a piece of shit and an untalented turd at that.'

Jerome grabs the edge of the table. 'You've got some nerve –'

He's cut off by the lights and twinkling jingle as Eloise appears.

The challenge is a rushed thing. Their game of truth or dare taking up far more screen time than the quick clip of

Rhys struggling to answer trivia questions and pretending he never cared anyway when he does not get enough right to earn a prize.

They continue drinking and chatting through the evening, and as it gets late, Isko sidles next to Rhys and toys with his collar.

'Want to alleviate some boredom?' he asks.

Araminta tries not to watch, and Rhys knows this is a test. They may not have discussed exclusivity, but Araminta is clearly territorial when the situation demands it.

'Nah, not tonight,' Rhys says. Isko waits for a reason: *I'm tired* or *I'm having fun* or *even I'm not in the mood.* But none comes.

He shrugs, disappointed but not wounded. 'All right.'

He wanders off to get another drink, detouring after to the confession booth.

Isko: *It was simply strange. I can't see why he wouldn't –*

'Isko,' Eloise's voice sounds, and the camera cuts to the other side of the confession booth to where the screen sits, normally filled with pointed questions or clips for them to watch and provide commentary on. Instead, their presenter appears. 'Our at-home audience has been voting, and you've been selected for an incredibly exciting opportunity to win some points. You are our secret agent on the island. You'll be given a series of tasks, and if you complete them, you'll not only win points but also have the opportunity to spy on another contestant's confessional footage.'

'What the hell,' Isko mutters, too drunk for this, staring at the screen like he doubts its existence.

This is not the show he signed up for.

'Do you choose to accept?'
But it's the one he's on.
'Yes, I accept.'

@StaceyK91

I love how we all said 'you want an agent of chaos? Isko is the only man we trust enough to bring this' because we are correct #Iconic

---

@RiotParadeOfficial

We'll admit, it's getting a little bit harder to be #TeamTheo with each passing day but we need him to win so he can buy our forgiveness with the prize money! For now, enjoy this playlist we've created: RiotParade Songs Where You Can Kind Of See The Band Conflict If You Read Into Them Enough #Iconic – love Al, Dante and Tyson

---

@Ianistired

Um, anyone else seen this? #Iconic SHARE: 'My dad worked in a shop' and 'you're too rich' Iconic's Kalpana Mahajan revealed as the daughter of Arjun Mahajan, owner of CHIMERA retail chain worth $53 million. rtvnews.au/Iconic/Kalpana-chimera-retail-chain

Kennard sits with Maes in the break room sipping burnt coffee and poring through their notes. In the corner, a boxy TV plays some local news station, reporters standing outside the walls of the precinct he sits inside. He can feel them breathing down his neck, pressing for answers, asking why they don't have them already.

When Cloutier appears, he throws himself onto the cracked leather sofa with a heavy sigh.

'That kid can talk,' he says.

'Who?'

'Jerome – classic nosy neighbour. Desperate to help us solve the case so he can brag about how instrumental he was. Avidly dodging all questions of his own legal and financial situations. Nothing on the cyberattack against AHX either. I could practically feel him planning how to monetize it – all the shows he'll appear on, the book he'll write. He's right; it'll probably earn him a fortune. What have you been up to?'

Kennard passes him the sheet, jolting as their fingers brush. This is ridiculous; they haven't worked a case together in a year – a long, arduous year – neither wanting to ruin their career over their inability to keep their hands off each other. And this is the case they get put on, high profile, the whole world watching.

'I think we're too focused on what we can see on the cameras. We should be focused on what we can't, what's not there that should be,' he explains.

'You could have gotten this from digital,' he says, nodding at Maes.

She hums her agreement. 'I'm going to get the footage of who enters those blind spots and when.'

'But,' Kennard interjects, 'I wanted to know which ones the contestants themselves were aware of: corners of the cellar, patches of trees too thick for the drones to fly through, the edges of the bathrooms. But that's the main one.' He taps the highlighted line. 'The smoking area.'

Cloutier scans the list, a scowl etching into his forehead.

'No,' he says grimly. He looks up at the TV, now streaming footage – namely Theo trying to save Rhys: black shapes in the black ocean with those black rocks, blurs of deeper darkness, barely discernible. 'That's the main one. Anything could have happened in that ocean.'

Iconic

Season 1, Episode 6

Araminta draws her knitted shawl closer around her as the biting night air cuts at her skin. Her stylists didn't pack her anything even remotely warm, and she wonders if she can steal something from Rhys.

Waiting on the patio when the house is still and the island impenetrably dark is disquieting.

Finally, Rhys bounds into the dim light of one of the soft lanterns.

'All ready,' he says, holding out an arm. 'May I?'

She bites back a smile and takes it.

He leads her to the beach, where a few haphazardly placed lanterns line the edges of the island, presumably an attempt at safety, letting them all know where it ends. Ahead, a soft glow shines, and she laughs when she realizes what it is.

'You didn't,' she says softly.

'I did. Is the bad-boy thing a turn-on now that I've become a criminal in pursuit of your heart?'

He's set up a picnic, its perimeter lit by artificial candles he's stolen from this morning's spa. She takes a seat in their glow, hating the thought that crosses her mind about cameras and lighting. In the distance, the lights of the AHX boats gleam, and she mistakes them for stars on a romantic horizon.

'If you steal my heart, I'll let you know.' She feels curiously unsettled by all of this. She is used to extravagant gestures – she's had many foisted upon her. But they always feel like they're about the person trying to seduce her, their own perceptions of themselves: *I am a romantic, look at what I will do, look at the lengths I will go to.*

But she keeps staring at the pile of blankets, unable to shake how deeply that hits her – that he might have thought *What if she gets cold?* Not just about how it will all look, and how overcome she will be, but someone who has thought to make her comfortable.

And suddenly she feels very sad that a thing like that could mean so much to her.

'There's champagne,' Rhys says, pulling a flask from the basket he's packed. 'But I thought the whisky might keep us warmer. Oh, damn, I forgot cups.'

'That's okay. We can drink from the flask.' She wants to share it – it feels . . . quieter. Which is a ludicrous thing to think on a date that's being broadcast, a drone hovering mere feet from them. But they're alone on the beach, on an island at the edge of the Atlantic, the four other inhabitants fast asleep in a house they cannot even see from this angle. 'What's your favourite colour?' she blurts out.

Araminta: *God, I'm really not helping that manic pixie dream girl thing.*

Rhys passes her the flask. 'Orange. Would you care to explain why you ask?'

The whisky is smoky, and cheap enough that it burns going down. 'I suppose the thing about being an expert in your field is that you're very good at controlling your self-image. I can feel it sometimes around the others, the performance of it all. But right now, I can feel it slipping away, and I realized I don't actually know anything about you.'

'Well, there are secrets on the wall if you're desperate.'

'Yes, but I thought I'd start with your favourite colour.'

'How do you know that's not up there?'

She laughs and takes another sip. She feels warmer but reaches for a blanket anyway.

'I'd rather hear about the secrets you didn't put on the wall.'

He smiles almost self-consciously and takes a moment to admire her before he speaks. 'I like green too. But if you want a deeper secret, I'm afraid I might be too ordinary to be here. Everyone else has scandals – I'm just a man. I mainly act on the stage, not even on the screen.'

'What is it you like so much about it?'

'The invisibility, mostly.'

'Invisibility? Everyone's watching you.'

'No, everyone's watching a character. Me? I disappear. Sometimes I get so into it even I forget myself until I take that final bow.'

She leans against him and he tugs the blanket over his lap too. She rests her head on his shoulder, not looking at him but ensuring they are framed properly. 'And what exactly are you hiding from?'

Rhys arches an eyebrow. 'Oh, the audience.' He looks straight into the nearest drone. 'I just hate attention.'

They both laugh and he takes her hand, running his thumb over the smooth lines in her palms.

'I love your laugh,' he says. 'It's almost lyrical.'

'Oh, for god's sake Rhys. What a line,' she scoffs.

But he keeps hold of her hand, and turns to her. She freezes under his examination.

'Why do you laugh off compliments?'

She hesitates, starting to make another joke before realizing that would only prove his point, and he's still looking at her so intently that she's suddenly asking herself: why *does* she laugh off compliments?

Araminta: *Rhys isn't . . . he's not what I was expecting, honestly. He's so different by himself, when he's not trying to impress the others. Some of the things he's done on the island, he might make you think he's just here for a good time, that everything is a joke to him. But it's not, and he's not — there's something deeper to him. Something . . . oh god, I don't know — the sort of thing you could fall for.*

'Why sculpture?' he asks when she doesn't answer.

'Power.'

He leans forward, a smile mirroring hers. 'Power?' he repeats, clearly delighted with the answer.

'Yes. To extract beauty from something so unwilling to give it? To take something so unwieldy and force it to take the shape you want? That's power.'

'And for you, power is alluring. When have you felt powerless?'

Araminta blanches and, worse, she feels it, the dip in her affected gazing. Something cold flickering behind the sparkling gleam of her eyes. Rhys is trying to get past the veneer, and for a moment it shakes her.

But she can package that emotion right back up. She's been told she has a habit of trauma bonding — a hazard of her profession, she supposes, to showcase her emotion in a filtered photo and hope someone relates enough to like her for it. But with Rhys there's a balance. To let him in and only him, to frame everything for general consumption while letting Rhys catch a glimpse of something more – and drive him to desperate lengths to try to find it again.

'I wasn't, obviously; with my amount of privilege I couldn't be. But I felt it,' she says, which feels a suitable compromise.

'Your family?' he asks. 'I heard that you don't speak to them anymore.'

She nods. 'It was just so messy. Your parents don't come out of the woodwork as terrible people; you just slowly realize they've been horrible your whole life. And when you've apparently been letting it slide for the last twenty-two years it's difficult to put your foot down and say enough is enough – especially when you know you'll lose everything. I can make my own money, but the emotional security is gone. I couldn't call my mother when my heart was broken. I found out my father was in the hospital from a tabloid. I spent Christmas at my friend's house, crying in her bathroom because I couldn't stand the way I felt around her family, like some jealous outsider. Which I was.'

'Araminta, what you did was impossibly brave,' he says, though she suspects it's only because he thinks it's what she wants to hear. Everyone says it. But every other comment on her socials implies she only did it for the credit.

It's how her head sounds sometimes: *you should have done it sooner and you never should have done it at all and you don't get to feel sad about it and you certainly shouldn't vocalize that because why are you making yourself the victim here when it's the people your father screwed over who are the victims and you got so much money off the back of it in raising your profile that it was probably only a publicity stunt in the first place and what a horrible daughter and they're lucky to be shot of a disgraceful, shameful slut like you and will you just shut up about yourself for five bloody seconds.*

She's self-aware enough to know she's victimizing herself for the cameras, weaponizing her pretty white sadness for votes. But she's not self-aware enough to know that being hurt does not make her right. And it doesn't stop the comments of a thousand social media accounts circling through her head.

'Anyway, that's me,' she finishes. 'Might as well know the baggage up front.'

'Baggage? No, that's character, Araminta. I don't want to be one of those jerks that suggests struggling makes you stronger, but whatever it did to you, who you are? Well, you're one of the most incredible women I've ever met,' he says, shifting on the blanket to face her.

'Can we go back to incessantly flirting?'

'Always,' he says in such a lascivious way it becomes flirtatious. 'As long as that's not just another way of pivoting away from a compliment.'

She lies down on the picnic blanket and he joins her, both of them facing the stars, and it's easier to talk now, to make their confessions.

A second drone comes to hover near the first, and she thinks that, if nothing else, the shot will be beautiful: the beach at night, the sound of the waves, the stars and the two of them, eternal and crystalline, a fragile moment between two fragile people captured perfectly.

'What's your life like back home?' Araminta asks.

'Back home?' Rhys blinks. 'That place hardly feels like it exists out here. But it's a tiny New York apartment, rehearsing lines, pacing across a stage, knowing the theatre won't even be full.'

'I love New York.'

'Not my New York. It's a thing you barely scrape through on the pennies you earn.'

'Oh,' Araminta scowls. 'I didn't realize poor people lived in New York – not in the city itself, at least. I would have thought it was too expensive. Why don't you just move?'

Rhys stares at her a bit too long.

Rhys: *Yeah, the tactlessness of the rich is going to take some getting used to.*

'I would love to see *your* New York though,' she says, worried she's said something wrong.

'Then I'll take you there – it'll be a real princess-and-the-pauper moment. I'll show you the dirty, cheap way I live, and then you can drag me to Chelsea and spoon-feed me caviar, and we'll be blissfully happy either way,' he says, an earnestness to him that can't be real – it can't be, it's been a single day – but she'll believe it anyway.

They talk on.

At points, Araminta forgets about the cameras. At points, Rhys remembers them.

'Araminta,' he says, voice lower, more serious, pulling her toward it, forcing her eyes to his, startled to find them so close to her even though they are right next to each other on the ground. He is lovely in the moonlight. The shadows cling to his every sharpness: the stretches of his cheeks, below his jaw, the hollows of his collar bone.

He presses his lips together as he goes to speak, and she can't stop staring at them, those two perfect lips. 'I don't know how it is that every word you say, everything you do, just makes me like you more. But this date has been one of the best of my life. And I've lived a very wonderful life.'

And oh, she knows he's just saying it for the swooning audience, knows that she is here because of them, but she likes him, and isn't it possible he likes her too?

In the years to come, she will be asked more times than she can count: Was it real? Or was it just for the cameras?

Both. It was always, even from the very start, both.

No one even tries to pretend Isko's challenges are related to the lofty claims of the show's intentions. But where the public may have been hoping for heightened tensions, the producers did not count on Isko's best efforts to side-step their manipulations.

When he's asked to take a card down and convince someone another contestant did it, he takes one of his own and sets his lighter to it, then tells Jerome that Kalpana took one – which is like throwing a stick into an inferno – an incremental increase to the fires of his rage.

Then he's asked to get Kalpana to speak about her father and he bristles, because clearly this is not about being an icon; this is just a shameless effort at more drama. So he lures her into a conversation about generational differences, and she briefly mentions her own parents, while ranting about what we owe future generations. Reluctantly, the producers declare it a success.

But the last task gets him.

'Your final challenge, which will win you access to another contestant's confessional footage, is to find out what Rhys and Araminta are hiding.'

Isko: *So I'm guessing they're hooking up, then.*

*

By the time Isko is tasked with finding out, Araminta and Rhys are naked in the ocean.

This is played on the edit as footage interspliced with Isko in the confession room, and when Eloise issues the challenge, it's spoken over lapping waves and smooth, bare shoulders disappearing beneath them.

But it had started on the beach, stolen moments around the back of the island, where the sand is a thin strip against the thicket of trees.

'Does it feel odd to you, starting a relationship and knowing there are secrets, having them pinned on a wall, mere yards from where you're claiming to trust each other?'

'I don't care to have secrets from you, Araminta. Other people, however.' He glances at a drone hovering nearby. 'Tell you what – how's about a leap of faith? I'll race you into the water, naked, of course. Whoever loses shares what's on the wall.'

Araminta bites her lip, playing up a nervous innocence, that she might be persuaded to do something so salacious by the temptation of those secrets. But they have always understood one another when it comes to the cameras, and though they might be waterproof, without clothes to clip them to, naked simply means *without microphones*.

'All right. One, two, three – go!'

She loses, but she doesn't care. It is simultaneously freeing and binding – to know the sword no longer hangs above her by a thread quite so fine, and to bond herself closer to Rhys. She even tells him the secrets that have already met the flames – all her mess laid bare. The guilt she can't admit to, the wounds heartbreak has left, the way she does not even know who she is anymore, just who she pretends to be.

Rhys holds her the whole time, his hands on her waist the only grounding thing in that ice-cold ocean.

'I'll tell you mine too,' he promises. 'But we should head back. Eloise could be starting the challenge at any moment.'

She's not, of course – the challenge has been pushed to a later time to make room for Isko to enact this final task.

He doesn't know where to begin, and soon everyone has retreated to their rooms to prepare for a dinner they assume he will be cooking them. He doesn't cook every day. If they want him doing it properly, he'll become a nightmare of demanded ingredients and shouts to get the hell out of his kitchen. But he doesn't mind making dinner tonight. If anything he hopes it will become strategic. In his time cooking for the elite, he learned one very crucial thing: people imagine the help can't hear.

When his knife skids across the chopping board he realizes just how angry he is.

They're screwing behind his back. Did Araminta use finding out about his own liaison with Rhys to get closer to him? Did she even think he might be upset about it? He wouldn't have been – if she'd told him. And Rhys, he wouldn't have cared if he'd said something, instead of passing him over last night without another word.

How long has it been happening?

Was there overlap?

Isko: *I'm angry that I'm angry at all.*

Isko opens the kitchen window to let out some steam and that's when he hears the quiet voices.

Of course. No one ventures around this side of the house except as a through route to get to the smoking area – and Araminta's balcony is right above.

They're not foolish enough to be out on it, but clearly, she has a window open too.

He can't hear what they're saying, only that they're there. And just as he's ready to give up, he remembers the cameras.

'God fucking dammit,' he whispers, knowing no audience will let him walk away from this and forgive him.

He abandons the food on the counters, heads outside, and starts to climb the flimsy trellis clinging to the wall.

Knowing that the producers will love this has him furious, and maybe if it were just the challenge, he wouldn't do it at all. But he has had enough of contestants keeping secrets.

Araminta's words tumble down to him on the choppy night air. 'I'm scared you'll break my heart.'

Isko recoils at the ridiculousness of such a statement. Hearing it, he sees it in a way he hasn't before: that Araminta always has one eye on the camera at all times, regardless of what the other is doing.

Rhys might be the actor, but Araminta is the writer, the producer, the director and all the roles in between.

'I'm not going to do that,' Rhys says, using the sort of tone he's never heard before, one that if he thought the man had capacity for it, he might call tender.

Isko listens a while longer, his grip on the rail tightening with each pretentious declaration of affection. When he can take it no longer, he practically jumps from the lattice, running to the confession room, food be damned.

Isko: *They're not just hooking up; they're dating. Is that it? Did I win?*

'Yes! Congratulations, Isko – wow, you really make an excellent secret agent! We'll have to bear that –'

Isko: *Great. Now show me Rhys's behind-the-scenes footage.*

'Good evening, contestants!' Eloise trills. 'You're nearing the end of your first full week on the island. How do you feel?'

Confused, because Isko is not here yet and they hadn't expected it to start without him. They glance around like he might suddenly have appeared, but it's just the five of them, sitting around the firepit.

'The winner of the popular vote tonight is . . . Araminta!'

Kalpana: *Oh, this is getting ridiculous.*

'If there's one thing that's assured when you reach a certain level of success, it's backlash. And what do we expect of our heroes? We expect them to be resilient! So tonight, Araminta, we're going to get you to read some rather critical social media posts about yourself. You can stop at any time, but to win you have to make it through all five!'

Araminta stills.

Kalpana stares incredulously at the screen. Rhys glances uncertainly at her as though not sure whether saying anything would blow their cover. Jerome and Theo barely react.

Before Araminta can agree, one is already on the screen, and she takes a sip of her cocktail and reads.

'"Araminta looks like the ghost of a Victorian child fucked Narnia's white witch,"' she says. 'That's rather more creative than just calling me an ugly bitch; I'll give it a seven out of ten.'

Rhys's eyes light up in that way they only do when they watch her play the game, and here she is again, not only dismissing the worst they can do to her, but with that rating, she reminds them all that just last night, everyone was begging for her kiss – that she is desirable no matter what these posts say.

Rhys: *I've never wanted anything as badly as that woman's brilliant brain consumed with loving me.*

'"LMAO just looked up Araminta's sculptures and I guess the only reason she's considered good is because no one else can afford to do it and compete,"' she reads. 'I mean, that's a fair comment – art should be far more accessible, and the elite do tend to be rich with gallery contacts, so whether art is good or the artist was just well connected is important to think about.'

Theo: *I'm beginning to see what Jerome meant by Araminta knowing her public image and working it to her advantage.*

'"Araminta is what happens when you send a bag of flour to Eton,"' she reads. She laughs and the others titter nervously. 'That one's quite funny.'

Jerome: *I didn't understand that one – Eton is famously an all-boys' school.*

'"Araminta Yaxley-Carter is a DISGRACEFUL choice for a show that's supposed to be about role models. Her sexcapades, her abandonment of her family, dragging their name through the mud while publicly insulting them and whoring herself out. I'd be ashamed if my daughters grew up to be like her,"' she says and fakes a laugh. 'Did my mother write this?'

Jerome snorts. 'Oh, that explains so much – daddy issues *and* mommy issues.'

Kalpana places a hand on her shoulder, and Araminta covers it with her own, appreciating the support.

'"Anyone know what work Araminta has had done? I know there must be some, but whatever it is, it's awful."' She raises her glass. 'The occasional Botox jab and some highlights in my hair. Thanks for noticing, I guess.'

'Wow, Araminta, you barely blinked! You really are resilient,' Eloise says. 'And your reward for winning is . . . a phone call home! You'll have five minutes tomorrow morning!'

'Oh my god,' Kalpana mutters wistfully.

'I would kill for that prize,' Theo says.

But Araminta can hardly think of tomorrow; she's too wrapped up in what's been said and how she might have played this all wrong. Isko's not even here to ask if she was too much.

Which is when he storms out of the house like she summoned him.

'It is funny, isn't it?' he says, marching right over to her. 'How Rhys was the one to nominate you for team leader. Tell me, were you screwing him even then?'

'What?' she scowls, thrown not only by his appearance but also the reference to a challenge that feels so long ago.

'He nominated you to fuck you, Araminta.' He throws these words at her and he doesn't really know why. Because he's annoyed they didn't tell him? But that's a mild feeling and this is more calculated.

'All right, so what if he did?'

'Well, I imagine it would be the sort of thing you'd like to know if he's offering you romantic sentiments – that he only cares about getting you into bed.'

142

'That's not true,' Rhys rushes.

'Yes it is,' Isko says, whirling on him. 'I just saw the confessional tapes.'

'Isko, what the hell is going on?' Theo demands. 'You saw the tapes?'

'These two are – god, I don't even know what – seeing each other?'

'What?' Jerome and Kalpana ask at once, turning to the two of them.

Jerome: *I mean, I don't blame Rhys obviously; he's a stand-up guy, but she really should have said something before leading me on like she did.*

'Why would you keep that secret?' Theo scowls.

'So they can keep flirting with the rest of us and manipulate us into giving them screen time. Or help in the challenges – I don't know what,' Isko spits.

'Wait, no, that's not it,' Araminta rushes. 'We're not . . . I mean . . .'

'That's why you keep winning the popular vote,' Kalpana realizes. 'You're giving the world a romance plot and they're eating it right up.'

'This isn't a plot and it isn't for screen time,' Rhys says calmly. 'Araminta and I wanted to explore whether there was something between us without the interference of the competition. And I think we established that there is.'

'Yeah, apart from that part where you're a liar and just want to bone, apparently,' Kalpana seethes.

'Yes, which brings me back to where on earth are you getting that from, Isko?' Rhys asks, still not looking at all put out by this. 'You watched the confessional footage?'

Isko feels the weight of everyone's attention on him.

143

'Eloise came on the screen and told me I'd been voted to do some missions – with the opportunity to win points and view one contestant's footage. One of the challenges was to find out what Araminta and Rhys were hiding, so I chose his footage to watch. He's disingenuous, Araminta.'

Rhys scoffs. 'Are you serious? Why would anyone believe a word you're saying when you just admitted you've been running missions behind our backs. What were they? I imagine you're the reason another card is missing.'

Isko nods. 'Yes but –'

'You said that was Kalpana!' Jerome's outrage seems to stem first and foremost from believing himself immune to this pettiness.

'Excuse me?' Kalpana whirls on him. 'You brought my name into your lies?'

'Whose secret was it?' Araminta asks.

'Mine. I burnt it.'

'You know what, fuck this,' Kalpana fumes, marching up to the wall.

'What are you doing?' Theo calls.

'What's the point in the rest of us leaving our secrets there if the show itself is making taking them down part of a challenge? Five points? That's what's on offer? Fine, guess I'll lose; this isn't worth it. And someone has to take one for the team.'

Kalpana: *Please – I did what you knew I was going to do. That wall was a source of conflict, so I turned it into a demonstration.*

She starts ripping them down, one after the next, throwing them behind her – some landing in the fire, some not.

The others swarm like birds after seeds, shouting for

her to stop, grabbing at cards, flipping them over to see if they're theirs. Secrets spill quicker than they can keep up:

My talent isn't enough
I think I hate my bandmates
I'm still in love with her
I'm scared to be here
I fucking hate my bandmates
The press
I miss my father more than I hate him
I want it back
I hate my bandmates

'Jesus, Newman – that's either some deep-seated vitriol or you wanted this out.' Jerome tosses a handful of cards at him.

Theo: *You know what, fine. I'm tired of dancing around this. I quit. RiotParade can do one. I'm going solo, and I hope I never see those arseholes ever again because the worst thing about all of this is I'm convinced I've only scratched the surface of their depravity, and I want nothing to do with it.*

Araminta rushes to throw cards in the flames before they can be read – she doesn't care; she's overloaded and overwhelmed. Rhys hurries to her side, asking her if she's okay, like the cards aren't even there.

And it soon becomes clear why he does not care.

Four blank cards are laid out on the table. And it's obvious from their reactions who pinned them to that wall. Rhys might be a liar, but only when he cares enough to do it.

'Are you fucking serious, Sutton?' Theo turns on him. 'The rest of us put everything on the line and you didn't write a damn thing?'

Araminta is so tremendously shaken that she is the only one not looking at him, instead staring into the distance and that dark ocean on the horizon where she shared everything. And he's never had anything at stake. Everything Isko claimed rings in her head.

Araminta: *Who even is he?*

'In my defence,' Rhys says, hands raised, jovial smile on his face like nothing of note has happened. 'I didn't know those cards would go on the wall. I thought they'd be burned right up. We were asked what was holding us back and, well, nothing. Nothing is holding me back. So that's what I wrote.'

Araminta finally turns to him, and in line with the others and their vicious glares, she is like something slotting into place. Even as they voted Rhys off the island, they were not united, not really, saving themselves without any strength of conviction. But here, for the first time, they are a unified force. A seething, hateful, frenzied force.

And at least for a moment, they think of all the ways they will make Rhys pay.

@killingyourjoy

Those posts about Araminta were disgusting and every single person who wrote one should be ashamed of themselves. #Iconic

---

@RiotParadeOfficial

We're sorry to announce Theo Newman's departure from RiotParade following his decision to pursue other ventures. We'll keep you updated as things progress, but rest assured this is not the end of RiotParade – love Al, Dante and Tyson

Cloutier places a cup of water on the table and Theo
reaches for it, only the slightest of shakes in his hand.

'So we'd like to go back to you finding the body,' he says.

Theo looks up at him like he's surprised to see him
there. When Cloutier looks at him, he sees nothing but
exhaustion. His whole body bends with it, but the fatigue
is concentrated in his eyes, something beyond mere
tiredness.

'Again?'

'Yes, just run us through what happened.'

'I . . . I went after him,' Theo says. 'I was too late.'

'That must have been incredibly traumatic,' Cloutier
says as Kennard glares. They anticipate the suspects seeing
right through their good cop bad cop shtick. They hope it
gives them a false sense of superiority that trips them up.
'What you did was incredibly brave, especially for a man
who said such nasty, provably false things about you.'

'Some might call it stupid,' Kennard says. 'An ocean like
that, at night.'

'It wasn't anything,' Theo says, shaking his head. 'Stupid
or brave – I didn't think. There wasn't time.'

'Stupid then,' Kennard determines. 'I believe not thinking falls under that category.'

And there it is, a brief flash of annoyance from Theo,
quickly masked with another shake of his head.

147

'Maybe. Probably. I just . . . god. Stupid or brave, it doesn't matter when it was worthless. When I couldn't get him out in time.'

'You retrieved the body,' Cloutier offers. 'It might hold the clue to what happened. At the very least his family has something to bury. You achieved something.'

'Did he?' Kennard snorts. 'We don't even know for sure he was already dead. Maybe he was fully conscious. You were still angry, weren't you, Mr Newman? And in that moment, in the water, you just wanted to finish the job.'

'He was dead,' Theo says again. 'His lips were blue, and there's no way skin is supposed to be that transparent and . . . and when I got him to the beach . . .'

'You performed CPR,' Cloutier finishes.

Theo nods.

'The victim didn't have any broken ribs. Remarkable enough from the fall. Especially remarkable for CPR.'

Theo looks like he could start crying at any minute – his eyes are wide and glistening, and he fumbles awkwardly with his fingers.

'How? I . . . I thought I – are you saying I didn't do it right? That I could have saved him?'

Kennard shrugs. 'Well, Mr Newman, I'm afraid we'll never know.'

Theo swallows. 'Look, I was worried about this. I assumed you'd point the finger at me sooner or later, and I'm not going to pretend I was his biggest fan. But if you really think someone did something to him because they hated him, then I had nothing on Araminta. She hated him more than any of us, and she was smart enough to do something about it.'

Cloutier doesn't disagree – it's almost always the partner. But without the lawyer they can't even talk to her.

There's a sharp knock at the door and Maes appears. 'If I could have a moment.'

The detectives follow her.

'You're seriously interrupting an investigation?' Cloutier demands. 'What could possibly be so important?'

Maes quirks an eyebrow. 'The autopsy results are in.'

Iconic

Season 1, Episode 7

Araminta taps nervously on the screen, waiting for her friend's face to fill it as the chirps of the dial ring out.

'Ahhh, scream!' a high voice trills – not actually screaming but saying the word – before her picture comes into view: slick, glossy hair, glistening cheekbones, and freshly manicured nails. She's as polished as Eloise and clearly prepared for her moment on screen despite her next words: 'Babe, I can't believe you chose to call *me*. God, I love ya.'

'I love you too, Binks,' Araminta says with a smile, genuinely overcome by seeing a friendly face, and she feels on the cusp of tears. She holds them back instinctively before realizing they wouldn't go amiss and letting them shimmer to the surface.

'Everyone is watching, Minty. They're so jealous of you on that gorgeous island.'

'Do they all hate me?'

'Of course not.'

'I don't need you to lie, Binki – I need to know what's going on.'

'I'm not lying. Everyone loves you!'

'Not our friends. The people online, the papers. I can't shake the feeling everyone thinks I'm horrible, especially after those posts.' What a convenient excuse they are – letting her ask about her reception without coming across like everything she's doing is a performance. It's all simply the social media posts messing with her head.

'No, babe, not at all. I mean, the papers that have dragged you for years are practically calling you a national treasure. And, oh god, everyone is obsessed with you and Rhys.'

'Rhys? Really?' They like Rhys and the way their relationship is going? So perhaps she should move on from the secrets, or lack thereof. But her chest tightens at the thought and it's not simple strategy – she's falling for this boy, and she's more profoundly hurt than she's been in years.

'Girl, please! That midnight picnic! Complete swoon. And he's so hot. And he's besotted with you.'

'But Isko said the confessional footage –'

'He's lying, kind of,' she says. 'Rhys said he only wanted to hook up, but you persuaded him to want more. He said he needed to marry you one day and he wanted you to fall for him and all this adorable stuff. Please, he knows how lucky he is to be with you and that's all I've ever wanted for you. Minty, you need to at least explore it! Besides, you can always –'

The call cuts out, replaced with text shining on the screen: *your time is up.*

Theo sits at the kitchen table, hunched over his coffee. He looks up at the sound of footsteps to see a mirror image in Rhys, lines creasing his eyes, his shuffling movements speaking of a lack of sleep. Maybe it's the tiredness that saps the usual bite and tension, but last night's anger is gone, and Theo feels no desire to tell him to fuck off.

'You look awful, Newman.'

'Fuck off,' Theo counters – but his heart's not in it.

'Well, I know why I feel the way you look – I might have ruined the best thing to happen to me before it could even happen to me. But why do you?'

Theo takes such a long sip of coffee he might be downing it. 'I quit the band last night.'

'Oh, shit.' Rhys falls into a chair. 'How are you feeling?'

'Don't pretend you care.'

Rhys considers. 'Look Newman, I'm not interested in much, but your cannibalistic relationship with music is fascinating. You'd let it destroy you for a taste of the glory you've always dreamt of – so yeah, I want to know how it feels to throw it away.'

Theo's certain Rhys is only doing this to provoke an argument, but he doesn't have the energy. And once again, Rhys is correct.

Theo: *It's not fair. It's really not fair that this is the guy who understands me best on the island.*

'I just committed to going solo, like I've always wanted to. Forgetting all the arseholes in the band I just cut ties with, I . . . I'm hoping that without all that in my head I might get back to the music. Because . . .' he glances up at Rhys and remembers who he's speaking to and no, he can't do this.

'Come on, Newman. You already hate me; it's not like you care enough about my reaction to risk it. You've got nothing to lose.'

Fine.

Theo finishes his coffee and stands to brew some more so he doesn't have to see the man he's speaking to.

'I've been struggling to compose lately,' he confesses.

153

'Writer's block? How utterly mundane of you.'

'It happens to the best of us.' Theo shrugs. 'It feels like more than that though. I can write. I've written loads, actually. But it's all so basic.'

'Is that a problem? Basic music sells.'

Theo looks at him and finds him staring right back in a way that's almost disconcerting. He's seen a lot of Rhys on this island. He's never seen him focused like this. When you talk to Rhys, it's on the off-chance he's listening.

He's listening now.

'I know. And music doesn't have to be deep to be important. But I suppose I'm hoping letting go of the band politics and the chaos of fame might help. I imagine a lot of people hate me right now. Maybe it will be worth it if I let it make me the musician I want to be.'

'Well, I know you're not looking for advice,' Rhys says. 'But I'm going to give it anyway, because my advice is excellent. You've spent most of your time here debating some of the most pretentious subjects I've ever heard. And I went to Julliard. No one wants to listen to a song about Plato. Why don't you focus on living a little? Let those tensions rise. Meet a beautiful girl and actually fall in love before you write another love song –'

'I'm bisexual.'

'That's not the point and you know it! Beautiful person then – someone to fall in love with. Do something. Feel something. *Anything.*'

Theo stares at him. Perhaps he should do more on this island – join in with the torrid affairs, start some drama. Maybe it wouldn't just be for AHX or his publicist; maybe it could be for himself and his music too.

Theo: *I just blew my life up on national TV and it's Sutton of all people — the man who dealt the first blow by stealing that card — helping me pick up the pieces.*

Coffee brewed, Rhys slides the sugar pot toward him before he can ask for it. 'No amount of outside approval is going to make you happy about your own work, Theo.'

Theo: *He's right. He's actually right. Honestly, that makes it worse.*

'And if all else fails, explore the abyss of your tortured soul.'

Theo is certain Rhys means it as a mocking sort of joke, but he finds himself nodding anyway. 'Is this really what you care about? Anyone else would be pressing me for details about the band and what happened.'

'I'm not stuck on this island with the band, Theo. And frankly your own fear is a bigger motivator and a bigger threat to me than squabbles with your coworkers. I don't think you'll win this competition to go solo, but you might do it to prove to yourself it's worth it.'

'Is that all that motivates you? Was Isko right? Do you just want to get with Araminta for the competition?'

Rhys gapes a little at the sudden pivot. The others know about the two of them now, which makes this the first time he has spoken about her to another person. 'I think she's special,' he finally says. 'And I think there might be something special between us too.'

'Then it's time for a grand gesture,' Theo says. Rhys glares at him and he shrugs. 'I might not have fallen in love well enough for a love song that would appease you, but I've studied plenty. If she's worth it, fight for it.'

*

Araminta returns from her phone call and gathers her things from her room: a shawl and a towel, her sunscreen and bottle of water. Enough that she can spend the morning somewhere decompressing.

She's not given a chance.

The moment she's on that patio her eyes track to the wall that's haunted them these last seven days.

There are secrets all over it – large, swooping letters in the blue ink they'd used on the cards, this time scrawled across the white walls themselves. Secrets, fears, the things holding them back.

I should have made it by now
The time I dated a journalist for the sake of a good review
The amount of debt I'm in
Someone using me being on this show for their five minutes of fame
Losing Araminta

Rhys steps around the corner and her breath catches. She forgets sometimes, surrounded by so many beautiful people, that Rhys has the smile and muscle definition to belong on a magazine cover. He is not the bland type of gorgeous these shows are filled with – he is distinguished, like young photos of iconic Hollywood actors. So interesting to simply look at that in a moment like this, he genuinely makes her heart skip a beat.

'Thank god it's you,' he says. 'I've already startled Kalpana and half-proposed to Jerome.'

Her laugh sounds nervous even to her own ears.

'What's this?' she asks.

'My secrets. I didn't write any because I thought they'd go up in flames. By the time they'd been turned into stakes and I knew I didn't have anything on the line, it was too late to level the playing field. I was going to tell you all these, and I should have when I had the chance, but I chickened out, scared that they'd be too much. That somehow, they'd just make clear how unworthy of you I am. But I'm hoping this might fix things. And I'm very much hoping it hasn't ruined whatever was growing here.'

She hadn't actually known what she was going to do. She'd wanted this morning to consider, but now it's so obvious. She's not on a reality show; she's in a movie, and she knows her lines.

They're the ones she's always dreamed of saying.

'It hasn't ruined it,' she confirms.

'Good, because I still owe you dinner.'

Everyone sits around the pool together, like a concerted effort has been made to heal after last night's tensions. At least by tearing all the secrets from the wall, Kalpana cleansed them enough to not be at each other's throats.

But they don't speak much.

Theo is focused on last night and this morning, letting himself feel all that can be felt right now.

Kalpana is still reeling from her self-sabotage, strategizing a potential win, and wondering if she needs it. She imagines the audience at home cheering her on, loving her frenzied destruction, racing to find out more about her and her work.

Jerome still plots revenge, though it's less a plot than idle fantasy with a formless shape, a mass with the vague appearance of Kalpana suffering. When he really thinks about it, what he wants is her listed on his app as he watches the one-star reviews come flooding in: *loud, bitch, ugly, catty, feminazi.*

Isko is no longer indignant over Araminta and Rhys, just trying to keep his head down, thankful that no one seems truly furious with him over his espionage challenge.

Araminta is all over Rhys. Not because she's pleased at their reconciliation, though she is, but because she catches the way Isko avoids looking at them – and with each ducked head, she grows angrier. He lied about what Rhys said in the behind-the-scenes footage; Binki said as much. So he was just trying to drive them apart? Just jealous? Fine. If he wants something to be envious of, she'll give it to him.

Her tongue is down Rhys's throat, her hands on his chest; she is the Nymph of Knightsbridge on full display. She would screw him right then and there if she thought it would cut Isko deep enough.

When they finally leave to freshen up before the evening, the others look up from where they had been carefully avoiding eye contact and burst into laughter.

'Oh, this is going to be a disaster,' Isko says.

'They do know that if this doesn't work out, they're stuck on an island together, right?' Kalpana asks.

Theo shakes his head with a wry smile on his lips. 'I assume it's crossed their minds, but who knows; they hardly asked for our opinion, did they? But he seemed pretty upset when he thought it was over.'

'He's an actor,' Isko says. 'Who could believe a word he says, let alone trust him enough to date him. Araminta's an idiot.'

'*He's* an idiot,' Jerome corrects. 'She's a man-eater. He hasn't thought this through at all. But the real question is when do you think they will bang? My money is on tomorrow.'

'Tonight,' Theo says.

Kalpana lowers her deck chair further, reclining a little more. 'Nah, Araminta will wait a few days. Jumping into bed with him wouldn't look right for the cameras. She won't want the world thinking she's easy.'

'Internalized misogyny aside,' Jerome says, continuing a conversation from a few days earlier that was cut for time – and interest – about how he really is a feminist, actually, and nearly wrote his thesis on Judith Butler. 'You're right – it's always the allure of what's happening behind closed doors that she turns into a scandal. I don't think she's the type that would have sex on TV.'

Isko snorts. 'She's the type that would roll around in paint and have sex on a canvas if she thought it would win her the evening's challenge.'

'I guess we will just have to see.' Kalpana raises her glass.

'Well, what do we get if we're right?' Jerome asks.

'The satisfaction.'

They all raise their glasses to hers because she's right – that is enough.

Araminta and Rhys arrive flushed when the alarm rings, the editing crew showing twelve seconds of their dinner date and fifty-four seconds of them kissing, which is an incredibly long time. The sort of time frame you don't realize is long until you're watching tongues on lips and fumbling fingers and two people trying to devour each other while clumsy music plays on top and the camera circles them in shaky spins.

The other contestants try to avoid looking at each other, knowing that if they do, they will start laughing. It seems stupid now, their anger at this relationship. It is too absurd to be annoyed by.

It's early, the sun not yet set, and Eloise flickers onto the screen with a knowing smile. Sometimes they forget the viewers, and it feels like it might be Eloise alone behind the cameras – her giant face on the screen, big blue eyes that seem to follow them. 'Good evening, contestants! Well, our first group challenge wasn't due to finish until tomorrow, but Kalpana, you certainly saw to the end of that. So we thought we'd give you a last-ditch effort to win back some points. Tonight, you're all going to take part, and we're testing your morality! That's right, we expect our icons to be morally outstanding citizens and –'

'No, we don't.'

Everyone snaps to Araminta, shocked that she'd interrupt the spiel, the unwritten code that they suspend their disbelief and play along.

'I'm sorry, but we don't,' Araminta says with a shrug. 'In fact, I'd argue the opposite is true – we like our icons to break rules, to push boundaries, to go off the rails every now and again. Though, I'll admit, in a sort of contained way without any real damage. Morality? Being an upstanding citizen is hardly iconic behaviour.'

Like now, for instance. There's no way the tabloid's favourite slut is going to win any morality contests, and she has no interest in being awarded such a title from the very people who would condemn her anyway. Better to play up to her brand instead.

Rhys had shuffled ever so slightly away from her almost instinctively, like he wants to distance himself from the fall-out. But he must realize what he's doing and how it looks, his face dropping into an easy, confident smile – the sort most are beginning to suspect he wears when most uneasy.

'Be that as it may, Araminta,' Eloise says with a patronizing smile, 'it's our at home audience's opinion on what's iconic that matters.'

Araminta: *[Laughter] I think you all just enjoy the conflict! And I have to say, excellent work.*

'So in the box left for tonight's challenge you'll find two paddles – one that says *I'd do that* and one that says *I wouldn't*. I'm going to read a series of prompts and you'll all raise a paddle.'

The cellar is littered with boxes – potential challenges just waiting for them. All of them are digitally locked, and in that moment, one of them pops open. Theo retrieves the paddles inside, and the edit cuts to them in hand.

'Would you ever cheat on a partner?'

All of them raise their paddle that no, they wouldn't.

'I've learned from my past mistakes,' Theo says and Rhys nods too, like that could apply to him as well.

'Would you cheat in this competition?'

They are divided – Theo, Kalpana, and Araminta saying they wouldn't, Isko, Jerome, and Rhys saying they would.

'No surprises there,' Kalpana mutters.

Isko: *Liars.*

'Would you hurt another contestant for the sake of winning?'

All of them say no.

Eloise smiles and continues on. Several rounds later, none particularly surprising, she laughs.

'Well, that was a fun warm-up, wasn't it?'

The paddles fall limp.

'I thought you wanted to win points?' She tries for something mischievous, perhaps even flirtatious. Something that works like sandpaper against their skin. 'Let's remind ourselves of where we are, shall we?'

The scores appear in a column down the screen.

Araminta: *5*

Isko: *5*

Jerome: *5*

Theo: *4*

Rhys: *4*

Kalpana: *0*

'Isko,' Eloise says abruptly, 'would you take a point if it meant stealing it from Jerome?'

Isko startles. 'What?'

'I have to press you for an answer, Isko.' A timer appears, counting down from ten.

Isko hesitates only a moment longer before raising the *I'd do that* paddle.

'Excellent,' Eloise chirps, and the contestants watch in grotesque fascination as the scores change.

Jerome: *4*

Isko: *6*

'Are you fucking kidding me?' Jerome seethes.

'You'll have your chance,' Isko spits back.

'Kalpana, would you swap scores with Araminta?'

Kalpana already has her *I wouldn't do that* paddle in hand and does not even hesitate to raise it. Perhaps if she'd lost points in another way, if it weren't the spiteful display of superior morality, she'd be tempted, but she would lose all credibility.

'Theo, the internet is awash with scandals. Would you like us to announce what we've unearthed on Kalpana for two more points?'

Theo hesitates. And, oh god, he hates that he hesitates.

Two points would place him at the top.

Kalpana's secrets might bury his.

If nothing else, the public might be too angry over him doing this to pay much attention to his past transgressions – and this is so much more forgivable.

Or would it be the blow that fells him?

Those ten seconds blink down far too quickly. He's not even sure which paddle is in his hand when he raises it – is as shocked to see *I wouldn't do that* as the others would have been to see any other answer.

Kalpana: *There was a moment there where I really thought he might.*

'Hmm, what about you, Jerome? You've certainly alluded to knowing plenty. Would you divulge a secret about another contestant for a point?'

He doesn't even bother to raise an answer, just turns venomously to Isko and snarls, 'Isko never actually graduated from culinary school.'

Isko's paddle clatters to the floor, masking his sharp intake of breath.

He's almost as angry at showing a reaction as he is with Jerome for chipping his carefully cultivated prestige.

'Hasn't stopped you from eating my food,' Isko hits back.

'And those Michelin stars you claim? I don't think busing the kitchens counts, Isko.'

Isko's nails tighten on his thigh, like he could tear right through the flesh.

Jerome: ʃ

'I'm still winning, though, aren't I?' Isko snipes. 'Was it worth it?'

'I've still got a long competition left to destroy you.'

'Your list must be long,' Kalpana says with an eye roll seen so often it verges on iconic in itself.

'Rhys, would you break up with Araminta to double your points?'

Gasps ring the firepit they sit around – shock and jealousy, affronted by the audacity of him even being offered this as an option.

Rhys throws his *I would do that* paddle into the fire and jumps to his feet with the other held aloft.

'Of course not.' He draws Araminta to her feet, pulls her close, and kisses her with antagonistic passion.

Araminta: *I never even doubted it.*

But she has. She's not sure, if pushed, she would have made the same choice – not because she doesn't like him, but because she is used to making sacrifices despite herself.

'And finally, Araminta, would you forfeit all your points to replace someone on the island?'

She had *I wouldn't do that* prepped in her hand, her glass in the other. But now she places her drink steadily on the other side and picks up the second paddle. She'd been so convinced she wouldn't do it, wouldn't even consider whatever they offered her.

But didn't she just make a point about being immoral?

She could get rid of Isko before he could manipulate her again.

Or she could cut Jerome – she saved him last time, but the longer he goes on the more she realizes he's going to incriminate himself and maybe make matters worse for both of them.

Or Kalpana, maybe, before she can push him far enough that it all comes tumbling out.

'Jesus Christ,' Isko mutters as the seconds tick down.

Jerome is perched on the edge of his seat, hands shaking.

Finally: *I wouldn't do that.*

'Well, thank you very much, contestants,' Eloise says, clapping, as though they are not still reeling.

As they realize what has happened, they offer small smiles to Araminta, like they're thanking her for her decision, like every one of them saw themselves suddenly cut from the show.

'And for those of you whose morals aren't as shiny as we'd hoped – perhaps Araminta is right. Maybe you can still prove to us that you're icons in the making.'

Theo claps Araminta on the shoulder as Eloise vanishes. 'I knew you wouldn't do that to us.'

As though she has sided in favour of her ethical code, and not in favour of five points being too high a cost.

Everyone rushes for more drinks. They are all shaken. That's twice now they've faced the possibility of someone leaving this island. Their positions are tenuous. Everything they need from this show is someone else's to snatch from their grasp at the slightest whim.

They are desperate to blunt the edge of that risk.

Jerome pours strong drinks, visibly, publicly, and pours them away the first second he gets.

Jerome: *I don't trust anyone here. Time to stop pretending like*

165

*we're in a fraternity and start taking this competition seriously.
When they're drunk, they're vulnerable.*

He plans to push them all to the utmost humiliation.
Mistakes they might never stop regretting.

He watches as they laugh and chat, drinks spilling, lip
curling when they demand music, and Theo rushes to acqui-
esce, hoping his solo efforts might garner some screen time.

It's Jerome who makes a joke to Rhys about him not
getting laid yet, Jerome who suggests they take it outside,
Jerome who brings up Isko's skinny-dip and mentions that
he's never done it himself and suddenly they're all clam-
ouring to go, racing across the sand, not realizing that
Jerome is lingering back as they toss their clothes aside and
go tearing into the ocean.

Jerome: *Absolute idiots.*

Rhys and Araminta collide in the water, her legs wrapped
around his waist as he lifts her to him, not caring that they
are naked and surrounded by the others, and the cameras
don't flinch from the suggestion of skin visible in the dark.

The others are still laughing but soon they get cold and
rush back to the firepit to warm themselves. Araminta and
Rhys are too drunk and too horny to care and crawl out of
the ocean only to roll on top of one another on the beach,
and he is pinning her arms to the sand beneath her when
the camera cuts back to the house.

It catches the sole figure of Jerome slipping back inside
its empty rooms in search of potential ruin.

@BethAdams99

Please, not Theo casually coming out and trying to use his
  apparent bisexuality to throw us off the fact that he tore his

bandmates apart and broke up the band live on air. A rainbow coloured look over there! FUCK THEO NEWMAN! #Iconic

> **@chordsbeforewhores**
>
> @BethAdams99 Let's get this trending! Fuck Theo Newman Fuck Theo Newman Fuck Theo Newman Fuck Theo Newman Fuck Theo Newman Fuck Theo Newman Fuck Theo Newman Fuck Theo Newman! #Iconic

---

@PhotographybyKenny

Oh my god, just when I thought Araminta couldn't be more of a champagne socialist – loads of her home rejuvenation workers are now claiming she got them to work for free in return for the exposure being featured on her channel would get them. Exposure doesn't pay the bills! #Iconic

'We've got a problem,' Maes says.

'With the autopsy?' Kennard asks.

'No, with this,' she says as she passes him her phone, inbox open.

'What am I looking at?'

'An email from Steiner saying he's been fielding calls from the Yaxley-Carter team of lawyers, Yaxley-Carter enterprises, and Rodger Yaxley-Carter himself.'

He scans the email, struggling to keep track of how often the words 'sue' or 'legal action' are used.

'She's not under arrest,' Cloutier protests. 'We haven't even managed to speak with her.'

'And we *have* arrested heiresses before,' Kennard dismisses, passing the phone back. 'I don't think they've ever successfully sued.'

'Yes, but those arrests normally involve car accidents or possession of illicit substances and normally result in light community service. This is different – they're saying Araminta went through too much on the island, had to watch her boyfriend die, has to cope with millions of people watching and dissecting her relationship, and the police have no right to compromise an already vulnerable person's mental health with an interrogation when what she needs is professional support.'

'I might agree if she weren't a suspect in a literal murder investigation. Besides, we're not detaining her; she agreed to be here.'

'If anyone is pressuring her to stay,' Cloutier adds, 'it's AHX, not us.'

'Oh, he also outlined all the ways he's planning on suing AHX for facilitating and encouraging everything that went down. It appears he's trying to buy his daughter's affections back. Anyway, I just wanted to let you know – in case the pressure wasn't already high enough – that we have a millionaire demanding we send his daughter home.'

'Great,' Kennard says, rubbing at his temples. 'Anyway, where's that autopsy?'

'Here,' she says, passing them a file. 'The coroner's running us through it in ten minutes but . . . well, it doesn't clear up whether it was a murder or an accident.'

'Cause of death: asphyxiation, likely as a result of drowning. Traces of Sertraline, must have missed a dose,' Cloutier begins as he reads. 'Light kidney damage – not a surprise with how much they were drinking; tar on lungs – not a surprise with how much they were smoking; aspirin, we come back to the drinking, although o.o blood alcohol, looks like the producer was right – wait, what's this?'

Kennard leans over to see which section Cloutier's looking at and feels his breath catch. It's not often he's surprised, but having assumed they knew the victim's every movement for the last three weeks, this one shocks him.

'How the hell did they get drugs onto the island?'

Iconic

Season 1, Episode 8

The competition is shifting tonight. The secrets are gone, and they do not know what AHX might put in their place, but they suspect something just as seductive and ruinous.

The day is filled with more of the pretentious chatter of previous days, but by the early evening, they're all wound so tightly and just want to take the edge off. So they start drinking to cover for the fact that they are finding solace through other means. It's remarkably easy, even on an island rigged with cameras, and even though AHX checked their bags before they arrived.

Araminta complains that she's too hot and that she's going to have a cold shower to cool down. She even puts up with the jokes about Rhys's effect on her person.

And when she is naked, when even the camera in the bathroom is not pointed in her direction – there solely for blurry shots of shower sex and girly conversations over makeup (yet to happen, probably won't) – she bends down to her conditioning mask, slips open the plastic pouch tucked inside and helps herself to a pill.

Jerome is more basic, having stashed his first pouch thinly beneath the cigarettes in their case. The others had been stitched into the lining of his jackets like he'd seen on TV. He only needs to wear one to the smoking area and tear the hems.

Kalpana is brazen. They had tested the medicine they brought in, every pill of it. They'd even put them in orange pill bottles so they wouldn't accidentally promote any brands on screen. But they hadn't touched her breath mints at all. There's a mix in there, all identical. But if she pops a pill into her mouth and it tastes like mint, she only waits half an hour to take another.

Isko thought himself ingenious when he had lined his cosmetics with plastic – his personal favourite an eyeliner pen that unscrews to reveal white powder. There are places on the island that even the cameras don't reach but if he wants to be flagrant, he simply reaches for his eye drops, thoroughly laced.

Theo is more careful than all of the others. He doesn't do the hard stuff anyway, but weed takes up so much more room than pills and powders and has more admin to it. But he got hold of a similar enough tincture, hid it in with his array of skincare, and can vape it without the smell alerting anyone. If he ever gets caught, he has medical cannabis certificates somewhere.

Rhys has no desire to use any of it. Even if he were interested in that sort of thing, he wouldn't risk the fame this show can bring him for a high.

He's the only one who doesn't touch a thing.

He never has – and he never plans to.

Kalpana stows her mints in her bedside draw before she steps into the hall, hears moaning from next door and determines she has no desire to do this sober. She slips one on her tongue, relieved when there's only recoiling dryness and no minty tang, before pocketing the rest for later and heading downstairs, where the others sit perched on the kitchen counter and haphazardly sprawled across chairs.

Joining them, she starts the arduous and particular process of making herself a drink, noting the rapidly depleting stock of limes as she begins slicing one.

'How long do you think that will last?' Theo asks, nodding at the ceiling, the tell-tale squeak of springs barely audible on the footage.

Isko picks at a hangnail. 'Two minutes in my experience.'

'Really?' Kalpana asks.

'No,' he says, turning a withering glare on her. 'That was obviously a joke. The sex was perfectly satisfactory.'

Jerome stares resolutely at his shoes as though terrified any engagement in the conversation might lead to more details about their sexual encounter.

'I meant the relationship,' Theo clarifies.

'Why do we care?' Isko says. 'Aren't we better than this constant gossip? I thought this show was supposed to be something different, something beyond the obsession with social dynamics and the constraints of the status quo.'

'Is that why you leaped at the chance to steal points from me?' Jerome mutters.

'Oh, get over it, Jerome; it's a game. You can't take it so personally.'

'Isko's right,' Kalpana interrupts, then rushes. 'About Rhys and Araminta – not about the competition; feel however you want about that. But I'm sick of us talking about this. I'm bored by myself.'

'Shocking,' Jerome coughs into his drink.

'Don't you care at all?' Theo asks Isko. 'It would be perfectly understandable if you did.'

173

'Any lingering desire I had for him was swiftly wiped out last night after all the theatrics with throwing the paddle into the flames,' Isko says, nose wrinkling with distaste. 'He's acting like a love interest in an eighties movie, Theo. And I certainly don't want him turning up at my door with a stereo.'

Isko: *You know, Theo is the first person here to consider how I might feel about all this. And I might not care, but it turns out I do care that none of them thought I might.*

'What do you think tonight's challenge will be?' Jerome asks, somewhat pointlessly given they have no way of knowing.

'Does it matter?' Kalpana asks. 'I'm sure you'll find a way to show the world what an untalented arsehole you are anyway.'

Isko: *I disagree – Jerome's very talented at being an arsehole.*

'Kalpana, you've made it very clear how you feel about me, so frankly, beat me in a challenge or shut the hell up,' he says, without rage, as though the words have been running through his head for days and he's finally spitting them out.

'Is beating you in a court of law not enough?'

'You haven't won yet. And your case is so ridiculous I doubt you ever will – especially when I get my hands on that prize money and spend it on the best lawyers money can buy.'

Kalpana drops lime wedges into her glass, and she's still clutching the knife in a shaking hand, and everything's still blurry, but gone is the calm the Xanax promised.

'Fuck you, Jerome. You're going down one way or another. Maybe we'll get lucky and you'll fall in all the ways you can.'

174

The creaking stops.

Theo glances down at his watch. 'Two minutes on the dot.'

The shot cuts to Eloise on the screen, gleefully greeting the contestants. They are practically on the edge of their seats – or, in Araminta's case, on the edge of Rhys's lap.

'Good evening, contestants! Well, that's our first full week complete. The competition is close, but it's still anybody's game!' Eloise says. 'And tonight, we launch our second, weeklong challenge. It's all very well being a stand-out individual, but no man is an island! To truly be exceptional you must be able to work together in a team. Which is why, this week, you'll be paired up, and each mini-challenge will be worth points for you and your partner to win.'

They stifle their discontent – not wanting to appear sneering of the very competition they volunteered for. But this goes against what this contest is supposed to stand for – being one of many, being incredible on your own merit and being better than everyone else on the island.

Araminta squeezes Rhys's hand, already thinking about how competing together will bring them closer and give them more opportunity for screen time.

'Our audience has also voted for your pairs!' Eloise says, and Araminta's confidence in their pairing falters, only to be thoroughly shattered. 'Isko and Araminta, you'll be our first pair, and at the top of the leader board, you'll be a match to contend with.'

Isko: *You're really going to put me with the girl rubbing her relationship in all of our faces?*

Araminta: *It won't be the first time Isko and I have worked* *together, but he's had moments of real cruelty here and . . . no, I'm not looking forward to it.*

It's not quite a lie and not quite the truth from either of them. They work well together, can read each other, and might have more in common than they care to admit. But there's no warmth there and certainly no trust.

'Rhys, you'll be with Theo.'

Rhys: *Excellent.*

Theo: *Absolutely not.*

'And Kalpana and Jerome, you'll be competing together.'

Jerome: *That's quite some sense of humour you have, viewers.*

Kalpana: *Is there any chance the first task will be to murder your partner?*

Having delivered so much information, Eloise now takes a moment to revel in it. Her smile is slightly too tight and makes obvious the work she's had done to keep the same face that first appeared on-screen decades ago.

'And we'll be kicking things off with our first challenge – because from now until this time tomorrow, you're going to be spending an awful lot of time with your partner – a whole twenty-four hours handcuffed together to be precise.'

'Are you joking?' Kalpana hisses. Jerome is just as angry, leaping from his seat and then standing still, like he doesn't know what to do with his outrage.

Theo: *Is this punishment? Tying me to Rhys in the hope that in comparison my old bandmates don't seem so bad?*

'You can forfeit if you'd like,' Eloise says. 'But I don't think you'll want to. Each of you will have a key, so if one of your pair decides to quit, it's over for you both. You either need to be the last pair cuffed or still handcuffed by this time tomorrow. If you are, you'll win five points each.'

'We've got this in the bag,' Araminta whispers to Isko who nods, albeit a little reluctantly.

Isko: *It won't be fun, but I don't imagine it will be hard.*

'Five points is not worth it,' Jerome snarls.

Eloise arches an eyebrow, and something lights in her eyes, like it's a moment she's been waiting for.

'Which brings me to my final announcement.' Eloise pauses for long enough to make eye contact with each one of them. It feels daring, like she would like to push them until they break. '*Iconic* has really taken the world by storm. And in return for making this competition into the phenomenon it has become, we're doubling your prize money. Whoever has the most points in two weeks' time will be walking away with half a million dollars.'

She doesn't even finish speaking before the handcuffs click shut.

@LolaLois
I've never felt a prouder part of the public than when I saw
those pairings lmao, we're all such shit stirrers #Iconic

@RiotParadeOfficial
The allegations being levelled against us are unequivocally false.
But we advocate supporting and believing victims – so
would like to prove our innocence to you rather than have
you take our word for it. Therefore, we've made the difficult
decision to postpone our upcoming tour while we
collaborate with investigators and allow this matter to be
settled in the proper manner.

@MeeraAWrites

@RiotParadeOfficial you're really gonna try the 'they're
false' card when those underage girls literally have
photos of the party in your hotel room? With the
three of you in?? Theo Newman was right to cut ties
with you, you're disgusting #TeamTheo #Iconic

Yesterday, Jerome had been keen to help, to tell them anything he could. But this morning he glowers as Kennard
enters, his nostrils flaring.

'So you weren't going to tell us they're airing the final
episode tomorrow?' he snaps. 'We all just had to find that
out ourselves from our hotel TVs?'

'We're the police, not AHX. Informing you of schedul-
ing decisions is on them,' Kennard says. He tries not to
look at the mirror, where Cloutier stands watching him.
He can't be in the same room without being distracted, but
without him he has no counterbalance, no one to even out
his harsh edges.

'That's not fair – it's disgraceful, actually. Rhys deserves
better than his death to become a finale.'

'I agree, and if we can prove a crime occurred, then that
won't happen. So I'd like to bring us onto why you spent
an exorbitant amount of time in the smoking area the day
he died.'

'I was smoking.'

'For so long? And you actually spent a while in there
most days, twice as long as the others. What would make
you cling to a space without cameras like that? Our forensics teams are scouring it, so perhaps the more appropriate
question is what were you doing?'

Jerome pales. 'It wasn't like that. It wasn't the cameras; it was them. When you're there, you can't escape them. There was always someone wherever you wanted to go. We all kind of respected each other's privacy in the smoking area – sometimes you'd go and someone would be there, so you'd head back later.'

'So you were avoiding your fellow contestants? Why?'

'Why?' he scoffs. 'Have you not seen everything that happened those last few days? Jesus, what are you doing here talking to me – go watch the footage.'

'Would you really like us to do that when we know you messed with the cameras?'

'I didn't do a thing to the cameras.'

'Then what did you do when you hacked into AHX?'

Jerome glares and says nothing.

'You know, Mr Frances,' Kennard says, leaning forward. 'I can't help but feel you want that episode aired.'

Jerome locks eyes with Kennard, lip curling up in a sneer. 'Maybe it wouldn't be fair on Rhys, but maybe I trust the public to get justice more than I trust the detectives wasting time talking to me when they should be interviewing whoever murdered him.'

Another knock at the door, Maes summoning them out again.

'The lawyer's finally here,' she says. 'You can talk to Araminta.'

Iconic

Season 1, Episode 9

The episode opens with an argument, a blur of rising voices that implies this has been going on for hours, but now it slows, becomes coherent, like a camera zooming into focus.

'You don't get to dictate our every waking moment, Jerome!'

'All we've had are waking moments – you were tossing and turning all night. I haven't slept.'

'Oh, grow up. I had to go with you to the fucking bathroom. I might never recover.'

'Why don't you sue me over it. The sight of a penis is something people go to court over these days, isn't it, Kalpana?'

'Are you really making light of indecent exposure?'

'You'll give a name to anything, won't you? This is why real issues are swept under the rug –'

'Jerome!' Kalpana screeches. 'Can we please go be around some other people, because if I'm latched to you for two more minutes, I'm going to indecently expose you to the sharp edge of a knife.'

'I've said yes, but I'm not sitting with you and Theo Newman while you discuss whatever nonsense you've decided is of the utmost importance today. You're like stoners, but without the drugs that might make it all bearable.'

Kalpana: *This is the worst thing to ever happen to me.*

Jerome: *Wow, what an incredible amount of privilege you must have.*

Kalpana: *Either let me out of these handcuffs or shut up. Is this not bad enough without me having to sit through the confessional footage with you too?*

'Fine! At this point I'd go sit with the leaders of the NRA and fucking Donald Trump himself if it got me away from being alone with you.' Kalpana rubs at her wrist, which is already chafed, despite the soft silken lining to the handcuffs. She's almost certain they're sex toys, which makes being bound to Jerome with them even worse.

'You know, I actually kind of like –'

'Do not finish that sentence if you don't want me to unlatch my handcuff right this second. How on earth are any amount of points worth this to you?'

'If I have to explain the appeal of half a million dollars to you, then I have some questions.'

Kalpana huffs and tosses her hair from her face. Unlatching this would be letting Jerome win by proving that he's getting to her.

'Besides,' he continues, 'we don't need to stay cuffed together all day. We just need to get the others to cave before we do.'

Kalpana stops fidgeting with the handcuff, and for the first time, she sees that she and Jerome might have something to work with in partnership after all – they are both conspiratorial and have no shame about being underhanded. They might both simply call such things *being clever.*

'What did you have in mind?' she asks.

Jerome straightens up, his smile smug and self-assured. 'There are dynamics already at play – Rhys and Theo hate each other, Isko isn't a fan of Araminta, and most importantly, Araminta and Rhys can't keep their hands off each other. Isko and Theo won't be able to stand it. I say we take all of that and push it to its absolute limit.'

The pair find Theo and Rhys sitting in stony silence, sipping at coffee they'd fumbled to make with their hands joined.

'Well, you look like you're having as much fun with this as I am,' Kalpana comments, noting the way Theo's hand tightens on his mug.

In the early morning, it's not quite hot enough for the shaded patio to feel warm, but the promise of the sun burns on the periphery, and Kalpana pours coffee over ice like she already needs the coolant.

'It's fine,' Theo says tersely.

'No, this is the worst,' Jerome agrees almost cheerfully. 'Agreeing that we both hate this is the first time we've stopped arguing.'

'I'm sure I can handle being latched to Newman,' Rhys says, batting his eyelashes at Theo. 'There must be dozens of teenage girls who would pay good money to be where I am right now.'

A vein in Theo's neck throbs.

Kalpana considers pushing that further, but she's not very good at improvising so she pivots to the track she'd planned. 'Still, you can't be happy to be paired with Theo over Araminta. I imagine you'd have a lot more fun handcuffed to her.'

Rhys's gaze cools as he turns to her. 'And is imagining Araminta and me in handcuffs something you've spent a lot of time doing?'

'Please,' she scoffs. 'You might be shocked to discover this, but you aren't my type, Rhys.'

'Araminta then. Do you wish you'd been paired with her? You could stop her escaping from you and force her to be by your side.'

Kalpana leans forward, narrowing her eyes. 'Is that how you see your relationship? Like you've trapped her?'

'Did I miss where this escalated?' Theo interjects.

'I just don't like a woman who kissed my girlfriend talking about her or our relationship,' Rhys snaps.

'It was a kiss,' Kalpana says icily. 'And it was before you were dating. If you want to talk about a double standard – Araminta is currently handcuffed to a man you fucked.'

'Besides,' Jerome says, 'everyone on this island has kissed Araminta. Hell, if the stories are anything to go by, half the population of London has kissed Araminta.'

'Theo, would you please come with me? I'd very much like to storm off now,' Rhys says.

'No, I'm quite happy right here.'

Rhys: *I did consider it, actually – just unlatching the handcuff. I don't want to do this – I want to be with Araminta. And maybe, for that opportunity, it would be worth losing. But I'm trying to think long term, of all the things that prize money could mean for us.*

'I'll unlatch the handcuff,' he bluffs.

'Jesus Christ, Sutton,' Theo grumbles, rising to his feet, coffee still clutched in his free hand. 'Fine, whisk us away in whatever dramatic exit you have planned.'

Jerome: *I think that went well, don't you?*

Kalpana: *Yeah, it was a good start. A bit alarming though. Rhys brushes everything off, but that struck deep? I never even wanted a relationship with Araminta, and he was acting like he'd bested me.*

Jerome: *Is that what you're mad at? The implied victory? Not him reducing Araminta to a prize?*

Kalpana: *Oh, get fucked, Jerome.*

Araminta and Isko are so at ease with the situation that it has crossed into a passiveness that is in itself awkward. They are amicable enough, but they are not deep or meaningful, their conversation all stilted pleasantries and vague necessities.

Isko is unbothered.

But for Araminta, it ruffles something at the edge of her mind, some lingering concern she'd done her best to avoid but now struggles to evade: loneliness.

She feels lonely on this island. All these people and no one to confide in. She has had to rely on her friends more than most, but now that something so exciting is happening to her, she has no one. She wants someone to gush about her crush to, someone to get as excited as she is every time Rhys makes her swoon, someone to squeal to after every date.

But beyond Rhys, who is there? At best it is this – courteous disinterest.

'Hey, I want to touch up my makeup,' she says, drawing Isko to the bathroom and ambling to the conditioning mask, slipping out her bag of pills and carefully pressing one into his hands. He lifts a singular eyebrow, which could mean too many things – amusement, curiosity, surprise – and swallows the tablet without question.

In part, she needs it. In part, she hopes the secret might bond them together, repair their fractures.

Isko appreciates it, but he also pockets the existence of her pill stash away for future leverage.

They take their high to the beach. The sun scorches like it's issuing a challenge. There is something almost Eloise-like in the way that it looms in the sky.

'Oh god,' Isko groans, and when Araminta looks up, she sees Theo and Rhys coming over.

'Rhys!' she beams unashamedly. The more she can be the excitable, innocent one in this relationship, the more she reshapes her own story. The thing they all miss when they scream about all the people she's dated, when all they see is proof that no one can suffer her long but might like the look of her long enough to try – they miss that it is also a list of how many times she has gotten her hopes up, and put herself wholly on the line for love.

Theo lets himself be dragged over to Araminta as Rhys reaches for her. As they kiss, Isko and Theo share a despairing look, far too close to one another.

'This is the world's worst double date,' Isko sighs.

'Can't we be a polycule?' Araminta jokes.

'Oh god, don't start,' Rhys says, shaking his head. 'I've just had to put up with Jerome reminding me of the many, *many* people you've been with. I don't need you lusting after more people in front of me. I much prefer you being my own personal minx.'

At this, he hooks his arm around her waist and draws her closer.

She's grateful for the closeness – too close for him to

see her face when he says that, time for her to work through her response, and how she wants to vocalize it.

'I'm not sure I love being called a minx,' she says with a breathy laugh.

Araminta: *It's not a big deal, but I don't know – it's just different, isn't it? When it's from someone you really like? Partly reinforcing all that slut-shaming, and partly introducing a degradation kink I didn't consent to.*

'What would you prefer?' Rhys jokes, smiling that captivating smile of his – one that is so bold and so bright, so centred on her that it feels like it holds promises of future happiness. 'Harlot? Jezebel? Nymph perhaps? That would be a nice "screw you" to the scandal-hungry press, to declare there's nothing wrong with liking sex and all that.'

'I think just Araminta would be fine.'

'Hmm, whatever you want, minx.' He leans forward and kisses her. She kisses him back almost immediately, all that teasing making her lightheaded even with its odd undercurrent.

Hands wrench them apart, their own wrists yanked away by their partners.

'That's enough of that,' Theo says with distaste.

Isko nods. 'You might not give a crap about forcing it down our throats the rest of the time, but for this challenge you're just going to have to cope with not launching at each other every two seconds.'

'You know what, I'm taking away the temptation,' Theo says, glowering at Rhys. 'Come on – let's go suffer this by ourselves. You can go back to the days where you pretended you weren't together.'

Rhys reaches back for Araminta with a joking

exaggeration, like they are lovers torn apart by great forces and not two irritated men. Araminta blushes, endeared all the same.

Jerome has decided to take this opportunity to start ranting that if 'her eco lot' actually wanted to save the environment they'd put their time and energy into innovation rather than blocking roads and throwing paint. In retaliation, Kalpana lectures him about the paradox of eco-conscious choices under capitalism, and they both threaten to dislocate their shoulders in an effort for more distance as the conversation spirals through various prejudices and fallacies until Jerome shrieks and buries his head in his unrestrained hand.

'How is this fair?' he snarls. 'If I were handcuffed to anyone else, it would be fine. The others are all going to get those points easily, but we've had the hardest challenge here and we won't even get more points for it.'

He's right – the others haven't suffered like they have. They deserve more.

And Kalpana resolves, as much as it cuts her, to push them to the brink. She does not hesitate, not even long enough to question what that says about her.

The wind picks up enough that the beach is uncomfortable, sand flying like tiny pinpricks, so they regroup on the patio, shielded from the worst of it by the house.

Kalpana sits next to Araminta and flirts – lightly and vaguely. The sort of way no one in their right mind would even clock as flirting.

But Rhys does. He's tautly across from her, and his hand clutches his glass a bit too tightly.

Jerome is busy distracting Theo, so he does not see the build to the outburst Kalpana is sure is coming.

'Okay, tell me honestly, are men good in bed? Like, do they actually make you come?'

'Some of them,' Araminta says with a smile, eyes landing on Rhys, who glares hard at her.

'Kalpana, that's enough,' Rhys snaps.

She tries to look innocent. 'What? I'm just saying, isn't it all over so quickly? With us girls' – she casts a look at Araminta, and Rhys's face twists like he wants to rip her damn eyes out of her head – 'you just have to call it. Otherwise, it can go on until morning.'

'She's right,' Araminta laughs, oblivious to the tension, and still feeling the numbness of the pill. 'My ex-girlfriend and I used to count a quickie as less than two hours.'

'Araminta,' Rhys growls.

'What?'

'I don't want to hear about your fucking exes – especially not about you being in bed with them.'

'Rhys, you have no reason to be insecure. You're –'

'I'm not insecure.'

'You sure sound it to me.' Kalpana chortles into her glass. 'Compensating for something?'

'Araminta, walk away from her.'

Araminta snorts. 'No.'

'Fine,' he hisses. 'Newman, can we go please.'

Theo turns from Jerome, eyebrows drawing together. 'What? No.'

Kalpana decides to stop being subtle.

'Shame all we did was kiss,' she jokes, 'They could have paralleled Isko and Rhys's ten minutes with our five hours.'

'I didn't realize longevity was the aim,' Isko adds without so much as looking up from the loose thread he examines.

'Kalpana, is there something you want to say?' Rhys snarls.

Kalpana remains calm, arching an eyebrow and says: 'I think I've been pretty clear. I could show your girl a better time than you.'

Kalpana: *it was gross, honestly. To challenge his machismo for his girl – blargh, disgusting. But I wanted to expose him for the misogynist prick he is.*

'Are you seriously going to sit there and let her say that,' Rhys demands, turning to his girlfriend.

Araminta stares at him. 'What does it matter? I'm dating you – who cares what Kalpana thinks?'

It is this that undoes him, eye twitching, Araminta pushing back, dismissing his rage.

He stands up, yanking Theo's arm like he is pulling a stubborn dog.

'Sit down, Sutton, for god's sake.'

Being locked in, his anger spikes. Like he is caged and snarling.

Kalpana coughs. 'Small-dick energy.'

'Fuck this,' Rhys says – and he's so quick, the key in his hand, the cuff twisted off, Rhys's heavy footsteps pounding off the deck before Theo can register the cuff hanging limply at his side. When he does, his rage could rival Rhys's, no time for breath between his string of curses.

Araminta stares after Rhys.

'Should I –'

'Absolutely not,' Isko snaps, reaching across and snatching her bag from her, where he knows her key is stashed.

Araminta looks back to where he's gone and swallows. 'Well, that's rather worrying, isn't it?'

The remaining four could fling the handcuffs into the fire when they finally come off, or else at the screen and smash Eloise's taunting smile into a thousand glass shards. She's so pleased with herself and too readily admits how much they've all struggled with the challenge – and how enter-taining it's been for the audience.

She dishes out their five points each, commiserating with Theo, whose nostrils flare with his attempt to force a calm what-can-you-do smile. Once the handcuffs are unlatched and the screen is off, Araminta goes to find Rhys.

He's on the beach, the wind considerably calmer now.

'Hey,' she greets, unsure where to start.

'Hi.' He turns, voice soft. 'I'm sorry. I don't know why that got to me like that. I think being kept apart from you all day had me already feeling on edge, and I just couldn't take it.'

Araminta hesitates. She does not know what to say. She knows the anger is a warning sign but he seems devas-tated, and genuinely apologetic, and that camera is whirring ever nearer. 'Shall we walk?' she finally offers.

It's too small for that, really. A lap of the shore takes five minutes – across the beach on one side, steadily upward to the peak of the cliff's edge on the other, and then back down to the sandy banks.

But they walk rings around it anyway, this wheel of an island, generating content for the audience.

And they talk.

'You just have to understand what it's like,' he says. 'When she's sat there flirting like that.'

'She's playing the game, Rhys. I knew what she was doing and I thought you did too, but as you proved when you opened that cuff, she clearly played it well.'

'My feelings for you aren't a game, Araminta.'

'I didn't say –'

'And you've kissed, I mean . . . look, you can't be talking to someone you've kissed like that.'

'I was laughing her off and spinning it back to you.'

Rhys glowers but turns it out to the ocean. 'You should have shut it down.'

'If she were genuinely making a move on me, I would have, but for god's sake, Rhys. There are six of us on this island; I can't just not talk to Kalpana.'

'And talking about your ex? Isn't there enough out there of your past sexual exploits? It's on every web page. I'm going to get enough details from everyone else – do I have to get it from you too?'

Araminta thinks this is ridiculous but suspects that may be because she came to terms with her sex life being public information a long time ago. She would not have a problem hearing about his previous encounters but supposes she can reluctantly see how he might struggle with it. She suspects the audience will side with him here too.

'All right,' she nods. 'I won't, now that I know it bothers you.'

Rhys sighs and takes her hand. 'They're just boundaries for me. Speaking of past relationships. Flirting with anyone, let alone people you've hooked up with. If that's not something you can do, that's fine, and we can go our separate ways. But Araminta . . .' His voice wavers, his tone different, and she turns to him, already startled. She knows that heaviness, knows it too well and already wants to brush it off – to brush him off before he goes too far. 'I never expected to meet anyone like you on this island.' And it begins, as it always does, with themselves – their wants, their explanations.

No declaration of love she has ever received (for this is surely what it is) has been about her. It's always the other person and the spectacle of it all, almost like they are saying these things for themselves, watching from afar, in the future, to look back and say *look what I gave to this girl*.

Maybe they think that if they can fake a feeling in language, or be kind, stretch what they are feeling that way, they can reflect on the passions of youth that she's not convinced exist.

Three drones hover.

'I never expected to meet anyone like you, period. You're the most incredible woman I've ever met,' he continues. This is what she wanted isn't it, for him to make it about her? She tries to cling to her skepticism, his earlier outrage, to protect herself in any way she can. But it's slipping away with every second he spends looking at her in the same way that she looks at sculptures.

She loves this every bit as much as she hates it. It's how she ends up in this trap again and again. Because she can deride them for their pretty words, but god, doesn't she love a pretty word?

'You've made my time on this island, and today has shown me that I don't even want to *think* about a single day without you by my side, here or anywhere. I know it's soon, but everything here is so intense and I have never felt like this before. So can we just do everything we can to make this work?'

'Rhys, I –'

'And I thought about it earlier anyway, and thought: no, I'll only make you think I'm some creep, and then everyone on the island will be out for my blood. But every time I think I can't like you more, you give these glimpses into the soul of yourself. Araminta, the way your brain works is a beautiful thing to witness. I love you, and I wanted to tell you that.'

She treasures the moment, conscious of the rush through her. And when Rhys turns to her, she wraps her arms around his neck and kisses him under the moonlight, the buzz of the drones drowning out the waves.

@ashareads23

Oh my god do I actually support Araminta and Rhys now? Is
    that something that's happening to me? They're so
    goddamn cute. #Iconic

> **@ChayleighLee**

> @ashareads23 I know right! It was so adorable how
>   protective he was!! And then that speech!!! #Arhys
>   #Iconic

@AkosuaNkrumah

I have to say something. Kalpana Mahajan has a reputation in
    the community for piggy backing off the campaigning of
    other activists and is widely seen as only looking to be the
    face of the movement, not the driving force behind it. For
    anyone watching Iconic, ask what sort of activist would go
    on a show like this, and what has she used this platform for?
    If you feel it's all a sense of performative superiority, here is
    a thread of people you should be following instead
    #Iconic

'Tell us what happened on that island,' Detective Kennard begins.

Araminta's lawyer, Cheryl Blythe, waves a perfectly manicured hand to stop her client, though Araminta had made no move to answer. 'I'm going to have to ask you to be more specific with the direction of your questions.'

'All right,' he agrees, fingers curling against his coffee cup. 'In your own words, how would you describe your relationship with the victim?'

Araminta takes a sip of her water. She looks tired, skin nearly translucent under the harsh fluorescents, blonde hair limp. Kennard wonders if AHX made the mistake of booking a four-star hotel. He doubts a Yaxley-Carter is used to anything less than Egyptian cotton. Or perhaps it was the guilty conscience keeping her awake. 'Variable.'

'Can you expand on that?'

'No, I don't think that I can,' she says. 'If I told you our relationship was wonderful, you'd pull up footage of us fighting. If I told you it was terrible, you'd show us having sex on the beach.'

'We just want a thorough picture of what went on,' Cloutier says.

'Do you?'

Cloutier meets Kennard's eye, and with the barest blink, Kennard suggests they move on. A year since they last worked together, and they can still communicate like this.

'Where were you when the victim died?' he asks.

'You have the footage,' Araminta says. 'I was in my room packing.'

'The finale wasn't for another week.'

'I was . . .' She glances to her lawyer, who nods. 'I was thinking about leaving. No, I wasn't thinking about it – I decided I was going to leave.'

'Why?'

'Because . . .' Araminta looks down like she can suddenly pretend to be bashful and innocent. These people have spent so long being audacious liars to each other they've forgotten the rest of the world isn't so fooled.

'Because of Rhys,' Araminta finally manages.

'You understand how that could be construed as a motive.'

'Of course,' she snaps. 'But it's not. I was leaving. I was getting out.'

'Perhaps you felt there was no way out. Perhaps you felt that leaving the show wouldn't be enough,' Kennard suggests.

'Did you have a question, Detective?' Cheryl cuts in.

'A lot of your fellow contestants have spoken about how after a certain amount of time on the island, nothing outside of it felt real. Did you notice a similar goldfish bowl effect?'

Araminta shrugs. 'A few times, I guess. I mean when I think of just how much happened, how quickly everything moved, I'm shocked. But it's hard to forget entirely about your world back home when there are drones flying around everywhere and cameras on every umbrella stand. So no, I didn't feel trapped by him. Quite the opposite – at its worst, I felt all I had to do was wait it out, and then I'd be home.'

Cloutier nods, before changing track. 'We've had the autopsy results in, so this question is pretty important. Do you know where one could find drugs on the island?'

Araminta shakes her head. 'You couldn't – they checked everything to make sure no one could get anything in. There must be some mistake.'

'Drugs?' Theo frowns. 'I'm not sure. I guess you would have to smuggle it in – why, did Rhys take something?'

'Christ, I *knew* he was on something. I thought he was just drunk,' Kalpana pops a mint into her mouth and arches a challenging eyebrow. 'They checked everything though. I'm not even sure how you could sneak it in.'

Jerome shrugs. 'You would have had to bring it in yourself, I guess. I have no idea how you would take anything, though, being on camera all the time.'

Isko snorts dismissively. 'If Rhys managed to get something onto the island, he's far smarter than I ever gave him credit for.'

Iconic

Season 1, Episode 10

Araminta did not say I love you back. She clings to that thought so tightly it keeps her awake. Did she react all right? Did Rhys catch anything amiss? Did the audience? She can rectify it with a moment of her own, she's sure. But does she want to?

Does she love him?

Should she? Would it be good for the cameras? Or is her confusion in its honest truth more relatable?

She decides that, for now, what she needs is space and time to miss him again. So she slips from the room and stretches on the beach. When she returns, she finds Theo at the kitchen table.

'Hey,' she greets.

He nods in her direction.

He can't be much of a morning person, not least because he's rarely up at this time. At this hour, he can hardly hold a conversation, and the more she presses, the more questions she asks, the more he retreats.

Theo: *Christ, who wants an interrogation first thing in the morning?*

And then Jerome joins, and for the first time, she is relieved to see him. He has a bad habit of appearing at inopportune moments and it's nice to know he can, occasionally, do the reverse.

She tries to chat to him, politely, civilly, as she always would.

But he just grunts in response.

Jerome: *Here we go – this is how it begins. They always come crawling back to you, always want you to be their shoulder to cry on.*

Later, she finds Kalpana on the deck, watching the waves crash on the distant shore.

She is hesitant, awkward, not wanting to blame her divide with Rhys on her.

But after greetings are divested with, Kalpana asks, 'So how were things with Rhys last night after his little tantrum?'

And Araminta knows it would be a betrayal to say anything about Rhys to Kalpana.

So she tries to change the topic but all she can manage is 'It's a nice day.'

'Imagine that.' Kalpana sips her coffee.

Kalpana: *My guess is he told her he loved her, then ejaculated prematurely, thus creating the tortured woman you see before you.*

She finds Isko by the pool. He hasn't said much lately, even when they were latched together it felt like he was in a world of his own, staring into the distance.

'Good morning, Princess,' he says, and she's too desperate to argue.

'Hey,' she says instead, and he turns in her direction.

Isko: *She clearly wasn't okay, but isn't that what she has a boyfriend for? To care about all that?*

'Another thrilling day out here,' she says. 'What do you miss most about being home?'

He considers. 'The ability to choose when I see people and how.'

Araminta looks at him, unable to tell if that's a semi-polite way of telling her to fuck off.

'That and Alex.'

And here it is, finally, a topic she can cling to.

'How did you two meet?'

'I'd actually rather not get into that. This island, this show, is already taking too much. I'd rather not give them my personal life too.'

'Oh, that's fine.' She falls back, defeated.

Isko: *I guess she didn't get my not-so-subtle hint to fuck off. Haven't we spent enough time together lately? Where's Rhys to stick his tongue down her throat when you need him?*

'Where did you go this morning?' Rhys asks, running his hands across her shoulders, pressing his fingers into the knots he finds.

She tries to relax into it. She doesn't have the heart to tell him how on edge all that touching makes her. But then she remembers their spa day and how it felt like that had started it all, their collusion – just the two of them against the others. Maybe she never needed anyone else.

'The beach.'

'Will the world end if you skip a day of yoga?'

'It'll feel like it.'

'Do you want to talk about it?'

She offers a weak smile. 'It's okay, honestly.'

'You know you can, right? That you don't have to keep it to yourself? I'm not going to think any less of you.'

'It's really nothing. It would be easier if there were something to talk about – trust me, enough therapists have tried and failed. Everything else I have answers for – with migraines I take pills; seasonal depression, I take a week-end in the Mediterranean or a holiday to the Caribbean. But anxiety just never leaves me. Sometimes I wake up feeling like my heart might burst, like I'm dying. Yoga helps me manage it.'

He nods, a concerned frown etched into his forehead. 'Is there anything I can do to help?'

Araminta: *I could tell he wanted to be like, 'Oh that's so horrible, I'm so sorry' but he didn't. Which is exactly what I need and just, god, even the fact I felt comfortable enough to tell him is more than I've ever done with anyone before. What exactly am I so scared of? He's perfect.*

She reaches for his hand. 'You being there when I return is more than enough.'

Theo is awful at this game.

He can finally admit it.

He doesn't know how to cause drama. He cannot throw himself into a romance for the sake of the cameras, cannot pick a fight for screen time or think of any way to command attention. Attention has always gravitated toward him. He thinks of what Eloise said when she first introduced *Iconic* to the world: You have always had to be one in a million, but can you even be one of six?

Out there he's special. But on this island with the others? Maybe he can't be the standout star.

So he gives up trying to find a clever way to use the information he has and figures that, if nothing else, this conversation will likely be aired.

He finds Isko filing his nails on a sun lounger by the pool, two bottles of water and a bottle of vodka next to him, and for a moment, Theo wonders if it might contain water too – if Isko is trying to cultivate some image by drinking vodka straight at 11 a.m. But the camera would have seen him fill it up, so it must be the real thing, though no less an intentional choice.

'Can I ask you something?' Theo starts, sitting next to him.

'Of course.'

'It's . . . well I suppose it's also a confession. And you'd be perfectly entitled to tell me to fuck off.'

Isko glances over the top of his sunglasses. 'You don't love me, do you, Theo?'

'I took a secret from the wall.'

There is no surprise, no anger, just Isko reaching for the vodka, slowly unscrewing the cap, and taking a swig. 'All right. And you're here, so it was mine. What was it?'

He hesitates just enough to show a remorse he's not sure he feels. 'It was about a girl, I think.'

'Just tell me what it was, Newman. I appreciate your efforts to keep from revealing it to the masses, but if you know, I'd prefer the whole world to.'

Theo: *It was horrible, hearing my own sentiments parroted back to me. All that hatred for Rhys when he took my secret from the wall, and I did the exact same thing to Isko.*

'It said: *I'm sorry, Juliet. Your «chou».*'

Isko nods. 'Ah.'

'Well, I was just wondering . . .'

'What it meant?' Isko offers when it becomes clear Theo is struggling to get the words out.

'Well . . .' Theo itches at the back of his neck.

'Go on,' Isko presses, leaning forward with a wicked

smile unfurling on his lips. His sunglasses are thick and dark, and Theo can't see the eyes behind them at all, just two big circles of black plastic. 'Theo Newman, say it. You stole a secret and now you want answers. It wasn't enough for you to merely take it from me; you're now audacious enough to come confront me and demand clarity.'

Theo swallows then shakes his head and snatches the vodka from the side and takes a long shot. 'Yes. I took a card, and what was on it has confused me ever since. Of course, feel free not to answer, to tell me I already got more than was fair of you. But I'd like to know, so I'm asking.'

To his surprise, Isko laughs. 'Forcing honesty from you all is like drawing blood from a stone, but what a delightful, thoroughly bloody thing it is. Sit down. I'll tell you about Juliet Moncrieff.'

Theo startles. 'Wait, I know Juliet Moncrieff. I think we had the same publicity team or something.'

'Well, they're shit. Fire them. Her publicists all but threw her to the wolves when things went down.'

Theo can't agree – they're doing a great job for him. He's here, after all. While the rest of the band awaits destruction, Theo's in the shelter avoiding the fallout.

On the other hand, he supposes, they did throw the rest of the band over to save him. But Theo would never be stupid enough to go to a party with fifteen-year-olds and take photos.

'I was her private chef for three years,' Isko says quietly. 'But Juliet didn't like thinking of herself as an employer. She really made an effort to make me feel like a friend – integrated me with her other friends and everything. She made cooking for her feel like someone respected my passion and was excited to see me indulge it. It was work, and the hours were long and she paid me, but working for Juliet was more than a job, it was a lifestyle. I wasn't entirely stupid; she liked collecting people and giving them cutesy terms of endearment like *chou*. I'm sure it made her feel thoroughly down-to-earth to befriend the help, but honestly, I liked all that about her.'

'Okay,' Theo says hesitantly. Because what does Isko have to apologize for; where does it all go wrong?

'My point is that I like Juliet a great deal and I still consider her a close friend. But I would understand if she didn't feel the same way. I testified against her at her trial, Theo; that's why I'm sorry.'

'Oh, that must have been so difficult. But you did the right thing –'

'So the system would like us to believe,' Isko says, a fierceness to his voice. 'I didn't know what I knew; I just answered their questions – who I saw coming and going from the house and when. I debated doing it for weeks but Alex finally convinced me that if Juliet was innocent, my testimony would help and if she wasn't, then it wouldn't be anything I said that put her away. But in the end, they did put her away, and I can't help but feel like I could have helped. I mean, who gives a shit about tax evasion anyway? Who ruins a friendship over financial fraud?'

'Yeah, of course,' Theo says with a nod. 'It can't have been easy. But what else could you have done?'

'That's what I'm saying, Theo. That's why I'm sorry – because we're told things are right or wrong by a system that locks away a girl who at worst misunderstood overly complicated financial forms and got famous enough that they thought to make an example of her. And if I could go back, I would have lied. I would have created any story, told the police anything to get her out. I'm sorry I ever believed you owed the police the truth. Every single investigator on Juliet's case was an asshole, and I should have screwed them over at every opportunity I had.'

They've replayed that clip so many times in the precinct they wonder if they're responsible for all the algorithms making it go viral.

It is marked in block letters on Isko's file: *Trust nothing he says.*

Araminta and Rhys have dinner alone together that evening, and Araminta appears in a fairy-tale dress – a soft pink number that glows in the golden light.

'My minx? Wearing colour?' Rhys gasps. 'Could this be?'

'I do wear colour on occasion,' she says. 'I have worn at least three colourful pieces on this island.'

'You should wear more.' His eyes rake her over. 'You look ghastly in white; in colour, you're a goddess.'

'Excuse me?'

'What?'

'I look *ghastly*?'

'Oh, I didn't mean it like that. I'm just complimenting the way you look now.'

It's not a compliment at all – but then she thinks of how quiet today has been and how it's not worth kicking up a fuss and ruining the first nice moment of the day.

And she does look nice in this dress.

'Well, I haven't been able to wear this one before. It clashes with my sunburn.'

They decide to rapid-fire some questions, like it will help them get to know one another. But it feels foolish – how could they possibly know each other better than they do? After spending a whole lifetime on this island, all that other time elsewhere is extraneous.

Araminta's answers keep falling back to art: her favourite travel location, where the best galleries are, her dream dinner party full of sculptors, her first kiss over an easel.

'You know what I like best about you?' Rhys asks.

She prepares herself for a compliment she'll only want to brush away.

'Your passion. Every single question I ask, you have a thorough answer. Everything you like, you adore.'

'So do you,' she says. So does everyone on this island. Has he not heard the arguments? She would argue that of them all, she is the most flippant, the most willing to dismiss a subject as trite. But perhaps he sees something in her that she doesn't.

'I know – that's why it means so much to me that you're like that too. I'm so passionate about everything I do – too much so. It's like I have to pick what to devote myself to because there just aren't enough hours in the day. I'd have loved to have thrown myself fully into my band, Hurricane Bay, but I couldn't do that *and* act, and in the end, acting won out. People who can't do anything without getting wrapped up in it are enticing. And no one is more captivating than you.'

She feels herself blush and looks away, unable to meet his eyes. He seems so sincere when he says things like that.

'Can I ask you something?'

'Of course,' he says, squeezing the hand he holds.

'It's just something I keep thinking about after, well, after you told me you loved me. Do you still, by the way?'

He gives her a withering stare. 'Yes, Araminta, I still love you.'

'Well, I just wanted to check it wasn't some high from being unlatched from Theo that you're now regretting. I won't mind, you know.'

'You won't mind?'

'Well, I would, but I'd understand. Anyway, given that you *do* in fact still love me, I just wanted to check something about what you said yesterday, just so I can't accidentally cross it again, about how I can't be talking to someone I kissed like that –'

'I never said that,' he says.

'Never said what?'

'That you "couldn't" do something – why are you making me sound controlling?'

'You know what I mean, about how –'

'Me setting a boundary is not me controlling you, Araminta. And I'd appreciate it if you didn't present it like that, especially on live TV.'

Araminta blinks, confused about where she went wrong but maybe shouldn't have brought their argument up anyway. 'Oh. Okay, never mind.'

'I love you so much, I just want this to be perfect,' Rhys says and forces a laugh. 'I don't blame you for misremembering. In fact, it's a good thing all this is being recorded, or with a memory like that, I'd have to remind you of this relationship when we get back out. I can't wait to just be alone with you. I'm going to spend the rest of my life making you feel like the most loved person in the world.'

But it's not just the words, it's him staring at her with his dark eyes so focused, the planes of his face in the torch-light, and she's overcome by his beauty and the way he gazes right back like he's just as captivated. 'Do you really think this can survive on the outside?'

'Of course it can.' He seems confused as to why it couldn't.

Frankly, Araminta could not even attempt to think of the outside world right now. 'Good,' she says anyway. 'Because I love you too. And it would be a real shame if what we have has some kind of time limit because of this show.'

The lights flash earlier tonight. And there it is on the screen again, a request that they all head inside while they set the challenge up. They do as they are asked, clinging to windows, barely able to see a thing once the boat draws close enough to dip beneath the trees. They watch as it leaves again, and the lights dance for a second time and the jingle plays and they are all summoned back to the firepit.

Eloise flickers to life on the screen. She's wearing enormous earrings, two black gems set in blue plastic; they half-expect the jewellery to blink.

'Good evening, contestants. Why, you look so much happier today,' she taunts. 'This evening's test is one of problem-solving and strategy. Each pair has received a series of riddles that will lead you to hidden letters around the island. You need to find all the letters and be the first pair to work out what the word is. There are three points each up for grabs!'

A buzzer sets them off running.

'*I help you ascend with each stride; to higher levels, I'll be your guide. Without me, progress is hard to find; what am I, in reality or in mind?*' Jerome reads, curling the paper so tightly his grip threatens to rip the page.

He can't stand this; intelligence is a trait he believes uniquely his on the island.

Kalpana skims the others like they might be easier. But she's just as infuriated – she dabbles in poetry! She should be able to find a double meaning!

By the time she realizes the answer is steps, the other pairs have already found their next clues. They finally dart inside to the staircase, just to realize that's impossible, that the crew were only crawling around outside and, after much running about, remember the metal rack leading down into the pool. By that point, the others are two letters down.

They're racing to their second when they pass one stapled to a lamp with *Theo and Rhys* written across the top.

Kalpana hesitates only a moment before she keeps going. Not because she does not want to rip it down herself, but because she cannot be seen to. Yesterday's subterfuge exposed the weaknesses and hypocrisies of the other contestants – this would be outright cheating.

Which is Jerome's field.

He snatches that page down and shoves it deep in his pocket, and Kalpana gets to pretend she had no idea he'd do that.

Meanwhile, Araminta and Isko stare at the page, two letters filled: *I, O.*

Two more to go.

But Araminta, expert at elusive phrasing, clocked that

the challenge was not to find all the letters, just to solve the word.

Araminta: *It feels fruitless in a way. Because I'm paired with Isko who's above me in the points table, every win just boosts him up too. It never closes the gap. But I guess if we take ourselves as far away from the other contestants as possible, I can put all my energy into beating him next week.*

'Icon is too straightforward,' Isko says.

'I agree, which is why I think they'd go for something adjacent – *Idol*, maybe? But how foolish would we have to be to guess that on a show called *Iconic*?'

She glances at the remaining riddles. Maybe one will be easy enough to push them in the right direction.

If I have it, I don't share it. If I share it, I don't have it.

It prickles her, a whisper that insists she knows the answer.

A secret.

The wall.

Rhys's admissions have faded to a pale blue – and on it a note is taped: *N.*

'Icon!' Isko and Araminta scream.

Isko: *So infuriatingly basic.*

Araminta: *But I guess you weren't really testing our intelligence anyway, otherwise why let us do it in pairs. No, you just wanted to see what we'd do.*

Gathered back together, Theo doesn't even wait for Eloise to award points before he kicks off.

'I've checked every lamp, lantern and bloody light bulb on this island,' Theo fumes. 'Someone took it, they must have.'

'Quite an accusation,' Isko refutes. 'How do you know you got it right.'

'What else is "it can fill a room without occupying space" supposed to mean?'

'Tension?' Araminta posits, with a wry smile. 'Now can we go back to our points, please?'

'Yes, congratulations Araminta and Isko!' Eloise beams. 'Let's take a look at what that does to the scores!'

Isko: *14*
Araminta: *13*
Jerome: *10*
Kalpana: *5*
Theo: *4*
Rhys: *4*

'Some real variation, but we're still early in the competition and anyone could win!'

The screen shuts off.

'So let's be clear,' Rhys says with his usual joviality, but his smile is taut, suggesting underlying anger sharper than the grin itself. 'Are we resorting to cheating now?'

'We're scavenging and solving riddles. And someone here feels the need to cheat to win? Sort out your priorities,' Theo adds, fury dulled into snarling derision.

Rhys: *I think Theo was mad because he was so pleased to have solved the riddle. Bless his heart.*

'Theo, I don't know who you're accusing, but no one here would cheat,' Kalpana says.

'Really, you're literally partners –'

'Sorry, let me clarify: the only person who would cheat was with me. He couldn't have.'

'All right, let's not argue this further,' Rhys interrupts, sliding his arm around Araminta's waist. 'Let's all just agree that from here on out, there'll be nothing underhanded – no cheating.'

'Fine with me,' Araminta says, smiling up at Rhys and leaning in closer.

Reluctantly, the others agree too.

Rhys: *Oh yeah, I have no intention of doing that. But now, I'm hoping I'll be the last person they'd suspect.*

And with what he has planned, becoming a suspect is the last thing he can afford to do.

@AzaOnTheNet

Can Araminta and Rhys stop being adorable for five minutes please? It's giving me unrealistic aspirations for my love life #Iconic

---

@BookishSaira

Love how Rhys's solution to cheating is to get people to promise they won't, like sure babe, that will definitely work #Iconic

---

@AdorableAmelie

Can we get more Theo Newman in the edited episodes please @IconicTVShow – I'm so tired of RiotParade dominating headlines and the one innocent member not being given a platform in favour of yet more Rhys and Araminta. Stop playing favourites with the edits #Iconic

AHX have ramped up their advertising for tomorrow's episode. It glares from Cloutier's phone: '*The truth: what really happened to Rhys Sutton – Friday at 8pm only on AHX.*'

He has the sudden urge to fling it across the room but instead shoves it into his pocket. It is a fact that the truth is not on those tapes: the drugs in his system that he never took, the water you never see him choke on. He can already see this becoming one of those great unsolved mysteries, fodder for dinner parties and podcasts.

Unbidden, his mind wanders to Kennard. They'll be named in the case documents, forever part of this. *Together.*

Before he can spiral, he pulls out his phone and throws himself back into the case. Already he can feel it slipping in importance, taking second place to his own life, his own problems.

He dials the producer again.

'Hello?'

'It's Detective Cloutier. I have some more questions.'

'You don't have much time, do you?'

'Before you become known as the network that made entertainment from this tragedy?'

'It's already entertainment. People are already watching it. We're just taking back control of the narrative.'

'Do you have any idea how much the victim's family will sue you for?'

'Yes, actually, our projections show that even taking that into account, we'll still make an incredibly tidy profit, which we'll need given we can't do the final live show. Eloise is refusing to take part, and we'd been counting on people tuning in for answers to the salacious questions everyone has –'

'Those questions – can you send them to me?'

'Well, we hadn't written all of them, but sure. I can send you what we have.'

Maybe they have been approaching this wrong.

They've been treating them like any other suspects – logical, in control, with some level of foresight. But maybe they need to be treated like contestants in a competition. Maybe that's still where their minds are. They are reality stars first, murder suspects second.

He takes that thought to the last person who definitively saw Rhys alive.

'What?' Kalpana snaps, chewing on a mint, glaring at him with new ferocity. 'Keeping something else from us? How many hours is it until the episode airs? Are you getting desperate?'

'Yes,' he says. 'And you should be too.'

He flips his phone to her and shows her the advertising.

She looks genuinely disgusted, which he marks in her favour.

'They're not just airing it, they're pitching it, marketing it, it's . . . fucking capitalism.'

'That's not all,' he switches to his pictures, to the screenshots he's taken from the #Iconic search: a string of *Kalpana definitely pushed him*, her winning in polls of who they think did something, people sharing their clips and theories about her.

'Okay, you've made your point.'

'A lot of people out there think you did it. And they're drawing their own conclusions as to why because we haven't given them a conclusion of our own.'

'My money's on Theo.'

'Really?' He's surprised – from what he's seen, they were close.

'He's as much of a liar as Rhys was. Even being there was a lie.'

'Liars don't necessarily make killers.'

'Liars covering up more scandals do. And they were fucking pouring out of Theo.'

He centres himself again, remembers what he came in here for – not to be distracted by her pointing the finger at another contestant. 'Look, Kalpana, we've seen the footage. *You* were the one on that cliff. If, for instance, you did something to protect Araminta, you'd become the hero of this narrative, the protagonist. I'm sure a judge would be –'

'I'm not protecting Araminta. If Theo didn't kill Rhys, then I think she probably did.'

'Excuse me?'

'I'm not protecting her. I think she was capable of murder.'

And damn it, this deflection works because it's the second time he's heard it.

So he goes back and pours over the clips.

No one has paid much attention to the footage of Araminta on the final day. She retreated to her room. She didn't spend time in blind spots. But Theo and Kalpana both think she did it, so there must be something.

And there it is, one moment – Araminta, gathering Rhys's belongings, muttering something under her breath.

'Et in Arcadia ego.'

He knows the painting, knows what it means.

Death. Even in paradise, there I am.

Iconic

Season 1, Episode 11

The show opens with Araminta's silhouetted form strad-
dling Rhys, the morning light just breaking through the
window, and when he flips her the scene fades, the logo
appearing.

They splice the footage with unnerving precision –
Araminta is sitting at the kitchen table, her head exactly
where it was in the previous frame. Kalpana sits beside her,
and though she's not where Rhys was, it's clear the producers want to draw a comparison between them.

'Have you two considered a good night's sleep every
once in a while?' Kalpana asks, nodding at the bruises on
Araminta's wrists. 'Christ, they're getting darker by the
second. How easily do you bruise?'

'What can I say? We're passionate,' Araminta sips her
smoothie. 'Jealousy is an interesting colour on you.'

'I'm hardly jealous,' Kalpana says. 'I've seen the way you
two kiss and frankly, I'd never want to embarrass myself
on national TV like that.'

Even Araminta laughs at that one.

But then she realizes they are back on dangerous
ground – she does not want to speak about sex with Rhys
to her. She gives a curt nod and it's only when her hair flies
back into place that Kalpana notices something is different
about her, though she couldn't say what.

Kalpana: *I've definitely felt a bit of a distance with Araminta over the last few days. She's dangerously at risk of becoming one of those boring girls that only spends time with her boyfriend.*

As they sit and chat idly, moving onto safer ground, Kalpana's chest tightens as she realizes what's different about Araminta: she looks more polished, more mainstream. She has always been beautiful, but in a quirky, try-hard way. All white tulle and white eyeliner, like a marble sculpture, like her own privilege embodied. But now, she's sporting careful black flicks across her eyelids and a tint of pink lip gloss, the brightest clothes she could find.

Something heavy settles in Kalpana's gut.

Kalpana: *I don't know what it is, but I think I'm worried about Araminta.*

The camera pans across the contestants playing chicken in the pool. Isko stands with Jerome on his shoulders as he tries to knock Araminta off Theo's.

The director takes satisfaction in the shots: the way Theo's abs tense as he takes a step back, the way Isko's knuckles pale as he clutches Jerome, and the way Theo's hands clasp Araminta's thighs, her skin dimpling, the water drops clinging to her skin.

Rhys arrives from the confession room and staggers to a halt, taking in the scene.

Theo slips but Araminta manages to knock Jerome off anyway, even as she falls herself a second later. She emerges drenched but cackling as Jerome stutters.

'I wasn't ready to fall!' he complains, snorting water.

Araminta hauls herself out of the water and sees Rhys.

'Hey! You missed it. Want to join the next game?'

He shakes his head. 'No, I'm all right. Do you have a moment? I want to talk to you about something.'

'Sure.'

'For god's sake, Rhys, lighten up,' Isko scoffs before diving under the water and away from his retort.

Rhys's brows draw tighter, and it's only then that Araminta sees his displeasure. She climbs onto the side but feels like she's sinking as she follows him back toward the house. As soon as they are out of sight he takes her arm and guides her off the path.

'What was that?' he demands, letting go as he turns to face her.

'Huh?'

'That thing in the pool?' he asks, an edge clinging to his words.

Araminta laughs, half amused and half uncertain.

'It's chicken,' she says. 'You've never played?'

His eyes flit toward the pool even though he can't see it shrouded by all these trees. 'Do you have any idea how it feels for me to walk out and see your legs wrapped around Newman's head?'

Araminta blinks at him. 'It's chicken.'

He snorts. 'Right. Is that what he told you to get you to do it?'

'Rhys, I hardly think it was a ruse to –'

'Do you want to fuck him?'

She's so shocked she just laughs more.

He regards her for a moment, his gaze darkening, and when he speaks, his voice is low and grave. 'Don't laugh at me.'

'I'm sorry. I'm just not sure how else to react to such a stupid question.'

'Don't call me stupid either.'

'I didn't. I called your question stupid.'

'You have your thighs wrapped around his head, legs clutching on to him for dear life while you wrestle with another guy, and I'm the crazy one? Not to mention that bikini – what, you need screen time, and your jiggling tits are the only way to get it?'

Araminta goes to put him in his place but catches herself. She's right: this is stupid. There must be a reason for this because Rhys isn't this foolish. 'Rhys, what's wrong?'

'Am I not telling you?'

'I told you I loved you last night, and now you're worried I want to sleep with another guy? Just because we were playing some childish game in the pool? And after the other day too? Are you really that insecure?'

He takes a breath, goes to say something but stops himself. He blinks, seems almost disoriented like he can't work out how he got here. 'I don't know. Maybe? Maybe I am.' He starts shaking his head, running his hands through his hair, gripping at the strands. 'I'm so sorry. I'm being an idiot.'

'It's okay.'

'I'm really sorry, I think maybe you're right, maybe I am that insecure. I haven't . . . I've had bad experiences in the past.'

'Rhys,' she says softly, reaching for him.

He sighs. 'I'm sorry that this bothers me, but it does. Is it really that much to ask that you don't do it again?'

Araminta scowls, adjusting the strap of her bikini, which

keeps falling. Perhaps he has a point: it is revealing. 'I mean sure, but –'

'Thank you,' his hand clutches her waist and he pulls her to him, envelops her in his arms and presses his lips to her head. 'I feel so safe with you, being able to open up with you. You're so patient and understanding, and god, I love you so much.'

She hesitates – but he's right, love is patience, and she's never had much to give. That's where she's always gone wrong before.

'I love you too.'

He smiles and it's so genuinely warm, so delighted. She's made people a lot of things in her presence: inspired, passionate, horny. Has she ever made them happy?

He nods in the direction of the pool and starts making his way toward it.

Araminta hesitates, still fiddling with the strap of her bikini. It's not worth her adjusting it all day; it will only annoy her.

She heads inside to change.

In the confession booth, Jerome regards the screen. The room is small, one of two padded, soundproof booths in the basement of the house. Its interior is bold and blue, just in case the audience forgets the show is set on a tropical island.

Opposite the sofa is a screen and a camera lens. Pulling the panels aside, he finds the computer itself. There's no mouse but that doesn't matter because there's a keyboard, and a few taps later he's navigating away from this programmed screen and past the blocks they've put in place to stop something exactly like this from happening.

Maybe AHX will kick him off the show for such an infringement, but he has bigger problems – starting with the woman who keeps screaming about all the things he's supposedly done wrong. Her lies. Her exaggerations. The sort of loud-mouthed bitch who could destroy a lifetime of well-intentioned work with one false cry.

Their temporary alliance has him under no illusions that she will not start up again the moment he's inconvenient. He knows because he's planning the same – to use her for as many points as he can while they're partnered and ensure she never stands a chance of winning the popular vote afterward.

And unlike everyone else on this island, he is capable of planning ahead.

He finds old chat rooms, old forums and old contacts – those who have taken the red pill and are ready to fight for it, activists in their own rights really.

Jerome sets the trolls digging and hunting, blurring the line between fact and fiction and sharing them just the same.

He's going to make her hated.

He's going to make sure no one believes a thing she says.

In the afternoon, their boredom mounts, and buoyed by the childish fun of their earlier game, they start throwing a watermelon between themselves. Isko and Kalpana abstain but the others take note of who drops it, each one deserving of a consequence until it finally smashes over Rhys, sticky juice clinging to all their hands as they rush back to the house to pour their penalty drinks.

Two shots for Theo, five for Araminta, nine for Jerome and a cocktail for Rhys – complete with all the sauces and condiments that they could find.

They chant for him to chug it like they are teenagers again.

Rhys finishes and slams the glass down in triumph. Jerome is sick after the sixth shot.

And then they start on *Iconic: The Game*. It is part drinking game, part marathon, part prank war.

The whole process is hampered by the shots slowly taking effect. Isko arrives to point out the holes and the flaws, and the footage cuts together various confession booth explanations from the contestants, all contradicting each other. The perfect montage of chaos.

Rhys: *You'd better keep these recordings; I need to know how to play this when I get out.*

Jerome: *You . . . what you do is . . . you just . . . you win.*

Isko retreats to his room to wash and change, but clumsy footsteps sound behind him and he turns, just as Rhys crashes into him.

'Fancy alleviating a little boredom before the challenge?' Rhys breathes in his ear and Isko can smell the alcohol on his breath, but there's a sharpness to his gaze that's almost wicked, and Isko isn't convinced for even a moment that Rhys is anywhere near as drunk as he's pretending to be.

But Rhys's lips are on his neck, pulling the door shut behind them, and Isko is too busy thinking *Does he want this? Does Araminta know? Why is Rhys doing this?* to actually stop him before Rhys pulls his open shirt from him, the mic wires tangled in its folds flying off too.

223

'Rhys, what are you –'

'Shh,' Rhys says, pressing his lips back to Isko, tracing the shape of his jaw as he rips his own clothes off, and the minute that mic is torn from him too, everything about him shifts – a little stiffer, a little more urgent, even as he leans back into Isko's neck. 'All right, those cameras are going to make it look like we're hooking up, but I assume if we whisper, the microphones won't hear us.'

Rhys's breath is still warm against him but it chills him, goose bumps prickling and he thinks of their last fuck and how readily he'd believed Rhys wasn't playing a game.

But of course he was.

'And why don't you want the microphones to hear us?' Isko whispers, hand reaching to the small of Rhys's back to further the ruse.

Rhys is right, the microphones don't pick up any of this – it's just a shot of two people making out while heavy, sultry music plays.

'I don't care but you might,' Rhys says. 'See, I overheard something you said to Theo. About testifying against Juliet.'

'So?'

'You said your fiancé encouraged you to do it.'

'Do you really want to talk about Alex while we're doing whatever this is.'

'Yes, Isko, yes, I do. Because I find it quite suspicious that your fiancé is an accountant and your former employer is in prison for financial crimes. How did you meet him again?'

Isko stills. 'Whatever you're implying –'

'You know exactly what I'm implying.'

That chill grows, running right down his spine. 'Alex would never –'

'Does it matter? Maybe he did and maybe he didn't, but do you want me asking you out loud, live on camera, in front of however many millions of watching fans? Maybe they'll reopen the case. Maybe he'll get fired. Maybe, at worst, his name will forever be associated with a certain suspicion.'

Isko's heart is pounding, and he can't believe Rhys is whispering all this against him like a caress. He can't believe Rhys is doing this at all, but a memory tugs at him: some hateful glint in Rhys's eye before Isko disappeared beneath the surface.

'What do you want?' Isko bites out.

'Correct response. What I want, Isko, for my silence, is for you to throw the challenges.'

'What?'

'You've been winning too many challenges and you're already at the top of the board. So you're going to sabotage your own team.'

'I'm on a team with your girlfriend.'

'I'm very well aware. Needless to say, you'll mention nothing about this to her.'

Isko drags his nails down Rhys's back, and the man gasps in pain that collapses back into that same, disorienting amusement.

'So is that a yes?' Rhys asks with an intimate smile, still playing up their connection for the cameras.

He wants to tell Rhys to get lost, or to at least assume that if Rhys has connected such things, a viewer might too. But Isko never has. He's never even considered it, and now he's spiralling because what if it's true? What if Alex is responsible somehow? If there's even a chance, he has to protect him.

He's committing to not winning. All that money, the lifestyle it could offer – but he'll still have the platform . . . still have the fame.

'I'm going to kill you.'

'Is that a –'

'Yes, it's a fucking yes.'

'Great,' Rhys says – before lurching away with a gasp. 'Oh my god what am I doing? I can't . . . I can't do this to Araminta. I'm sorry, I . . . oh my god.'

He grabs for his clothes – and his microphone – and runs from the room. When Isko turns and pounds his fist on the wall, the internet believes it's just out of the pain of losing Rhys.

Isko hides in his room until the challenge, and no one had realized he wouldn't cook for them until far too late in the day. Again, the alarm rings early and asks them to go inside, where Araminta and Rhys run around the kitchen, throwing carbs together in an attempt to sober everyone up, interrupting their own efforts by snatching each other around the waist and pushing one another up against counters, kissing with clumsy desperation laced with their own intoxication.

By the time Eloise appears on screen, most of them are fine, if a little disoriented, but Jerome is lucky to be standing. Worse, his carefully gathered information is leaking from him.

'You're a . . . rich . . . poser fraud thief,' he slurs, pushing Kalpana's hand from him as he tries to stand.

226

'Right, sure Jerome,' she sighs, propping him up anyway.

Kalpana: *I would like to just say thank you once again to the voters who put me in a team with this man.*

The alarm blares, and Isko finally arrives to join them. He sits beside Araminta without a word.

'Are you okay?' she asks, genuinely concerned, though it's not clear how much of it is simply for her own success.

He stares forward, waiting for Eloise to appear, and gives a curt nod.

Isko: *I . . . yes, of course it's awkward being in a team with Araminta when I was making out with her boyfriend a few hours ago.*

'Good evening, icons! How are we all doing today?' Eloise asks.

Araminta and Theo offer kind smiles for the sake of the cameras but everyone else just stares at her, waiting for her to get to the point.

'We have an exciting challenge tonight that will test your ability to communicate with your partner and to trust them. There are three obstacle courses set up at the back of the house. One of you will be blindfolded and the other will have to direct them through it. The first to the end wins.'

Kalpana regards Jerome, trying to work out if she'd rather receive drunken instructions from him while she herself is blindfolded or instruct him.

Kalpana: *I guess it comes down to the challenge itself, and I'd rather drunk Jerome trust me than put my trust in that intoxicated arsehole.*

She helps him secure the blindfold.

'What do you think?' Araminta asks.

'I don't care,' Isko says, still staring off into the distance.

She thinks of her own perception and all she's trying to change: sculpture and home improvement. What is it if not proof that she is not afraid to get her hands dirty?

'I'll be blindfolded then,' she says, reaching for the slip of fabric.

'Make sure you keep hold of that for later!' Rhys calls.

'Do you still have the handcuffs?' she tosses back with a smile.

Theo, on the cusp of tying his own, offers a final filthy look in his partner's direction before hiding such expressions behind opaque fabric.

Kalpana, Rhys, and Isko take their spots at the end of the course.

The alarm blares for them to begin.

There are nets to crawl under, hurdles to climb over and a dozen different things to dodge.

Isko is slow on delivering his instructions, calling notes a split second too late and he winces as Araminta, too enthusiastic, bashes her shin into the first bollard.

Maybe Rhys doesn't notice because he doesn't react – he's too busy yelling for Theo: *'Right, then a few steps; okay, stop and duck.'*

Araminta takes slower, more careful steps, but Isko's instructions are barely instructions at all.

'All right turn like . . . to eleven o'clock. No, no, sorry – one o'clock, other way. Take a half step. Okay, and another two half steps – yeah, that would be a whole step, yeah, I guess.'

'Isko!' she shrieks after a while. 'Can you please get better at this!'

Surprisingly, Jerome is farthest ahead – too intoxicated to care about bruises and plowing right through, feeling his way around obstacles without listening to Kalpana at all.

He crosses the finish line as Araminta's foot tangles in one of the nets and she goes crashing to the floor.

She shrieks, more from surprise than pain. But it does hurt. It really does, actually.

Rhys seems to suddenly notice his girlfriend on the floor, and with the buzzer signalling the end of the competition, he runs over.

'Are you all right?' he asks, crouching to feel the tender lines of the wrist she's cradling.

She nods despite the tears welling in her eyes. 'I'm fine, I think. Just landed hard, and my wrists are dodgy anyway.'

'Too many hand jobs?' Jerome calls.

'Too much heavy lifting and not admitting I need help,' she spits, climbing to her feet, limp wrist still held in her other hand.

Rhys puts his arm around her waist like she might need help standing.

Isko slowly makes his way over. 'Well, if we were going to lose to anyone, I'm glad it was them,' he says pointedly, with a fierce glare at Rhys.

'There's always tomorrow,' Rhys says with a bright smile at odds with his injured girlfriend hanging off his side.

'Congratulations, Kalpana and Jerome!' Eloise calls. 'Let's go back inside and let the crew come to tidy up. Araminta, if you want to stay, someone can look at your injury.'

She shakes her head. 'No, it's okay. I'll just go ice it.'

'I'm afraid we have to insist,' Eloise says. 'It's our policy.

Everyone else please venture inside, and Araminta, a medic is on his way.'

Rhys presses his lips to her head and leaves her in the sand, watching as a smaller speedboat appears. The medic does not introduce himself. He's rather quiet as he works, and Araminta traces the deep lines around his eyes, the curls of greying hair escaping from beneath his cap, and wonders how this invasion of someone to the island can make it feel all the more isolated. He is right here and still something keeps them separate.

He bandages her wrist, and after consulting someone on the radio about whether she should come for a scan, leaves her.

That's it – that's all she gets.

'All okay?' Rhys asks as she returns, finding them all in the living room. She nods, not really knowing how to explain the absurdity of what just happened, that a slightly standoffish man could leave her spiralling like this.

Eloise flickers onto the screen.

'Well, Kalpana and Jerome. Congratulations on winning three points each. I hope you're all ready to win it back tomorrow!'

Eloise flicks her off and Rhys scowls.

'They shouldn't make you do the challenge tomorrow,' he says to Araminta. 'You need time to rest and heal.'

'I'll be fine,' Araminta insists.

'Araminta,' he says sternly. 'You're injured. I suppose we'll see tomorrow, but if it's physical, I really think you should sit it out.'

'It's a sprained wrist, Rhys, and I'll do whatever I please, thank you.'

Rhys doesn't look particularly happy at this, but at the last moment, he remembers himself. 'Of course, my love. Is there anything I can get you?'

'I think I'll rest it,' she says. 'I'm going to bed.'

'I'll come with you,' he says instantly. 'Just in case you need anything else.'

Isko doesn't care to stop himself from glaring as he watches them go.

Isko: *Rhys is a bastard and he deserves whatever he has coming for him.*

@onlyinthemovies
Oh my god as if Rhys just cheated on Araminta and is
carrying on like nothing happened! What a dick!!
#Iconic

> **@IslaRae**
> @onlyinthemovies I'm not sure I'd consider a drunken
> kiss cheating but he definitely needs to tell her asap!
> I was really enjoying the two of them, I can't believe
> he'd do this!

@NickMillerFanClub
frantically taking notes on Iconic: The Game
checks how much alcohol is needed
I am going to die.
#Iconic

@KarenRWinters
Okay but would all reality shows be this engaging if they drank
this much? Someone deliver a crate of wine to The Circle
asap #Iconic

Cloutier pushes a tablet across the table and Araminta watches stony-faced as the clip plays.

Cheryl doesn't react either, except for those ways detectives are trained to see: her fingers tightening on her pen, tendons in her neck a little more prominent, lips thinner than they were before.

'Could you please explain what you meant by this?' Cloutier asks.

Araminta blinks. 'What do you mean?'

'Well,' Kennard says beside him, 'it looks to me like you're predetermining death on the island – like you're admitting you've done something to make that happen.'

'I don't understand,' she says, turning to her lawyer.

'Could I have a moment with my client?'

The detectives leave the room, barely glancing at each other until the door shuts.

'This is it,' Cloutier says excitedly.

'No, it's not,' Kennard snaps.

Cloutier looks at him. 'Are you okay?'

He shakes his head. 'Working this case is taking a toll.'

'In what way?'

'You're going to make me say it?' Kennard hisses and glances down the hallway, checking that the coast is clear. 'I'm struggling to work with you. I can't stay focused. All their drama is just making me think of our own.'

Cloutier smirks, and Kennard isn't sure if he'd like to slap the expression off his face or remove it in a far more enticing way. His fingers curl.

'Am I really so distracting?'

'Yes, which you know. Can we just do separate interviews?

I'm not sure I can keep pretending we're a competent team when . . .'

'Well, we *were* highly competent.'

'Jacques,' Kennard growls, but the man just laughs again and holds up his hands in surrender.

'Fine, fine. Besides, this is it – we have it.'

The lawyer pokes her head out the door and summons them back.

'Go on,' she says. 'Tell them what you just told me.'

Araminta's lips are pursed and she swallows like she's swallowing her own irritation. 'Cheryl just told me what that phrase means. I didn't know.'

'Pardon?'

'I didn't know,' she admits again. 'I'd heard people say it. I thought it just meant, you know, even when things should be amazing, they still suck. It was my way of saying that even though I was on a glamorous island, on TV, I was still miserable. That I was quitting.'

'You didn't know it refers to death in paradise?' Kennard repeats, clearly not buying it.

'What?' Araminta finally snaps. 'Is this what you want – fine! I'm not as smart as I make out. None of us are. It's all posturing. No one wants to admit they don't understand what anyone else is saying, so we're all led to believe it's profound, and it's all just a circle jerk of nonsense. That's the show. So no, I don't know what random Latin phrases mean. And I didn't know it was from a bloody painting either.'

'But you're an –'

'Artist, I fucking know. It's all fake, okay? Are you happy?'

Iconic

Season 1, Episode 12

It's so hot today – or rather, the heat has changed. The air is sticky and pulls at them, so close and oppressive, like the whole island is a rubber band snapping together.

Sweat beads on the backs of their necks and their faces turn red, and no amount of fanning cools anyone down. The sea is too cold for any long-term solution, and jumping in and out of it is only making them hotter. Even the shade is sweltering, almost more humid for the lack of sun to blame it on.

They lie beneath umbrellas, close to the ocean, where the tide brushes their feet in cooling strokes.

'This is it,' Rhys says. 'This is how it ends.'

'Don't be so dramatic,' Theo says.

'Maybe it's already ended. Maybe I'm already in hell. Does this feel like one of the circles to you?'

'You're here, aren't you?' Theo mutters.

'Seventh,' Kalpana answers. 'Violence against neighbours, I think. All those plunderers and tyrants immersed in boiling blood.'

'That sounds about right,' Isko mutters, carefully not looking at the others.

Isko: *Am I going to tell Araminta about Rhys? No, I think, like all things, it's whatever Rhys wants. If he wants to tell her, he can.*

'Corrupt politicians are in the eighth circle in boiling pitch. Do we think we're there yet?' Araminta asks before anyone can respond to Isko. It's too hot for drama, even for her.

'No, blood feels a closer match; it's more humid than pitch,' Rhys says. 'It's not where I thought I'd end up. I always thought I was a shoo-in for the second circle. All that lust.'

'What do you think?' Theo asks Isko.

Theo: *He just didn't really seem present, not since he vanished on us last night at dinner. I was trying to draw him back in.*

'I think that all the things I would want from heaven are the reasons I'm going to hell,' Isko says. 'No sex in the afterlife, that's lust. No food, that's greed. I mean, what is there to live for? What's the point of paradise?'

'Where are you residing then?' Theo asks. 'You can't just say all the sins are sexy.'

'All the sins *are* sexy,' he says. 'But let's see – cheating? But no, *I'm* in an open relationship. Sodomy? That's too easy.'

'I bet Araminta knows about sodomy,' Jerome laughs, glancing around the circle like they are all in on the joke. 'You know what they say about girls with daddy issues.'

Rhys: *Jerome is such a bastard at times, isn't he? [Laughter] He's not wrong though.*

'That's the sixth circle,' Araminta explains, looking directly at Isko and refusing to acknowledge Jerome. She'd used Dante's circles of hell as inspiration for one of her first collections and is too delighted by this conversation to let him derail her. 'Heresy – you're condemned to a desert with blazing sand and rain made of fire.'

'Not so different from this then,' Isko says.

'Theo?' Rhys asks, challenging smirk already in place like he's daring Theo to say something real rather than a practised lie for the cameras.

Theo meets the challenge with an answer that would be comedically over the top were he not entirely serious. 'Oh, all musicians are false prophets. People worship our texts, kneel at our altar, and are embodied by a spirit of some sort or other.'

'Deifying yourself?' Rhys asks.

'I'm not deifying myself. I'm competing with God, and I'm winning.' He grins, but still no one is sure if he's actually joking.

'Eighth circle is a fun one,' Araminta says.

'You should know. Seducers are being whipped in eight, right?' Rhys grins.

Araminta scowls. 'Not sure I'm a fan of being reduced to the number of boys who fall at my feet.'

'But there are so many of them,' he teases. 'My minx, nymph of desire, men falling one by one. Writing songs about you and everything.'

'Okay, but I've asked you not to call me —'

But he's already singing Peppermint louder than she can talk and soon everyone else is laughing and singing along, and Araminta can only glare and fling her middle finger up at them all before collapsing back onto the hot sand, too exhausted to fight them more.

Jerome: *Okay, but it's not like . . . normal to have the circles of hell memorized, is it? What sort of a conversation was that, and how are they all like this?*

*

237

By midday everyone's miserable but none more so than Araminta. Her wrist has swollen even more in the heat, and the freezer can't make ice quickly enough. She's in pain. Jerome's comments are starting to get to her, and it's too hot to even find solace in Rhys's arms.

Ironically, the house is bearable – the air-conditioning limited, but the fans powerful, the shade cooler than outside.

But she's the only one to cave and choose it over the hum of the cameras pleading for beach views and glistening skin.

'Hey,' Kalpana says, standing awkwardly at the doorway of Araminta's room.

'Oh, hi, what's up?' Araminta puts her mascara down.

'I wanted to talk to you about something.' She perches nervously on Araminta's bed.

'Sorry, could you not sit there?' Araminta says, glancing at the door.

'Oh, yeah, sure,' Kalpana says. Araminta sits on the only chair, pulled up to a vanity desk, so she just leans against the wall instead.

'So I kind of overheard some of what Rhys said to you yesterday.'

'What about?' Araminta asks, but her hand pauses as it reaches for lipstick.

'The game of chicken. About how he didn't like you playing.'

Araminta's jaw clenches so tightly it's a wonder she can still talk. 'That's not what he said. He had a problem with my legs around – you know what, actually, no, this is none of your business. Don't ruin such a lovely day.'

'I don't want to intrude. But he forced you to change

238

outfits, and he was so possessive during the handcuff challenge, and I'm just worried –'

'Don't be,' Araminta snaps. 'I can handle myself.'

Kalpana: *Christ, how do you say to your friend 'I think your boyfriend is manipulative and selfish and you're better off without him'?*

Araminta: *Is she stalking me? How did she know about that? Maybe Rhys had a point – maybe she wasn't just flirting for the competition.*

'Besides, there's no point getting into all this – it's the island, right?' Kalpana continues. 'It's such a goldfish bowl, I keep forgetting just how much is waiting for me outside of it.'

'Rhys and I will be just fine outside of this island.'

'No, of course. But it's not the be all and end all that it is here, right?'

Araminta still regards her suspiciously. 'Is there something you want to say, Kalpana?'

Kalpana shakes her head, knowing that if she pushes too far Araminta will go running from her – and likely into the arms of that prick.

And then she wonders too at how this looks: Is she too involved? The saviour swooping in? Has she said something wrong that the audience will pick over? Is she being condemned for not doing enough?

Suddenly, any sense of what is right or what is clever vanishes, and there is only a vast expanse of watching viewers in her mind, waiting for her next move.

'No,' Kalpana finally says. 'I just wanted to check that you were okay.'

'I'm fucking fantastic.'

*

239

By the time Eloise flickers onto the screen, the heat has broken and so have they. They are exhausted, weary from surviving the day.

The alarm asking them to go inside was their first relief. Now Eloise calls: 'Are you ready for your next challenge?'

They nod their heads blankly, knowing it is what the producers want.

'We've got another physical challenge for you all, but this one is about achieving equilibrium with your partner – reading and responding to one another.'

Outside they find some sort of inflatable, a gladiator arena of sorts with six discs and long cords connecting them to the ones opposite.

It reminds them a bit too much of the trial all those days ago.

'You need to stand opposite your partner, pick up the rope and try to balance as the discs move beneath you. You'll have to be in tune with your partner, their body and their movements.'

Jerome: *I'd literally rather die.*

They suspect the joy in this challenge may simply be in making them all look like fools again, people who think so much of themselves forced onto a glorified bouncy castle.

'Whichever pair can balance with their partner the longest wins three points each!'

It's over fairly quickly.

Araminta is struggling, her injured wrist throbbing after only a few seconds, but she grits her teeth and tries to power through. The discs shift beneath them and they have to twist and turn, always with that rope gripped, threatening to lurch their partner off if they move too suddenly. Maybe it's the surprise – the sound of a body crashing into the cushioned mat beneath – but as soon as Jerome hits the ground, Isko falls too, though Araminta is certain she felt no sudden shift.

They are back around the firepit and Eloise lights up on screen.

'Congratulations, Theo and Rhys! That's three points each! Tomorrow is our last day competing in pairs, so enjoy your final opportunity for a sense of camaraderie before you're all turned against one another again!'

Rhys snorts. 'Oh god, is that what we were supposed to be doing?'

'I think we failed miserably in that case,' Jerome says.

Eloise's voice cuts through over the speakers: 'It's weird, isn't it?'

They all freeze for a millisecond before turning as one back to the screen, where Eloise has turned away from the camera but is still very much projected on it. And talking to someone else, not them.

She should have disappeared. This is a glitch, a transmission they were never supposed to receive – unless they are? Who can tell on this island? Surely everything is under AHX's control, right down to the phase of the moon and the stars in the sky.

'Talking to them while all this happens out here is starting to feel like lying. Like, how am I supposed to be like "Oh, well done, Theo. There's a point – isn't that great!" without being like "Oh, by the way, your old bandmates are all being accused of paedophilia and grooming a bunch of fifteen-year-olds. They definitely did it too. There are pictures. Of them at a party full of teenagers. It's all anyone can talk about, but good job ditching them! Excellent timing!" I just can't help but feel like he ought to know, you know?'

Someone says something off-screen, and suddenly Eloise is turning back to them, wide-eyed as she realizes, and the screen goes abruptly black.

'Oh fuck,' Kalpana whispers, the only one to speak as they turn to Theo.

But after a lingering moment of shock, he stands. 'I need ... potentially a whole pack of cigarettes. Jesus Christ, those poor girls. Those arseholes. I . . . RiotParade is dead and those motherfuckers deserve to burn with it.'

@LilyWylkes

I didn't even think about the fact Theo Newman had no idea this whole time, god that poor boy. He deserves the world after what that band has put him through #Iconic

---

@ElliotASanders

Can we not let Theo Newman distract from the fact Rhys Sutton is a manipulative piece of shit. I'm so glad Kalpana is there because there's no way she's going to let him get away with it and when she finds out about him trying it on with Isko? Oh it's all over #Iconic

---

@AzaOnTheNet

TBH they're all icons at this point – the things they've put up with and all the drama they've gloriously given us and then being like oh btw which circle of hell are you in? More determining of icon status than 'here balance these ropes.' Award them all #Iconic

Kennard only sees Cloutier for a handful of moments the next morning before the team gathers.

'Are you okay? I saw the news this morning – you were . . .' He places a hand on his shoulder without thinking, then worries that withdrawing it would only be stranger.

'Yeah,' Cloutier says darkly. 'I saw you too – guess we're famous now.'

'This is insane – we haven't had this kind of media attention when we've investigated serial killers.'

'Serial killers don't tend to be reality stars.'

They start with a briefing, everyone working the case assembled – not just Maes and Kennard and Cloutier but everyone: the whole team on the ground in Lisbon, and those working back in the Lyon office. They're surrounded by screens, so many people calling in.

The irony is not lost on Kennard that he is now the one performing for a camera.

'Let's start with our lead suspect,' Cloutier says. 'The girlfriend, Araminta Yaxley-Carter. Two witnesses are convinced she did it, and she said something incriminating the day he died. In terms of motive, the relationship was rockier than most, but none of the usual motives are going to hold up because she was a week away from getting off the island and away from him. Unless she provided the cocaine, there's no way she did it.'

'Speaking of,' one of the agents says, 'we've found trace amounts of cocaine in the smoking area and some inside, on the stairs. We've found pills in Araminta's hair conditioner; tests are running to confirm what it is, but it won't be cocaine. We thought we had that in Andrada's room – we found a powder, but it's Oxycodone. And there's a tincture of marijuana in Newman's room. So we don't know who had the coke, it was probably a few of them, and this close to the end, they'd probably used up their stash. Possession isn't necessarily a crime in Portugal, just intent to supply, and as we've said, it easily could have been Rhys himself who brought it in.'

'Which makes that line impossible to prove. Even if we found out someone had it, the defence can always say it could easily have been one of the others that got it to Sutton.'

'Unless they confess.'

'Well, that would solve everything,' Kennard sighs.

'Either way, that's not enough to convict anyone, let alone Yaxley-Carter.'

'Let's move on,' Cloutier says. 'Kalpana Mahajan. There's plenty of footage of her admitting she hates him, which of course isn't a crime in and of itself, but if we're discussing motive, that's it. There's also an argument to be made that she liked the girlfriend. It's all over the internet that she pushed him, but let's be clear: we have the footage and that didn't happen. But maybe she intentionally led him to the edge hoping the drugs in his system would take over.'

Cloutier continues. 'Then there's Francisco Andrada, goes by Isko – let's consider him the jilted ex. We don't really know the depth and validity of their feelings for one another, but on paper? It's a motive. He fought with Rhys the day he died, but cranial bleeding was light.'

'What about Theo Newman?'

'There's tension throughout, they argued on the day, and he claims he tried to save the victim.'

'That's not much.'

'No,' Kennard agrees. 'Then there's Jerome Frances. We have evidence to say he liked the girlfriend, Araminta. Maybe he thought with Sutton out of the way he'd have more of a chance. On the day in question, Jerome accessed the AHX servers, but unless he hacked Sutton to death, it might not be relevant.'

Someone stands up. 'With all due respect, this is weak.'

'Yes. Unfortunately, it's all we have.'

Iconic

Season 1, Episode 13

Everyone but Theo is gathered around one of the tables outside, sunglasses on and makeshift fans gripped tight, as the heat creeps up to rival yesterday. Their exhaustion lingers, morale dragging lower at the thought of another scorching, oppressive day.

'Has anyone seen him?' Isko asks, and even though they all shake their heads, they're waiting for Kalpana to answer – she's his closest ally after all.

'No,' she says. 'But I'm not surprised – I mean, can you even imagine? Guys he's known his entire life, who he built his band with, and they turn out to be creeps?'

'Theo was lucky he got out when he did,' Jerome nods. 'Something like that could bring him down.'

'Guys in bands get away with stuff like that all the time,' Kalpana says. 'Hell, guys in general get away with that all the time. But I think it says a lot about Theo and his character that he said enough was enough when it was nowhere near as bad as it is.'

Araminta leans her head on Rhys's shoulder. 'And to find out like he did? Gosh, the poor thing.'

Rhys scoffs. 'Yeah, real poor thing. Newman will be fine – this will propel his solo career and he'll come out a hero. I'd say the whole thing has worked out pretty well for him.'

'I just hope the girls are okay,' Araminta says, slightly quieter, withdrawing the second Rhys's dismissal appeared.

Kalpana catches it all.

Kalpana: *Maybe I've been too distracted with Jerome to realize Rhys is even worse.*

'They partied with rock stars – I imagine they're better than okay. They'll be telling that story for years,' Jerome says. 'Besides, do we even know they were actually fifteen? DateRate had a massive issue with teenagers joining. They all look twenty nowadays and it's really difficult to tell.'

Kalpana: *Or maybe they're both the absolute worst.*

'The thing that bothers me most is the way it all came out,' Rhys says.

Kalpana almost spits out her coffee. '*Really? That's* what bothers you most about this?'

'Absolutely. Do we really think it was a glitch? Or, just possibly, do we think the *Iconic* producers are trying to stir something?'

'Does it matter one way or another?' Jerome asks.

'Sure, because if it was intentional, then this time they came for Newman.' Rhys glances quickly at Isko, then away again before anyone can catch it. 'Next time they might come for one of us.'

They disperse when Theo finally emerges. Rhys heads off for a cigarette and runs into Kalpana as she leaves the smoking area. At the edge of the garden there's no shade and the sun is so hot it pulses, the air wavering.

'Wait, Rhys,' Kalpana calls as they start to pass each other. 'Has Araminta seemed down lately to you?'

'Not particularly. Then again, she does quite like being around *me*.'

Kalpana grips her cigarette case tightly and takes a step toward walking away – but then her grip tightens, case crushing in her hand, and she spits out, 'You should treat her better.'

'Excuse me?'

'You tell her who she can talk to, what she should wear –'

'I never told her what to wear.'

'So you didn't insult her so much she stopped wearing white altogether?'

He rolls his eyes. 'Oh, come on, that is not –'

'You don't call her "minx" like it's an affectionate term?'

'It is an affectionate term. It's a fucking joke, Kalpana, but I can see why that would go over your head.'

'You didn't say she couldn't play games then?'

'Okay, first of all, I haven't told her she can't do anything, I've just said certain things bother me. Men deserve to talk about their feelings, Kalpana, and setting boundaries is healthy in any relationship. Secondly, it's none of your business. And actually, if we're calling out shitty behaviour, she spent last night ranting to me about how creepy you are – she's not interested, love; read the damn room.'

Kalpana reels from the accusation. Rooted to the spot, she watches with tensed jaw and shaking hand as Rhys abandons his planned cigarette and walks back to Araminta, ready to take his anger elsewhere.

'Want to explain to me why Kalpana just accosted me?' Rhys demands. Araminta is on a lounger by the pool, still damp from the dips she's taking to stay cool. The others have opted for the beach, where a breeze might be more readily enticed.

Araminta laughs. 'About what?'

'About you,' he says coldly, and she startles, her humour gone quicker than he can blink. 'About how apparently I'm not treating you right.'

'She *what*?' Araminta spits, jolting upright in her seat and shading her eyes with her hand to see Rhys and all his hurt better.

'So you're not happy with this, with us, is that right?'

'What? No, of course I am. I have no idea what she said, but –'

'Really? Because she seemed to have a pretty thorough understanding of plenty of conversations we've had. So you just go bitching to her about how horrible I am?'

'No!'

'She just berated me on camera about what a horrible, abusive person I am.'

'That's ridiculous! Rhys, please, what did she say?'

'Why don't you ask her? You clearly love talking to her.'

'Rhys!' Araminta yells because he's walking away from her and she can't stand this. 'Rhys, I'm sorry. I –'

'I don't want to fucking hear it!' he snarls at her. 'I've put up with so much, ignored so much, and I'm done. There's only so much I can handle, Araminta!'

'What are you saying?' She feels something tightening in her chest. 'Are you breaking up with me?'

'Of course not – not if you set her straight and never talk to that bitch again.'

*

Araminta plans on running to Kalpana immediately, to find out what exactly she said, but she bursts into tears the moment he's gone and they're not quiet tears either but loud, choking sobs that shake her whole being.

Araminta: *It's like we've been living this perfect little holiday romance and suddenly Kalpana's stuck her neck where it doesn't belong and . . . I can't lose Rhys. I've lost everyone I've ever cared about – I'm not losing him too.*

Kalpana is the one who finds her, and she can't breathe enough to scream at her.

'What the hell did you say to him?' she gasps instead.

'Nothing he didn't deserve,' Kalpana says. She sits on the chair next to her and leans forward to comfort her, but Araminta leaps back.

'Don't touch me. Don't bloody touch me.' She scrambles up because she will not cry in front of her. Well, not any more than she has already.

'What did he say to you?'

'Nothing *I* didn't deserve,' she sneers. 'I told you everything was fine. I told you I was happy. Why would you try to ruin that?'

'I didn't try to ruin anything, I just called him out on a few things.'

'You had no right to do that. You really hurt him and I love him – hear that, Kalpana? You really hurt the man I love. So screw you.'

Kalpana: *If me saying what I said to Rhys was enough to cause all that, then he's a bigger prick than I thought.*

Araminta waits a few hours before she joins the others on the beach. They're sitting on the ground by a huddle of trees, and she appears in the bright light, skin washed out, wearing Rhys's favourite dress – so figure-hugging it shows the outline of her bikini beneath it.

'Hey,' she says, greeting the guys. Kalpana is conspicuously absent.

They awkwardly nod at her but Rhys doesn't look up, not even as she sits beside him.

A few moments later he asks how everyone is feeling about the final paired challenge.

'Oh, I'm sure it will all go perfectly well,' Isko says, and there's not even harsh bitterness there anymore. He can appreciate the strategy of the game played. And now that his anger has faded, he's left with a vague sort of amusement. In pushing himself out of the competition, he feels like a spectator. And watching, he is ready for Rhys to fall.

'How does one acquire your level of confidence?' Rhys asks Isko.

'You acquire my level of talent.'

'Rhys has nothing to worry about in that department,' Araminta says.

Rhys rolls his eyes. 'Yeah thanks, dear.' His belittling words lash at her, their disdain, their contempt. *Dear.*

He turns back to Isko. 'Well, no one is denying the considerable size of your . . . talent.'

'Bored of flirting with your girlfriend?' Isko asks – this time with a cold bite.

Isko: *Should I tell her he came on to me? He should say, shouldn't he? Is it even a big deal, or am I just trying to insert myself into some sort of love triangle?*

He has no qualms about exacerbating that fall for Rhys. But if he does, Rhys will bring up Alex and Juliet, so he'll stick to pointed behind-the-scenes comments that save grace for the watching audience.

'Oh, she knows I love her,' Rhys concedes. 'But flirting's an art form that requires two talented parties – I'd like some back and forth at the very least.'

Araminta glares at the sand before her, and it's taking all her effort not to turn those furious eyes on him.

Araminta: *I know he's hurt but . . .*

Theo: *I mean, she was right there and he's talking about her. But then, I'm not sure what she was expecting from him. It's no surprise to the rest of us that he's an arsehole.*

'Well, I'm not about to shower you in compliments,' Isko says.

'Would you care to shower me in something else?'

'Two out of ten,' Theo mumbles.

'I do not need hecklers, Newman.' Rhys grins. 'If you're so desperate for my attention, you're more than welcome to join this hypothetical situation.'

'Hypothetical is where it will remain,' Isko says.

Rhys grins. 'I'll convince you yet.'

It's still too warm when they dine, and Araminta sits, radiant tonight with shimmer across her cheeks and her usual salt-crisp curls ironed flat. Rhys sits next to her but doesn't so much as look at her, and she is ramrod-straight as if she breathes too hard, she might make things worse.

Theo makes a comment about other reality shows – Araminta's not really listening, too busy trying to eat her food and not glare too obviously at Kalpana, who carefully avoids her gaze while still managing to throw murderous glances at Rhys.

'Who wants to watch people fake relationships on TV?' Isko asks.

'Maybe they're not faking it,' Rhys says.

And it's her olive branch, so she reaches for his hand, and he flinches, *actually* flinches, and she's adrift once more.

'Of course they're faking it,' Isko says. 'Trust me, I'm an expert at faking it.'

'Not in my experience,' Rhys grins. 'But no, some of them are faking it. That's what makes it so irresistible – everyone watching closely, trying to discern who is and who isn't because, like it or not, reality TV is art – and art reflects life. And if they can see the falseness reflected back at them, maybe they'll spot it in their own lives.'

'Or maybe it's not that deep and everyone wants to believe in love, fake or not,' Kalpana suggests.

As Araminta stares at Rhys, the thought crosses her mind that he could be faking all of this, every single part of their relationship. He's an actor, he's a liar, it's what he does.

But she doesn't believe it, even for a moment.

And that somehow hurts more.

Rhys and Isko take the dirty plates in, and Kalpana turns to Araminta.

'Can we talk?'

'No,' Araminta snaps. 'No, we can't. And if I wasn't perfectly clear before, you may never do so again. Leave me alone, leave Rhys alone and maybe do us all a favour and swim to another island.'

She stands and Kalpana is incensed because look at her, just *look at her*, she's too good for that boy. And she's twisting herself for him like she wasn't already perfect — like her sun-scorched, sandy, bare skin isn't better than this made-up version, like her usual artful, joyous flicks of eyeliner aren't a thousand times hotter than these doe-eyed wings.

And she's so distracted by all this that she doesn't see that Rhys has come out, has heard everything Araminta just said, and grins approvingly at his conquest, who doesn't know he's there yet either, who is flustered and harried and desperate for his approval.

Kalpana, catching this, expects disgust, doesn't know what to think when it doesn't come.

Rhys looks to her and smiles a victor's grin.

When the alarm trills, they gather from paired conversations to sit around the screen. The heat combined with the dark fall of night has brought insects that bite viciously at their skin, undeterred by the fire in front of them.

Araminta: *I'm too tired for this. I'm exhausted.*

'Hello, contestants!' Eloise says with a forceful grin.

Theo: *So she's not going to acknowledge what happened yesterday?*

'Are you ready for our final pairs challenge? Great!' She doesn't even wait for them to respond, and her energy has shifted distinctly toward that of a children's television presenter. 'This one is simple and you'll need to fetch those blindfolds again! You'll take it in turns to wear one while your partner is shown different words on screen. They'll have to describe it without saying it, and the team who gets the most correct within two minutes combined will win as many points as they successfully guessed.'

It soon becomes clear that this is no innocent game, and the thought that the producers may have turned against them is suddenly unshakable.

When Jerome is blindfolded and Kalpana has to describe words like *lawsuit*, *sexism*, *date*, and *bankruptcy*.

Or they spin it around, and Kalpana's having to guess *environment*, *fraud*, *wealth*, *fashion* and *clout*.

Theo and Rhys breeze through theirs, neither particularly fazed by the blows levelled at them: Theo not blinking at *break-up* or *scandal* and Rhys thoroughly unfazed by *cheating* and *lies*.

But it all comes apart with Araminta and Isko.

Affair. 'When two people are seeing each other when one of them is already in a relationship it's a . . .' Araminta rushes.

Isko's face scrunches up behind the blindfold. 'Uh, betrayal?'

'Yes, like that, keep going.'

'Um, hook-up? Sex? Dating?'

'No, no, behind someone's back.'

'What?'

'Or um, oh, oh, the news would be described as current "blank."'

'Wait, what's the news got to do with it?'

They swap places, Isko only guessing two points and taking a while to get there.

Father. 'Um, it's like, uh . . .' Isko stalls, catching Rhys's eye and noting how thoroughly entertained the man is by his efforts to throw an incredibly easy challenge. 'You know, like in the church,' he stumbles. 'Like one of the people who wears a collar.'

'Priest! Reverend! Pastor!'

'Yeah, but like, um, you know . . . a title.'

'Archbishop! Cardinal! Pope!'

'Uh. No. And if you made a confession you'd say . . .'

'Oh! Father! Father!'

Rhys cackles.

Theo: *Yeah, something was up. I don't think even Isko could be that bad.*

When the buzzer goes and Araminta has three points, she rips the blindfold off and glares at Isko with unrivalled fury. She practically vibrates with her anger as Eloise announces that Theo and Rhys have each won seven points and declares the up-to-date scores:

Isko: *14*

Rhys: *14*

Theo: *14*

Araminta: *13*

Jerome: *13*

Kalpana: *8*

The moment Eloise vanishes, Araminta turns on Isko. 'You threw that game on purpose!'

'Oh, don't be ridiculous,' Isko dismisses. 'We're just clearly not on the same wavelength.'

'No one is on your wavelength, and I don't believe you are either,' Araminta insists, believing herself more with every word because there's a hint of panic to Isko's expression, and he is only ever calm and dismissive, even if he's furious.

He might be the only one on the island incapable of acting. And she knows she's right.

'You did, you absolutely did!' she shouts, slapping another mosquito tearing at her arm. 'Wait – the others, did you . . . oh my god, you threw those too. I injured myself, Isko! You hurt me just to make us lose a challenge – why?'

The others watch on, staying silent, until the moment Isko realizes it's fruitless.

'So what if I did?'

And the others start shouting.

'Are you serious?' Kalpana demands.

'Why?' Theo asks.

'Araminta's right – she got hurt,' Rhys fumes. 'So you'd better have a really good explanation.'

Isko's anger floods back to him, and for a moment, he considers exposing him. But he can almost feel Alex's hand in his, holding him back.

'Because it's a fucking game,' Isko says. 'And I'm sorry you got hurt, but I didn't make you trip. AHX ran that risk when they set the challenge. But it's all a contest, right?' He locks eyes with Rhys for this part. 'And we're all making decisions based on strategy. I'm winning, and it's foolish for me to carry on dragging you up and away from the others in the chart. It'll be harder for one of them to over-take you. So yes, Araminta, I sabotaged us in the challenge so that overall I can win the competition.'

'You're a prick,' she spits, and something in her comes loose. 'We were a team, and I trusted you, and you hurt me and embarrassed me, all in the name of a few points! You're a disgrace who couldn't win by genuine means. Fuck you.'

She turns on a delicate silver heel and storms off toward the darkness of the barren, sprawling beach and the darker edge of the ocean on the horizon.

*

Rhys finds her curled up on the sand, knees drawn to her chest, arms wrapped around them, staring past the blinking, flickering torches and into nothingness.

'Hey, are you all right?' he asks.

She shrugs and doesn't even look up. She feels him sit next to her. He runs his hands along her arms – night has finally brought the bitter cold it promises on this island, and she's freezing.

'That was quite a reaction,' he says.

'I need to win, Rhys,' she says curtly. 'I *need* it. I can't . . . stay like this for the rest of my life. Famous for my parents and my fall out with them and who I'm fucking and who I'm not fucking and – I need to win and I need that prize because the thought of . . .' she gasps, struggling for breath. 'Of having to rely on someone for money . . . my parents used money to control me for so long and winning this? It would fix everything, Rhys. My bloody head and my shitshow of a life and . . . I was trying so hard and Isko just decided it didn't matter.'

'Of course, my love.' Rhys nods. 'That's a lot of stress, and well, I imagine that's not all that pushed you over the edge this evening.'

She curls her fingers around his, thankful for the warmth.

'I think you know it's not.'

'Yeah, that's . . . look, I overreacted earlier,' he says. 'I was really upset, and I think rightfully so, but you're clearly sorry about it and you've apologized, and I think I've been a dick about it.'

She takes a shaky breath. 'Yeah, I was going to mention it.'

'I forgive you,' he says.

'You do?' she asks, hating the way her voice wavers, the hope and the need to please that she's never heard in her voice before, but it's nothing compared to the happiness of knowing he wants her again, that they're okay.

'I know it won't happen again. Look, you're not the only one with daddy issues. When I was younger I . . . I saw my mother with another man. And when my dad found out he was almost angrier with me for not saying anything. I was a kid, I didn't know what I was seeing, but somehow it was my fault.'

'Rhys, I'm so sorry – that's terrible,' she says, turning toward him like she is drawn to him by his tragedy. Maybe she is.

'Maybe it's made me paranoid. That's my problem, not yours. But if I'm . . . overbearing, or concerned by things that seem innocent, that's why.'

'I understand.'

'Thank you,' he says. 'It really means a lot that you get it, that you won't push me too far on these things. I'm sorry it took me so long to forgive you for earlier,' he says, running a finger along her cheek, letting it linger at her jaw like he wants to take a moment to savour her. 'I've missed you, a lot, my beautiful minx.'

'I've missed you too,' she admits, though she's not sure that word explains just how much she's felt today, just how much she's wanted to be closer to him.

And she does feel calmer, just being with him. When he kisses her, it chases all the spiralling thoughts from her head, and she wants to keep kissing him, to never do anything but kiss him.

'You're our lead suspect. We've spoken to the other contestants,' Cloutier says, careful not to say suspects. If they
want to think they're still on a show, he'll let them. 'And
when we asked them who would want to kill Rhys, they all
said you.'

'Hardly a surprise,' Araminta says. 'I was his girlfriend.'

Her lawyer reaches forward, taps her arm. 'Remember
what I said,' she says in a low voice.

'Listen,' Cloutier says. 'We've all seen that footage – it
would be perfectly understandable if you were to –'

'Were to what?' the lawyer interrupts. 'You haven't even
told us how he died.'

'He drowned,' Cloutier says.

Araminta raises an eyebrow, glancing to her lawyer like

this could mean something. Something beyond *the fall didn't kill him.*

'And you're investigating for murder because?'

'Because something got him off that cliff and into the water,' Cloutier says.

'I didn't even see him.'

'You wouldn't have to see him to give him cocaine.'

If Araminta looked surprised before, she looks more so now.

'You just said drugs before, but *cocaine*?' she asks softly. 'Rhys told me he didn't do drugs.'

'Which is why we think someone gave it to him.'

'Or he's a liar.'

'Was he?' Cloutier asks.

Araminta shrugs. 'He wouldn't class it as lying – he'd call it performance, an artistic rendering of reality, or a misunderstanding. But yeah, he was a fucking liar.'

'Araminta,' her lawyer starts.

'Enough of a liar that you'd kill him for it?' Cloutier asks.

She glares at him, not so much for what he has said but that he would say it, the audacity of believing that might push her into a confession. 'I wouldn't kill anyone. No matter what they did.'

'I've spoken to several of your fellow contestants,' Kennard says, just like they'd agreed. At this point, nothing short of a confession will do. 'And more than one of them has pointed us in your direction regarding Mr Sutton's death.'

'Deflection, obviously,' Jerome says. 'I think the only thing I said to Rhys the day he died was "Should I leave the milk out." He'd been distant, you know, since he started

262

dating her. Spent more time with her than he did any of the rest of us.'

'And you didn't like her?' Kennard asks, though of course he knows the answer.

Jerome considers before finally shrugging. 'I liked her well enough, I just don't think they were well suited for one another. She was the kind of girl who complained when her boyfriend was an asshole like she didn't pick the asshole. And he clearly only liked her because of a lack of better options.'

'So you admit he was an asshole?'

Jerome glares at him. 'I don't think I said that at all.'

'Well,' Kennard says, moving on. 'I'd like to circle back around to the drugs found on the island, in the smoking area, no less, where you spent forty minutes the day Rhys died. And then, I'd like to discuss this write-up filed at your workplace for an incident involving white lines at a Christmas party.'

'They never concluded anything.'

'No, but they're HR and we're Interpol, so we'll take our chances.'

Kennard and Cloutier finish their interviews simultaneously, emerging into the hall and nearly colliding. Which means they both notice the looks from the other officers at the same time, passing them on the way to their unofficial office.

Maes is waiting for them, angrier than Kennard's ever seen her, and he's worked with her for years – her whole body stuck in rigid lines, barely able to talk, as she just spins her computer screen to face them.

It takes a moment to realize what he's looking at – some partiers in Berlin, a video of a bar. And then he sees it, him and Cloutier in the background, clearly visible as they laugh, their faces turning toward the camera, not realizing it's there. He watches as they turn back to each other. He remembers this, during those brief weeks they thought they could make it work – how it felt easy. Kissing him felt so easy.

Cloutier reaches out, clutches him, nails curling into his skin as they watch their undoing.

'It's everywhere,' Maes says. 'You've gone from passing mention to the centre of the scandal – is Interpol even investigating properly? Or are their lead detectives too busy fucking each other to pay attention to the murder? And frankly, I'd love an answer to that one too.'

Iconic

Season 1, Episode 14

The day passes quickly, the heat muted into a hazy, sleepy warmth. The contestants chatting amicably for the most part, Araminta rarely leaving Rhys's arms. And he's so much nicer than he ever was.

Isko: *I have lost count of how many times I was nearly sick. We get it. You've fucked and made up. The unending stream of compliments was worse than the times they tried to apparently eat each other.*

Araminta: *I'm still annoyed with Isko, but, well, I'm optimistic. I'm only a point behind and we're only halfway through the competition. I think I can win this.*

As the afternoon dims into evening, Araminta announces she is going to go shower before dinner.

She expects Rhys to accompany her but he just calls after her: 'Wear that blue thing I adore, will you?'

Kalpana wants to shake her when she nods without a second thought.

Over dinner, the contestants gather around the table discussing *Desert Island Discs*. No one can follow it given they all pick the most obscure songs they can think of, and by nature, no one else has heard of them.

'Four a.m. in an Empty Room,' Rhys says, and Theo looks to him, waiting for the smirk or the laugh that should accompany Rhys naming one of his songs.

'Really?' he asks, when none is forthcoming.

Rhys nods. 'I've never denied your talent, Theo; you just need to direct it better.'

'That sounds like a challenge,' Theo says.

Then he leaps to his feet, grabs an empty wine bottle from the side, and readjusts his actual microphone on his collar to make sure it can hear him in full clarity. He launches into a song.

It's so abrupt that for a moment they don't know what to do with it. But it's exciting, and more than that, he's good, incredible really – the sort of voice that you feel in your spine, in your very skin, and actually having something interesting to watch is a thrilling break from performing interest to a camera.

Araminta: *Most people would have to pay a lot of money to see Theo Newman perform like that, wouldn't they?*

The song is new, a slightly different vibe than RiotParade's. It's angrier, certainly, but more soulful too.

Rhys cocks his head to the side to watch.

Rhys: *He's clearly on his way to something, but, well, let's not make the mistake of believing the strategy only comes out during competitions. I would say he's doubling down on launching his solo career. It makes you wonder if this was always his plan.*

He finishes with a bold final note, and they all begin a gentle applause.

Jerome clears his throat. He suspects he is not being given the screen time he deserves, that he needs, if he's going to win in the court of public opinion before the actual trial. So he will force himself back into group conversations no matter how much they try to cut him out. 'I believe it was my turn, actually, on the song I'd take to a descrt island. Before that . . . interruption.' He turns his cruel eyes on Araminta. 'And I'd choose "Peppermint."'

She doesn't even look like she hears him, too busy trailing circles across Rhys's thighs and, now that Theo is done, staring out at the ocean.

'I never answered either. I'd probably go old school,' Theo says. 'The Who or something.'

'Didn't the drummer murder someone?' Kalpana asks.

'He accidentally ran over his bodyguard – hardly a criminal mastermind,' Theo scowls.

'I'm sorry, is there a certain level of masterminding required for something to be considered murder?' Rhys asks with an exhale that is equal parts derision and amusement. 'Since you're apparently an authority, how would you do it?'

'Poison,' Jerome says instantly. 'Something innocuous, like mushrooms, and if I have to buy it, then purchased in cash. Something that could be an accident but probably isn't.'

'Poison is weak,' Isko says.

'Exactly. It's a woman's weapon, which means if they're looking at all they won't be looking for me.'

'Yes, the police are so easily deceived.' Araminta rolls her eyes.

'And how would you do it?' he asks.

'With a chisel, probably.'

'You'd hardly get away with that,' Jerome says. 'You might as well carve your name into the corpse.'

'Who said anything about trying to get away with it?' she counters. 'If I killed someone, I'd want the world to know.'

267

'Femme fatale with five minutes of fame?' Rhys asks.

She just smirks back. 'Sure, or maybe I think I'd only kill someone if it was righteous – not an act to be hidden, but held aloft. An example, if you will.'

'Okay, that's hot,' Rhys says.

'I'd suffocate them,' Isko says. 'Hold a pillow against their face – no mess and difficult to prove.'

Rhys laughs. 'And with what upper-body strength would you do this?'

'I'm sorry – do you need a reminder?' Isko appraises Rhys, like he would just as soon stab him as fuck him, but there's something unnervingly erotic about it regardless.

'A syringe full of air,' Kalpana says, 'in between the toes – it'll look like a heart attack.'

'Christ, that's psychopath shit,' Theo says.

'No, it's not; it's a viral social media post,' Araminta sighs. 'Next you'll be saying to bury the body beneath a dead dog.'

'As long as it's vertical,' Kalpana says, grinning.

'Wouldn't you pay someone else to do it for you?' Jerome asks Kalpana.

'That would leave a trail, surely.'

'Family connections, then,' he suggests. 'Rich people have those, don't they?'

'I don't know what you're admitting, Jerome. I had no idea Silicon Valley was crawling with potential hitmen. Then again, you'd have no problem getting on the dark web.'

'Google works just as well,' Jerome says, then adds under his breath, 'especially when you're a retail tycoon.'

No one else hears, but Kalpana does, snapping to face him with eyes that are wide and terrified.

Jerome: *She's not my partner anymore, is she? I have no need to keep her filthy secrets.*

Kalpana reaches for her drink, running through ways to spin this: To declare it boldly and pretend she never hid it, simply didn't mention it? To refocus on all the positive changes she's made? To ignore it? She's hardly the only activist to keep rich parents quiet – it doesn't fit the vibe, and it's a distraction when people yell at you for it rather than the real issues.

'What about you, Newman?' Rhys asks.

Theo shakes his head. 'You know, not everyone sits around plotting murder.'

'I've yet to meet someone who hasn't toyed with the idea, just once.'

Theo shrugs. 'I'd confess the moment the police so much as looked at me. Probably best not to let it get that far.'

'Good evening, contestants!' Eloise calls from the TV screens. 'Are you ready for your challenge? We want to give you all the opportunity to claw back some points, so this week you'll all be competing against each other. But the popular vote will still be awarded and the victor given an advantage in the challenge. Are we ready?'

They glance at one another uncertainly.

'We had a tie in our vote tonight between expecting our icons to be generous or cunning. Which is exactly the choice you'll have to make – one by one you'll enter the confession booth and face a simple challenge. Complete it and you'll have the option to either sabotage another contestant or reward them. Which will win, your tactics or your kindness?'

The contestants glance at one another, waiting for the catch, until Kalpana finally asks what they're all thinking: 'Why would anyone choose to reward another contestant?'

Eloise nods like she was waiting for it. 'Because you aren't rewarding them in the competition. There are no points this time around, just the opportunity to set yourselves up for future success. Because your prize is to give another contestant a letter from home.'

So this is the choice: an edge in the popular vote by making the nice choice, or an edge in the challenge itself with an advantage over an opponent.

Araminta is the first to react, which surprises only those who have not been paying attention. Sure, she might harp on about her estrangement from her family, but there are five cameras on her at this moment.

'Oh my god! A letter from home!' She blurts, unable to think of anything better to say.

'Alex,' Isko breathes, leaning toward the screen as though enraptured.

The others feign excitement, but it's too tinged by fear to appear quite real. Letters like that could say anything. At their best, they could destroy the version of themselves they've created for the show, could drag the people they are away from this island into the spotlight. They'd almost rather someone gain an advantage against them than deliver those letters into their hands.

The tasks themselves are easy puzzles that they finish in moments – clear that the real challenge is the decision itself.

Jerome doesn't imagine there's much benefit to the advantage – he already knows so much – and choosing the letter might redeem him a little and entice the public to his side. It would go against the image she conjures of herself if Kalpana picked anything other than the letter. Theo feels like any other option is taking something he himself would kill for away from someone. Araminta knows her own family situation will be at the forefront of everyone's minds, and what better way to play on sympathy than to sacrifice herself for someone else's well wishes from home. And Rhys chooses the letter only so he can imagine hand delivering Araminta's to her himself.

But Isko doesn't hesitate.

He slams the button for an advantage, and when asked who he'd like to sabotage, he punches in Rhys's name.

There are no points to be won, and no reason Rhys would read him winning a letter for another contestant as a means of disobeying his command to throw the competition. It's a weak taste of a revenge he was beginning to believe he'd never get.

Which means that when Rhys finishes his challenge and chooses the letter, a new reel begins playing on his screen. A string of close-up shots of every time someone has touched Araminta, her thighs around Theo's head, her arms around Kalpana's waist, her bound wrist against Isko's.

Rhys's sabotage is his own jealousy, and the flames of it lick with such vitriol he can hardly contain it. He throws the door to the confession booth open with so much force it slams into the wall behind him as he leaves.

His arm is tense around Araminta and he does not cool so much as bury the fire deep. It is almost worse, to see him simmer rather than boil over.

Theo finds the boxes with letters on the beach, each one with a digital lock that has opened in response to their success. He piles them all in one box and hauls it back to the firepit.

'There are only five,' he says. 'Looks like someone chose sabotage.'

They look at one another – wondering who and, worse, if they are the victim, if something might happen to them when they least expect it.

Rhys: *Of course, I didn't say anything. If I had to see that, then they can simmer in their fear that it's coming to them.*

'Never mind that now,' Araminta says. 'Not when there are lovely notes from home right there. Let's celebrate that and come back to the other options later.'

Theo digs through the scrolls before looking up at Jerome. 'I'm sorry, mate. It looks like it was your letter that wasn't won.'

'Are you fucking kidding me?' Jerome starts rooting through the box himself, like it might be hiding.

Jerome: *That's what I get for being a good fucking person.*

Kalpana: *Whatever. He probably chose sabotage himself.*

'Then forgive me if I don't stick around for your happy family reunions,' he spits, tapping his pockets for his tobacco and marching away without another word.

The others stare, not quite feeling guilty that Jerome doesn't have a letter, but perhaps wondering if they should pretend they do.

'Shall we read each other's aloud?' Kalpana asks, just to break the silence.

'I suppose we'd better,' Araminta says because she knows the cameras better than anyone else. And no one wants to watch someone read something in silence. Besides, she's used to milking her tragedies to entertain an audience.

'I'll start,' Theo offers, when no one moves. He reaches in and grabs a scroll at random, *Kalpana* scrawled in gold, looping letters on the side.

Kalpana: *If it's anyone reading it, I want it to be him.*

'Kalpana, I'm not even sure how to encapsulate just how proud of you we all are.' Theo grins. *'It's been a blessing to watch you flourish and show the world what you can do. Keep up the fantastic work, and don't let the haters and the press and all that nonsense get you down. We all love you so much, and we can't wait to see what you make next. Love, Divya and Anika.'*

Kalpana buries her face in her hands, surprising herself by crying. Theo wraps his arms around her and she holds him for a moment.

When she pulls away, she is smiling, tears still running down her cheeks.

'I didn't even know how much I needed to hear from my sisters,' she says.

What press? What haters?

She needs to win, because donating that money to some charitable cause would silence whatever anyone is saying. Winning is her salvation.

She sighs. 'Go on then. I'll read the next one.'

Isko passes her the box and recognizes the writing pressing through the page before she can even turn it to the name. 'Oh, that one's mine.'

'Darling,' Kalpana reads, *'I cannot tell you how much I miss you and how furious I am to be proved wrong — you can last on this island, and clearly you can outshine the rest of the competition, make*

the whole world jealous of me for being engaged to you, and make me miss you more than I ever have. I love you, and I can't wait to hold you in my arms once more, Alex.'

'Awww,' they chorus, mostly because they know it will annoy him.

Araminta: *I can't believe the fiancé is real, honestly.*

Theo: *I guess an open relationship really can work.*

'I guess I'll read one,' Isko says, unable to quite dismiss his smile. 'Araminta, I have yours. Okay um . . . *Babe, you are totally rocking this thing! I'm so impressed! Can't wait to celebrate your win (because I'm certain you will) and blow all your prize money on a villa in the Med (that is the plan, right?). See you as soon as you get back home, Binki.'*

Araminta smiles. 'That's nice.'

'Who's Binki, and why do her parents hate her?' Kalpana asks.

'My friend from art school,' she says. 'And I always assumed it was a nickname, but she's from Chelsea so you never know.'

Isko: *So we're all out here getting letters from family and fiancés, and Araminta gets some random girl she went to college with? I know she's estranged and everything, but was everyone else busy?*

Theo: *I don't think I've ever wanted to hug someone more. She looked like she could shatter.*

'I can't wait to meet her, minx,' Rhys says, squeezing the hand he holds.

'My turn, I suppose,' Araminta says, a touch too forced. She draws a scroll. 'I have Theo – oh you're going to have to read your own, Rhys.'

Rhys shrugs. 'I'm good with that.'

'*Newman! Stop bad-mouthing us, man. I swear we can change, haha!* Oh god,' Araminta gasps. 'This is from before . . .'

'The allegations,' Theo finishes softly, staring at the letter aghast. 'Should we even finish reading it? I don't want to give those bastards a single moment of a platform.'

He can barely keep a straight face. He gave those bastards a platform for days before the allegations came out – as though he didn't know, as though he didn't come in here to distance himself from it when it all hit the fan.

'Well, I,' Araminta hesitates. 'I think if anything that makes reading it more important.'

'Oh, you are absolutely reading it,' Rhys encourages. Sitting opposite Theo, they can hardly see each other for the flames of the pit.

Araminta reaches for her drink before continuing. '*You will not believe what is happening out here. We've been booked for Coachella, we're up for seven Turntables, and last week we performed on* It's Friday Night. *The phone hasn't stopped ringing – though obviously you are very much missed – even if you aren't missing us, you grumpy bastard. Hurry back and let's turn all these tensions into chart success – Al, Dante, and Tyson.*'

'I hope they all rot in a prison cell,' Theo seethes.

Rhys dramatically unfurls his scroll.

He freezes for a second before the lazy grin falls back in place.

'You know, surely the whole joy of this is watching someone else react – and you don't really get that with me reading it, so let's just move on.'

Isko is quick to his feet and quicker at yanking it from Rhys's fingers.

'*So I'm guessing we're over. Valerie,*' Isko reads.

'What?' Araminta yelps.

'*PS, I left your shit in a garage. You'll need to pay the bill.*'

They stare at Rhys and his eyes flit around them all like a cornered animal.

'Something to tell us, Sutton?' Theo asks.

Rhys is caught, hesitating for longer than he ever has before.

Araminta keeps her eyes on the scroll, blinking quickly. 'You have a girlfriend?'

Kalpana: *You could hear the lump in her throat. It was fucking heartbreaking.*

'Had, clearly,' Isko says, turning the scroll over like there might be more, but that's it.

'No, well yes, I have an ex,' he turns to Araminta. 'You know my crazy ex – I told you about her. This is her. She must have convinced AHX we were still together so she could write this and they could have a dramatic TV reveal. I swear, I'm many things, but I'm not a cheater.'

Isko has to turn away before he says something Rhys will want revenge for.

Araminta glares at him, unsure whether to believe him.

'I have no idea what you're talking about,' she says.

'What do you mean? I told you about this – about her!'

But he hadn't. Rhys has made it very clear how he feels about discussing exes.

Araminta shakes her head. 'I . . . I need to be alone right now.'

In the confession booth, Araminta clutches a tissue, her eyes red like she has only just stopped crying. But now she sits straight, like she has come to a resolute decision.

Araminta: *I believe him. AHX should have done better checks on this girl. As far as I'm concerned it didn't happen. Rhys and I are happy — that's all that matters.*

@KylaPayne

'I'm many things but I'm not a cheater' RIOTS! RIOTS IN THE
STREETS! WE RISE AT DAWN!! If you too hate Rhys
Sutton, may I direct you to my etsy for public enemy number
one shirts #Iconic

@EmptyRoomBlues

Okay but the fact we all know Al wrote Theo's letter just
because of the coffee comment! Please, this band will be
back together again in no time and it will be amazing
#TheoToWin #Iconic

> #### @ErikaDolson
> @EmptyRoomBlues are you just . . . seriously ignoring
> the allegations?
>
> #### @EmptyRoomBlues
> @ErikaDolson oh sorry didn't realize allegations were
> the same thing as a verdict in a court of law.
> Innocent until proven guilty. And maybe with
> deepfakes and AI photos you shouldn't believe
> everything you see on the internet

@RealiTea

'AHX asked me to encourage Araminta to date Rhys on
that phone call and I really wish I hadn't listened to
them' – Araminta's Bestie Binki Rose speaks out on behind-
the-scenes secrets www.realitea.com/iconic/
binki-rose-speaks-out #Iconic

Cloutier's swearing so quickly the words are blurring together and Kennard just keeps staring at Maes. This is it. It's over.

He gave up everything for this, gave up Cloutier for this, and it didn't even matter.

'Well?' Maes demands.

Cloutier's phone rings in his hand.

'It's Steiner. I need to take this,' Cloutier says, answering the call and running from the room.

'That was a year ago,' Kennard finally manages.

'And you expect me to believe it's stopped?'

'Yes.'

She slams the laptop closed. 'You know what, fuck both of you. A man's death will be aired on television because of you two, and worse, a murderer could walk free. At best, you haven't given it your full attention, and at worst, you've given any defence lawyer immediate grounds to have the case thrown out! You've just spat in the face of every single person working on this.'

'I didn't, I . . . look, we haven't done anything. We've even interviewed separately, tried to avoid each other –'

'Tried to avoid your partner! Do you hear yourself? You should have told them you couldn't work this case the minute you were both assigned.'

'I thought it wouldn't impact it.'

'How could it not impact it?' She stands from the desk and goes to storm from the room but Cloutier reappearing blocks her way.

'Well?' Kennard asks.

Cloutier can't even look at him. 'We don't have time for them to take us off the case – a new team wouldn't get here

278

quickly enough. So we have the day, and then we're suspended. There'll be an investigation and a disciplinary hearing.'

'Shit.'

'We can still do this,' Cloutier says.

Kennard can't even think.

'We need to act – to prove that we can manage this.'

'To deflect, you mean,' Maes sneers. 'To get the press focused on something else.'

'That, yes, but also to pressure AHX not to air the episode. To maybe get the world focused on the fact a man died, horrifically, and maybe someone caused it.'

Cloutier and Kennard both go to the room, police stationed outside the door, but they can't imagine there will be need for the extra manpower.

'Francisco Andrada,' Cloutier says. 'You are under arrest in connection with the murder of Rhys Sutton.'

Iconic

Season 1, Episode 15

The scene opens in split screen: Araminta asleep on the sofa and Rhys wrapped in the linens of her bed. He'd practically moved in, his suitcase on her floor, his pills on the bedside table, his products all over her bathroom.

After all that happened last night, he still felt like he could exist in her space.

Araminta: *I do trust him. I do. But I couldn't face it last night. I needed time.*

The scene jumps to Rhys and Araminta together, clutching mugs of coffee in the morning light. The camera manages to find the one angle where they are framed by palm trees and exotic flowers, rather than the beige pool patio or the firepit still littered with the glasses and mess of last night.

'So what happened?' she asks.

Rhys sighs. 'I dated Valerie for a few months about a year ago. She's been obsessed with me ever since. She'd call me at all hours and message my friends on Instagram to find out where I was. When I did *A Doll's House,* she booked a ticket for every single show. It must have bankrupted her. And she'd throw things on stage, notes or flowers or her underwear. I ended things with her in October last year, but I guess she managed to convince AHX that she was still my girlfriend – I mean, she never even *was* my girlfriend. We were never exclusive.'

Araminta nods, drawing her knees to her chest. 'That's . . . a lot.'

'Yeah.'

'You never mentioned her though.'

He turns to her sharply. 'Yes, I did. Nice to know you can't even remember my crazy ex-girlfriend stories. They're some of my better ones.'

'You didn't.'

As Rhys turns to her, something about his gaze is inquisitive and something is hideous. 'I'm not the only one with crazy exes, Kalpana attacks me every other day about you.'

Araminta: *One stupid, drunken kiss.*

'We don't need to bring Kalpana into this,' Araminta says bluntly. 'We've covered that.'

'Really?' He snorts. 'Do you think she's somehow going to not say something about last night? And are you going to be on my side when she does?'

'Of course,' she snaps. 'I don't care about her. I care about you. And I don't give a shit about your ex-girlfriend, even if the letter was true. You love me and I love you. It's simple.'

' *"Even if the letter was true."* Oh, I'm sorry – do you not believe me?'

'Yes, I believe you. I'm just saying,' she adds, shrugging. 'I've had crazy ex-boyfriends too. The best of mine wrote songs about me. The worst . . . there was this one guy I dated for a few weeks who started turning up to all of my art shows, even followed me home a couple of times. One show he turned up with a hammer and started smashing a sculpture to pieces, and I just *knew* he wished it were my face.' She shudders. 'Actually, it wasn't even just terrifying when it happened; it's terrifying now. I still have to triple-check the security on my events.'

Rhys gazes across the pool, toward the dip of the beach. 'Valerie . . . it's ridiculous. How the hell did she manage to convince AHX we were together?'

Araminta falls silent, her knuckles paling around her coffee cup.

'So last night,' Kalpana says.

Isko: *Do I have the energy for this ordinarily? No. Do I have the energy for this before I've even had coffee? Absolutely not.*

'Yes, that sure was a night,' Isko replies.

She doesn't pick up on his mocking tone. 'I can't believe Rhys has a girlfriend – on the outside, I mean.'

Isko: *I can!*

'It's not fair on Araminta,' she continues. She has to – she can't back down now. 'He treats her terribly anyway, and now this.'

'How exactly does he treat Araminta terribly?' he says, before immediately regretting encouraging her.

'Oh, I don't know – the insults, the controlling behaviour, the gaslighting.'

'Gaslighting? Oh, there's a term people love to throw around. Where's your proof?'

'He literally did it last night, saying he told her about his crazy ex – which, by the way, do not even get me started on. That phrase is –'

'Please save the feminist rant,' he says. 'Rhys is simply bringing entertainment. If it bothers you so much, why don't you say it to his face?'

'Because I don't want to cause any conflict.'

'Then why are you here? For god's sake, woman, actually do something about it rather than bitch to me because as I believe I've made very clear – I don't care.'

Isko: *Look, to be honest this Valerie thing is a relief. Now Araminta's been shown who he is, she can decide whether she still wants him, and it has nothing to do with me.*

Kalpana tries the same thing on Jerome later.

'What the hell is wrong with people nowadays?' he asks. 'Abuse is being hit, Kalpana; it's being hurt. Not lying or telling slightly mean jokes. Stop devaluing actual abuse victims by saying shit like this counts.'

And with Theo.

'I say this because I like you – you just have to let them get on with it. You're only hurting yourself.'

And all she wants to do is talk to Araminta, but she can't. Every time she so much as looks at her, the other girl pointedly ignores her or glares so viciously it's a wonder no one turns to stone.

Araminta hadn't realized how tiring pretending to be fine was. All she has left are her feelings for Rhys, and she is manipulating them so she doesn't lose them. Because what is she without them? Without him?

She feels like a person whose edges are diametrically opposed – like the parts of her that are at war might split her open in their haste to race apart.

It feels good, his kisses, his hands, feeling this wanted in the face of everything, and it feels gut-wrenchingly awful to think, but she cannot stop her racing mind.

'Rhys, something else about Valerie –'

'God, can you not, please?' he begins harshly, but as he carries on speaking, he softens. 'Please, Araminta, I know it's messy, but this woman stalked me, hurt me, and now she's trying to ruin the best thing to ever happen to me. Just . . . I know you have questions, but my ex-boundary exists because of her. Thinking about her is traumatic for me. Can't you respect that?'

'I . . .' she starts, confused. She doesn't want to needle at sensitive parts of himself that he has so bravely shared with her. 'Of course, I don't want to hurt you. Excuse me – I'm just going to the bathroom.'

But she goes instead to Isko.

She's not sure where she stands with him. It seems to fluctuate. She thinks he's more loyal to Rhys than to her. But mostly she thinks he's not loyal to anyone, which works for her purposes.

'He says she's an ex,' she says.

Isko had been in the middle of mixing a drink, but now he puts the soda he had been about to pour down and shoots the rum straight.

Isko: *Have I, somehow, made myself the emotional support for everyone here? I cannot tell you how terrible a decision that is.*

'Do you believe him?'

'Yes,' she says instantly.

Isko: *I guess this is my opportunity to tell her without telling her, you know?*

Isko looks at her shrewdly. 'Darling, you know better than that.'

'You don't believe him?'

285

'I don't believe anyone. But he has a thousand reasons to lie and none to tell the truth,' he says. 'But then again, what harm is there in believing a lie if it makes life easier.'

'I'm not interested in making my life easier. I want the truth.'

'No, you don't,' he says. 'You wouldn't be talking to me if what you wanted was the truth. There's nothing wrong with easy, Araminta. Isn't everything hard enough anyway?'

She considers, but part of her is distracted: *How much longer until Rhys wonders where I am? What would he say if he found out I was speaking to Isko about this?*

'What would you do?' she finally asks.

'Me? Christ, don't come to me for advice. A boy like that? I wouldn't believe a single thing he said and I'd love him anyway. I'd lie to myself a thousand times for a single chance at happiness.'

'This is deep.'

'I know.' He unscrews the rum. 'Let's not do it again, hmm? We're in paradise. Go act like it.'

'Can I just –'

He smashes the bottle back onto the counter. 'For fuck's sake, I've answered your questions, haven't I? Why is no one on this damn island capable of talking to each other. I've tried to be polite, but frankly, I don't want to talk to you about the man who –' He is desperate for breath when he catches himself. 'I'll talk to you about a lot, okay? But I don't want to talk to you about this.'

Isko: *I tried. My conscience is clear.*

'Has Kalpana spoken to you?' Rhys demands.

Isko: *Busy day for me. I'd better be getting screen time.*

'Yes,' he says.

'About me?'

'Yes.'

'This is ridiculous,' he says, fuming. 'Jerome just told me she's telling everyone I'm abusive.'

Jerome: *Of course I told Rhys. He's my boy.*

'Yes.'

Rhys swears and kicks the trash can. It falls and rolls across the floor. They both stare at it.

Rhys takes a deep breath. 'Araminta doesn't think that, does she?'

'I didn't get the impression she did, no.'

'So you've spoken to her too.'

'She asked me what I thought of last night.'

'And you said?'

'That I thought your excuses were bullshit but I'd believe them anyway for an easier life.'

'Mate, what the hell?' Rhys turns on him.

Isko just sighs. 'Oh, I know you're not trying to convince me you don't have a girlfriend. Do you think I was born yesterday?'

Rhys just shakes his head. 'Araminta is something else. I . . . everything I left behind, it's not *her*, you know? It's not like I could grab a phone and call Valerie and tell her it was over.'

Isko: *Pretty sure he slept with me too, just before any of you go buying his whole 'Yes I have a girlfriend, but then I met Araminta' excuse.*

Isko feels that rope lassoing toward him, an opportunity to pull Rhys further into the flames. The world thinks they hooked up, after all.

Isko wouldn't put it past Rhys to out the truth if he did, but to say nothing and pretend it never happened is equally as suspicious. And what if Rhys realizes it was he who sabotaged him yesterday? Has AHX even enacted whatever they had planned? He feels like he's unravelling, panic seizing his chest at the idea that, whichever way he falls, Alex could be hurt. The wrong decision feels so easy, even accidentally, to make.

'I think Kalpana is getting to her,' Rhys says, filling the silence with more anguish. 'Araminta was accusing me of stuff earlier today.'

'What stuff?'

'Of being like her ex that stalked her.'

'*What?*'

'I know,' Rhys says. 'Apparently, he smashed her art at a show. Apparently, that's what this situation is like.'

Isko takes a sharp breath. 'That's not the same thing at all.'

Rhys goes to run his hands through his hair, but they still, grasping at the strands instead as though in anguish. 'Maybe I shouldn't have started all this. Maybe I should have just carried on pining for you.'

'Pining?' Isko takes a sip of his drink. He doesn't believe him for one moment and it takes damn boldness to say such a thing to a man you're blackmailing. But it's a confidence that's oddly appealing – no doubt speaking to some inner problem, some kink to be used and tossed aside.

Araminta is not the only one drawn to Rhys as if the current is dragging them under.

Rhys's eyes latch on to his. 'Sometimes I think you're the only one here I can stand.'

*

'Good evening, contestants!' Eloise says when the bell rings. 'I hope you all enjoyed your letters from home!'

'I certainly did,' Jerome says with a smirk.

'Today's challenge is one we're all excited for. The winner will take five points, the runner-up four, third three, etcetera, until the final participant, who will get zero. One thing we expect of icons? They need to be versatile! Not just a singer but a dancer, not just a mogul but a visionary, not just a social media star but a fashionista. So we've decided to shuffle up your areas of expertise! Araminta, you'll get an acting challenge; Theo, you'll have a sculpting challenge —'

Araminta: *Ah, so now I'm a sculptor but when it's my challenge I'm an influencer?*

'Rhys, you'll have a music challenge; Kalpana, you'll get to come up with and pitch a new dating app; Isko, you'll have to give an impassioned speech about a matter close to your heart; and Jerome will have a cooking challenge.'

Jerome: *This is bullshit.*

'Theo, you're the winner of the popular vote so you'll get an extra half an hour. Congratulations!'

They splice together a montage of chaos: Jerome failing to crack an egg, Theo cutting himself on the wire he's sculpting, Rhys wincing at his own flat notes, Araminta bashing her head against the wall of the recording booth, and Kalpana throwing a pen down in frustration.

Jerome goes first: dishing out something they might not think is food if it didn't come out of a saucepan.

Isko refuses to even try it, saying he can't abuse his palate like that; it would be a risk to his livelihood.

Then Kalpana: 'So you take a test, like a political

alignment test, then match with people based on similar values rather than looks.'

'Right, so how do you stop people from lying to exploit the results? Or even stop it from being used to radicalize people on the cusp of such an alignment?' Jerome counters, to which she has no answer.

Theo presents what looks like a wire rabbit, but he explains it's supposed to be a treble clef. 'Well, RiotParade won a Treble, so I figured this could be the first award I get as a solo act.'

Isko launches into his impassioned speech, throwing the competition by ridiculing it: 'And that's why I firmly believe everyone should be imprisoned on an island for a month in their life. It's truly character building.'

Rhys picks up a guitar and starts singing.

Theo: *I can't believe there was a guitar in this house all this time. I know it was in a locked box, but I would have shattered that thing to get my hands on it. And then I had to watch Rhys butcher it.*

Rhys's style is different from Theo's – all rugged lines and dregs of pain to Theo's smooth, rolling meander. The talent differential is stark: Rhys is a contender at an open mic night and Theo is the future headliner of Glastonbury.

Araminta's acting challenge is pointed in another way – a list of phrases with instructions to say them with different emotions:

'You lied to me – happy!'

'I forgive you – angry!'

'Maybe this could be my happily ever after – sad!'

And when Eloise declares the challenge over, encouraging

the audience to get voting, Rhys plucks up the guitar again and passes it to Theo.

'Come on, man,' he says. 'Entertain us for the evening.'

Rhys: *Gotta help the solo career, right? Maybe he'll remember me when he's famous.*

After an hour of songs around the firepit, Theo puts the guitar down and they carry on drinking, Rhys and Araminta becoming so grossly affectionate that Isko snaps for them to *get a room or an ocean or go literally anywhere else that isn't right in fucking front of us.* So they go for a walk, sticking close to the lights so the cameras can see them best.

'I want to talk to you about something,' Rhys says nervously. 'But I don't want to ruin such a nice day.'

Araminta's heart leaps.

Araminta: *God, what now?*

The camera zooms in on the circles his thumb traces on her skin, the way she leans into their held hands.

'I really love you, Araminta. Which is completely ridiculous because, Christ, I've only known you for a couple of weeks but . . . I don't think I've ever been this happy. But sometimes I'm not sure that you love me like I love you.'

'What?' she yelps. 'Rhys, how could you possibly think that? I love you —'

'I know,' he says with an attempt at a sad smile, but something about it is satisfied. 'It's not you, Araminta. It's this island. It's like you said when we first started dating — it gets in your head. And these people are doing everything they can to tear us apart. But I have an idea to resist them, to put us before the competition.'

'What?'

She hates how his every sentence shakes the ground beneath her, cannot stand how unsettled she feels.

She cannot remember the last time she felt stable.

'We love each other beyond this show, and I think that should be our driver in everything, don't you?'

'Yes.' Her voice is filled with trepidation, with the certainty she is being led into a trap.

'That money could set our lives up together. It could buy us a future. I think we should work together for it. If you love me as much as I love you, then I think we should combine forces, work as one to make sure one of us wins, and then we can split the prize money.'

She feels his eyes on her like a sniper. One wrong blink, one smile he doesn't want to see, and he could take the shot.

She's too focused on how she should react and what he wants to see to really process the words, or the way she feels about them.

Is this all he's ever wanted? Is this all it's been for?

'And the person to win would be –'

'We can discuss that. But it would make most sense to be me, wouldn't it, given I'm ahead in the polls? But I'm just being strategic here. The point is I love you. I don't want to win. I want our love to.'

He pulls her close – which is a mistake on his part, because it's easier for her to think when she's not looking at him, when she's in his arms rather than caught in his eyes.

I don't know. I don't know. I don't know.

But I do, I do love you.

But no, she does not think that love is enough to throw the competition.

And no, she does not think she can tell him that.

She knows there's only one answer and she gives it. 'Yes, all right then.'

But she's not sure she's telling the truth. And she's not sure how Rhys will react when he figures that out.

@SerenaHarper

How are Rhys and Araminta able to make colluding look so cute?? I want to be in cahoots with my partner!! Also really loved the healthy communication earlier – Rhys being able to unpack the reasons behind his behaviour and them able to move past it? They're gonna get married, I swear!!! #Iconic

>   **@LuluLime**

>   @SerenaHarper are you kidding me this is the post with the highest notes on the Iconic hashtag? NO IT IS NOT OKAY THIS IS LITERALLY A MANIPULATION TACTIC

@KimRobinson

Really don't get how Araminta has gone from being one of the best contestants to the worst in days. HATE girls who change their whole personality to get a boy to like them. No way past Araminta would have been doing anything other than screaming 'YOU CHEATED!!!' and 'ABSOLUTELY NOT, WIN THE COMPETITION YOURSELF' during these conversations #Iconic

The press moves away from Cloutier and Kennard, straight to the news of an arrest – though the police haven't told them who yet.

But the mystery of the arrest only has people more

excited for the final episode – an episode AHX is refusing to pull.

'But there's an arrest,' Cloutier protests. 'It's now going to prejudice an active crime.'

'Yes, and the injunction doesn't have time to go through, and AHX is willing to take the risk of us pressing charges. They'll probably blame it on a mid-level member of staff, fire them, and collect their earnings.'

'They know as well as we do it's not a murder charge,' Maes says, throwing the file down. 'This is cowardly.'

'He assaulted Rhys.'

'That didn't kill him.'

'The blood loss and the internal bleeding could definitely have made him dizzy enough to fall off that cliff.'

'If you believed that, you would have arrested him two days ago,' Maes says dismissively. 'Anyway, his lawyer will be here in half an hour and they'll get the charge thrown out.'

'Can we get all of them lawyers?' Kennard asks. 'I don't care if they've refused them; I don't want another reason for the press to think we've handled this wrong.'

'Agreed. But if it wasn't Isko, who was it?' Cloutier says, glancing up from his screen. He'd only checked whether his own name had disappeared from the headlines, and now he's deep in message boards bursting with excitement for the episode.

'Araminta,' Kennard says. 'We've got the most evidence on her, and I think she's close to cracking. Besides, look at the show – when it came to Rhys, didn't it always come back to her?'

*

Cheryl Blythe taps on her screen when Cloutier and Kennard enter.

'Well, I'm surprised to see you two lovebirds still here,' she smirks. 'I've just been reading the latest.'

'This remains our investigation, and your client is still a suspect.'

'Please, this alone will make it easy to get any charges dropped. Just let the poor girl go home.'

'Could you get her please?'

'You've already arrested someone. Why are you still interested in her?'

'There are aspects of the death that remain unexplained. I see no reason multiple arrests couldn't be made.'

Cheryl tuts and fetches Araminta from the room they've been meeting in. Kennard was right – she does look on the brink of breaking.

'Araminta, have you heard of coercive control?' Kennard asks.

Araminta freezes, though it's difficult to tell why. Shock? Anger? Trauma?

'What's your point here?' Cheryl asks.

'I would imagine that's quite clear, Miss Blythe,' Cloutier says, throwing a reassuring smile to his partner. 'We believe your client killed the victim. But we believe, as has been argued successfully in previous cases, that it was a reasonable response. Self-defence if you will.'

'I dated Rhys for two weeks,' Araminta snaps.

'Two weeks on that island? A lifetime, from what I hear.'

'Maybe it was and maybe it wasn't,' Kennard says. 'Maybe if he'd had more time, it would have progressed from there. That's not actually on us to prove; that's on your lawyer. All we have to do is charge you with murder. But you see, we're reluctant to do that given these circumstances. We'd much prefer we were able to come to an arrangement.'

'Do it,' she snaps.

'What?' Kennard and her lawyer say at the same time.

'Go ahead, charge me with murder.'

'Araminta,' her lawyer starts.

'I'm either under arrest or I'm free to go, right?' she says, standing up. 'I'm here of my own free will, helping you. I'm done. So arrest me.'

Kennard and Cloutier sit stunned.

'Go on. Here, I'll give you what you want: I hated him. He deserved what happened to him. I'm glad he's dead. There – is that enough to arrest me?'

'Araminta,' Cloutier tries, 'we just want to talk about what might have happened –'

'I don't care,' she says, with a smile she hasn't worn since the show – smug, self-assured, moneyed. 'I wish you gentlemen the best of luck with your case.'

Iconic

Season 1, Episode 16

Yoga, title card, and a far-off shot of the island, tiny in all that sea, the towering glass house barely a pixel.

Araminta makes breakfast, nodding to Jerome when he enters the kitchen, shortly greeting Theo when he does the same. Her hand stills on the knife as she slices fruit.

Araminta: *It just kind of hit me hard this morning, you know. Like, who exactly am I waiting for? I'm not talking to Kalpana, Isko apparently hates me, Theo has said a handful of words to me this whole time, and Jerome's said more but they haven't exactly been nice.*

The camera cuts to her bringing breakfast to Rhys. He stirs as she enters, blinking sleepily up at her.

'Balcony?' she asks.

Rhys runs his eyes over her – the skin-tight leggings, the flash of midriff, the tangled hair swept on top of her head. 'What do you think about putting breakfast aside and doing something else first?'

Araminta blushes. 'Well, I'm certainly not averse, but if I don't eat something soon, I might faint and that would kill the mood somewhat.'

'Somewhat,' Rhys agrees, rolling out of bed with a grin. The camera lingers on his body, all on show in the pants he wears – muscular thighs and clearly lined abs. Filler footage has shown them all working out, at points, but he is in better shape than when he got here – or at least he looks it, so little food, slightly dehydrated, muscles sharp and hard – and the camera loves it.

He takes the tray from her, bending as he does so to kiss her still-swollen lips.

Araminta: *At least I have Rhys. At least I'll always have Rhys.*

They cut a montage together – Theo's 'fuck *off*, Sutton' practically a catch phrase by this point, Isko swimming lengths of the pool, Kalpana and Theo in yet another pseudo-scholarly debate, Rhys stroking Araminta's arm as he passes her, Jerome carrying drinks to the others and Kalpana glaring at them all.

It's interspersed with more shots of the island, more than they've ever shown before, so that any joke is punctuated by a crash of waves, any wistful glance directed to the sea.

It doesn't look like a reality show, this cut. It looks like an indie film and feels like a social experiment.

It attempts to make up for the fact that nothing at all happens, really, nothing all day.

The night is another story.

The alarm trills, though it needn't. They're already sitting around the firepit, already facing toward the TV on the wall, and waiting for whatever Eloise has planned.

Rhys wraps his arm around Araminta, and she nestles into his side like a comma curled against him.

'Good evening, contestants!' Eloise calls. Tonight, she wears a fluorescent green dress – a screen within the screen, and they transpose her with images of their own

298

expectations of the encounter – all of them anticipating something dark-edged and chaotic.

'Before we get into tonight's challenge, I have the results from last night! In first place with five points is . . . Theo! In second with four is Kalpana! In third with three is Araminta! Fourth place for two points is Isko! And fifth with one point is Jerome! Which means, unfortunately, Rhys you came last and won't be getting a point tonight.'

They tense because Rhys's song was one of the better entrants – and that means the vote is not of their talent but of public opinion. So what does that mean for the rest of them?

The scores spill out on the screen and Araminta doesn't dare exhale, lest Rhys catch it and question her commitment to the competition, which he has made her commitment to him. Because he's lower than she is now, logically he should try to make her win, but if he sees a shift in her behaviour, he'll think she did not care so much when she had more to lose.

Theo: *20*
Isko: *17*
Araminta: *17*
Rhys: *15*
Jerome: *15*
Kalpana: *13*

Rhys: *No, it's too late to change the plan now. Maybe if each challenge were worth a point, but they're often worth more, and that board can shift suddenly. I'm sure Araminta agrees.*

'Tonight, we're challenging your ability to adapt. After all, icons need to have longevity and not feel threatened by the next rising star,' she says, and they move from resigned

299

curiosity to concerned alarm. 'Your spot in the ranks of the great can always be threatened by a new face. We're over halfway through now, and you've had too easy a ride.'

The camera cuts to a shadowy figure walking up the beach, lit only by torches, clothes carefully androgynous.

'So this evening you'll be competing for more than just your points – you'll be competing for your spot on the island.'

They're past the sand now, stepping onto the cobbled stones that lead up to the house.

'A spot that will be decided by a vote. And not by the public but among yourselves.'

Kalpana: *Fuck.*

Jerome: *Fuck Fuck Fuckety Fuck.*

'Why so panicked?' Eloise grins. 'Have you not had two weeks to prove to one another what icons you are? Do you really think someone else could beat that in the twenty-four hours we're giving you to get to know them before you cast your votes? And the ranking you decide will determine how many points you each receive tomorrow. May the most iconic remain.'

The figure is at the patio now, but the others are glued to the screen, not listening for footsteps that could never be heard over the distant waves.

But they do hear a suitcase dropping to the floor, and they spin to see who's there.

'Hi, everyone,' a glittery voice says, two words containing such promise of sweet revenge. 'I'm Valerie.'

On the AHX server, the episode crashes, a sudden influx of casual viewers driven by the demands on social media.

AHX will fix it, of course, and ensure it never happens again – enough that by the time Rhys dies, it can sustain the millions of people who flock to watch him fall.

But in the edited episode, they all seamlessly rise to their feet, and the camera tracks to Rhys like it could catch a reaction from a man who has one talent: contorting his emotions. To look shocked or horrified would give Valerie an advantage, perhaps even what she wants, so he defaults to his usual amusement. If he laughs at the disturbances of the world, he can pretend he is in control of them.

Araminta deposits her drink carefully on the table, nudging the glass away from the edge, and as everyone else approaches this newcomer, she slinks away inside.

In the confession booth, Araminta stares in utter shock.

'So you're Rhys's . . .' Isko asks, because someone has to.

'Crazy ex-girlfriend, apparently,' she says with a saccharine smile. She's not unlike Araminta, but smaller, with long, coppery hair and the metallic glint of a tongue piercing. 'I'm also a director. Award-winning director, actually – most recently a Tony for *A Doll's House*. Rhys was an understudy in it.'

She falters as she realizes Araminta isn't there.

'Where's your girlfriend, Rhys?' she asks.

'Hello, Valerie. Lovely to see you again,' he tries, his voice the kind of charming he hasn't used much of on the island.

'I'm sure it is,' she says. 'And I have some questions.'

'Hit me.'

'They're not for you.'

Rhys sighs and sits back down, leaning back with his

arms spread casually across the backs of the chairs. 'I'm sure you jumped at the opportunity to come here and put me in my place. But I'm happy, Val, impossibly happy, and I'm not letting you destroy that.'

'I think you've destroyed that, actually,' Kalpana snaps. She steps forward to shake Valerie's hand. 'I'm so happy you're here.'

Valerie takes her hand, but her eyes keep cutting to Rhys. 'Lovely to meet you too – *big* fan of your work.'

Valerie: *God, this is power, isn't it? It feels unreal, knowing all this stuff from the outside. But unfortunately, Daddy's Little Activist and the Tech Bro Incel are probably my best chances of getting to stay here.*

'I'm here because I'm an award-winning director and you're a disgruntled bit part,' Valerie says, turning her ire back on Rhys. 'And I deserve a spot on this show more than you do.'

'Makes sense to me,' Kalpana says.

'Come now, Rhys has proved himself several times over,' Jerome says, crossing to sit with him. 'I don't see why we should believe a thing this woman says over him.'

'Yes, I'd like to know that myself,' Araminta says, appearing in the door frame. 'I'm perfectly willing to accept two sides to every situation, but it strikes me that when someone invades a show like this with the clear intention of creating conflict in their ex's new relationship, one side might be more than a little biased.'

'Araminta, please,' Kalpana snaps. 'It's getting pathetic now, the way you unquestioningly swallow that man's lies.'

'Thank you, Kalpana, for your much-wanted opinion,' Araminta says without tearing her gaze from Valerie.

302

'You're right, I have reasons to lie. Embarrassing your ex on TV – who wouldn't want that?' Valerie shrugs. 'But I've watched the show well enough to know that you're more aware of your self-image than anyone else. And how would it look, Araminta, for you not to believe another woman? When you choose the man everyone on the outside knows is trash over the sisterhood trying to protect you.'

'I don't feel very protected,' Araminta snaps. 'And let's not make this a matter of belief. I'll hear you out, but ambushing me like this is a clear manipulation. I imagine breaking Rhys and me up will be great for ratings. So you'll forgive me if I take my time processing what you've said rather than believing you on the spot and destroying what is, let's be clear, a very good relationship.'

Kalpana: *God, she's right. It's an ambush and they forced her to his defence. She was on the cusp of turning against him, and by over-playing their hands they pushed her right back to him, and fuck, I thought it would be so easy to vote for Valerie over Rhys, but would that make it worse? To send her awful boyfriend home and leave her on an island with his ex?*

Araminta steps back, her hand reaching, and Rhys grabs it, squeezing it tightly, as if to say how well she's doing.

'All right,' Valerie says, shrugging. 'Believe what you want. But I'm obviously an ex-girlfriend, not the fling he tried to make me out to be. We were together for a year. But you don't want to hear about me – so let's go with what else he's keeping from you. Oh, how about the fact that a few days after he said he loved you, he launched himself at Isko? They've been keeping that little hook-up quiet.'

Rhys might be an actor, but from the way his hand slackens in Araminta's, she feels the truth ring through.

'I know,' Araminta says, tossing her hair from her face. 'Rhys told me.'

'What?' Isko turns to her.

She shrugs. 'Anything else?'

Valerie falters. 'Rhys never told you. It wasn't –'

'On air?' Araminta asks. 'Yes, he didn't want to embarrass me like that. He confessed it quietly, when we were in bed, microphones on the other side of the room. I forgave him. So was that it, Valerie? Was that all of your ammunition?'

Rhys is still and Araminta is hollow, lying to save face, stiff upper lip, and anything real or true or hurting – fucking bleeding out, screaming for attention – is stifled under her determination to not break down in public. Good lord, anyone paying attention would see that all her scandals are surface-level affairs, because nothing real happens in front of the cameras. The world doesn't deserve to see her cry.

And she's not being cheated on live on TV. That's not her narrative. That's not how this story goes.

'I . . . all right, the way he's treating you he treated me for months, and I never realized until seeing it play out on hyper-speed –'

'As we are now exiting the world of facts and entering a realm of opinion and speculation, I must stop you,' Araminta says. 'I have no interest in your viewpoint or your judgment.'

'But –'

'You have twenty-four hours on this island, yes? Very well, but I don't see why I should have to suffer it.'

She releases Rhys's hand and turns back toward the house. On the other side of the glass doors, she falls against the wall and starts to shake – hidden by the lights, and the gauzy curtain and the cameras finding something else entirely more fascinating.

She's done all she can for this show, for this platform – and for a moment she feels almost like its chosen favourite: all the right choices, all the spectacle and plot. But they wanted to throw her to the wolves, to embarrass her in front of the world, and she feels every blinking camera lens like a surgical scan.

A moment later, she's pulled herself together enough to grab her cigarettes and head to the one place on this island without cameras to watch her break.

'Well, I certainly have no interest in talking to you any further,' Rhys declares.

'Me neither,' Jerome says, as Rhys had likely hoped from the way he turns to him expectantly.

Valerie shrugs and takes a seat by the fire. 'That's fine, Jerome, though I have to admit I'm a little disappointed. You were the person I was most excited to meet.'

'Really?'

She nods and ducks her head away, tucking a strand of hair behind her ear. 'Yeah. Magnetic tech genius who's still a really nice guy? You were part of the reason I agreed to be on the show.'

'Oh, give me a break,' Rhys mutters.

'No one's making you stay here, Sutton,' Theo snaps. 'In fact, you might want to go check on your girlfriend, who just ran out of here.'

'Oh no, I think I want to hear every single thing that lying bitch says.' He smiles at Valerie and leans into the corner of the bench. 'Don't mind me. Go on as you always planned.'

'You think she's lying because she's more impressed by me than the rest of you?' Jerome asks, his voice low. 'Why is that so unbelievable?'

Kalpana scoffs. 'Do you want a list?'

'Look, man, you're my favourite guy on the island,' Rhys says.

Isko: *Rude.*

'But she's a manipulative hag who will say whatever she needs for five minutes of fame.'

Valerie brushes Jerome's arm as though reaching for him in shock.

Jerome glances at her fingertips, so close to him, and then turns to Rhys with a steady glare. 'I think perhaps Theo is right. Maybe you should go and check on your girlfriend.'

Jerome: *He probably just didn't like his ex-girlfriend hitting on me. But I'm not turning down a girl like that just because Rhys is mad about it. Besides, if he's as into Araminta as he claims, why does he care?*

Rhys stands. 'Araminta was right. This whole thing is a farce to stir drama and leave people hurt. I'm frankly disgusted you'd all play into it like this.'

Valerie acts as though she's been there from the start. She jokes and laughs and spins their questions back on them so they can speak about themselves. She feels she already knows them, and they respond to that familiarity in kind.

The dramatic entrance, the power of lights and music and all that confrontation might have the audience convinced she is a soap opera character rather than a reality TV contestant, but she's not really that either.

She doesn't want fame or victory.

She's just a woman whose boyfriend cheated on her live on TV, then made her the butt of the joke.

But she would like to stay, to drag this out, to have days to get vengeance for her still-broken heart. So she flatters and entertains and drip-feeds information in the hope that she might earn their favour, to make them at least like her more than their most hated competition.

'You know that clip of you singing yesterday has gone viral. Everyone loves it – you're primed for a hit single the moment you leave this island,' Valerie tells Theo.

She reassures Isko that he is an audience favourite, that sympathy is very much on his side. But he doesn't care anymore because this is his victory – it has to be. The sabotage he chose to bring on Rhys? He does not know about the video or how long the producers have had this planned, does not realize this is so much bigger than himself, and sees it as wholly his action that brought this woman here.

But instead of elation he just feels calm. This is closure. This is him making things even. Now he can respect a game well played by both sides and hope that even as he throws the competition, enough footage of him cooking airs and he'll win opportunity if not the prize.

Valerie tells Kalpana she has a hardcore group of fans – which is true; she simply does not let on what a minority they are. And she flirts with Jerome, even as her stomach turns. But Rhys has dragged her name so low there's not much room left for her to sink. So she swallows what's left of her pride, stares deep into Jerome's eyes, and smiles like he is the only thing worth seeing.

Valerie: *I might usually be the one behind the camera, but I know how to sweet-talk sponsors. I'm giving it a damn good try.*

Rhys can't find Araminta on his cursory search of the house, so he spends some time in the confession room ranting about how this challenge is designed to hurt him specifically and it's thoroughly outrageous to direct a whole challenge at one individual.

When Araminta finally returns to their room, Rhys rushes to her side. She clings to him, folded into his arms as he whispers reassurances for hours. Slowly she feels herself pouring back into her skin, or whatever mold it is she's left to fill.

Rhys does this to her, makes her feel whole, and more than ever she feels that all she needs is him, just the two of them against the world. Or against the show, which is effectively the same thing.

'What do we do?' she asks against his skin. 'How do we make sure you win this whole thing?'

Everyone starts to go to bed, and the logistics of this challenge arise. Where is Valerie going to sleep? Did AHX even think this through?

Rhys is in Araminta's room – do they expect his ex-girlfriend to take his bed?

'You're more than welcome –' Jerome starts, but Theo cuts him off before he can make sleeping with him a condition of his vote.

'I'll take the sofa. You can have my bed.'

'Just share with me,' Kalpana says, and there's something about the way she says it, like it is the most obvious conclusion, that the others do not push. But Valerie sees the intentional gleam in her eye, knows that this is an opportunity as much as anything else on the island.

Because the first things to come off as they dress for bed are their microphones.

And when the lights shut off, no one can see them talking – and if they can, perched by the headboard, they will assume it is harmless, girls talking at a sleepover. Didn't Araminta herself put this idea in their heads, microphones off and quiet words whispered over satin sheets?

'Thank you for calling him out,' Valerie starts, sitting cross-legged on top of the comforter, facing Kalpana's dim outline in the dark. 'You were the only one who ever did.'

Kalpana takes a breath. 'Of course. But Valerie, Araminta is in such a difficult place right now. I worry that all of this is too much, and I think if we voted Rhys off in favour of you –'

'I don't want Rhys voted off.'

Kalpana snorts. 'You could have fooled me with the way you were flirting with Jerome.'

'I'd like to stay, sure. But I think my ideal outcome would be Jerome votes to save me but loses the vote to stay in the process. I certainly don't want to be here without Rhys. It would be too easy. But giving him screen time? Letting him show himself up more and more? I want to give him a platform so high that when he falls, he breaks his damn neck.'

'I understand you're angry – he hurt you . . .'

'It's not just that,' Valerie hisses.

It is. It is exactly just that. But that's not what will hook Kalpana.

'It's every man worshipping him, every man inspired by him, learning from him, sitting taking notes. I want to make an example of him, Kalpana. You don't know what it's like out there, how many messages of support he has. I want to show every man watching that there are consequences when you behave like this.'

Kalpana knows what she's doing, can practically feel the hook drawing through her flesh.

But it lodges there all the same.

And she has her own rage thrumming through her, wrapping around her, ensuring she can't escape its snare.

'They're not really supporting me on the outside, are they?'

Valerie regards her before giving a small shake of her head. 'They think you're cosplaying poverty for clout. But some – not all, obviously – are really rooting for the way you're going after Rhys.'

And there it is. This is how she survives this show.

She hates Rhys, she's furious at how he treated Valerie, and she's angry that he treats Araminta like that, angrier still that Araminta lets herself be treated like that, and angriest of all that neither of them is listening to her.

But she's going to make them listen.

'Help me expose him,' Valerie pleads.

Kalpana does not entirely know what she is agreeing to. But if she is honest, she never really does – swept up, believing in a message, in a slogan, in a root cause. '*Teach men a lesson*' is certainly one she can get behind.

'Okay, let's do this. Let's point those cameras right at him, and let's bring him down.'

@Xena_Z_Art

Here's the petition to get Rhys off the show. God this is
   sickening – AHX you should be ashamed of yourselves. At
   some point don't we have to take responsibility for the
   things we let happen in the name of entertainment? #Iconic

   > **@FeliciaTru**
   >
   > @Xena_Z_Art chill babe, it's hardly the hunger games.
   >   Just let people enjoy the tea because it is PIPING

@LulaLaney

Valerie is great but Rhys was so funny reacting to her. Almost
   made me like him again tbh, like does nothing faze him???
   That man would laugh at the end of the world #Iconic

@CarrieOn_6

You do know that Rhys can just be a cheating piece of shit and
   he doesn't have to be abusive like . . . these claims are WILD
   and GROSS, stop making everything into something

A local officer opens the door for her and there she is: eyes red and dry from a return trip to New York, chestnut hair twisted into a fraying bun, arm in a sling it wasn't in two days ago. Valerie.

'Thank you for coming to see us,' Kennard says, rushing to his feet.

'No problem,' she says, ignoring his hand and taking a seat. Her voice is flat. Hollow. The sort of thing they might think was sad if they hadn't already read the various interviews she's managed to find time for. 'So you arrested Isko?'

'Yes, but we're looking at all avenues,' Cloutier says.

'I assume you don't think I did it.'

'No, but we think you might hold the clue to who did. You were with them. You saw them in a way that no one else did, and maybe you picked up on dynamics not visible to the camera.'

She swallows, her fingers toying with the edge of her sling.

'I think any one of them could have done something.'

'Could have? Or do you think they did?'

'I think it was just an accident. But my boyfriend just cheated on me on international TV then fucking died. I haven't slept in days. I think I've thought through every avenue you're looking at.'

'We're listening.'

She tells them everything, every dynamic at play, every blind spot and way that someone could have done something. Everything she herself could think to do – everything she did, the things AHX might have used her to set in motion. Her scheme with Kalpana, Jerome turning on Rhys, how it all ended . . .

'And . . . no, don't worry, it's stupid.'

'Stupid might be the answer.'

Valerie's lip wavers, her head shaking slightly like she cannot bring herself to admit it. When she speaks, it's like she's choking.

'But I also wouldn't put it past Rhys to have planned it all himself. To have orchestrated it – maybe he didn't mean to die and maybe he did. Because this pandemonium is exactly the sort of way he would have wanted to go out.'

More confused than ever, and with time running out, they have one last round of interrogations. They start with Jerome. Once, they thought him the least likely killer. Now they think they're all as guilty as each other, spinning circles in the interrogation room, lies falling like the heavens themselves have opened.

'You and Rhys argued over Valerie, didn't you?'

'Oh please, it's a bit late in the day for this, isn't it?' Jerome scoffs. 'I didn't kill him, you know it, I know it – you can't even tell me how I possibly could have.'

'You hacked AHX. We could arrest you for that.'

His lawyer goes to speak, but Jerome just laughs in their faces. 'God, how embarrassing would that be. Are you fellas not being humiliated enough without scrounging for arrests on charges that aren't murder? Tell you what, why don't you hit me up after this. When you lose your jobs, know that Soltek is always looking for new assistants.'

Cloutier takes the lead with Kalpana.

'I need you to understand, Miss Mahajan, that just because this man is dead, we do not believe him to be a good person. Whoever killed him may have done the world a service.'

Her new lawyer looks at her and gives a subtle shake of his head.

Kalpana rolls her eyes. 'Thanks, I caught that one myself. Look, I didn't kill him.'

'Okay,' Cloutier says with a nods. 'But if you did, well,

that's going to come out eventually. But a confession? An explanation? I know several prosecutors who would be sympathetic to ridding the world of a man like that, of saving the next girl. A deal could be struck.'

Kalpana doesn't even consider it. 'I didn't care about saving the next girl; I cared about Araminta – and there was no saving her. What could killing Rhys possibly do to help? It would only make things worse. Why are you wasting everyone's time? I watched him fall. This is nothing more than a tragic ending to a horrible man –'

'Kalpana, I –' her lawyer starts.

But she silences him with a glare, looks at Kennard and Cloutier, and raises her chin in defiance. 'What a fucking pity.'

'Mr Newman, we've compiled quite a lot of evidence against AHX,' Kennard says. 'There's certainly a case here that if something happened to Rhys, and we're not saying it did, the person who did it wasn't in their right mind. With the right lawyer, this might not even go to trial. But only if they cooperate. If the truth comes out later? There's not much I can do.'

'Mr Newman has the right lawyer,' the woman in question intervenes. 'So if you want a deal, you discuss that with me, not my *innocent* client.'

'Is that true, Mr Newman? Are you innocent? Or on that island, away from everyone and everything you knew, did you see Mr Sutton as a threat? As a danger to the women with you? One might even go so far as to say that if someone did do something to him, they were a hero.'

Theo stays silent, refusing to look at anyone but his lawyer.

'You don't have to answer that,' she reassures him. 'It's an inane question.'

Isko's lawyer arrives while they're interrogating the others, so once again Maes is pulled from her tapes to assist.

'You said you'd never hit anyone before,' she says. 'Yet you managed to do quite a lot of damage to Mr Sutton. There was internal bleeding.'

'Mr Sutton didn't bleed to death,' the lawyer counters.

'No, he drowned,' Maes says. 'Hence the arrest for aggravated assault and murder by negligence.'

'Given the circumstances of that show?' the lawyer says, satisfied smirk unfurling on his face. 'Trying to charge Francisco Andrada for a punch is not going to stick. With the lack of safeguards, AHX would be lucky if the only thing that happened on that island was someone throwing a punch. Let him go. You've embarrassed yourselves enough already.'

Isko takes a breath and looks up at Maes with tired eyes. 'I hit him. We all know I hit him. So if you can prove that got him into the water, then fine, I'm under arrest, show me to my cell. But if you can't – if he could have sustained that bleeding from the fall, or if the drugs sent him off, or if he was just a drunk idiot standing too close to the cliff's edge, then what more is there to say?'

And they're right; the charges were never going to stick. So the final brick falls as the clock pushes on toward 8pm, and the world prepares to change the channel to AHX.

Iconic

Season 1, Episode 17

Kalpana wakes early and finds Araminta posing on the beach, spandex stretching over taut muscles as a drone hovers nearby.

'I want Valerie off the island,' Kalpana says.

Araminta lowers her foot slowly, giving herself time. Her first thought is that she's lying, that it's a clear effort to manipulate her even more than Valerie being on this island already has. But what if it's not? Could it be possible that Kalpana's and Rhys's interests align? And what does that mean for her if they do? Rhys would never be happy with her talking to Kalpana, let alone colluding with her.

She should go back to the house immediately and tell Rhys she spoke to her before he can hear it from someone else.

'No you don't,' Araminta says, snatching up her water bottle like she's about to walk away.

'I think this whole situation was messy enough without her,' Kalpana says. 'It's not her fault, but she's made everything worse.'

'Sure.' Araminta takes a step.

Kalpana: *Valerie wants to expose Rhys and so do I. But I'm not keeping Araminta on here as some tool to reveal the worst of him. We do differ in one key way: I want Araminta to lose. I want her to go home tonight.*

'And I don't think it's fair that someone could come into this competition so late in the game and potentially win.'

Araminta's breath catches and she knows she should carry on walking away, knows she should not entertain this.

But her heel drags, her reluctance palpable. Finally, she shuts her eyes and says, 'I'm listening.'

While Kalpana distracts Araminta, Valerie goes to Rhys. He's on the patio, rubbing tanning lotion into his calves, skin glinting in the sun. When he looks up, there's a split second where her gut does not remember all the hurt, where her brain misfires on old signals that have her attentive and aching.

When his lip curls, her mind rights itself in a painful lurch.

Valerie: *The thing you have to bear in mind is that up until two weeks ago, I was Araminta.*

'You're still here then. I'd half hoped it was a nightmare.'

'Rhys, please,' she says, letting that hurt seep in. All the pain she replaced with anger she dredges back up. 'I . . . I'm sorry.'

Rhys huffs derisively. 'For what? Your behaviour? For coming on the show at all?'

'For whatever I did that made you leave me.'

He perks up at this, though he tries to hide it by rubbing lotion into his arm. 'I made it perfectly clear what I expected in a partner. You always pushed it to its limit. And then to come on here and yell at me in front of everyone? It's pathetic.'

'I know I shouldn't have done that.' She nods, voice

small. She crosses to sit beside him. He doesn't tell her not to. 'I didn't realize how much it would hurt me to see you with her.'

'So you reacted like a child throwing a tantrum? Congratulations, Val. You would have struggled to find someone who treated you as well as I did and who loved you as much as I did anyway. After that little performance you've just ensured no decent man will ever look twice at you.'

'Maybe the only decent man I care about is looking at me right now,' she says, making her eyes big and wide and pleading. She's going to throw herself at this man's feet, knowing he'll trample her.

Rhys hesitates at that, and something shifts in his gaze – cold rage to pity and, as she expected, a hint of desire. Rhys loves broken things; it's why he creates them.

'I'm with Araminta,' he says. 'I love Araminta.'

'I think you love me too,' she says, reaching for him, trailing her fingers along his arm, and when he does not swat her hands away, she reaches for his face, strokes the smooth planes of his cheek, and leans in. 'I came here to win you back.'

He leans in too, barely a breath apart. 'And why would I dig through the trash for scraps I discarded weeks ago?'

Valerie: *Which means no matter how much I hate him, no matter how much I wish I could become some femme fatale vigilante, he's always going to have the upper hand. He's always going to be able to hurt me.*

She wasn't aware she had anything still standing in her heart to crumble until it falls.

'If you didn't love me, you wouldn't enjoy upsetting me

so much. That's what you always said, right? That I ignited some extreme passion in you, that everything was so intense with me?'

'Those fires have died.'

She lets her hand fall and stands abruptly. 'Fine. I'll see if Jerome cares for my affections instead then, shall I?'

Rhys catches her wrist and spins her back to him. 'Don't you dare,' he warns, voice low and smooth.

He notices the goose bumps that shiver across her skin.

'Rhys!' Araminta is on the deck, arms folded, glare murderous and voice terse. 'Can I have a word?'

Behind her, Kalpana stares, horrified, like this was not always the plan.

Alone with him, Araminta unleashes her tirade in a sweeping tide. 'I can't believe you! Why would you give her the time of day, let alone do whatever that was. I –'

'Araminta, Araminta.' Rhys repeats her name in a breathy laugh. 'My love, I was using her!'

'She was flirting with you!'

'Yes, she was trying to manipulate me. She was just playing the game – you can't let her get to you like this.' He holds Araminta's arms like he would reassure her, but she breaks out of them, nearly slipping on the sand in her haste to step away.

'*She's* not the one getting to me!'

'I was humouring her! Trying to find out what she wanted, why she was here. Stop overreacting.'

'I'm not overreacting; I'm reacting!'

'What about how I'm reacting? Have you once thought to ask me how I am with all of this? I told you how deeply triggering Valerie is for me and how much she's scarred me. Yet all I've done from the moment they blindsided me with my worst trauma is make sure you're okay.'

Araminta presses her lips together to stop from crying. 'God, you're right. I'm so sorry, Rhys. If we were on the outside of course I wouldn't care, but this place is too small, these challenges too enormous. I'm not sure I'll cope if she stays. What if she wins the vote tonight and is here until the end? I . . . I just want her gone.'

'Okay.' Rhys closes the distance again, and this time when he holds Araminta, she doesn't push back. 'If you want her gone, then we'll make that happen.'

All seven of them lounge on the beach, Valerie locked in conversation with Jerome in a way that straddles her position: leading him on enough to make him believe he stands a chance but not so much Rhys thinks she genuinely wants him. It is clear he is always the goal.

She tries with the others too, but Isko doesn't care. He might vote himself out – after all, he cannot win anyway, not with Rhys still dangling that leverage, and Theo is already sold on her over nearly everyone else.

Theo: *Honestly, the only one I wouldn't trade Valerie for is Kalpana.*

It is not relaxing; they are just pretending it is. The tension is palpable, the number wrong, and everyone wants to speed to the end of this challenge for the world to right itself.

Araminta and Rhys are so wholly absorbed in each other that it takes everyone by surprise when Araminta surfaces to say, 'Anyone in the mood for a game?'

Maybe it will be a way to expel this energy, or to at least

remind them that it is not that serious, just a competition – just entertainment. Or maybe it will allow them some small taste of the victory they crave.

In their hunt to invent activities, Jerome presents flag football, or the variation of it they can concoct on this island. Suit ties tucked at the edges of their shorts and bikini briefs, and teams assigned, a simple task: Try to get the other ties without losing yours. First team to get all three of their opponent's ties wins.

Rhys runs his finger around the edge of Araminta's bikini, drawing her tight. 'I know who I'm trying to get first.'

Then they are separated: Kalpana, Araminta and Valerie versus Jerome, Rhys and Theo.

Isko referees.

The game is ridiculous, full of loud squealing and yelping as people duck and weave. In the edit, they overlay it with upbeat music that makes the whole thing comedic – but the reality is vicious. When lunges miss, they bristle – when someone gets too close, they could bite.

Kalpana is out first, Theo reaching her before she can react.

Then Jerome, Valerie laughing as she draws the tie from him, winking at him like the whole thing is flirtatious.

Back in the game and they are running, panting, desperate for the win.

It happens quickly – Rhys running for Valerie, feinting toward Araminta and turning back at the last moment, losing his balance and colliding into her.

They both go down hard.

Valerie screams.

Rhys rolls off her, apologies falling from his lips, crouching down to help her.

He's shoved aside by Kalpana, who turns on him even as she tries to help Valerie to her feet.

'You fucking arsehole, you did that on purpose!'

Valerie's shock is wearing off and the pain is blistering to the surface.

'Of course it wasn't on purpose!' Rhys protests. 'My foot sank in the sand.'

'It looked pretty intentional to me,' Theo spits.

Valerie is sobbing now, clutching her shoulder. Theo tries to examine the wound, poking carefully at swollen flesh, and Valerie howls.

'Old . . . injury,' she chokes out.

Kalpana turns back on Rhys, nostrils flaring, fists curling.

Kalpana: *Of course it was intentional – he lunged at her. He knew she had a problem with her shoulder, and he did it knowing she'd go down on that side.*

A tender is already approaching from one of those AHX ships.

When it arrives, a handful of people jump out – the medic who examined Araminta, the driver and a man with a clipboard who calls for them all to go back up to the villa or the pool and wait for AHX's clearance before returning to the beach.

They leave Valerie crying in the sand.

The moment Kalpana steps from the rough dirt path onto the tiles of the patio, she rounds on Rhys.

'Well?'

'Well, what?'

'You tackled her on purpose.'

Rhys shakes his head and moves past her. 'I'm not dignifying that with –'

'Yes you are,' Theo snaps. 'You hurt her.'

'Yes, and I feel awful about it, Newman! Dear god, what is wrong with you all? Do you really care so much about this competition that you think someone would injure another contestant over it? Let alone . . .' He glances at Araminta almost nervously. 'Look, Valerie and I are messy, but that history between us? It means something to me. I don't want her harmed!'

'I don't know, guys,' Jerome says nervously, glancing from Rhys to the beach. 'I really doubt he did that on purpose.'

'I'm sure that's what he'd love us to think,' Kalpana says, seething, her nails piercing her arms in her fury.

'Isko, you're the referee; what do you think?' Rhys asks.

Isko meets Rhys's eye with something like a challenge. Does he truly want to keep pushing him like this?

But then Isko checks out, no longer caring much at all and happy to let Rhys pull the strings.

'Of course it was an accident. Pull yourselves together. Is this whole thing not dramatic enough without you writing in more melodrama? Now can we please do what we do best and go get a drink?'

But it's not enough to stop the wary glances, or the suspicion taking root that maybe everything Rhys does is intentional. And maybe the people who stand in his way get hurt.

*

Araminta and Rhys collapse into one of those wide, shaded sun beds and spend the whole afternoon fully entwined and vacillating between soft, gentle caresses and passionate grasping.

Araminta: *Of course Rhys didn't hurt Valerie on purpose. He wouldn't do that. Besides, even if he knew about the injury, you have to be quite specific to hit a shoulder, right? Besides, what does it achieve except for Valerie losing an hour or two to convince us to keep her. And even if – no, no, of course he didn't do it intentionally. He said he didn't.*

But an hour later and Valerie hasn't returned, and two hours later when they check the edges of the beach there's no one to be found.

'They might have taken her somewhere for tests, but I'm sure she'll be back,' Theo assures Kalpana, who cannot settle without knowing what's happened.

By the time they sit down to dine, there's still no sign of her.

Rhys's arm stretches across Araminta's shoulders, and she leans against him unconvincingly.

Araminta: *I hope she stays gone, but I also feel guilty about that and am terrified for whatever the next challenge is, given what the last one brought. Honestly, I'm just so, so tired.*

Rhys is lost in a story – the worst audition he ever had, a role he so richly deserved.

Kalpana stabs a piece of lettuce with such force it scratches the enamel off the plate.

Rhys arches a deliberate eyebrow. 'My dear, if it offends you so much, don't eat it.'

'The salad isn't really what's offending me,' she mutters. 'Though I'm sure I'm thankful for your concern.'

Rhys rolls his eyes. 'Alright then, Kalpana. Why don't you tell us what is offending you.'

'You mean beyond you shoving your ex-girlfriend and winding your current one even further around your finger? Oh, you mean in that story? Sure, let's recap – you turned up fifteen minutes late to an audition and asked the female director to get you a coffee. But somehow holding that against you is unprofessional because it has nothing to do with the art. Which she probably didn't anyway – you just weren't good enough, but you think you're entitled to everything and not giving it to you is a disgrace.'

'And what are you basing that assessment of my character on? Or is this where you call me a Libra?'

'No, it's where I call you a self-entitled prick.' She doesn't miss a beat.

Rhys grips the table. 'Why are you such a bitch all the damn time?'

Kalpana shrugs. 'Entertainment? And I can't fucking stand you, so that helps.'

'Stop it,' Araminta says quietly.

Kalpana rolls her eyes. 'Oh, don't you start. Just because he's got you to shut up and sit pretty doesn't mean he gets the rest of us to do it.'

Araminta doesn't even blink.

'Don't turn it to this again,' Jerome groans.

Isko takes a long sip of wine and leans back in his chair.

'Go on, Kalpana. Do you have something to say?' Rhys asks.

'I have several things to say,' she snaps.

'So I've heard – and so has half the island, right?'

326

'You know what your problem is?'

Rhys gives a bored sigh that doesn't erase the contempt lingering in his voice. 'No, why don't you tell me what my problem is?'

'That you're a deeply boring person and you can't bear it, so you create all this turmoil to appear interesting because you're terrified of being normal or anything less than the centre of attention.'

Rhys's expression is calm, but his eyes are so intently livid that Theo's skin prickles in anticipation. 'Sutton,' he warns, tone careful, like he's approaching a feral dog.

Rhys turns that glare on him and speaks like his very name is a sneer: 'I should have known you'd take her side on this, Newman.'

Theo sighs. 'Why is everything a fight with you?'

'Because someone here has to have a backbone,' Rhys says. 'And I'm not sure you'd know one if it was arched on your bed screaming your name.'

'How's this for backbone: fuck off.'

'Inventive.'

Isko pours more wine, his eyes dancing with joy.

'Rhys,' Araminta says at the same time Kalpana says: 'Theo.'

Their eyes meet.

The alarm rings.

'Good evening, contestants,' Eloise says, greeting them in solemn tones. 'I'm afraid I have to deliver the sad news that Valerie has had to step back from the competition for now to seek further medical treatment. She's all right, and wishes you the best of luck, but needs some time to rest and heal. She wanted to say that she hopes to see you all very, *very* soon.'

Kalpana: *Rhys looked so fucking smug.*

Araminta: *Kalpana spent over an hour this morning telling me how much she wanted Valerie gone. And here she is, seething about it. I'm so sick and tired of everyone but Rhys trying to manipulate me.*

'That does mean that we're having to call this challenge short. While we do still want your rankings of each other, we think we'll save it for tomorrow when we challenge you in our most exciting contest yet. Enjoy your evening – it might be your last before you're all out for blood!'

They stare as the screen flashes black. At this point, they can only assume Eloise has a sick sense of humour.

Kalpana turns to Rhys, and when she speaks her voice is dark and furious. 'I assume you're happy.'

He doesn't answer, just stands and grabs Araminta's hand to pull her with him, pausing only to snatch up his glass before they disappear.

'He's taking this ridiculously personally,' Jerome says with a shake of his head. 'I should be the one storming off – the girl I was growing to really like just got kicked off.'

'Yeah, must be hard to have your five minutes of fame vanish,' Isko says, his voice quiet but carrying, like he doesn't care one way or another if Jerome actually hears him.

'I don't need a girl to get screen time, Isko.'

'Please, this show is about them. It is about Araminta and it is about Rhys. We are all incidental. I gave up on hoping for fame or even the prize long ago. I suggest you all do the same.' Isko finishes his drink and stands to get another.

Theo and Kalpana don't really care. Kalpana doesn't need to win – she needs to salvage what she could lose, and Theo is sure he's had enough screen time to survive.

But Jerome could throttle him. Worse, that rational, analytical part of his brain recognizes that Isko's right. He hadn't thought it mattered all that much – that the people he needs to impress will gravitate toward him. And maybe it would have if the lawsuit weren't happening. He's not going to get followers like that; he needs to be so wildly successful that no one cares about his faults – a Musk-like figure who can bleed failure without his fans detecting a drop.

And that means he needs this competition to have a lasting impact – for himself, even on the periphery, to be eternal, not wiped out with the latest season. He needs a scandal, the type that will go down in history.

He just needs to figure out when and how.

And who.

Rhys leads Araminta through the house and out to the garden on the other side of the kitchen, the trees tall, dark tombs in the shadows.

He takes a long swig of whisky before he speaks. 'If I'm near Kalpana for one more fucking minute I'm going to kill her.'

'Just ignore her.' Araminta tries not to sound weary.

'Ignore her? When she's always attacking me for no good reason?'

Araminta knows it's a losing battle, so she stays quiet, just walks up to him and wraps her arms around him. After a beat he sighs and leans into her as he strokes her hair.

'You're the only thing keeping me sane here,' he says quietly.

They've spent so much time wrapped in each other today that she can still feel his hands on her, his lips trailing her skin, his leg pressing hers wide. Now, with his fingers in her hair, words whispered in her ear, she tilts her head back in surrender.

He kisses her tenderly, none of the desperation of earlier, none of the desire, just the need for something deeper. His thumb brushes the pulse jumping on her neck, and she pulls him closer.

'God, I love you,' he breathes.

'You should,' she says, smiling against him. 'I'm pretty fantastic.'

He laughs and they break apart.

And then his smile falls. He looks toward the house. Only Jerome is visible, scouring the fridge for leftovers.

'They're really getting under my skin tonight. All of them,' he says.

'Yeah,' Araminta admits. 'I've actually been feeling kind of . . . oh, never mind.'

'What?' he asks, coiling a strand of her hair around his finger.

She shrugs. 'I don't know – lonely? I feel like I can't talk to anyone here.'

Displeasure flashes across his face before it settles into concern. 'You can talk to me.'

'Of course,' she hurries. 'But the others – Isko hates me, Kalpana's a bitch, Theo is a prick and Jerome is a creep. The way they all sided with Valerie, didn't even try to –'

330

'Am I not enough?' he asks, pulling away from her.

'Of course you are,' she says, clutching at his hand, trying to draw him back. 'But we're stuck on an island with them, and the fact this dynamic is so twisted is hard.'

Rhys rolls his eyes. 'Yes, but you'll make a big deal out of anything.'

'It's not a big deal; I was just saying. Forget it, don't worry.'

Rhys sighs. 'Can you just, I don't know, be there for me without making this about yourself? You took Valerie being here so personally you didn't even stop to think about how I felt. Add to that the fact Kalpana has spent weeks tearing me apart and you're making this about you.'

'I'm not.' Araminta pushes his arm off her and steps away. 'I'm telling you I feel isolated and alone, and you're telling me I'm making a big deal out of nothing?'

'I never said that,' he growls. 'Fucking hell, Araminta. There's not enough shit going on here without you making things up?'

'I'm not making things up.' Araminta crosses her arms, but every second she spends staring at him feels a colossal struggle.

'Yes, you are. Why? Does it make you look better if you turn me into a villain?'

'I'm not saying –'

'We both know you're not exactly in the right headspace to see things as they really are.'

'What the hell is that supposed to mean?'

'You literally have an anxiety disorder. So what does this look like in your head? Poor Araminta with her cruel boyfriend who never listens to her? The whole world out to get her and none more so than me?'

Araminta shakes her head, nostrils flaring. 'You've been a real arsehole lately, you know that?'

'Incredible, you can't prove a point so you're resorting to swearing. It's not cute, Araminta, acting like a spoiled brat all the damn time.'

'I *am* a spoiled brat.' She tosses her hair over her shoulder. 'Haven't you heard?'

'Oh, go cry me a fucking river, or better yet, run off to Kalpana and cry in her arms. She'll love that. Were you even going to tell me what she said to you this morning? Yeah, don't think I didn't catch that while I was talking to Valerie, you were speaking with her. What were you doing, planning your next hook-up?'

'I don't want to be with her,' Araminta snaps. 'And I don't know how many bloody times I have to tell you that.'

'Don't you dare speak to me that way.' Everyone must be able to hear him now.

'And right now, I'm not sure I want to be with you either.' Now she's shouting too.

'Is that right?' His eyes flash and his voice falls to a deathly quiet.

She swallows. 'Maybe.'

They stare at each other, for the first time in all of this feeling like the only two people on the planet, no drones, no cameras, no microphones digging into their hips.

'I'm going to give you one chance to apologize right now.' His words are low, slicing through the close, humid air.

Isko opens the door, he and Kalpana walking out with packets of tobacco and cigarettes clutched in their hands that suggest they weren't planning on being in frame

332

right now, and from the way they look at Rhys and Araminta, it's clear they weren't expecting them to be out here either.

'Arguing again? You two need to chill out,' Isko says.

'Go,' Rhys says, barking at him. They don't have to be told twice.

He watches them leave, and Araminta can feel every step they take even if she can't see it, something in her tightening with every inch away from her they get. Rhys turns to her, anger twisting still but something colder too, something cruel.

'I'm waiting,' he snarls.

Araminta fights it, that desperate urge to appease him. A tear escapes from the corner of her eye, and she rubs it away before he can use it against her.

He sees it anyway and laughs. 'You're fucking pathetic. You know why you're not going to break up with me? Because no one else on this island can stand you. If you didn't have me, you'd have no one.'

She risks a glance over her shoulder and sees that Kalpana and Isko have stilled on their walk, have turned to watch them.

Rhys watches her.

'What?' His anger swarms back and there's no room for her out here, where his fury takes up all the space. 'Why don't you run after her then?'

'I'm sorry,' she says quietly, and she'd like to shrink into herself, to disappear, but still there is relief at saying the words, at finally having them out there. 'But I can't do this right now.'

'What the hell does that mean? You –' She is turning,

moving away. The glass is in his hand and then it is not; it is smashing against the wall.

Araminta screams and jumps, drops of his whisky clinging on her skin.

'Don't fucking walk away from me when I'm talking to you!'

Araminta stares at him, just stares and stares, and he is looking at her, chest heaving.

Kalpana practically tackles into her. 'Are you okay?' she asks, glaring at Rhys like it's taking all she has not to kill him right now, not to grab one of those shards and tear into him. Araminta's skin is icy, and Kalpana doesn't know what she's expecting – Araminta to lean against her for support or to push her away in disgust, but she doesn't even flinch, might not even know she's being held.

'It was only a fucking drink,' Rhys growls.

'Don't talk to me again,' Araminta says. She wants it to sound strong, inflexible, stable at last. It's sturdy like glass – cold and capable but threatening to shatter at any minute. 'Don't touch me. Don't even look at me. Get your things out of my room and leave me alone – we're done here.'

She shakes Kalpana off too, and this time when she turns, no one stops her.

Rhys practically runs and Isko follows him. When Rhys reaches the beach, he sinks to his knees in the sand, and Isko hovers behind him.

'You're an idiot,' he says coldly, simply.

'I know,' Rhys exhales, staring out at the ocean. After a moment, he speaks again: 'Do you think I've destroyed my chances?'

Isko considers. 'No, I'm sure she'll take you back once she calms down.'

'That's not what I – never mind.' Rhys stands and turns to face him. He seems . . . Isko isn't even sure. Whatever this expression is, it's not one he's seen before. 'What do I do now?'

'Damage control, you mean?'

'I can't believe she did that,' Rhys says, and it's almost like Isko isn't here, like he's talking to himself, but he's staring at him so intently the entire time.

'What, broke up with you? Are we really going to talk about what she did and not what *you* did? What on earth were you thinking?'

'I wasn't,' he says, rising to his feet.

'Well, I'm not sure if that makes it better or worse.'

'It was a theatrical moment. You know how we all get swept up in feeling.'

'No.'

'Well, I do, Isko.' Rhys takes a step closer. 'Everything always – a performance of emotions but it's not faking it, it's recalling it – you feign crying by thinking of something sad, elation the same, every emotion a memory. Sometimes, I just get swallowed whole by a feeling and it's so intense, and this time it was anger.'

Isko stares at him.

Isko: *I know how it sounds, but . . . well, it's true. That is what he's like – a thousand emotions all at once, and it's a lot, but it's intoxicating. He draws you into it.*

'You don't throw glasses at girls –'

'I didn't throw it at her; I threw it at the wall. Christ, is that what everyone's going to think? That I tried to hurt

335

her? I was angry. I wanted the glass to smash for god's sake, that's all.'

Isko arches an eyebrow. 'Well, I know that – I saw what happened – but don't smash things when there's a camera on you, regardless of the depth of your emotions.'

'Fuck the cameras, fuck all of this,' Rhys says. 'I didn't date her for the cameras, and we didn't break up for them either. I feel the way I feel and I'm so fucking sick of considering an observer.'

'And us?' Isko can't help but bring himself to ask. 'I'm comforting you, Rhys, and how many times have you screwed me over in the name of an observer.'

Rhys stills and the calmness makes every second slow, like they're both lingering in this moment. 'I'm not sorry.'

'I know.'

'But I'd like to know you without concern for an audience,' Rhys says, and this time when Rhys looks at him, he feels more like he is being seen. He feels, possibly, like no one has ever seen him until now. Rhys looks at him like he's the answer.

'Without the game?' Isko asks.

Rhys swallows and Isko watches as his throat lifts and falls. There's something about him, something that goes far beyond attraction. Something Isko is almost afraid of.

'Without the game,' Rhys confirms, voice quiet, breathy.

Isko: *I didn't even consider it. It wasn't a decision. It was just instant.*

Isko grasps Rhys's T-shirt and pulls him closer.

Rhys collides with him like it is the last thing he will ever do.

336

Which it isn't — he has another twenty-two hours of life left.

@HenryHarrett

Me, every time Rhys does anything: huh, I wonder if this will be
the final straw

AHX: this is fine

Like what's it going to take for them to intervene? He's a
gaslighting, manipulative, ABUSIVE arsehole and it's
disgraceful that he still has a platform on the show.
Petition below — sign and share! #Iconic

@ZoeTheWriter

Hey it's actually possible to feel sorry for Araminta and
ecstatic at Rhysko being canon again at the same
time. #Iconic

@QuinnSimmons

⚠ PS A ⚠ The editing on that episode was REALLY
misleading. Rhys was telling the truth, look at the footage
on website! He didn't throw that glass anywhere near
Araminta. It was an expression of anger, not a threat!!!
#Iconic

> **@ElMarsha**
>
> @QuinnSimmons you know that's not the point,
> right? Every time a man is violent even if not in
> direct violation of you it's a threat — every time a
> man punches a wall in anger or yes, throws a
> glass, it's a way of saying look at what I could do
> to you

The press has stopped calling them *witnesses* or *suspects* and started calling them *the survivors*. Worse, they surround the precinct, making it impossible to get them out, to let them go. Now that AHX has heard Isko has been released, that the charge fell through as soon as it was made, they're furious – emails stream through that say the contestants were expected at the hotel an hour ago, that between the accommodation and the lawyers they've spent enough funding their case, that there is a line that has been crossed when it comes to their 'good will.' It all ends with a thank you for the free publicity.

The suspects don't talk as they wait in the foyer. They don't even meet each other's eyes. Jerome reads the posters, Theo draws up his hood to block them all out, Kalpana chews on a mint, and Alex, rushing through the doors after a series of interconnected flights, throws his arms around Isko and doesn't let go.

They've been kept separate even at their hotel, police outside every door. The sight of them together now is almost anticlimactic.

And then all at once, they're gone.

In the break room, Maes finds Cloutier and Kennard packing up their belongings.

'I'm sorry we couldn't solve it.' She doesn't need to say more. They've lost enough without her berating them further.

Kennard nods. 'Thank you.'

Her phone buzzes – a notification, set to pull her away from work so she could enjoy that nightly episode with her daughters. *Iconic, five minutes.*

'Well,' she says, 'do you want to?'

Kennard takes a shaky breath. 'Yeah, might as well see this through.'

They pull kitchen chairs around the small, boxy TV. Cloutier takes Kennard's hand. Kennard rests his head on the other man's shoulder.

And like millions of other people around the world, they wait for the final episode to begin.

The contestants go to their hotel rooms and seal themselves off from the world and from each other. They haven't said a word to one another since they left that island.

And they have an episode to watch.

Araminta makes it fifteen minutes before she abandons the screen. It's a cement block of a hotel, near the airport, a whole floor secured for them so they won't encounter the public, security at the doors to the stairs. She can't go down so she goes up, a brick kicked against the door to the roof, and suddenly it's a perfectly good smoking area.

She lights her cigarette while leaning so far over the railings she's not sure falling would even be a choice; it's simply up to fate. She watches the lights of homes in the distance and wonders how many people are watching her right now, not the version of her smoking on a rooftop but the version she was there, the version she will always be to the people who will forever wonder if maybe there was something more to Rhys's death.

Isko doesn't see her until it's too late to turn around and pretend he wasn't there. She looks up, meets his eyes, and neither says a word as he heads to a different spot on the roof. He sits on a vent and flicks the lighter.

They smoke in silence, marvelling at how it still feels like they're on that island – all this humid air, the scorching metal beneath their fingers.

'So did you do it?' Isko asks after fifteen minutes, so quietly he doesn't expect Araminta to hear.

But she does, and to both their surprise, she laughs. 'No,' she says, still not turning to him, still staring off at the planes taking flight in the distance, at the cars whizzing past below. 'I wish I did it.'

Isko exhales sharply. It's exactly the answer he should have expected, but it catches him off guard nonetheless.

Jerome arrives then, nodding awkwardly and skirting to the side. Araminta should go back inside, back to her hotel room. But she doesn't want to. So she lights another, just for the excuse.

Jerome takes his time. He has to roll his first, and he thinks of how many he rolled on that island, in that little box of a smoking area.

Theo nearly turns around when he sees the others out there – seeing them gathered makes him think of a beach and desperation.

But he can't bear the hotel room either, so he steps out onto the roof thinking that he hopes he never sees them again and also wondering whether there will be a reunion show.

Kalpana joins soon after.

'So none of us could take it then?' she asks but no one answers. She takes the remaining corner, doesn't even want to look at the others, keeps her head down.

She'd thought it was over, had clung to that relief as she left the station. But then she switched on the TV and realized it will never be over – this will always mark her, she'll always be a suspect, and if the police don't reopen the case one day, the public will put them all on trial in other ways.

The thought has her struggling with her lighter, and her fumbling fingers send it flying. If she squints, she can see the green dot on the ground below.

'Fuck,' she says. The others look up, can only guess what happened.

'Here.' Isko tosses his and she just manages to catch it, brings the flame to the edge of her cigarette before going to throw it back.

'Keep it; Alex will have one. Besides, hopefully that's my screen time over with,' he says, heading back inside before anyone can say anything else.

Kalpana's eyes trace the horizon, so much further than she could see on the island, where blue just merged with more blue. But her eyes are drawn back to that dot of green on the ground again.

It's an awfully long way to fall.

Iconic

The Finale

The scene opens on blurry, black-and-white footage of two figures – one moment pressed against a wall, lips together, hands clutching at whatever they can grasp, and then something moving beneath a sheet.

Chilling, eerie music plays – after all, everyone watching knows how this ends.

The *Iconic* logo appears.

It starts raining at midnight. By four, the lighter sleepers give up. There are several hours during which they toss and turn and contemplate rising, but they manage to do it together. In the hallway between their rooms, Isko collides with Araminta.

He has hastily thrown an unbuttoned shirt on, and his hair is dishevelled as he emerges from Rhys's room. Araminta's eyes are red, her skin pallid. She stares at him like he's crushed her.

'Araminta,' he says softly, but she's already running down the stairs. He hesitates, just for a moment, contemplating letting her go. Then he runs after her.

He doesn't know why he follows her other than to prove that he can, that he isn't scared of her. He had sex with her ex-boyfriend just a few hours ago. He could run in the opposite direction, but he doesn't; he follows her.

She stops in the kitchen, staring outside at the haze of

rain, and he wonders if she will run out into it. It seems exactly the sort of thing she would do, to insist on more drama, always more drama, the perfect shot.

But she turns.

'Isko,' she says, nodding like nothing is wrong. 'Good morning.'

'Good morning,' he says.

She watches him, waiting.

He goes to speak but can't think of anything to say. He doesn't want to apologize; he's done nothing wrong. But he can't bring himself to ask if she's okay, because what if she's not?

'Well?' he demands.

'Well, what?'

'Say something. I can't stand this silence.'

She looked on the verge of falling apart but now she stands straighter. He has shocked her out of it, and now her outrage contorts and her lips twist and she folds her arms across her chest. 'All right, how was it?'

He rolls his eyes. 'Oh, for fuck's sake.'

'Okay, how many times was it? Do you need me to find out what he thought again? Oh, should we maybe exchange contact details, you know, just so we can compare STI tests when we get home?'

'You're ridiculous,' Isko says.

'Well, what did you want me to say, Isko?' she asks, feigning shock. 'What exactly were you hoping for here?'

'I thought you were better than all this cattiness.'

'Well, I'm not.'

'You took him from me first, you know.'

'Seriously? You're *engaged*!'

344

'I'm just saying you don't get to be annoyed at me for sleeping with someone you slept with when you did the same thing.'

'You slept with the man I love so that he could avenge himself. Presumably mere minutes after we broke up.' Her eyes run over him, a quick look up and down, the perfect disgusted sneer.

Araminta: *They literally hooked up when we were together! I'm not angry with Isko, but I'm not going to pretend he's not twisting the knife Rhys stabbed me with.*

'You didn't break up because of me.'

'No, I broke up because of him. But if you're looking for my blessing then you're not going to find it here.'

'I slept with him because I wanted to,' Isko says. 'I just . . . wanted to be clear it wasn't about you. I didn't do it to spite you.'

'No, that was all him.'

Isko laughs. 'Well, not just that. I'm sure I hold some appeal. I don't think us having sex is wholly about his revenge fantasy.'

Araminta just stares at him for a moment. And then the worst thing happens: he sees pity. 'Oh, darling,' she says, 'you know better than that.'

She struts from the room without another glance.

He watches her leave, trying to ignore that voice in his head saying *she's right.*

Araminta: *I . . . I don't even think it's just the heartbreak. It's that I'm heartbroken* again. *And to realize the truth of all the things that I spent so long denying and fighting against, because of course that couldn't be true, because that would never happen to a girl*

345

like me. Because I'd know better. God, I think maybe he really did intentionally hurt Valerie too . . .

Tears still run down her face when she leaves the confession booth and runs right into Rhys.

She squeezes past him, brushing against the wine bottles, racing toward the stairs with her head bowed low. Even down here she can hear the wind howling outside, and right now she wishes she were out in it.

'Wait,' Rhys calls.

'No!' she screams, slowing her steps, turning to him, waving her arms like they can force distance between them.

She is not crying but sobbing – messy, choking wails that shake her whole body.

'Araminta,' Rhys says softly, holding out his hands like he is surrendering.

She supposes this is it, what she has avoided for so long, breaking down in public. Her suffering projected to a nation.

And here he is to witness it.

'Are you happy now?' she demands. 'Is this what you wanted to see?'

'No,' he says quickly, the word catching like the mere thought that this is something he wanted hurts him.

She laughs like a wounded animal. 'If this isn't it, then what is? You tore and you tore and you tore, for what?'

'I didn't mean to hurt you,' he says.

'Which part? The entirety of our relationship? The glass? Isko?' she asks, letting the tears flow freely now, but they are at least just tears; the full wracking sobs have dissipated.

Rhys shuts his eyes like a man trying to get his story straight. 'I'm not saying I didn't hurt you. I did. I know I did. I'm just deeply sorry about it.'

'Great. Can you leave me alone now?'

He nods. 'If you want, I just . . . are you okay?'

'No.'

'And I don't suppose there's anything I can do to make that better.'

'No.'

He sighs. 'I can't help, I know that. I caused this, but . . . Araminta, don't be upset because of a man like me. I'm not worth it – especially not to someone like you. Someone who can do so much, who will be so much regardless of me.'

Her jaw tightens. His compliments have a way of slicing her when she isn't looking.

'I'm sorry,' he says. His hand brushes her shoulder.

When did he come so close?

Using his words to creep nearer. That shouldn't surprise her at this point.

'You were the best thing that ever happened to me. And I'm sorry I let you down. For what it's worth, I still love you. I think part of me always will.'

She flinches away from the words. Suddenly, she sees what he's doing – the way he's using her, has used her from the start. Maybe he loves her too, in whatever way he can, whatever it means to him: some corrupted, twisted thing that wants to possess her, to use her talent to bolster his own, to take her reputation and use it to elevate his.

He wants her back to win this game.

Part of her wants to laugh. Part of her, something deeper than her heart, breaks.

The door at the top of the stairs opens, the other contestants appearing.

'We heard shouting,' Theo says, watching Araminta closely.

Theo: *Kalpana told me what happened last night and I swear I could have murdered him. I can't believe he threw a glass at her. But she said Araminta wouldn't want me fighting on her behalf. Right now, I'm not so sure that matters — someone needs to clock Sutton, and I'm more than happy to take one for the team.*

'It's nothing,' Rhys says, watching her too.

Isko: *We had sex a few hours ago and now he's not even looking at me. If I had any lingering doubt that he had sex with me to use me, either as a distraction or as revenge, that's vanished. [Pause] Maybe I'm mostly angry at myself for letting myself be used.*

'I'd rather she told us that,' Isko snaps.

'Araminta,' Kalpana says stiffly. 'Come join us.'

Araminta swallows, risks a glance at Rhys, who nods and steps back, and she hates it, hates that she still feels like she needs his permission.

She runs past them all, Kalpana following her quickly, the others still staring at Rhys like they don't know what to do with him.

Jerome: *I overheard Kalpana telling Theo last night. It's horrendous.*

He does not actually think it is. It was a broken glass, and they're all acting like it was Rhys's fist and her jaw.

But Jerome knows he needs a scandal if he wants this show to become legendary.

And now it's obvious Rhys needs to be at the centre of it.

Kalpana goes with Araminta to her room. Outside, the rain has become desperate, demanding, and all encompassing. It's the kind of rain that hammers on the windows

348

like it's trying to break through, the sort of wind that rips up trees and blows from no one direction but from all around.

She expects Araminta to sob harder away from the others, but she catches her breath as she crosses the threshold and swallows the tears. She throws herself heavily down before her mirror and grabs a makeup wipe, ready to clean up the mess, like she could erase the pain just as easily.

Kalpana doesn't know what to do. She feels like she's intruding, but how could she be when this is being broadcast.

'I heard what he said last night,' she says after a long moment of silence. 'About how you have no one. That's not true.'

'Isn't it?'

'I'm here, aren't I?'

Araminta watches her, like she's searching for something, and Kalpana doesn't know what reassurance to give – a smile, a steady gaze, a nod. So she does nothing until Araminta looks back to her mirror.

'We didn't speak for days. And yesterday when you approached me . . . you were using me, right? Saying you wanted Valerie off the island.'

'No, no, I wasn't using you,' Kalpana rushes, and she perches herself on the edge of Araminta's bed, wondering if she'll be asked not to sit there again. 'But I admit I was lying. I wanted you to go home.'

'Me?'

'Yes.' She doesn't even attempt to sound apologetic, her voice as righteous and just as ever. 'I didn't see a world

349

where you realized what Rhys was doing while you were both still on this island. I thought you needed to escape him. Get some distance and gain some perspective.'

'He's the one who should leave this island,' Araminta snaps. 'Not me.'

'Well, this was before we knew his danger was a physical kind. I can't believe he's still here.'

Kalpana: *Seriously, what does he have to do to get kicked off the show? And Araminta . . . do you know when a woman in an abusive relationship is most at risk? When she tries to leave him.*

'Did you think he would accept his loss and walk away?'

'He threw a glass at you.'

'I mean, not quite; he threw a glass near me.'

Kalpana: *You could have licked the whisky off her. I'd say that's pretty damn near.*

'Then why did you break up with him?' Kalpana asks.

Araminta glares at her but she doesn't drop her gaze. She needs to know: needs to know what support Araminta needs, needs to know what she's dealing with – what the situation is.

'I broke up with him because I was scared,' she says at last, voice steadfast but cold. She reaches for her make-up bag so she can become polished once more. 'Several times during that argument, actually, I was scared. I didn't realize until the glass shattered. And I simply shouldn't feel fear in a relationship with anyone, no matter how bad the argument.'

Kalpana nods. 'Right, you shouldn't. And no one should be stuck on an island with someone they're afraid of. They can't –'

The moment the liner touches her lid Araminta flinches,

drawing a line across her face, and she throws it from her hand, swearing incessantly. 'Fuck, fuck, fuck.'

'What?' Kalpana is up. Does she have a black eye? Or is it something else, is everything she's holding back about to come spilling forth courtesy of a makeup error?

'I don't even like that eyeliner.' Araminta waves her hand at it, her movements shaky and theatrical, tears already brimming over again. '*He* likes that eyeliner. You know it took me ten minutes just to pick an outfit this morning? I couldn't look at a dress without seeing his reaction to it.'

Kalpana: *I came up here to check she was okay, but I don't think I was actually prepared for her not to be. I'm not exactly someone you go to for comfort.*

It seems to do more for Araminta than the glass did, realizing the depths of his infiltration.

As their eyes meet in the mirror, Araminta's reddening once more, Kalpana sees her opportunity.

She wants to launch into a speech about how she can do so much better, about men in general. To use Araminta as a launch pad for something greater – something that can resonate. Kalpana could be a voice for downtrodden women everywhere.

They'll remember her for this, not her gilded upbringing. All those other movements will pale in comparison.

But actions speak louder than words.

'If AHX won't kick him off the island, maybe we can,' Kalpana proposes.

'How?' Araminta asks, tossing the eyeliner in the trash.

'Ice him out, make him want to leave. Or give the show an ultimatum – all of us or him. Maybe someone knows something too. I'll speak to Theo. I'm sure even three of us taking a stand would be enough. Imagine, a protest on the very show itself.'

Araminta's enthusiasm pales. After so long spent evading the way everyone was using her, she seems to be seeing it everywhere.

But she nods and Kalpana rises to her feet, excited in a way Araminta has never seen in her. She's practically bubbly. And when she leaves to speak to Theo, Araminta stays, staring at her reflection in the mirror and the eyeliner streak cutting across her face, trying to reconcile all that she is with the image before her.

She sees evidence of Rhys, reflected in the mirror.

He never collected his things. If she looks up she can see his towel, his deodorant, his medication, his clothes, and even a pair of underwear screwed up on the floor.

She wants him gone.

It's only another week, but that suddenly seems insurmountable, such a long stretch of time. Is her relationship with Rhys not testament to how much can happen in a place like this in so few days?

Kalpana's protest will take time. AHX will probably spin a distraction – a challenge or a secret that will shift their course, dissolve their solidarity, and by then she might cave again, because she knows how close she came this morning, how sweet his apology sounded . . .

And didn't Rhys himself show her just how to get rid of someone on this island?

An accident. An injury.

She rises to her feet and steps over to her bed, to where so many of his belongings are scattered, and starts throwing them together, so he can come grab them and leave without lingering long.

She tosses a sweater onto the pile and it slips off, taking his deodorant and medication with it.

She falls to her knees to gather it up.

When she replaces the pills, no camera can see that his antidepressants are now further under the bed, her aspirin in its place, though many people will realize in years to come that the boy who said he was allergic to aspirin should not have had any in his system at the autopsy.

One allergic reaction – that's all she needs, and they'll send a ship. She doesn't know how allergic he is. She doesn't know what his reaction might be. She hopes it's unsightly and painful. She hopes he leaves here in agony.

Hell, she hopes he might leave here in a body bag.

No one treats a Yaxley-Carter like this.

She makes sure the orange jar is right at the top of the pile, like he might walk in and immediately realize he hasn't taken his meds today.

'Et in Arcadia ego,' she mutters.

Because if that doesn't work, there are plenty more ways to try.

She might never stop thinking of ways to hurt him.

While Araminta and Kalpana talk, the others brave the smoking area. It's sheltered, but as soon as they step outside, they realize the short walk has become a dangerous one, the wind howling, grass slippery, and even though it's mere yards away, it is a journey deserving of its own epic.

Audio from the smoking area rarely makes it into the edited episode, but this time it does, even though it's bland, to imply with that cold black screen and crackling audio that there are aspects of this island we do not fully know.

Theo hovers at the entrance, craning his neck toward the horizon.

'I can't see far enough to say. It's all mist. I can hardly tell what's rain and what's ocean.'

'They have to be gone,' Jerome says. 'There's no way a boat could be on that ocean right now. Especially not one that's part of something like this. AHX would be sued for putting employees at risk.'

'So we truly are alone for the first time in all of this and trapped on this island together? Fuck, with this rain, trapped in the house?' Isko asks.

'I guess so,' Theo says. 'Right. I'm going back. I'm too bloody freezing.'

They are all drenched from their run – the rain so cold it lashes where it strikes. But they'll be back repeatedly, to escape the house, for a moment of peace.

'Me too,' Isko says.

'Yeah, I'll come,' Rhys adds.

He has said nothing the whole time they have been out there, just drawing smoke into his lungs and staring at the heavy rain. At first, Jerome thinks he's forgotten there is no camera on them. But then he thinks it is simply that Rhys is performing foremost for them.

The clip ends with the three racing back to the house.

But Jerome stays, claiming he wants another.

The moment they leave, he withdraws the little sachet of coke from the lining of his pocket and taps out a thin stripe that he swiftly leans down to inhale.

As he pulls his head back, he clocks a battered pack of

cigarettes in the corner, right where Rhys was sitting. Even if he hadn't been there, Jerome would know they were his. A singular pack, all hand-rolled but prepared in advance. Jerome frequents this place the most, and by now he knows Araminta and Theo smoke manufactured cigarettes that come in cartons, Kalpana uses menthol papers, and Isko takes care rolling each one before he drags it to his lips.

At first Jerome ignores it and smokes two cigarettes while he thinks. Nothing to pick up on the mic, just him despairing over his forgetability, his inevitable erasure from the public consciousness.

The issue isn't just him; it's the show.

He's spent too much time on this island wrapped up in drama with Kalpana, and he has so much more to think of – the empire he's trying to build, the investors he'll have to sweet-talk if, and only *if,* Soltek goes under.

He needs something that will simultaneously distract and focus – draw them away from the problem and give them something to care about even more. Throwing a glass at Araminta on TV, that's great. But it's not enough. He needs something no one will forget, something that will make this show legendary.

The cameras don't show Jerome pouring yet another line of white powder onto the bench, don't see him snort it up or the way his eyes catch on those cigarettes as he does.

Oh, perfect.

He could wait, of course. He's sure the others will do something ridiculous and noteworthy soon.

But why do that when he can control the narrative. In

fact, he's pretty fucking sick of letting AHX take the reins. He's the genius here. Time to give them a show they'll be thanking him on bended knee for.

And no reporter will ask him about his legal woes if they're too interested in what it was really like on the island with someone as unhinged as Rhys.

Sorry Rhys, you don't deserve this, but you do what you've gotta do.

It takes nearly twenty minutes that are laden with constant twitching glances toward the entrance, his heart hammering with every second he spends there, none of it helped by the cocaine racing through his veins.

But he leaves the cigarettes exactly where he found them, each one replaced with his own, not only lined with the coke but mixed into the tobacco itself. He's just spent a small fortune.

But it's done.

'I had no idea he had a problem. I was his best friend on that island and I didn't know he was struggling with addiction.' He can see himself now, chatting on a morning television show.

He could develop something too, leverage it – augmented reality treatment or AI therapists, *inspired by, to raise awareness of . . .*

He'll get everything he's ever wanted.

And the cameras will never know.

The contestants sit in the living room, clutching mugs of coffee in their cold hands. They can't work out where the heating for the house is, if such a thing even exists, and the bedrooms are too cold for Araminta to hide in for long, so they're all forced together by necessity. The rain drums on the windows, echoing through the house, and the whole thing feels fragile suddenly, like it could collapse under nature's fury.

Soon, nearly everyone is drinking, which helps, because no one is talking.

Araminta: *Imagine that agonizing, can't-catch-your-breath, can't-think-straight pain of a break-up where you're convinced deep in your gut that you've made a terrible mistake. And all that time he's right there, watching you, practically begging for another chance. Of course I started drinking.*

Jerome doesn't, though once again he pretends. And Rhys only manages a few sips before he goes out for a cigarette, and afterward, the whole world feels slanted. He doesn't touch his drink, just clutches at the arms of his chair like they might steady him.

Kalpana heads to the kitchen to speak to Theo, and it doesn't take her long to convince him to take a stand against Rhys. He would have been ready to do that from the first day.

But like Araminta, he doesn't think a quiet protest will be enough to get rid of him.

Theo: *Rhys is conniving. And manipulative. And worst of all, clever. I think the only way to get rid of him is to surprise him, to bring in something he couldn't possibly plan for.*

And he keeps thinking about those boxes in the basement – the preparation for future challenges and the tools of their former tasks.

He doesn't know what he's hoping for – a camera or recording device maybe, to let Rhys think he's out of range or in a blind spot and catch him saying something he shouldn't, or a phone that could access the internet so they can confront him with something that will push him over the edge, let him show his true colours once and for all. Jerome could access the internet, of course, but Theo doesn't know that, and even if he did, he doubts Jerome would use that power against Rhys. They're too close. Even Valerie couldn't successfully come between them.

So when he goes back into that ice-cold room with those solemn, silent people, it's an easy thing to suggest.

'God, we need to liven this up. There's a guitar downstairs, right?' He'd had to put it back in the box after their task swap challenge was complete. 'Jerome, do you think you can open them? There might be other things too that could make this more fun.'

Jerome's eyebrows shoot up. 'Really?'

He cannot believe what Theo is daring to ask – and under any other circumstances, he'd say no, absolutely not.

But today it's perfect. Rhys is jumpy, his fingers tapping on the chair, and he's only smoked a single cigarette – Jerome needs to amp this up. As he sits in a chair, saying nothing, people might not realize he's on something. He needs a show, an opportunity, a party for Rhys to smoke more, say more, make himself undeniably the star of the show.

And if, in the process, Jerome can prove that he can code well too, that he is not some charismatic schmoozer who swindled his computer scientist co-founder out of millions but an educated innovator in his own right, then all the better.

'Yeah, come on, it'll be worth it, right?'

Jerome heads to the confession booth and slides the panels back to bring out what he needs.

The boxes are just outside, ten of them for various

different challenges and rewards. Each one is digitally locked and remotely signalled to open or close. It's easy – they're hardly high-tech pieces of kit.

But AHX must have learned from their mistakes last time – the walls are tighter to get past, the access limited.

Worse, they're actively fighting back.

This is ridiculous – they can't have hired a hacker. This must just be a bog-standard IT technician on the other end of their computer, trying to stop him.

So they know, which means there will be consequences, but fuck it, he was never going to win this competition anyway, and taking down the defences of a company as big as AHX will do more for his investment potential than half a million dollars ever could.

He shuts them out. Completely.

Oh, the cameras are still streaming, mics still pushing their voices across oceans; everything is still feeding out of this island. But nothing is coming in.

And past that – he finds more than he was ever looking for.

It's ridiculous, not hidden at all, just in an easy little tab on a browser: *history*.

Oh, this is perfect. This is better than he could have hoped for. Why take one of them down when he can have a scandal that ricochets?

So he sets up a code, the simplest he could manage, the thing everyone learns: *If. Then.*

If Eloise appears on the screens.

Then reveal it all.

It's a little more complicated than that – full of ways that AHX might try to push the stream through to the

TVs, their access routes, how they connect themselves to all these remote devices. But the gist is that tonight's challenge is his to set.

He feels like god. He needs to snort less coke.

And before he can forget, he taps a few buttons and every box springs open.

They haul the boxes upstairs and spread them out. Some offer tantalizing suggestions of fun to their bored minds: jump ropes, pads of paper, paints – even a karaoke machine. But none offer the solution Theo is looking for – not unless they want to tie him up with the rope and take the hammer they once nailed secrets with to his skull.

It's clear Kalpana and Araminta wouldn't necessarily rule that out.

They rush to the smoking area together, discussing strategy. When Eloise appears, they decide. That's when they'll make their stand – declare that they won't be participating anymore unless Rhys is removed.

Araminta: *I'm not sure if they were just humouring me. But yeah, having Kalpana and Theo really helped.*

'I wish we could get one more person,' Kalpana says. 'So it's a clear majority. Are you sure Isko wouldn't?'

'He slept with Rhys this morning,' Araminta snaps.

'Oh, yeah.'

Araminta: *But then again, I'm not really sure they were there for me at all.*

No one much feels like karaoke, and Theo's efforts on the guitar are lukewarm. They alternate between drinking and smoking cigarettes and sneaking away to swallow pills or snort lines. Any conversation is clipped and tense and silenced altogether by their efforts to spend the day numb.

When the rain finally lets up, they take their haul outside, like they can reset the energy and maybe find something in those boxes that interest them after all.

It's still overcast, still grey. It's hard to tell how much time has passed.

But when the light darkens and there's no glint of sun on the horizon, it's difficult to believe something isn't wrong.

'Do you think the storm cut out communications?' Kalpana asks, staring at that TV where Eloise should have appeared by now.

'Didn't she promise a big challenge tonight?'

'Do you think anything is working?' Jerome asks. 'You know, are the cameras still feeding out?'

'I don't see how we'd ever know,' Theo says.

They fall silent, the idea that they might be alone having never occurred to them. If they're not even being watched, what do they do? Who do they become?

'Shots?' Isko proposes.

Shots, they agree, and it's only when they tap their glasses together, even Rhys, long past the point of caring about the erratic way he feels because it feels good too, that the alarm blares.

Jerome: *Finally fixed it, eh?*

Rhys is so startled he drops his shot glass before it can reach his lips, and Araminta jolts back at the sound of it shattering.

'Hello, contestants – sorry about that, we had an issue with the –'

Eloise cuts off, the screen momentarily black – and then filled with . . . they squint – what is that? A screenshot of a web browser. A long list of search terms. And it doesn't make sense until Araminta gasps: 'The date!'

RiotParade party
RiotParade photos
RiotParade underage

Theo's search history from the honesty challenge. Where he'd won access to the internet and done the most cursory of searches to check whether the news had broken.

'You knew,' Kalpana says quietly. Ironic that, after all of these challenges and heartbreaks, this is her first betrayal.

'Is that why you came on here, Newman?' Isko says, his grin growing wider with every second. 'Distance yourself from the band so that when the news broke, you wouldn't go down for their mistakes?'

'That's low,' Rhys says before hysterically laughing, and it's that laughter, that careening cackle that strikes right at Theo's heart. It's Rhys thinking that Theo is lower down even than he, that he is something to laugh at.

'You know what, Sutton, you smashed the wrong fucking glass.'

That hammer is in his hand, and then it is swinging into the screen.

Shards spray outward, and contestants shriek as they race to shield themselves.

But Rhys laughs harder. 'Yes, Newman! Come on, you can do better than that!' He grabs the hammer from Theo's hand and hurls it at the nearest camera. The metal screeches and the falling camera smashes to the ground, louder than the thunder still crashing on the horizon.

Around them, the lights flicker. Then everything goes dark.

'Rhys!' Araminta calls, almost instinctively, into the pitch-black night.

A second later and the whir of a generator can be heard, the lanterns flickering back on, dimmer than they were but enough to see by. The light dances in the reflections of the broken glass.

Rhys rushes to Araminta's side, where she has crouched and covered her skin from the spraying shards.

'Are you all right? What's wrong? Are you hurt?'

Araminta stares at him, lips fumbling for words she doesn't know how to say.

'Araminta,' he says, reaching his hand out. Hesitantly she takes it and rises back to her feet. Rhys seems to take this as permission to speak, and as erratically as his frenzy appeared, it vanishes. 'Araminta, I don't really know what to say. I know I messed up, I know I'm hard to love, but god, please, I couldn't live with myself if you believed for one moment I didn't love you as much as I do. To be honest, I'll struggle to live with myself without you anyway, but I need you to know: I love you. You're all that I've ever wanted. You're incredible, you're iconic. You deserve everything.'

His words are fierce and slurring; he's leaning ever closer. Everything he ever was is made clumsy and crystal clear.

But it doesn't stop the fear in Araminta's chest.

She should have shoved him in the dark, thrown him onto those glass shards and hoped it hurt like hell.

Why didn't she think to do that?

'That's enough,' Isko says, stepping closer, placing his hand on Rhys's shoulder. 'You've made your point.'

'I can't do this,' Araminta says, stepping back – then turning and bolting.

Araminta: *I'm packing. Send a boat. Send the quickest one you have because I'm getting out of here. I quit.*

Kalpana hesitates a moment, glancing between Isko and Rhys, then swears and goes chasing after her.

Rhys laughs, though there's something sour about it. Isko doesn't know what sort of performance Rhys is aiming for, but he's sick of it already. 'Enough of what, Isko – just jealous I'm flattering her instead of you?'

'I don't need your fucking love bombing, and neither does she.'

Rhys grabs him as he goes to move past him, sloppily pulling at his arm.

'How drunk are you?' Isko hisses, pulling free of his grip. 'You know, you nearly had me fooled. That the glass was an accident, but it wasn't, was it. You –'

'Stop, stop,' Rhys says, shushing him. He even puts his finger over Isko's lips, and Isko could kill him.

Isko shoves him off, hard.

'Isko.' Theo takes a hesitant step forward, hands raised to either side like he might have to intervene.

Rhys's face falls, his nostrils flaring, and this, this must have been what Araminta saw. He staggers forward, straightening up to his full height.

'You're an idiot, Isko,' Rhys shouts. 'That's what you're angry about. You don't hate me for playing the game; you're angry at yourself because you thought I wasn't.' He punctuates his words with sharp taps to Isko's chest.

'Rhys!' Theo shouts, taking another step forward but not sure how to help. Jerome just watches, sipping his drink and unable to stop a grin from slipping onto his face.

'Don't try to physically intimidate me, Rhys,' Isko says, struggling to stay calm. This is all too familiar. He has never been in a fight before, but he's been here, at its precipice. He's just always managed to stop the situation from escalating.

'And if I do? You're pathetic. What are you going to do about it?' Rhys asks, giving his shoulder another shove. 'Glare from a corner? Go crying off to Alex? Your dodgy little account —'

Isko hits him. He's not sure he even decided to. His hand just reaches out and strikes his chest.

Rhys laughs and that grin falls back into place. 'Oh, you do fight back. Tired of being walked all over? Some people are just meant to be used, Isko.'

And this time he does decide to, because there's nothing he can say right now that will feel better than his hand colliding with Rhys's face.

Isko flinches as sharp pain lances up his arm from the fist he didn't know how to curl.

Rhys's head cracks to the side, and Isko isn't even sure he's hurt him because this is all so theatrical.

But then Rhys turns and his eyebrow is slit, caught on Isko's engagement ring, and even in the dim torchlight, Isko can see the crooked tilt of his nose, the blood trickling in a thick swell, and the bruise blossoming beneath his eye. It'll be black within the hour.

Rhys's pupils are huge, staring at him in shock.

Isko gasps, pulls his hands to his mouth. He can't believe he did that. Nor can Theo or Jerome, stunned into silence.

Rhys touches his face, pulls his fingers away, sticky with blood that he stares at with amazement. There's not a lot of it, but it's enough.

He looks up at him and grins. Why does he always smile? Is it just to unnerve them all? Or is it simply a reflex?

'You know,' he says, '*I* never actually hit Araminta.'

'You need to shut the fuck up, Sutton,' Theo says, fuming, stepping in front of Isko as though he were the one hurt.

'Going to hit me too, Newman?'

'I should.'

'Go on then.' Rhys opens his arms out wide.

Theo could. It would be so easy. He's never been in a fight before – arguments, yes, many of those, but not a fight.

'Whoa, this is a bit much,' Jerome protests, feeling like he should probably say something before he becomes complicit.

Theo plows on. 'You need to leave this island.'

Rhys's expression darkens. 'No.'

'This competition isn't more important than all you've done.'

'And you really want to finish this competition without me?' he says, cocking an eyebrow and staring him down.

And Theo's anger rises because no, he doesn't. He's not even the biggest threat, nowhere near, but he's the one Theo wants to beat.

'This isn't about the fucking competition,' Isko shouts,

staring up from his bruised hands. 'You think we still care about that?'

'I think Newman does,' Rhys says, smiling, and there's blood on his teeth. 'I think he's the most malicious person here. He came onto this competition to deflect, isn't that right? You're conniving. Selfish.'

Theo grabs him by the collar, fist curling into his shirt, and steps forward with menace.

He's shocked to find himself in such a position.

But Rhys isn't – he just smiles. 'That's exactly what I thought.'

Theo stares at his own hand like he doesn't recognize it. He lets go.

'Doesn't fit with your image, does it? You're supposed to be the nice one of the band,' Rhys smiles, his eyebrow arched. 'But you know what I think?'

They're just words, but they're lacking the usual hollow bravado – they're heavy and firm and solid. Theo's hair stands on end, and he doesn't want to know, though he already does.

'I don't give a shit what you think,' he says, turning to walk away.

Rhys can't stand that, someone walking away from him. His face falls and it's livid, eyebrows drawn, eyes hateful. This is what he has always wanted from Theo: his attention. And he'll go to any lengths to get it.

'I think you were at that party, Newman.'

Theo freezes and Rhys laughs.

'Oh shit,' Isko says, glancing between the two of them.

'I'm right, aren't I? You didn't just come on here to avoid the scandal but to slice your name from it. You were at that party with the rest of the band, but unlike them, you didn't get caught. Underage girls, Newman? Now that I think about it, I'd say you're even worse than I am.'

'Children, Theo?' Jerome asks, aiming for aghast and ending up at elated. 'Children?' he repeats, like he was not the one making jokes about fifteen-year-olds mere days ago.

'Of course not,' Theo snarls. 'I wasn't there.'

There is no evidence.

But that doesn't matter. The seeds have been planted.

Rumour can kill a career before it even starts.

Rhys turns to Jerome. 'Do you want to get a hit in too, or am I free to go look for my girlfriend?'

Jerome arches an eyebrow. 'I think you'd better have another cigarette first, think things over.'

Rhys points at Jerome, shirt crooked, eye rapidly swelling. Blood splattered. 'I knew you were the only one here with a lick of sense.'

Rhys does not bother with the smoking area. He heads to the beach instead, where the waves hurl loud and angry onto the sand, the waters rough and turbulent. The wind whips with a ferocity that has the skies themselves roiling, clouds tumbling tumultuously like the slightest whim might entice them to storm again. It all feels too close, the deafening noise, the resentful waves and bitter sky pressing nearer, trapping them on this tiny rock in its centre.

The camera shows a dim red speck in the harsh darkness. Slowly it fades and another takes its place, Rhys lighting a new cigarette whenever the last one burns away.

He makes it through two and a half before he sees Kalpana, up by the cliffs.

She'd been planning on following Araminta. But when she ran into the confession booth, slamming the door so firmly behind her, Kalpana had needed a moment to herself.

And the sharp edge of the island seemed like the perfect place, at once violent and peaceful, like the raging anger and aching sorrow inside her.

He stomps heavily up behind her and she scrambles to her feet, confused more than scared until the moment he opens his mouth.

'You! You're a fucking bitch.'

She's so confused by the outright anger that it throws her. She has no comeback, though later she'll think of several. She is too shocked to respond, does not do anything other than turn to face him.

'A fucking bitch,' he repeats. 'You've been trying to take Araminta from me for weeks.'

'I didn't take her, Rhys. She left you because you scared her. Because you've spent weeks hurting her. And now she's leaving the competition.'

'Things were fine with us before you got involved. You kept trying to stick your nose where it didn't belong. You turned her against me.'

His words roll into each other, and she doesn't think he's blinked this entire time.

'Rhys, you're drunk,' she says, biting back the tirade she wants to give. She can berate him later, when he's sober. 'Let's go back inside.'

She eyes the edge of the cliffs warily. They aren't close, and they're lit up more than other parts of the path. They'll be fine. Then she eyes the darkness on her other side, the thicket of trees between her and the house. The fact she's stuck out here in the dark with an angry man.

Her pulse jumps, eyes locked on the camera hovering nearby in a desperate plea for help. The lights of the boats have never looked so distant.

'You had it out for me from the start,' he snarls, staggering toward her, and she takes an instinctive step back, closer to that edge. She realizes it's not a shadow clinging to his face but blood arcing down it.

'We can discuss this inside,' she says firmly.

The light catches him and she clocks his red eyes, the manic gleam.

He's high.

Which means he's not rational. Which means he's even more dangerous.

He points an accusatory finger at her, his other hand clutching at something she can't see on his chest.

A drone hovers nearby, a moth to a light.

'You're just a bitch.'

'Guys!' she screams, terrified, and now even more so, scared her shouts might startle Rhys into doing something stupid. 'Theo!'

The waves are so loud, she doesn't know how anyone will hear.

'Oh, are you scared of me, Kalpana? Does that fit your fucking narrative that I'm some terrifying, abusive monster? And not a man so fucking in love it hurts – a love you fucking fucked, you . . .' He trails off with more mumbling insults. He takes a breath and tries again. 'Araminta is just confused. She thinks you –'

'I am not the reason your relationship fell apart. And

370

frankly, Rhys, I don't think you actually care about that at all. You're just upset it fell apart on *television,* and you weren't even the one to do the dumping. You're angry the world knows exactly what you are: a horrible, cruel little boy.'

Rhys staggers forward again. 'You need to stay away from me.'

'You came to me.'

'You need to stay away or I'll . . .'

'What, throw a glass at me?'

He stares at her, eyes catching the flame of the lanterns driven into the edges of the island.

'Rhys! Mate, can you come here a second!' Theo appears from somewhere and Kalpana can't even see him, but she's so relieved she could cry.

Rhys scowls and looks around, and the rage seems to fall from him. 'She hates me. They all hate me. Everyone in the world.'

'Probably,' Kalpana confirms. She has no sympathy for this.

'Maybe I should just step off the edge.' He nods to the cliff.

'I don't think that's going to solve anything,' Kalpana says, something tightening in her stomach. Would she stop him if he tried?

'Hey, Rhys, come on – let's talk,' Theo comes into view, walking slowly like he's approaching a wild animal.

'How far down do you think it is?' Rhys takes a step closer to it, his movements jerky, and he careens forward, like he has no idea just how close he is.

'Rhys, get away from there.'

She can barely see the edge, where the sharp line of cliff

371

meets the night. Rhys staggers like it does not exist at all, like the sudden drop is luring him closer with siren song.

'Relax,' he shouts again. 'God, you're always so uptight.'

'Rhys, please,' Kalpana screeches as he takes yet another step. He's so close.

She says nothing, reaches out an instinctive hand to steady him.

He flinches back.

He's still a step from the edge, but he's high out of his detestable mind, his movements are too much, too big, too off kilter.

He doesn't even need something to trip over.

Kalpana leaps forward as he tips, manages to clasp her hand onto his, and it's hot and slippery with sweat.

Everything happens so quickly. Isn't time supposed to slow?

A stumble, a lurch, a clasped hand, wide eyes locked onto hers.

And a decision to let go.

The slightest movement as her hand opens and he slips free.

Rhys falls.

He doesn't make a noise at all. That's the worst part. Maybe he didn't even know he was falling. Maybe he didn't care. Maybe he thought it was funny, thought he was invulnerable, and this would all be a story to tell one day.

That hand in hers, and she does not think of it as a self-righteous good, or as a sacrifice she makes for the rest of the world. As she uncurls her fingers, she thinks that if she's going down, then so is he.

But when he hits the water, the horror of it all washes over her and she screams.

She leans as close as she dares, ripping the torch from the ground. She can't see a thing.

She turns to Theo, but he's already gone, running down the cliffs, pulling his shoes off.

'You can't go down there!' Kalpana shouts, her voice panicky like it's never been before. 'It's too dangerous – you could drown.'

'But he will if I don't!'

He runs.

Theo gets halfway down the cliffs before he dives into the water. It's freezing, so cold that it calms his heart, which began racing the moment he heard Kalpana scream.

He pulls himself through the water, rough waves hitting his face, rocks catching at his legs.

He can hardly see at all. Once or twice, he finds the cliff edge worryingly close, has to propel himself further. The water is always dangerous – heavy waves and turbulent currents, and now it's churning all the more from the earlier storm.

Rhys.

Rhys could die, might already be dead.

He could die too.

He glances up, hoping to see Kalpana standing at the point where he fell, but he can't see the land, just straight up the rocky edge to the indifferent stars.

He can barely see his own hands pulling him through the water. The cameras can't even make them out. How is he going to find a body – *Rhys*, find Rhys in this?

But then the moonlight hits something pale and Theo springs toward it.

He clutches Rhys without thinking, starts to sink beneath the waves, and has to let go and hold him again.

He finds his face, his eyes closed, a nasty cut down one side of his head and the barest traces of blood. That's good, right? He can't be that hurt if there is that little blood.

Unless he's already dead. Do dead men bleed?

He's struggling with him in the water, needs to get him out, but there's no way he can do that here. So he cups his chin and starts swimming, positioning himself beneath him to pull him through the water toward the beach.

He can't die. Men like Rhys don't die. The world would be too kind a place if they did.

Theo's teeth start chattering, and his limbs feel so heavy as he kicks through the water.

'If I die for you . . .' he says angrily.

'Theo.'

He freezes. Did he hear that right – is Rhys alive? It was the barest whisper; maybe he imagined it? The microphones certainly don't pick it up.

All at once, it flashes through his mind. All the sympathy Rhys will get from this, enough to move past what he's done to Araminta, what he's done to all of them. The times he made Theo doubt himself, told him he was nothing special. The constant barrage of it all.

Hate. So much hate.

Not least because there's something else lingering there, something he hates more than anything. Something about how forgivable it all is, how he's willing to let it all go, all of Rhys's worst behaviour, for the right line in a song.

That feeling of kinship he's never been able to shake. Like he might be just as awful. Everything Theo has been trying to save – his passion, his career, his future. And Rhys destroyed it all with a single line: '*I think you were at that party, Newman.*'

He hears a glass shattering. A screen. A camera.

He doesn't realize he's holding him under the waves. At least, that's what he'll mutter to himself over whisky at 4 a.m. That he didn't know. That he didn't mean to do it. That he wasn't as bad as Rhys, wasn't as bad as his bandmates, who knew how old those girls were when he didn't because he was already in a room with one of them before anyone thought to ask. He was in a room when they took photos. In a room before they could even see him there. It was just a mistake. He's still a good person. Rhys's body going still in his arms. He didn't know.

When he does realize, he's not sure whether it's too late.

But he holds on for a moment, just in case.

For Araminta, and all the women like her, all the ones waiting for Rhys to hurt them. At least, that's what he'll cling to when he's sober and trying to hold it together. Nothing about him, nothing about the anger he's harboured for weeks.

Because he's a good fucking person.

The world is a better place without Rhys Sutton in it. That's the thought he can't shake, even as he drags his body closer to shore.

Isko comes first after hearing the screaming, sprints back to the garden for more torches, and soon they are all there. Araminta is crying, her gasps somehow echoing and silenced by the nothingness around them. Jerome stares blankly at the horizon. Isko and Kalpana try to provide Theo some light.

They've got the solar torches and begin throwing them into the water, where they bob for a few moments before suffocating beneath the waves, so much angrier at night, so much darker too.

'I think he's got him,' Kalpana says.

Araminta continues to cry.

'He's taking him to the beach,' Isko says.

They run, hoping to help.

When he appears minutes later, Araminta hurls herself into the water, Isko following after, and together they help pull Rhys onto the sand.

Theo throws himself onto him, slamming onto his chest, pressing his lips to his though he knows you're not supposed to do that anymore, only how can he say he did everything to save him if he doesn't?

Araminta breaks down again.

'He's dead,' she says. 'Look at him – he's dead.'

One little pill – a swollen throat, maybe, or dizziness that got him off the cliff. Something that made it easier to drown, something that turned an accident into something so much darker.

'Theo,' Isko says gently, minutes later, when he still presses himself onto Rhys's chest. 'He's gone.'

He won't even realize the role he might have played until the police thrust it in his face. Who knows what bleeding on the brain can do? Get someone off a cliff edge, certainly. Maybe even stop them from swimming for the surface. He might not realize that now, but his knuckles sting as the water trickles into his open cuts.

Theo shakes him off, pushes back to Rhys. He tastes salt, and he can't tell if it's the seawater on Rhys's lips or his own tears.

His conviction is gone, some deeper awareness taking root, a truth he's been denying. If he were actually a good person, he would regret this or, rather, would see reviving Rhys as the priority, not making it look believable. But he's not a good person. None of them are.

Kalpana pulls Theo back and he staggers, staring at the corpse on the beach. Aren't dead bodies supposed to look like they're just sleeping? Aren't they supposed to look at peace?

'You did all you could,' Kalpana says reassuringly.

All she had to do was hold on; all she had to do was try. And shouldn't she feel guiltier than this? Shouldn't she be looking at him and thinking anything other than *good riddance*?

Jerome stares at the horizon, unable to believe the sun isn't rising, that this night isn't over yet.

Unable to shake the feeling that this scandal isn't the one he wanted, but god, no one will forget them now, will they?

'Look.' Araminta nods at the ocean.

They turn. The ships are enormous, closer than they've ever been and racing toward them. Other people, watching the show live, and too late – far, far too late.

The contestants shuffle closer to one another and this tiny island, clinging to it, hoping that despite all its cruelty, all its reckless abandon, it might keep them safe.

They do nothing but watch as the impending world crashes toward them.

Reading Group Guide

1. Do you expect 'reality' from a reality TV show? Why or why not?

2. What do you think of the commentary of the contestants during the show? Do you believe they're being more truthful in the commentary, or is it all part of the act?

3. Araminta consistently wishes to be seen as a sculptor, an artist – someone other than who she is seen as in the media. Do you think this is possible? If someone has a reputation, is it possible for them to change it?

4. Is causing a scandal the best way to get famous? Would doing something extremely positive or altruistic give you as much fame or media coverage?

5. The contestants of *Iconic* put a lot of emphasis on money in relation to success and fame. Is money the best indicator of success? How do you measure success?

6. Araminta claims that the public doesn't want their icons to be moral or upstanding people. What do you make of this statement?

7. Is it possible to have true relationships if you know you're being watched the whole time? How would your actions and behaviours change?

8. What are the warning signs that Rhys isn't treating Araminta well? What sorts of controlling and manipulative behaviours does he exhibit?

9. How do the storylines of the *Iconic* show and the police officers' love affair parallel each other?

10. Are all the contestants culpable in Rhys's death? Is there anyone more guilty than the others?

11. How culpable is AHX (the producers of *Iconic*) for the events of the show?

12. Would you watch a show like *Iconic*? Why or why not?

A Conversation with the Author

What inspired you to write this story?

I love books and have to read a lot for my day job, which means that sometimes when things are really busy, I struggle with fiction in TV too. So I watch a lot of reality TV and documentaries instead – and at some point, all the true crime and reality merged. I was thinking about murder live on air, about how to get away with it – and about how some of the horrible behaviour I'd seen on reality shows paralleled that of the documentaries. And there I was, part of the problem, enjoying it. I wanted to push it further and explore that question of 'What do we let happen in the name of entertainment?' and so *Then Things Went Dark* was born.

Why do you think we enjoy reality TV so much?

I think mostly it's just very fun, and the setups are always so ridiculous. They have this simultaneous awareness of how silly it is while also treating it incredibly seriously. It's both intensely high stakes and so removed from reality that the stakes feel low. But I think what I particularly love about it is trying to work out what's real, who is only behaving that way because a camera is on them, and dissecting what the edit is trying to convince us of – especially spotting changing food or drink throughout conversation and realizing it's not as real as the producers want us to believe!

Who is your favourite of the contestants? Who was the most fun to write?

This is such a hard question when I went into this book with the intention of writing six of the worst characters to have ever existed and making them each a different brand of awful. Rhys was actually very fun to write because he has such a careless glee to him, and in so many of his interactions, he's trying to get a reaction from someone else, which makes for some very fun scenes. But I think my favourite is probably Isko. I just love the jaded disinterest, judgmental wine sips and snarky one-liners.

What do you want readers to take away from your book?

Mostly I just want them to have a fun time with this self-absorbed, deluded, and pretentious cast! But in terms of the serious heart of the book, it was really important for me to explore toxic male behaviour in ways that I was seeing amongst my peers – especially the weaponizing of therapy language and emotional manipulation. Araminta is someone who knows the signs and knows red flags but still gets caught up in it because *anyone* can. Abusers will always find new ways to manipulate – and Rhys is intentionally doing it on a show where the truth is subjective and murky because he can turn that to his advantage. So I suppose if readers did take something in that regard, it's that abusive relationships vary and you can know all the indications of abuse, value yourself, and still fall into a toxic relationship.

Acknowledgments

This book was a labour of love and I'm so excited that it exists! And it's in your hands! Right now! That wouldn't be possible without the support of several people so thank you to the following:

Firstly, to Hannah Schofield, my incredible agent. I finished *Then Things Went Dark* the day Hannah offered to represent me, and I knew she was the one when, having queried a YA rom-com, she was just as excited at the prospect of my satirical thriller. She's always been my biggest supporter, talks me out of many crises, and is the ONLY reason this book exists.

Thank you to the entire team at Sourcebooks: Cristina Arreola, Anna Venckus, Sarah Brody, Tara Jaggers, Jessica Thelander, Deve McLemore, Gianni Washington, and Sara Walker. The biggest of thank-yous to my editor, MJ Johnston – especially for giving me license to always make the book even more dramatic.

Thanks also to my international publishers and to my UK team at Michael Joseph: Hannah Smith, Stephanie Biddle, Ciara Berry, Phillipa Walker, Serena Nazareth, Alice Mottram, Riana Dixon, Christina Ellicott, Laura Garrod, Kelly Mason, Sophie Marston, and Akua Akowuah. I cannot stress how incredibly supportive Penguin have been, and I've loved working with the MJ team – thank you for making publishing this book so fun!

Thank you to my family, especially my grandparents to whom this book is dedicated – I wish my granddad had seen my books publish. I know he'd have been impossibly proud – even if slightly alarmed at the subject matter. And on the note of grandparents, thank you to Carol Welsford, who we miss so much every single day.

Given the suggestions of how to list my friends included 'sending in our receipts of who preordered first' and 'if we beat a Beholder in DND, can we be first,' I have elected to go in NO PARTICULAR ORDER: Jess Rome, Megan Salfairso, Ellie Brown, Amanda Wood, Dora Anderson Taylor, Liberty Lees-Baker, Kristina Jones, Claire Kingue, Aoife Prendiville, Fraser Wing, Laura Grady, Saoirse McGlone, Izzy Everington, Sara Adams, Hannah Ainsworth, Annie Gardiner-Piggott, Isabel Lewis, Natalie Warner, and Sophie Eminson.

Finally, thank you to Christine Baranski, especially for that one scene in *Mamma Mia!* You were right: little boys who play with fire get their fingers burned.